DAUGHTER
OF THE LOOM

Books by Tracie Peterson

www.traciepeterson.com

Controlling Interests
Entangled • *Framed*
The Long-Awaited Child
A Slender Thread • *Tidings of Peace*

BELLS OF LOWELL*
Daughter of the Loom

DESERT ROSES
Shadows of the Canyon
Across the Years

WESTWARD CHRONICLES
A Shelter of Hope • *Hidden in a Whisper*
A Veiled Reflection

RIBBONS OF STEEL†
Distant Dreams • *A Hope Beyond*
A Promise for Tomorrow

RIBBONS WEST†
Westward the Dream • *Separate Roads*
Ties That Bind

SHANNON SAGA‡
City of Angels • *Angels Flight*
Angel of Mercy

YUKON QUEST
Treasures of the North • *Ashes and Ice*
Rivers of Gold

NONFICTION
The Eyes of the Heart

*with Judith Miller   †with Judith Pella   ‡with James Scott Bell

TRACIE PETERSON
AND
JUDITH MILLER

DAUGHTER
OF THE LOOM

BETHANYHOUSE
PUBLISHERS
MINNEAPOLIS, MINNESOTA

Published by Bethany House Publishers
A Ministry of Bethany Fellowship International
11400 Hampshire Avenue South
Bloomington, Minnesota 55438

Printed in the United States of America by
Bethany Press International, Bloomington, Minnesota 55438

ISBN 0-7394-3251-6

To my three J's—
Jim, Justin, and Jenna—
with love and thanks for
being my support team.

—Judy

TRACIE PETERSON is a popular speaker and bestselling author who has written over fifty books, both historical and contemporary fiction. Tracie and her family make their home in Montana.

Visit Tracie's Web site at: *www.traciepeterson.com.*

JUDITH MILLER is an award-winning author of five novels and three novellas, two of which have placed in the CBA top-ten fiction lists. In addition to her writing, Judy is a certified legal assistant. Judy and her husband make their home in Topeka, Kansas.

Visit Judy's Web site at: *www.judithmccoymiller.com.*

CHAPTER 1

Lowell, Massachusetts
Monday, September 1, 1828

"I will not fail," Lilly Armbruster whispered into the early morning dawn. Setting one foot in front of the other, slowly, methodically, she continued onward until reaching the bridge over the Hamilton Canal, the bridge that would take her into the Appleton textile mill.

How different life might have been if only Lowell could have remained unchanged. How different her life might have been if only Matthew had remained unchanged, as well. Lilly tried to dispel the memory of the only man she'd ever loved. He was her enemy now—as clearly as the others who had marred her beautiful East Chelmsford with their monstrosities of brick and iron. Even worse, they had renamed it *Lowell!* She shuddered at the thought.

"Progressive industry," Matthew had called it, pleading with her to understand. "It will be to the betterment of everyone concerned," he'd promised. But it hadn't been to her betterment—nor to her father's.

The sun was beginning its ascent into the gray eastern sky as Lilly crossed into the mill yard by the only open gate, the one that would permit her entry into the fiefdom of the Corporation, a fiefdom that had been carefully planned and cultivated by a group of Bostonians, now referred to by the locals as the Boston Associates or the lords of the loom. Powerful men—men with money, connections, and an unrelenting passion for the creation of the mill town they had named after their visionary, Francis Cabot Lowell. These same men had given special attention to every detail, completing their architectural wonders with moats, fortified walls, drawbridges, and serfs—many, many serfs.

Step by step, Lilly moved farther into the mill yard, her attention now drawn toward the dull, rumbling noise seeping through the thick brick walls of the taller buildings that formed the outer perimeter of the fortress. She had never noticed the sound before, but she had never been this close to the mills before, either. The reverberating din seemed to be pounding out a message of doom.

Despite a chill in the morning air, a rivulet of perspiration trickled down the small of her back. Swallowing hard to gain control of the bile that now rose in her throat, Lilly paused momentarily to deposit her bags before entering the building. There was no sense in dragging them along with her, especially since she was already exhausted from carrying them all this way.

She took a deep breath and smoothed down the pleats of her bodice. Her gown wasn't very fashionable or stylish, but she couldn't imagine that would matter to the men inside. Squaring her shoulders, Lilly knew the moment of truth had arrived. She had to go through with her plan. She had to see this through, no matter how distasteful.

A middle-aged man was perched at a desk near the doorway; probably a clerk or bookkeeper, she decided. He looked up from his papers, gave her an agitated glance, and nodded toward a single chair near his desk. With her fingernails biting into the flesh of her palms, she seated herself and waited while the clerk continued writing in his ledger.

What would Father think if he could see me in this place? She pictured him cupping large worn hands to his mouth, calling out from the gates of heaven and warning her against such folly, shouting that she didn't belong among these evil men who had lied to him, breaking his heart with their wicked schemes.

Lilly watched as the clerk laid down his pen and scratched his balding head before giving her his attention. "Applying for a position, I presume?"

Lilly forced herself to look him in the eyes—brown, wide-set, beady-looking eyes that sent a dark message. "Yes." It was all she could manage. Her heart raced in a maddening staccato. It seemed to beat out the words *You fool! You fool! You fool!*

In a slow, lingering manner, the man let his gaze travel the full length of her body. "How old are you, girl?"

Lilly knew her slender figure and petite frame often caused people to believe her years younger than her actual age. "I'm twenty," she said, straightening her shoulders. She wished silently that she'd pinned her hair up instead of leaving it in a single braid down her back. Then, too, her bonnet was at least five years old and much too childish for a young woman.

"Twenty, eh?" The man looked as if he didn't believe her.

"Yes, I'm twenty." Lilly stood her ground, offering nothing more.

The man gave a *harrumph*ing sound, then shook his head. "We have no openings. Did one of the boardinghouse keepers send you?" he asked, glancing about the room while giving her a smirk that revealed uneven yellowing teeth.

"I'm applying for a position as a weaver or perhaps a drawing-in girl. My name is Lilly Armbruster, and I think if you'll check with Mr. Boott or Mr. Appleton, there may be a position available for me." Her confidence swelled. She would not let this man deter her.

His lips curled into a mocking sneer, his beady eyes now narrow slits in a too-thin face. "Well, since Mr. Boott and Mr. Appleton aren't in the immediate vicinity, why don't you tell *me* why you think one of them would be willing to create a position especially for you, Miss Armbruster?"

She struggled to maintain her decorum, wanting to reveal neither her fear of this leering man nor her abhorrence for seeking employment in one of the mills. "Mr. Boott attended my father's funeral last week. While at the cemetery, he told me there would always be work at the mills for our family." She paused, giving him what she hoped was a look of complete innocence. "Do you think he was insincere, merely making consoling remarks to a bereaved family?" she asked, intoning concern.

The clerk shifted in his chair and shoved a bony finger under the soiled collar of his dingy white shirt. Exhaling deeply, he shoved his chair away from the desk and excused himself. Lilly watched as he scurried off and whispered in the ear of an older man across the room. Wagging his head first in one direction and then the other, he occasionally stole a glance at her from under hooded eyelids, his appraisal making Lilly feel somewhat less than human. Finally, the older man turned back to his work, obviously bringing the conversation to an end.

The clerk returned to the desk and settled into his chair. "Mr. Nettles tells me there will soon be an opening in the spinning room and you can begin a week from now. Come with the others at the first bell. Report to me, and I'll take you to your assignment. I'm also to tell you that there's an opening at Adelaide Beecher's boardinghouse, number 5 Jackson Street. Mr. Nettles has sent one of the doffers to advise Miss Beecher of your arrival. She'll be expecting you."

His smug look had vanished. "And *your* name, sir?" Lilly inquired, putting her innocent act aside.

"Arnold. Thaddeus Arnold. I'll have your contract ready for signature when you arrive next Monday."

"Thank you, Mr. Arnold." She lingered for a moment, watching as he took up his pen and went back to his ledgers. "Good day, Mr. Arnold, and again, my thanks for your kind attention." When his head snapped up to meet her eyes, she knew she had failed to keep the bite of sarcasm from her reply.

"It's not wise to make enemies of those in authority, Miss Armbruster." His thin lips barely moved as he hissed the words across the desk at her.

A tingling sensation coursed through her body, and she could feel his glowering stare follow her every move as she rose from the chair and exited the building. Though her instincts told her to run and never come back, she held herself in check, straightened her back, and raised her head high until she was out of his sight.

Gathering her luggage, Lilly moved away from the mill and the disgusting man. Once she'd rounded the corner of the building, she stopped and leaned against the cool brick wall. Would she never learn to control her tongue? There was no changing things now, but perhaps it would be wise to try and make amends with Thaddeus Arnold next Monday. For now, she'd best gather her wits and make Miss Beecher's acquaintance. The boardinghouse was just down the street, and a friendly face and a cup of tea would be welcome.

A row of three-story brick boardinghouses flanked by smaller white frame houses at each end lined both sides of Jackson Street. A few children were playing outside one of the houses at the end of the square, and Lilly paused momentarily to watch their carefree antics. Had she ever been so young and lighthearted? It seemed impossible to recall such a time.

Trudging down the street, she paused momentarily in front of number 5 before ascending the two steps and firmly knocking on the front door. The door opened, and a plump woman with a winning smile stood before her. "Welcome, welcome, welcome, my dear. Do come in and let's get you settled." Wasting no time, the older woman took Lilly's satchel and started toward the parlor. "Don't stand there gathering flies, dearie. Bring the rest of your belongings inside, and let's get acquainted. I'm Adelaide Beecher."

Grabbing her bandbox and a small trunk, Lilly entered and shoved the door with her backside. She nodded in satisfaction at the clicking sound as the door latched. "Mr. Arnold sent me. I'm Lilly Armbruster. Where to?" she asked as the plump woman moved aside, permitting an unobstructed view of two long dining tables surrounded by what looked like as many as thirty chairs.

"This way, dearie. We've several flights of stairs to climb, so you may want to make two trips," she warned.

"No need. I'm accustomed to hard work, Mrs. Beecher," Lilly stated firmly, knowing her small frame might suggest otherwise.

"Suit yourself. And it's Miss Beecher. I've never been married. The girls call me Miss Addie—you do the same. Unless my sister's around, of course," she giggled. "Then they call me Miss Adelaide. My sister's name is Miss Mintie Beecher. She's a bit of a stickler for formalities and barely suffers the use of our given names. She's the keeper at number 7 across the street. She houses some of the men, so her quarters are off limits for my girls."

Lilly smiled and nodded as she continued trudging up the stairway. "How much farther?" she panted. The first flight of stairs hadn't been so bad. They were slanted at an easy angle, and she'd hardly lost her wind. But this flight was steeper and narrower. Her feet seemed to barely get a decent toehold before striking the back of the step, threatening to topple her backward.

"Almost there. Just one more," Miss Addie cheerily called back over her shoulder. "You can leave one of those satchels and come back for it if you're having difficulty. The next flight is a bit steep."

Lilly heeded the warning and dropped her bandbox at the foot of the stairs. It was a wise decision. The ascent seemed never ending, and Lilly had truly despaired of reaching the top when Miss Addie finally announced, "Here we are."

"I guessed this might be it. We couldn't have gone much farther unless you planned to put me out on the roof," Lilly jibed as she touched the rafter with her outstretched hand. Instantly she worried that her words had been spoken out of line. She looked to Addie to ascertain if she'd offended her, but the woman merely smiled back at her.

"I like your sense of humor, Lilly. A sense of humor is a true gift from the Lord. I don't know how I would have survived the last six months without mine. I must admit, however, some of the girls don't share my opinion, so don't be surprised if you hear some of them say they're looking to change boardinghouses. Seems no sooner do I get a new girl than I lose another. Which does bring to mind the fact that two girls moved out yesterday, and I didn't need to bring you clear to this attic room after all," she admitted with a chuckle. "Unless you'd prefer to be up here by yourself?"

"I'm not sure," Lilly panted, still winded. The lumpy mattress sagged in protest as she dropped onto one of the four beds sandwiched into the tiny, airless room—there was barely room to store her baggage. Two small chests were wedged into the small space on either side of the two narrow attic windows. It appeared that opening the top drawer of either chest would be impossible without hitting the wall, and she had to turn sideways to walk between the two beds.

"You get two drawers in one of the chests, and you'll share the bed as new girls move in. The previous keeper told me she sometimes had eight or nine girls up here, but most times just six or seven."

Lilly laughed. "I like your sense of humor, too, Miss Addie! Eight or nine girls. Why, there's not room for more than four in this room at best. It's not so bad in here right now, but the heat in summer and cold in winter would most likely be dreadful."

"I'd like to tell you that I'm joking with you about the accommodations, miss, but what I've told you is truly the way it is. 'Course, if my cooking doesn't improve, there may never be more than one or two up here. These girls put great store in having good food and plenty of it. But I'm afraid my cooking isn't quite up to the boardinghouse standard yet."

Lilly gave her a wilted smile. "Let's take a look at the second floor."

Miss Addie nodded and led the way back downstairs, stopping in one of the two large bedrooms on the second floor. Lilly glanced about the room. It, too, had four beds, and the chests that lined the wall were similar to those in the upper room. However, this space was larger, and she determined that not having to contend with sloping rafters was a distinct advantage. "How many girls in each of these rooms?"

"Eight—two to a bed and two drawers in the chest. There's a bed open in this room. Well, at least half a bed is open." She grinned. "Nadene lost her bedmate and will probably be glad for the company. It can get rather cold up here at night."

Lilly had no idea who Nadene was. It seemed strange to be agreeing to bed down with folks she didn't even know, but apparently that was how things were done in the mill boarding-houses.

"I think I'd prefer to be down here," Lilly stated. "I'm afraid Mr. Arnold didn't give me much information regarding the boardinghouse. I have no idea how much you charge for room and board."

"The Corporation pays me twenty-five cents, and you pay me one dollar and twenty-five cents per week. Washing your bed linens is included in the price. I've a list of the boardinghouse rules downstairs that each girl must agree to abide by. Remind me to have you read it over and sign the contract. I'm rather forgetful about keeping up with the paper work." She looked over her shoulder as if to ascertain if anyone else would overhear her before adding, "That's frowned upon, don't you know," she said in a hushed voice.

"I'm not sure I can afford to pay before I begin working at the mill. I can ill afford to spend the little money I have," Lilly reported.

Holding a finger to her pursed lips, Miss Addie creased her brows in contemplation. "That does present a problem. I don't suppose you know how to cook for a crowd of hungry girls, do you?"

"*That* I can do," Lilly replied, untying the ribbons to her bonnet.

Miss Addie chortled and clapped her hands together. "Can you teach me?"

Lilly carefully removed her bonnet and placed it atop the dresser. She ran her hand through the chestnut curls that had escaped her braid, knowing she must look frightful. "I'm not sure I can turn you into an expert cook in six days, but I can certainly help you on your way. And you can always ask me questions after I've begun to work at the mill."

Miss Addie's rounded cheeks took on a rosy hue, and her deep blue eyes sparkled. "I think we've solved the problem of your room and board. I knew we were going to be great friends the minute I laid eyes on you. Come along. You need to begin my lessons. The girls will be coming home for dinner in two hours, and my preparations are far from complete. You can unpack after dinner while I wash dishes and clean the kitchen," she instructed, already three-fourths of the way down to the first floor.

Lilly followed along obediently, listening intently as the older woman explained that the largest meal of the day was served at noon and that the girls would arrive at five minutes past the hour. "The food must be on the table when they arrive. They have only half an hour to get from the mill, eat their meal, and return. Their schedule demands that the boardinghouse run smoothly in order for them to eat and return to work on time. I do have one little doffer who helps serve—I don't know what I would have done without her—but there's still more work than I can manage. I'm hoping that once I get all the beds filled, I'll be able to hire someone to help a little more, especially with the meals. But for now, I'm on my own."

"This shouldn't be much different from cooking for the farmhands during harvest," Lilly replied. "How many are you feeding?"

Addie hesitated a moment. "Fifteen, including us."

Lilly nodded. "That shouldn't be too hard. Show me what you've already done."

Two hours later the pealing of the tower bell that had tolled over the city for the past five years announced that midday had arrived. Lilly placed the last bowl of food on the table as the front door flew open. Twelve young women had soon crowded their way into the dining room, with chairs scraping, silverware clanking, and voices competing to be heard above each other as they called out for bowls or plates to be passed. The noise was deafening after the preceding hours of quiet camaraderie in the kitchen with Miss Addie. For a moment, Lilly found herself staring at the group of girls. Instead of exhibiting the manners of genteel young ladies, the girls wolfed down the meal with little attention to etiquette or polite conversation. There was no time for such social amenities here.

"This is so-o-o good," one of the younger girls commented, her mouth still full of rice pudding. "You've been holding out on us, Miss Addie. This is the best meal I've had in ages!"

Several others nodded in agreement and one took a moment to ask, "How'd you do this, Miss Addie?"

All gazes were fixed on the older woman, some faces filled with amazement, some with doubt, and some with what appeared to be undying devotion. "Save your praises. It wasn't my doing; I merely helped. It's our new boarder you have to thank. Meet Lilly Armbruster."

"You've hired a cook? Isn't that what *you're* supposed to do?" Prudence Holtmeyer inquired.

"Indeed, it is one of my duties, but I'm hoping to become more skilled, and Lilly has agreed to help. However . . ."

Before she had completed her explanation, the girls were pushing their chairs away from the table, grabbing their cloaks and bonnets, and rushing toward the door. Several took an extra moment for one last bite of the rice pudding before scurrying off. Minutes later, all was once again silent. Lilly glanced over the table in amazement, for she'd never seen anything like it. Even the farmhands that she and her mother had cooked for took longer to relax and eat the noon meal. These girls were like a colony of locusts swarming in, devouring everything in their path, and moving on. There was one difference, however: the girls would be returning in only a few short hours to repeat the routine.

"I was certain we'd prepared too much food," Lilly commented to herself. She'd thought Miss Addie a bit touched when she'd continued to pull food from the cupboards as they prepared the noon meal.

"Oh, dear me no," Addie replied, already reaching for two empty serving bowls. "The work is terribly hard. They build a powerful appetite, which is why they grow most discontent when their meals are tasteless or ill-prepared."

Lilly thought of the hard work and tried to imagine herself

joining the girls at such large meals. The idea struck her as almost amusing. There was no possible way she could ever eat as much food as those girls had eaten. Why, her waist would get as thick as . . . as thick as Miss Addie's! Matthew had always liked her tiny waist.

Matthew! How he seemed to plague her mind at the most awkward of times. Lilly knew she wouldn't mind it half so much if the ache in her heart wasn't yet so pronounced. *I cannot allow myself these feelings,* she told herself, pushing aside the chance to relive her girlhood dreams of becoming Matthew's wife. There was no sense in remembering the ivory satin wedding gown her mother had promised to make. There was no need to dwell on the way her heart fluttered whenever Matthew flashed her a smile. Lilly sighed and forced her attention back to the job at hand.

Addie seemed not to notice Lilly's contemplation. Already she was humming a tune and making order out of the mess. "I'll clear the table and wash the dishes. You go upstairs and unpack. There's fresh water in the pitcher so feel free to freshen up. I'm sure someone as pretty as you is used to being able to see to her appearance, but around here, you have to grab what opportunity presents itself. When you've finished, we can decide about supper."

"Perhaps we should plan the menu first. It doesn't appear there's much bread remaining. I'll need to start now if it's to be ready in time for supper. By the way, what time is supper?"

"The girls will be home at six-thirty. The lighting up doesn't occur until September 21. Then supper will be later, not until seven o'clock," Miss Addie explained.

"The lighting up?"

Miss Addie smiled. "Mercy, but you have a lot to learn. September 21 marks the date when the winter hours begin. Work commences a half hour later in the morning, but you make up for it by working a half hour later in the evening. Folks call it the lighting up because it's dark in the morning when you go to work and dark in the evening when you return home—the lamps become necessary both morning and evening. Then, come March 21, there's what they call the blowing out. The days start becoming longer once again and the lamps aren't needed so much."

Lilly nodded and reached for one of the dishes. She scraped the remnants of dinner from the serving platters into an empty serving bowl. "Seems like a sensible plan." But Lilly reminded herself that if her own plan went well, the mills wouldn't even be around come March 21.

Miss Addie clucked in agreement as she took hold of Lilly's thin wrist. "Oh, but that's not the best part. Sit yourself down for a minute while I tell you."

Lilly seated herself on one of the dining room chairs while Miss Addie poured a cup of tea, added several spoons of sugar, and began to vigorously stir. After taking a sip of the brew, the older woman leaned forward and spoke in a hushed tone. "The very best part is the balls. There's a Lighting Up Ball and Blowing Out Ball. Very, very fancy, I might add. Not like the parties I knew in Boston, mind you, but very tastefully done for a town the size of Lowell."

Lilly began to rise, but when Miss Addie motioned her down, Lilly plopped back into the chair. "I really should start clearing off the dishes, Miss Addie. I'm not interested in balls or parties, but I do thank you for explaining the lighting up."

"Well, you may not be interested right now, but you will be come the twenty-first day of September. Attending the ball is a must for all the mill girls. It's required. Well, perhaps *expected* is a better word. Those two balls are the only time when there's socializing among all the people who work at the mills. Why, the supervisors dance with all the girls, even the little doffers. Those are the little girls who sometimes hire on for lesser jobs like helping in the boardinghouses or removing empty bobbins in the mills."

"Children work in the mills?" Lilly asked in stunned disbelief.

"Well, the doffers don't work all that much. No more than fifteen minutes or so at a time. They're usually the daughters of women who work there, and they have plenty of playtime and still attend school. They benefit from the money they earn, for usually it helps their family a great deal."

"Still, they're just children. They shouldn't have to work in the mills." *I shouldn't have to work there, either,* Lilly thought.

"Oh, don't you concern yourself about it." Addie continued, "Let me finish telling you about the balls. They're quite the event. Mr. Boott makes an appearance, along with some of the other Boston Associates. The girls look forward to those two dates all year long. You mark my words—after you've listened to the girls talk about the balls, you'll be ready to don your prettiest dress and dancing slippers when the time comes."

Miss Addie obviously expected her to become smitten by the whole affair. Any further denial of interest was only going to cause additional delay in the cleaning-up process, so hopefully a neutral answer would suffice. "We'll see, Miss Addie. We'll see."

Addie nodded and rose from her chair. Each of the women skillfully balanced an armload of dirty plates and bowls and headed toward the kitchen. While Addie put the dishes to soak, Lilly began to take stock of the larder and what they might prepare for supper. Her thoughts ran rampant.

I'm actually here. Here, where God can use me best, Lilly reasoned. Although she had struggled in her spiritual walk, even going so far as to give up her Bible readings and church, Lilly knew God had a purpose in bringing her here to the mills. He would use her to make right the very thing that had brought such tragedy to her family.

Then everything shall be better, Lilly assured herself. *I will find a way to drive the mills out of Lowell, and God will reward me and bless my life.* Lilly looked over her shoulder, almost fearful she'd spoken her thoughts aloud. Addie was nowhere in sight.

Lilly breathed a sigh of relief to find herself alone. Addie would never understand Lilly's feelings. Addie didn't know what it was to have the Association come in and destroy the land she'd come to love—demolish her father's hopes—steal her inheritance. Had Lilly truly not felt led of God to come here to the mills, there was no telling what might have become of her. Women without protectors suffered greatly.

Well, it is certain the mills will offer me no protection, Lilly reasoned. She picked up a bag of flour and balanced this with a can of lard. "I can do this," she whispered. "I can do whatever I have to, to make it all right again."

"Did you say something, my dear?" Addie questioned, popping into the room.

Lilly smiled. "I was just saying that I've found the ingredients to make bread. Come and I'll show you what's to be done."

Scooping heaping cups of flour into a bowl, Lilly then began measuring lard and scalding milk. "Why in the world did you ever take this position if you don't know how to cook, Miss Addie?" she inquired while continuing to prepare the ingredients for a half dozen loaves of bread.

Addie wiped her hands on her apron, then blotted the hem against her perspiring neck. "It's a long story. Suffice it to say, our father managed to die while owing more creditors in Boston than either my sister or I knew existed. Mintie and I were reared in a family of privilege and position—Boston society," she explained proudly. "But when the Judge—that's what we always called our father—died, the creditors came calling, and there was no stopping them until we'd sold our home and almost all of our belongings. Suddenly Mintie and I found ourselves not only penniless but friendless. People of class want nothing to do with you once you've lost everything. We had to find some way to support ourselves, and we read in the newspaper that they needed boardinghouse keepers, as the mills were expanding. Of course, the Judge had once been against the mills. He figured them to be full of spies. In fact, he wouldn't have anything to do with them."

"Would that more men were like him," Lilly muttered.

Addie didn't seem to hear the remark and continued with her explanation. "Mintie sent a letter of inquiry to Tracy Jackson, one of the Boston Associates. He and the Judge had been friends, and I think he took pity on us. In any event, after receiving Mr. Jackson's reply, Mintie decided it was a magnificent opportunity for us to take employment here. She said it would be a job of great virtue for two spinsters. She's very practical, you know." Then with a twinkle in her eye, the older woman added in a hushed, almost ominous tone, "She also thought it a good way to keep an eye out for British spies."

Lilly couldn't help but giggle. The very thought of anyone harboring such ideas was amusing. The war had been over for a very long time, and England was now considered an ally. How strange that Addie's sister should still be worried over such a thing.

"During our years at home, Mintie was always in the kitchen helping cook and run the Judge's household. Like I said, she's very practical. She's tried to help me with my cooking, but she has twenty men to cook, clean, and wash for in her own board-inghouse. So she's busy all day and most of the evening," Addie confided. "Sometimes that's a relief and other times it leaves me quite lonely."

A mixture of sorrow and pain lingered on Adelaide's face. Lilly wondered if her memories of the past, mixed with her pres-ent failures at the boardinghouse, caused Miss Addie undo grief. "You don't need to explain further, Miss Addie," Lilly whis-pered, giving the older woman a reassuring smile. "I find myself in much the same predicament."

Addie nodded and wiped away a stray tear that had managed to escape and roll down her plump cheek. "You'll not have long to suffer, I'm sure. With your beauty, I don't know how you've managed to remain single this long. You'll no doubt be married before you're even here a year. You're such a pretty little thing, so young and full of life. Why, you've just begun to live. Now, Miss Mintie and I, that's a different story. At our age, we don't have men lining up at the door anxious to pledge their devo-tion."

"Neither of you ever married?" Lilly blurted, immediately wishing she could take back the words as a look of sorrow once again returned to Addie's face.

"I was betrothed years ago, but father insisted that I wait to marry until Mintie found a proper suitor. He argued that the eldest should marry first. Unfortunately, a proper suitor didn't come along, and my young beau tired of waiting. Not that I blame him. He was quite a handsome man, my Charles, even if I do say so myself. We were well suited. Both of us enjoyed laughter and wanted lots of children. Last I heard, he and his wife had seven children and a multitude of grandchildren." She hesitated for a moment and sighed. "Now, why don't you tell me about all the beaux who must have come knocking on your door, Lilly. I'll wager we don't have enough hours remaining in the day for the telling of those tales."

"Quite the contrary, Miss Addie. In fact, I've had only one beau; and much like your courtship with Charles, my relationship with Matthew Cheever was destined for failure." She paused, transfixed for the briefest of moments. "But no matter," she continued. "We've chosen our separate paths." Silence hung in the room, creating an emptiness that needed to be filled, a void that too closely resembled her barren heart.

CHAPTER 2

Boston, Massachusetts

Matthew Cheever watched closely as Nathan Appleton glanced toward his wife at the end of the table. Appleton nodded his head and the couple rose in unison. "Shall we adjourn to the library, gentlemen? I believe there are cigars and a fine bottle of port that need our attention. Ladies, I'm certain my wife has some new piece of needlework or a book of poetry she wishes to discuss with you in the music room."

The two groups took their respective cues, the men following Nathan to the library and the women trailing along behind Jasmine Appleton in customary fashion. The meal had been superb, but it was obvious the men now longed to be done with the formalities so that they could finally get to the business at hand—the *real* reason they had gathered: to report and discuss their successes and formulate their plans for the future. Men's business. Aside from obvious social impropriety, their wives' total inability to comprehend matters dealing with business forbade any interesting discussions at supper. They had managed a brief conversation regarding their good fortune in escaping the disastrous results of the depression that had devastated many of their friends. But with their money invested in the Lowell project, none of them had been adversely affected. When Jasmine realized her husband was discussing such a disturbing topic while their guests were being served crème brûlée, she had lovingly chastised him and called a halt to their conversation.

"Finally, gentlemen," Nathan remarked as he offered a humidor filled with an array of pungent imported cigars. The men stroked the tightly wound tubes of tobacco between their fingers, sniffing them the way their wives inhaled the sweet aroma of summer's first rose. Finally, after much ceremony, each of them clipped off the cigar's end and settled back to puff on the aromatic offering.

Matthew felt enthralled by the scene unfolding before him. It was difficult to believe that he could find himself among this group of influential men. Strange, he thought, how opportunities arise from the most unexpected circumstances.

"Listen and learn," Kirk Boott instructed in a barely audible tone.

Matthew nodded, chiding himself for getting caught up in his own thoughts, even if only for a few moments.

"As I was saying at supper before my wife cut me short, we've been most fortunate, gentlemen. Many here in Boston have been suffering great losses, and I fear they will continue for at least the remainder of the year. Not a major depression, perhaps, but certainly those who have invested at the wrong time and in the wrong places have suffered dramatically. Fortunately for all of us," Nathan commented, surveying the room filled with men, "we've experienced nothing but profit. Our project has been every bit the success we had anticipated."

"That's true enough, Nathan," Tracy Jackson remarked, "and with the Appleton Mill opening just last month and three other mills slated for opening next year, we'll see even greater profits in the years to come. Textiles will be our future and fortune. My only regret is that Francis didn't live long enough to see his plan to fruition."

"Agreed, Tracy, but your brother-in-law will never be forgotten. I can think of no greater honor we could have paid than to make the town his namesake."

Tracy nodded his head. "That's true, although I think perhaps some of the locals resented the town's name being changed to Lowell. It appears they're now becoming accustomed to the change, and with the daily influx of newcomers to the town, I believe the name has taken hold."

"I'm not so sure the old farm families have accepted the renaming of East Chelmsford just yet," Matthew interjected. A wave of embarrassment washed over Matthew as he realized he'd spoken the words aloud. He was here to listen and learn, not to necessarily voice an opinion.

All heads turned toward him, making his embarrassment even more complete. Kirk Boott gave him a slight smile before turning to the others. "I believe all of you know Matthew Cheever. He has strong ties to the Chelmsford farming community. He keeps me abreast of any unrest that may be stirring among the locals. Most of it has been settled by now, of course, but Matthew can tell you that many of the old East Chelmsford landowners still resent us—particularly those of us involved in purchasing their land."

Tracy Jackson swirled the deep purple liquid in his snifter. "Don't tell me they're still contending they were duped."

Boott looked to Matthew. "Go ahead," he encouraged.

"I'm afraid so," Matthew responded, feeling strengthened by Boott's approval. "Many say you deceived them."

"How so? They were paid a fair price," Appleton retorted.

"It's not the money, although they do believe they were underpaid," Matthew replied. "Those landowners truly believed the land would continue to be used for agrarian purposes. They sold their acreage based on that belief and say that Mr. Boott told them he planned to plant crops and raise sheep. Now they deeply resent the industrialization of their land."

"Surely they didn't believe Kirk was going to become a country squire," Tracy jibed. Several of the men chuckled. "What they're angry about is the fact that we've been able to put their land and water rights to profitable use."

"Since Mr. Boott is the visible member of the Boston Associates, the one with whom the locals have had personal dealings, their anger toward him runs deep. They have even gone so far as to make up a song about Mr. Boott," Matthew replied.

Tracy Jackson shook his head and laughed. "Ah, you've been memorialized, Kirk. I hope they haven't portrayed you too shamefully. Why don't you sing it for us, Mr. Cheever?" Jackson encouraged.

Kirk shifted in his chair. "If it's a musical offering you're wanting, Tracy, I'm sure the women have something to offer in the other room."

"Come now, Kirk. It can't be all that bad," Tracy taunted. "Give us the gist of it, at least, Matthew."

Kirk nodded his head. "But no singing," he admonished his young protégé.

Matthew made a show of himself, clearing his throat as he walked to the center of the room. Gone was all hint of embarrassment. The other men applauded in delight as he gave an exaggerated bow. "No singing," he promised as he turned toward Boott and received what he knew to be a forbidding glance. "Besides, I'm afraid my voice would send the gentlemen running out the front door. Now, let me see if I can remember a verse or two of that little ditty.

> "There came a man from the old country,
> the Merrimack River, he happened to see.
> What a capital place for mills, quoth he,
> Ri-toot, ri-noot, riumpty, ri-tooten-a.
> And then these farmers so cute,
> They gave all their lands and timber to Boott,
> Ri-toot, ri-noot, ri-toot, riumpty, ri-tooten-a."

A thunder of applause filled the room while he gave a slight bow and returned to his chair. Matthew sensed that Kirk was carefully observing him. He didn't want to do anything to estrange their relationship, yet truth be known, he was enjoying the attention of these powerful men.

"You have the boy well trained, Kirk. I notice he ceased his recitation and came running back to his chair the moment you appeared bored by his presentation."

Matthew ignored Paul Moody's remark but was somewhat surprised when Boott nodded, gave his friend a wry smile, and said in a voice loud enough for all to hear, "Let's hope so. I believe I've earned my reputation among my business partners as well as the Lowell community." The comment irked Matthew, who was no child. At twenty-five he was no one's trained boy.

Nathan leaned forward and offered Kirk more port. "The last I heard, they were referring to you as the tyrant-in-residence."

Holding out his glass to accept the offered drink, Kirk shook his head. "I'm not sure it's quite so bad. I may be quick to exact punishment, but I believe I am fair."

"And what of that young boy who felt your riding whip upon his back last week? Would he believe you to be fair?" Nathan asked.

"Ah, word does travel quickly, doesn't it? Just remember, gentlemen, none of you wanted to live in Lowell and create civilization out of mayhem. You willingly granted me the position of tyrant-in-residence, and I believe the town is better for it. That boy was an impudent scoundrel who needed to feel my whip. And in the event you haven't heard, I fired a foreman last week for disobedience. If any of you have a grievance with my methods, please speak out," Boott challenged.

A silence fell over the room as each man cast sidelong glances at the others. Matthew could hardly agree with all of Boott's methods, but he admired his ability to lay everything out on the table. Leaning back in his chair, Matthew crossed his arms and waited to see if anyone would take Boott to task.

Nathan broke the silence. "Now, Kirk, you know we have nothing but praise for your efforts in Lowell." Matthew smiled to himself. He might have known Appleton would rise to the occasion and smooth any ruffled feathers. Nathan Appleton knew the importance of keeping Boott content in his position. As Boott had mentioned, no one else wanted the job of turning chaos into order.

Nathan continued when no one else joined in to comment. "There's not a man here who would challenge your ability. After all, we chose you in large part because of your demanding personality. You have the paternalistic temperament necessary to manage the town. None of us is equal to the task, nor do we want it."

Boott placed his arm around Matthew's shoulder, breaking the tension that had filled the room. "Well done, my boy. Now that we've been entertained, let's get down to business. Nathan, would you like to begin?"

Matthew breathed a sigh of relief as they waited for Nathan to settle behind his large walnut desk and then begin rummaging through a stack of papers and drawings. "Well, gentlemen, as you know, the textile mills are expanding at the approximate rate we had planned, and the profits have exceeded our expectations. As these additional mills are constructed, we're going to need more girls to operate the looms. Kirk, why don't you tell us what you're doing in that regard? You might also give us a bit of information regarding the Irish. Have you been able to keep them contained?"

"Hiring more farm girls won't be a problem. The girls themselves spread word of their good fortune through their letters and occasional visits back home. Their friends and relatives come to Lowell seeking the same opportunity to earn money. However, I did take an added precaution and hired two men to travel farther north into New Hampshire, Vermont, and even Maine, spreading the word and bringing back any girls that may be ready to come. We still have openings at the Appleton, and then there are always those that want to go home for vacations or leave due to illness—the usual turnover.

"As for the Irish, don't concern yourselves. Although they are the one thing we seem to have overlooked in our planning, aren't they?" Kirk questioned as he glanced about the room.

Matthew knew only too well the concern Boott and the others had in regard to the Irish. Ignorance of Irish culture, beliefs, and attitudes made this necessary element of laborers an unneeded worry. But they'd brought it on themselves. The Irish provided dirt-cheap labor—men who would break their backs from dawn to dusk, day after day after day, for a quarter of the pay other men would demand.

Paul Moody raised his hand to the back of his neck and smoothed down the fringe of hair that circled his balding head. "I guess I always thought they'd return to Boston. Of course, I didn't consider the fact that as we continued to build, we'd need them in Lowell digging the canals and helping construct the mills. We should have realized they'd begin to bring their families and squat on some of the land. Not much we can do about that now."

"They're a necessary evil, and that's a fact," William Thurston concluded. "Dirty bunch of beggars for the most part—heathens, the whole lot of them."

"They're papists, William, not heathens," Nathan interjected.

"Same thing. More witchcraft than Christianity, as far as I'm concerned. Superstitious miscreants. You'd think so, too, Nathan, if you'd take some time and go down into that mess of shanties they've patched together on the Acre. It's a blight to our fair city, and so are they."

Nathan's lips curled into a wry grin. "Really, William. I didn't know you were spending so much time among the Irish, but since you've become such an authority, perhaps you've devised some sort of plan. What solution do you propose?"

Irritation crossed William's face as he pulled a linen handkerchief from his pocket, wiped his forehead, and moved away from the blazing fireplace. He stuttered momentarily as all eyes shifted in his direction. "I didn't mean to give the impression that I spend inordinate amounts of time with the Irish over at the Acre. I visit only when it's necessary to question Hugh Cummiskey and assure myself things are progressing when I make my occasional trips to Lowell."

"I guess the rest of us rely upon Kirk to give us that assurance," Nathan put in. "After all, he's the one that we've charged with the task of building and supervising the operation of the mills and canals—a monumental task, I might add, Kirk. It's no wonder you're in need of an assistant." Nathan allowed his gaze to rest upon Matthew for a moment. "Ah, well, I digress. You still haven't told us your solution, William."

William had moved to a chair across the room from the fireplace, but the pinkish-purple flush continued to splotch his cheeks. "I don't have a solution, but that doesn't negate the fact that there is a very real problem. Left unchecked, the situation will only worsen," he replied, his remark tinged with irritation.

Matthew watched intently. It was apparent William Thurston was upset with the lack of support among the Associates, though Boott stroked his chin while giving Thurston his exclusive attention. A look of gratitude washed over Thurston's face when he realized he had been successful in garnering Boott's attention. Finally Kirk rose from his chair and sauntered toward Nathan's desk. Slowly he turned toward William and casually leaned against the oversized desk. "I agree with your observation that the Irish presence in Lowell was unplanned, William. We must always keep in mind, however, that although I've been successful in luring men away from the farms and out of Boston to work as mechanics and in the offices of the mills, there are few men willing to perform the heavy, dirty work of mucking out the canals, clearing the land, and constructing the buildings. I need pure brute labor to accomplish this work—not just animals, but men, too. The Irish may not offer much in the way of skilled labor or intelligence, but they've strong backs and, more importantly, they're hungry. Even if I could find others willing to do the manual labor, the Irish tolerate lower wages. In that regard, it seems prudent to continue employing the Irish."

"Hear, hear," Tracy Jackson replied, holding up his glass toward the others. "Kirk is doing an excellent job protecting our investment. Don't forget, William, you're a major stockholder. I would think you'd be more interested in a good rate of return on your money than the plight of the Irish. Besides, they're a pitiful lot of humans who have low expectations from life, especially from England and her descendants. Why not let Kirk take care of dealing with the Irish in Lowell? You'd serve us all better by remaining in Boston overseeing the banking business. I'm sure it would make your wife happier if you weren't off to Lowell every week or ten days," he added, giving William a perceptive glance.

William patted his linen handkerchief across his forehead. It appeared he didn't quite trust himself to speak. Matthew watched closely, knowing that wisdom required Thurston to align himself with Boott and the Associates. But why was Thurston so hesitant? It was obvious he was a minority of one. Continuing to argue would only cause a breech—a breech that would cause problems for the other Associates, and one that Thurston surely couldn't financially survive.

"You're right, gentlemen. We need the Irish and they need us. So be it," William finally replied. "I thought perhaps Daniel would be joining us this evening."

Kirk smiled, nodded, and then leaned toward Matthew. He held his hand over his mouth and spoke quietly. "Mr. Thurston's an intelligent man. He knows when to fight for a cause and when to give it up. Changing the subject was an intelligent tactical decision on his part."

Tracy Jackson blew out a long, spiraling curl of smoke before answering William's question. "Daniel was detained in Washington but hopes to be in Boston by mid-October. He sends nothing but good reports and continues to spread word among Congress that our venture is successful. Fortunately, our backers in Congress remain supportive—and Daniel assures me the federal funds will continue. Good news to all of us since that reduces our risk considerably."

Matthew glanced around the room, his questioning gaze settling on his mentor.

"My young friend hasn't been privy to information regarding our financial windfall and, I believe, is a bit perplexed by your comments, Tracy," Kirk commented.

Nodding in agreement, Matthew turned toward Tracy Jackson as he stated, "Nothing difficult to understand, my boy. One learns early on the importance of choosing a lawyer who is not only well versed in the law but who has the proper connections. The Boston Associates decided on Daniel Webster. Daniel is well connected to members of Congress and a close friend to several of us."

"An excellent lawyer, too," William Thurston added, the ash

on his cigar turning bright orange as he inhaled deeply.

"Absolutely—Harvard educated!" Tracy agreed. "When we were in the early stages of planning our textile revolution here in New England, each member of the group agreed to pledge personal funds toward the financial stability of our plan. Of course, additional financial security was a concern. It was Daniel who relieved us of that worry. He managed to secure a million-dollar windfall from Congress, which is being paid out over the course of our development of the Lowell project." Tracy leaned back and blew a grayish-blue puff of smoke, a slow smile creeping across his lips as he watched the cloud inch upward into a circle and then rise toward the ceiling.

Matthew took a deep breath and slowly exhaled. Had anyone other than the principal stockholders of the Boston Associates told him that the Congress was financially involved in this venture, Matthew would have denounced the revelation. There was, however, no sound reason for him to question the truth of what he was told. In fact, he found the information intoxicating. That he, the product of an East Chelmsford farm family, was sharing drinks with men who had the ability to influence the spending of Congressional dollars was surely one of his finer moments. A sense of power washed over him, and he wondered if Boott ever had such feelings. The improbability that he should be sitting in the midst of the Boston elite was mind-boggling, and there was no doubt in Matthew's mind that he would find a way to make this situation beneficial to himself. He glanced toward Boott and was met by his steely gaze.

Later, as they prepared to make their way to the carriage, Boott spoke. "You remind me of myself in many ways, Matthew. I could almost hear your brain at work trying to determine how best to capitalize on your newfound place among these men of power and position."

Matthew felt the heat rise in his cheeks. "I count you foremost among these men, Mr. Boott."

Kirk gave Matthew a wry grin as he slapped him on the

back. "I'm sure you do, my boy. I'm also sure that you bear watching."

Matthew knew the words were not spoken in jest. Boott would be watching him very closely in the future. If he was going to achieve his goal and become a member of the Boston Associates, he must be careful to do nothing that would cause Boott discomfort or concern. He chided himself for taking center stage earlier in the evening. He would need to remain low-key in the future, he thought as he followed behind Boott, shaking hands and offering his thanks and farewell to the men and their wives as they left the Appleton residence.

Soon they were settled into the carriage that would return them to Lowell. "It was obvious you enjoyed yourself this evening," Kirk remarked.

Matthew leaned forward with his arms resting across his thighs. "Absolutely! I feel rather the fool for not realizing what an important role the government could play in a private business venture."

"It's merely your youth and inexperience that prohibited you from gaining such knowledge—coupled with the fact that such information isn't bantered about among strangers. As a matter of fact, I was rather surprised when Nathan broached the subject in front of you. On another note, however, I'm interested in what thoughts you might have on Thurston's comments regarding the Irish. Do you view the situation as problematic?"

Matthew leaned back in the coach and thought a few moments before answering. "I believe there are some valid concerns. Although Thurston was speaking of the larger settlement, there really are two separate groups settled in fairly close proximity to each other. But I'm sure you're aware of that."

"No, I don't spend any time in that area. Hugh Cummiskey is my contact with the Irish workers. When necessary, I've sent one of the men from the machine shop to fetch him. So the Irish are squatting on more land than any of us realized, and there is a problem. Is that what you're telling me?"

"I'm not certain the Irish occupy any more land than you surmise. I merely wanted to point out that there are two Paddy camps on land located slightly outside the edge of town. Two groups that do not get along very well, I might add. Depending upon how you plan to enlarge the mill community, it appears those Paddy camps could end up in the middle of town. On the other hand, you can't build without the Irish laborers. It's become evident the young farm boys are interested in becoming mechanics and working for Mr. Moody on the locks and canals, but—"

"But they'll not count themselves among the lords of the spade. Not that I blame them, of course," Boott concluded. "The infighting . . . now, that could present a challenge. The Irish have always been a factious sort—my years in England taught me that much. If they want to survive, they need to outgrow that clan mentality they've brought with them."

Both men remained silent as the coach continued to lumber through the countryside, swaying both of them back and forth—unmercifully at times. Matthew would have much preferred Nathan Appleton's offer that they remain in Boston for the night and depart the next morning. Boott, however, had adamantly refused, obviously convinced the mills and newborn community could not survive without him. Although Boott verbalized trust in his managers' judgment, Matthew knew that he never gave them the opportunity to exercise much authority.

Finally Boott broke the silence. "John Farnsworth will be arriving from England within the week. Of course, I'll be meeting with him upon his arrival, but I would like for you to be present also. In the meantime, make arrangements for him at one of the better boardinghouses. I'm sure he'll expect a house to himself, but we can negotiate that after his arrival."

"Farnsworth. He's the expert you hired for calico printing, isn't he?"

Boott nodded his head, a wry smile crossing his lips. "Quite a negotiator. Did I tell you about my meeting with him in England?"

Matthew leaned forward, his eyes alight with interest. "No, I don't believe so."

"When we first discussed the possibility of calicos, Francis—

Mr. Lowell—mentioned the talented artisan he had met when he toured the mills in England. Said the man was one of the most brilliant craftsmen he'd ever had the pleasure of meeting. When we ran into difficulty producing our calicos, the Associates agreed that I should attempt to locate Farnsworth."

"And he was obviously willing to leave England."

"After a bit of dickering about his wage. When I asked what wage he would require, he told me five thousand dollars a year."

Matthew's jaw dropped. He couldn't believe his own ears. "He was joking, of course."

"I'm afraid not. When I told him that was more than we paid the governor of Massachusetts, he replied, 'Well, can the governor of Massachusetts print?' I had to tell him the governor could not and that I needed him more than I needed the governor."

"The Associates agreed to a salary of five thousand dollars? That's difficult to believe."

Kirk reached for the small cushion he carried with him whenever he traveled. "It's bad enough that my back gives me problems when I sit in a comfortable chair, but riding in these coaches is going to be the total ruination of my spine," he stated, pushing the support behind his back and settling farther into the seat. "Where was I? Oh yes, discussing the merits of John Farnsworth's wages. 'Tis true the man will be paid more than any of us, and that was a difficult pill to swallow—harder for some than others. However, we came to the conclusion that he will be worth that figure ten times over once the Merrimack is producing quality prints."

"I don't doubt you've made a sound decision."

"There isn't a man among the Associates who would doubt the validity of the man's worth. After all, if there was anything that Francis Cabot Lowell knew, it was the looms and textiles."

"I'm sorry I didn't have the opportunity to meet Mr. Lowell before his death."

Kirk stared out the coach window for several minutes, seemingly lost in his thoughts. Matthew had settled back, the motion of the coach beginning to lull his senses, when suddenly Kirk leaned forward, slapped Matthew on the knee, and issued a challenge. "Well, my young friend, if you were the agent in charge of this project, how would you reconcile the problem of the Irish? Would you remove them from the land? Order them to quit their fighting or suffer the consequences?"

Matthew cleared his throat. "I would work through their religion. As Mr. Appleton pointed out earlier this evening, they're all papists. No one has more influence over the Irish than a Catholic priest. If you could somehow manage to have a priest assigned to them, it could help. Many of the men now have their families with them. A strong religious leader could keep the men in line and possibly alleviate the feuding."

"I *knew* you were bright. I believe you have an idea worth exploring. I'm personally acquainted with Bishop Fenwick. I believe I'll send an invitation for him to visit in the near future—or perhaps I should travel to Boston and pay him a visit myself. Excellent idea, excellent."

Matthew basked in the adulation for only a moment before Boott fired another question in his direction. "Is there anything else you learned this evening that we haven't discussed?"

Matthew thought of a great many things he'd tucked away for future reference. He had no desire to share them with his employer just yet, but of utmost importance was the earning of Boott's trust. Not only that, but Matthew hoped that by cultivating their working relationship with sound judgment and positive initiative, Boott would soon come to see him as an invaluable asset.

"Well, it did appear there is a hierarchy among the stockholders, but I wasn't certain. I thought perhaps there was deference shown due to those men holding more stock." Boott nodded and motioned for him to continue. "I learned it's imperative to cultivate influential friends."

"Absolutely!" Boott exclaimed, slapping Matthew on the leg. "Think about the fact that there is no single member of the Boston Associates who was powerful enough to influence Congress, but several of us doggedly pursued our friendship with Daniel Webster. It has reaped a multitude of benefits. You must keep this lesson in the forefront of your mind, both in your business *and* personal life. If you do, you'll go far, my boy. A wife must be chosen with no less intelligence and cunning than one chooses a lawyer or business partner."

Matthew grinned. "I would imagine that to be true enough, but I never have cared for the way my lawyer wears his hair or fashions."

"Looks can be deceiving," Boott said, sobering. "Just remember that. Things are not always what they appear to be, and this is especially true when dealing with people."

CHAPTER 3

Lowell, Massachusetts

Lilly trudged up the narrow stairway and made her way down the hall. Her back ached, and she longed for quiet and the comfort of a good night's sleep. Carefully, she turned the doorknob, fearful she might awaken the other girls with her late arrival to the room.

"Welcome to our humble abode," the girl known as Marmi greeted in a none-too-quiet manner. Six girls sat gathered together on one bed.

"Shhh!" Prudence Holtmeyer warned. "Keep your voice down, Marmi."

"Sorry, I always forget," she replied. "Lilly, in case you haven't met everyone, this is Katie, Sarah, Beth, and Franny. Nadene's asleep, but I think you met her earlier."

Lilly smiled as she closed the bedroom door. "Thank you for the welcome," she said in a low voice. "I thought you would all be asleep by now. I was afraid I'd awaken you coming in this late."

"Not us—we always stay up late chatting, except for Nadene," Katie replied.

"She's the early-to-bed girl. You needn't worry about

39

waking her. She falls into bed after supper, and nothing seems to interrupt her sleep," Franny added.

"We rearranged your things closer to your bed," Prudence said. "Hope you don't mind, but we thought it would make it easier for you when you're getting ready for work in the morning. You won't have to crawl across the bed to get to your clothes."

"Thank you again," Lilly replied. She had half expected the girls to act aloof since she really wasn't one of them, at least not yet. Apparently they weren't given to drawing class distinctions among themselves.

Marmi bounced across the bed. "There I went and made all the introductions, and we haven't been formally introduced. I'm Margaret Mildred Tharp, but everyone calls me Marmi. I know you met Prudence earlier at supper."

She pointed toward the figure cocooned in a log-cabin patterned quilt. "Nadene is from Vermont. Prudence and I hail from New Hampshire, and the others are from around the state. Whereabouts do you come from?"

"I suppose if we're making proper introductions, I should say that my name is Lilly Armbruster, and I'm from right here, East Chelmsford—that would be Lowell to you."

Prudence raised her eyebrows ever so slightly. "The girls that hail from Lowell usually live at home."

"It saves them the cost of room and board," Beth threw in as if Lilly couldn't discern that for herself.

"Why did you decide to live in a boardinghouse?" Prudence questioned.

Marmi glanced toward Prudence and shook her head. "You don't have to answer any of our questions you don't want to. We all tend to be a bit inquisitive."

"Nosey's more like it." The cocoon had spoken. All the girls turned to peer at the multicolored quilt. A tangle of copper-colored hair appeared, followed by two light blue eyes and the palest complexion Lilly had ever seen. "They'll be asking you questions until sunrise if you don't put a stop to them early on," Nadene said, nodding her unkempt curls toward the ensemble.

"I'm Nadene Eckhoff. We're to share a bed."

Lilly smiled. "Pleased to make your acquaintance."

"What are you doing awake, Nadene? You usually sleep through no matter how noisy we get—and we're talking quietly tonight," Prudence quickly added.

Nadene slipped her legs over the side of the bed and pulled on a thin cotton wrapper while shoving her feet into a pair of broken-down work shoes. "Need to go to the outhouse," she answered.

"Want me to go with you?" Marmi offered.

Nadene shook her head. "It's you that's afraid of the dark, Marmi, not me. But thank you anyway." The girls stared after Nadene as she trudged out the door carrying a flickering candle.

"She has beautiful hair—and her skin, it's so pale it's almost translucent," Lilly whispered.

Prudence nodded. "She's sickly, that's why. No matter how much sleep she gets, she's always tired—and pale," she added.

"Maybe it's just her natural coloring," Lilly offered.

"No. One of the other girls who came at the same time as Nadene told me Nadene had color in her cheeks and was healthy looking when she first arrived at the mills. I think she's gotten worse since they transferred her over to the Appleton. She used to work at the Merrimack, but when they opened the Appleton, they took some of the most experienced girls and moved them over there to teach the new hires. Nobody can match Nadene when it comes to spinning, so it didn't take long for the supervisors to decide she should become an instructor at the Appleton. They're working her too hard," Prudence explained.

Marmi nodded in agreement. "That's probably true enough, Pru, but Nadene doesn't take care of herself, either."

Franny added, "She doesn't keep herself warm enough in winter and won't even go see the doctor when she needs to."

"She doesn't keep enough of her money to pay for a doctor visit," Beth declared. "She sends it to her family."

Sarah, the quietest of the group, shook her head. "I think it's nice she sends her pay home to help her family, but she carries it too far, never willing to use any of her wages to care for herself."

"Her money, her choice," Prudence replied.

Footsteps quietly echoed on the stairs and Marmi put a finger to her lips. "Talk about something else," she whispered.

"You never answered my question about why you're living in the boardinghouse," Prudence remarked, turning back toward Lilly. All the girls seemed to await her answer in great interest.

"My parents are both deceased. We lost our farm when the Associates decided to make East Chelmsford the site of their industrial community."

Nadene turned sideways as she wove her way through the narrow aisle between the beds and dropped onto the lumpy mattress. "You never give up with your questions, do you? Now look what you've done—you've caused Lilly to dredge up sad memories. Now she'll never get to sleep," Nadene scolded, pointing toward the gloomy expression etched upon Lilly's face.

The girls glanced in Lilly's direction. "We're sorry," they chorused in unison.

"And don't you tell them it's all right, Lilly, or they'll just keep on with their unending questions until they've learned and repeated every detail of your life," Nadene interjected.

The girls giggled. "She's right. We don't know when to stop asking questions."

Lilly glanced toward Nadene, then chose her words carefully before answering. "Your apology is accepted."

Nadene nodded her approval.

"We truly do appreciate your cooking skills," Prudence said, obviously not wanting to go to bed. "I'm only sorry you can't remain here at the house and be our cook. We all like Miss Addie, but she's a poor excuse for a culinary artist."

"Oh, listen to you, *culinary artist,*" Marmi mimicked, causing all of the girls to giggle.

"Do you know where you'll be assigned once you begin at the Appleton?" Franny inquired.

"I've been told the spinning room, but I'm sure that it's subject to change since I haven't actually signed a contract yet. The thought that we're required to sign a contract seems to imply that the owners don't believe women will keep their word. As if women might not be responsible employees, don't you think?" Lilly inquired, hoping to elicit the girls' attitude toward their employer.

Nadene leaned back against her pillow and tucked the quilt under her chin, obviously willing to remain awake a bit longer.

"They require contracts from *all* employees—the men, too," Prudence replied. "I think the contracts are a good thing. That way there's no misunderstanding. We're all given the same information about the rules and what is expected of us."

Most of the girls nodded in agreement. Nadene didn't respond.

"So you don't mind any of the rules?" Lilly ventured.

"Some of the regulations may seem harsh—we're certainly expected to give a long day of hard labor for our pay, but that's to be expected. At least the Corporation has eliminated the required pew rent at St. Anne's Episcopal," Nadene stated.

Lilly was aghast at the remark. "Pew rent?"

Nadene nodded. "Thirty-seven and a half cents a month."

Franny added in a conspiratorial whisper, "They held it out of our pay, but we raised enough of a ruckus that they finally stopped."

Nadene continued. "The pew rent was an easy way for Kirk Boott to recover the cost of building his Episcopal church. My feeling was that if he wanted an Episcopal church, that was fine, but why should I pay for it? I'm a Methodist."

Lilly folded her arms across her chest. "Such behavior by Mr. Boott and the Boston Associates shouldn't come as a surprise to me. Every one of those men is self-serving, set upon nothing but the almighty dollar. Not one of them has any concern for others. Those men and their greed have caused untold suffering to the farmers of East Chelmsford. I have no doubt they'd sell their souls to the devil to turn a profit."

Prudence's mouth dropped open. "How can you say such things, Lilly? Why, the Boston Associates are forward-thinking men who have finally given women an opportunity to be of value in this country. I personally applaud what they've accomplished. Perhaps you haven't given thought to how you would have supported yourself upon the death of your parents if these mills hadn't been here to provide you a job," she countered.

Lilly clenched her fists, her expression hardening as she fought to control her voice. "If the Boston Associates hadn't invaded this countryside, my father would still be alive, and if he weren't, I'd at least have a farm to provide my living, Prudence. You'll not convince me that those evil men have done me any favors. Had they ventured into New Hampshire and stolen land from your family, I'm sure you might think differently."

Lilly knew she'd gone too far. Exhaustion made her vulnerable and free with her thoughts. Why couldn't she be sweet spirited like her mother? *Mama would be so ashamed of my attitude.*

Marmi placed an arm around Lilly's quivering shoulder. "I'm sorry for what's happened to your family's land, Lilly, but the mills are here to stay, and if you're going to work in them, you need to forget the past. If you can," she added quickly.

Lilly took a deep breath before exhaling slowly. She was alarmed that such random conversation could elicit her anger so quickly. It was obvious she'd made a spectacle of herself the very first night. The girls were all staring at her.

Forcing a smile, she glanced about the room. "I see my performance has left you all in awe. My father always said I was born to be an actress. Do tell me more about all these fees for church pews."

Marmi, Prudence, and the others visibly sighed in relief while Nadene appeared to be calmly evaluating her behavior. It was apparent that Nadene was not easily deceived.

"One thing about the fee at St. Anne's: you were told when you were hired that you had to pay. At least the Corporation didn't steal the money like old Elder Harley over at the Freewill Baptist," Marmi said, once again taking up the banner for the Associates.

"Same thing as far as I'm concerned," Nadene replied. "Neither one of them had consent to take the money."

"Yes, but at least Mr. Boott used it for the church," Beth

said, her eyes wide as if she suddenly knew a great secret. "I heard Elder Harley did unspeakable things with his ill-gotten gains."

Prudence laughed. "Who knows what Elder Harley did with all the money the girls donated to him."

Lilly curled her legs beneath her, listening to the tales, surprised at how sheltered she had been from this information while living so close. "Whatever are you talking about? Did one of the preachers steal money from the mill girls?"

Marmi's head bobbed up and down. "Indeed, he did. He told the girls he needed funds to build a church, which would be a good thing for the community. In order to raise the money, he offered the girls interest on any funds they loaned him. All of the Baptist girls as well as girls from other denominations loaned him money. Then he absconded with their funds, having never laid a cornerstone."

"Cornerstone! He never even turned a spade of dirt," Prudence chimed in.

"I heard he had a mistress," Katie offered.

"Katie! That's gossip, pure and simple. The rest of this we know firsthand," Franny admonished.

"Are you planning to attend St. Anne's?" Marmi inquired. "That's where most of us attend church."

"I haven't attended in a long time. I'm not sure that I'll be going to church, at least not in Lowell," Lilly replied.

The girls gasped in unison. Nadene merely gave her a wry smile.

"Why are you smiling at me like that?" Lilly asked.

"You'll attend. It's in your contract. All mill employees must regularly attend church or be subject to dismissal. And yes, they do check with the boardinghouse keepers to assure themselves of our attendance. You may get by with staying abed for a Sunday here and there, but be assured, such behavior will not be tolerated frequently."

"Besides, why wouldn't you want to go?" Sarah asked softly.

Lilly had so long been troubled in her spirit that she'd given up trying to understand it. She wanted to do the will of God, but at the same time, God's will seemed very uncertain—very unclear. It was almost as if He were playing a game with her. Testing her. Teasing her.

"I was very sad throughout my father's illness," Lilly said, reluctant to confide her true reasons. "I haven't felt like going to church and being around a lot of our old friends."

"Well, that makes perfect sense," Marmi said, patting Lilly's hand. "But now you'll have all of us and you shan't be sad for long."

Lilly wished that were true. If only she could know for sure that her plans were what God wanted. At times she felt confident—almost as though God had written them out on a tablet like He'd done for Moses with the Ten Commandments. Then other times she felt so confused, wrestling whether or not God even heard her prayer—whether He saw her misery.

"I don't know about the rest of you, but I must get up early in the morning. I think we should all get some sleep," Nadene remarked. Without waiting for a reply, she snuffed out the candle, sending the room into immediate darkness.

Lilly quickly realized there was nothing to be done but prepare for bed. She slipped into her nightgown, thankful she had removed it from her trunk while there was still candlelight in the room, then crawled into the empty space beside Nadene. She could hear the other girls settling in for the night, the swishing of sheets and the groaning protests of the bed frames breaking the silence.

Lilly clung to the edge of the uncomfortable mattress. Never in her life had she shared a bedroom, much less a bed, with another person. She attempted to relax, but it seemed her body had stiffened into a rigid column, unwilling to yield to her command. Sounds of deep, relaxed breathing soon turned to soft snores, interrupted by an occasional mumbled, unintelligible word. Yet sleep would not come. Thoughts of pew rent, stolen church funds, contract signings, and beady-eyed clerks skittered through her mind until she finally sat up along the edge of the bed, holding her aching head in her hands.

"You'll get used to it after a while," Nadene whispered

before breaking into a deep racking cough.

"I'm sorry I wakened you. I tried to be quiet, but I'm not accustomed to sleeping in a room with anyone else."

"You didn't waken me, Lilly. The girls don't realize that the reason I'm so tired is because I'm awake for long periods of time every night. This cough won't let me sleep, so I come to bed and get rest when I can. Strange thing is, my cough never seems to bother them."

"Why don't you see a doctor? Perhaps there's an elixir that would help."

"There's no elixir going to help me. My lungs can't seem to bear up under the humid conditions at the mill. I suppose one day it will be the death of me, but for now, it's salvation for my mother and brothers."

Lilly turned toward Nadene, stunned by her cavalier attitude. She could barely make out Nadene's form in the darkness, but somehow she knew Nadene was awaiting her response. "Life is a precious gift from God, Nadene. I think we're meant to protect it as best we can. Death won't serve you or your family well," she whispered in reply. She felt Nadene's weight shift the bed. "I promise I won't spend my time telling you what you should do, Nadene. I know how tiresome that can become. Let's just agree to look out for each other. Would that be all right?"

Nadene reached out and took Lilly's hand. "Yes, Lilly, that would be all right. I think you and I are going to get along just fine."

"I hope so, because I surely could use a friend. I wouldn't tell the others, but I'm frightened about going to work in the mills. I'm used to being outdoors, coming and going at my pleasure. I fear being cooped up all day. Is it terrible?"

"It's like most things, Lilly—after a while you get used to it. But I won't tell you there aren't times when I truly long for the quiet of home. I can remember thinking that a colicky baby was more noise than I could bear. Now I know different. The sounds of a crying baby would be a mere lullaby compared to those clamoring machines in the mill. And heat—I'd be happy to stand over a wood cookstove for the rest of my life if I didn't have to suffer the mugginess that they create for us to breathe."

"I don't understand, Nadene. There are windows in the buildings—I saw them. Why don't you open the windows and let fresh air circulate in the room?"

"Ha!" The remark sent Nadene into another fit of coughing. When the hacking finally ceased, she leaned against the headboard of the bed, gasping for air until finally her breathing returned to normal. "The windows, dear Lilly, are nailed shut. If the air in the room is dry, the threads break. Too many broken threads make for a shabby piece of fabric. On the other hand, moisture in the air helps prevent broken threads. Since a good product is more important than the health of the employees, our windows are nailed shut. After all, workers can be replaced. The reputation of the Corporation rests upon the fabric we produce."

"So you dislike what's going on here as much as I do," Lilly ventured.

"Probably not. I need the work, so I'm thankful for a job that pays well. Were it not for the mills, my family would be starving. I dislike the fact that the conditions are unhealthy—at least for me. Some of the girls seem to have no problem working in the humidity. Now you'd better try and get to sleep. My guess is that you have to be up even earlier than the rest of us in order to help Miss Addie with breakfast."

"Thank you, Nadene."

"For what?"

"Offering me your friendship," Lilly replied simply. She pulled the sheet across her shoulders and tried to adjust the meager pillow. But no matter how much she plumped the ticking, the bundle of feathers inside fell flat. Finally she quit struggling with the pillow, laid her head down, and began to pray.

CHAPTER 4

Only the continual pumping of John Farnsworth's right hand overshadowed Kirk Boott's verbal welcome as he ushered Farnsworth into the vestibule of the Boott residence. Matthew stood back watching the exchange, studying both men as they eyed each other. They could have passed for brothers, both tall and lanky with thick wavy hair, both exuding an air of confidence. And while Farnsworth was the elder by at least ten years, his physical agility belied that fact. There was a vibrant assurance in his step and an obvious eagerness to greet life's many challenges.

"I hope you don't mind that we're meeting here in my home rather than at the Merrimack," Kirk said as he led the men into his office. His large walnut desk stood in front of two large windows overlooking the flower garden. Boott's prized mums, goldenrod, asters, and dahlias, all dressed in their autumn finery, were in full view. "Sit down," he requested, gesturing toward one of the leather-upholstered chairs opposite the desk. "Tea will be here momentarily," he continued while ringing a small gold bell.

Although Kirk hadn't invited him to be seated, Matthew lowered himself into the chair alongside Farnsworth who, at the moment, appeared somewhat nonplussed by Boott's fawning behavior.

Farnsworth settled into the chair and turned his attention toward his host. "I generally find the meeting place of little concern. Rather, it's the outcome of such interaction that is of interest."

"Exactly! I couldn't agree more. However, I find that information discussed at the mills sometimes makes it way through the entire Corporation before I've left the building. Consequently, when I want to assure myself of privacy, I conduct business meetings here at home."

"Ah, I see. Well, perhaps it's not the place where you hold your meetings but the trustworthiness of the employees who attend those meetings?" Farnsworth suggested.

Matthew glanced up as a mobcapped maid entered the room. Boott pointed to a spot on his desk and then watched as the woman dutifully placed the tea service where he had indicated.

Massaging the back of his neck, Boott directed a steely look at Farnsworth. "You may be correct, Mr. Farnsworth. If so, I hope you won't prove to be one of those gossiping employees."

"I can give you my word on that, Mr. Boott, but only time will prove if you have my loyalty," Farnsworth replied as he took the cup of tea being offered.

Matthew turned his attention toward Boott, who hesitated a moment. "That's a fair enough answer, Mr. Farnsworth. Truth be told, people never know about loyalty until it's put to the test, do they?"

Farnsworth nodded his agreement and took a sip of his tea. "This is your meeting, Mr. Boott. What would you like to discuss?"

"Most important, the improvement of our calicos. After that, we'll need to discuss arrangements for your housing and detail your position at the Merrimack. I believe we have any number of matters that must be resolved prior to your first day on the job. And, of course, you need to sign your contract."

"I'm pleased you didn't include my salary as one of those items under discussion, Mr. Boott. Otherwise, I would be looking askew at *your* sense of loyalty," Farnsworth replied, with the corners of his mouth turning up ever so slightly.

"If there is one thing I learned from the Englishmen who arrived before you, it is to settle salary negotiations before paying for passage to this country."

"Did my English brothers give you a bit of trouble when bartering for their wages?"

Boott nodded his head in agreement. "They gave me more than a bit of trouble. They decided that unless I met their salary demands *and* provided them with housing that met their specifications, they wouldn't work for me. I thought they were bluffing and told them I wouldn't agree to their requirements."

"I take it they called your bluff?"

"They did. I turned and walked away, thinking they'd knuckle under. Instead, they loaded back into their wagons and left town. I thought they would merely go a short distance and make camp, thinking I would come running after them."

"And?" Farnsworth asked, his eyes sparkling.

"They were well into New Hampshire by the time we found them. They had no plans to return. I met their every demand as well as a few extra incentives in order to convince them to turn around. That is why I insisted we agree upon your wages prior to your departure from England. You'll recall that I expected you to drive a hard bargain—and you didn't disappoint me in that respect. I am, however, pleased that the matter of your wages was settled while I was in Lancashire."

Farnsworth rose from the leather-upholstered chair and shoved his hands deep into his pockets. "We came to this country at great risk. You know very well that the law was against us. We weren't to divulge information or bring drawings related to the mills under threat of great penalties. The money had to be worth our while. After all, it would be very hard for us to return home once word got out that we'd aided the competition. I, for one, would fear the consequences."

Matthew heard the bitterness edged with sorrow in John's voice. He knew the man spoke truthfully. England wanted to keep America dependent upon her for textiles. The fact that

Americans had taken the initiative to plan their own textile mills had not gone over well at all. The matter of Frances Lowell touring the English mills and walking away with the knowledge embedded in his memory was even more distressing.

Farnsworth put the matter behind him and pressed a question. "Why don't we begin by talking about the calicos? I know you've hired me to improve the quality of your prints. How would you say they currently compare to English imports?"

Matthew glanced toward Boott, and the two of them laughed. "I apologize, Mr. Farnsworth. It's just that when anyone asks about the quality of our calicos, we're reminded of the story that frequently circulates about the city," Matthew said.

"If the story gives you cause for laughter, I would enjoy hearing it," Farnsworth responded.

Kirk nodded at Matthew. "It is said that one of the female residents of Lowell purchased a piece of Merrimack calico, intent upon making herself a new frock for special occasions. She worked diligently until she had completed her sewing. The following Sunday morning she appeared in her new dress, expecting her family to be duly impressed. Her brother, however, took one look at her and advised that it was good she was planning to wear the costume to church because that dress was certainly holier than she could ever hope to be."

Farnsworth nodded his head in recognition but didn't laugh. "You do have a problem, gentlemen. If the best you are currently producing is a piece of cloth that is full of holes and you're passing it off as calico, we have much to accomplish. But accomplish the task, we will. By the time we've fine-tuned the Merrimack's machinery, we'll be producing cloth that will make the English envious."

Boott leaned forward, focused upon Farnsworth's words. "That's the attitude I want to hear," he said, slapping his hand upon his knee. "I knew you were the right man for this corporation the minute I laid eyes upon you."

"Well, I thank you for your confidence, Mr. Boott, but there's much work to be done before we'll actually overtake the English. It will take your continual cooperation—and the funds for necessary changes to the equipment."

Boott rose from his chair and came around the desk. "You'll have no problem with either of those items. I'll make myself available to you at any time."

"Thank you. I'll remember that promise. Now, I believe you mentioned something about housing earlier. I would like to get settled before taking a tour of the Corporation's holdings. I trust you've made arrangements for my accommodations?"

Boott appeared to squirm at the question. "I believe I may have mentioned there is an area of housing known as the English Row. It is, however, full at this time. Since I wasn't sure what you might prefer in regard to housing, I took the liberty of seeking out a room in our best boardinghouse."

Farnsworth was silent for a moment. Kirk pulled a linen handkerchief from his pocket and pressed it against his forehead. The room was apparently becoming uncomfortably warm for him.

"A boardinghouse will suffice until a house can be provided, but I suspect it would be best if we address housing in my contract so that there is no misunderstanding."

"Of course, of course," Kirk quickly agreed.

"My father has agreed to come to America when his health improves. I would want to have adequate accommodations prior to his arrival," Farnsworth added.

"We can begin plans for a house as soon as you tell me what you'll need. We can add another house to the English Row—or build something else, if you prefer."

John smiled, a faraway look in his eye. "I find it unnecessary to live alongside my English brothers. In all honesty, I'd prefer a house that had a bit of land around it for a garden such as you have out there," he replied, gesturing toward Boott's backyard. "Though perhaps a bit smaller. We wouldn't want folks to think I'm trying to outshine the Corporation's agent."

Boott laughed, but Matthew sensed he was not completely pleased that Farnsworth wanted a home apart from the English Row. It was obvious, however, that Farnsworth's request would not be denied.

"I have your contract here in my desk if you'd like to sign it," Kirk offered, pulling the paper from a drawer.

John carefully folded the pages and tucked them in his coat. "Why don't I take this with me and read it over. I'm sure it's in proper order, but I prefer to read binding legal documents several times before signing them. I'm sure you understand."

"Of course, of course," Boott concurred. "We can meet again tomorrow—if that will give you ample time," he quickly added.

"Tomorrow morning should be fine. Eight o'clock?"

"Yes, eight o'clock. Why don't we meet here at my house? Once the contract has been signed, we can go down and walk through the mills."

John nodded and rose from his chair, then hesitated. "What about a horse and carriage? I'll be in need of transportation from time to time."

"I can make arrangements at the livery. You'll be able to use a carriage any time you desire," Kirk said with a smile.

John furrowed his brows ever so slightly. "Quite frankly, I was thinking more along the lines of the Corporation furnishing me with my own horse and carriage. Of course, you could board them at the livery stable until my house is constructed. Perhaps young Matthew and I could take a look at what they have available at the livery on our way to the boardinghouse."

"Certainly. Matthew, why don't you stop at Kittredge's and see if he has any good horseflesh available? Check about a carriage while you're there, also."

Boott and Farnsworth exchanged their good-byes with Farnsworth once again agreeing to read his contract before returning the next morning. Kirk stood on the portico watching after them as they rode off in the carriage, his earlier exuberance seeming to have waned. Matthew could only imagine what thoughts were now flying through his mentor's mind.

The carriage had barely begun to move when Farnsworth emitted a chuckle. "Well, my boy, how do you think our meeting went?"

Matthew glanced at his companion. He wasn't sure how to

answer the question. He didn't want to offend Farnsworth in any way—after all, he was an important asset to the Corporation. On the other hand, he didn't want to appear disloyal to Boott. "I believe it went quite well, Mr. Farnsworth," Matthew cautiously replied.

Farnsworth laughed a thunderous, reverberating guffaw that seemed to begin at the bottom of his feet and work itself upward until it exploded into the crisp autumn air. "Good for you, Mr. Cheever. It's a wise man who guards his tongue with a stranger. Now, let's see if Mr. Kittredge has any horses."

Matthew yanked back on the reins, pulling the horses to a halt in front of the combined hardware store, wood yard, blacksmith shop, and livery stable. "The livery stable's out back," Matthew announced, leading Farnsworth toward the rear. "Would you look at that—what is it, I wonder?" he asked, pointing toward a huge pile of black rocks.

"Quite a mess, I'd say," Farnsworth replied.

They could hear a number of voices in the blacksmith shop, the noise escalating as they grew nearer. "Appears you threw away forty hard-earned dollars, Kittredge," one of the men hollered. The comment was followed by boisterous laughter.

Matthew and Farnsworth stood to the rear of the crowd, watching as Jacob Kittredge ignored the guffaws and remained intent on the task at hand. Curious, Matthew edged his way a bit farther in. Moments later he returned to where John was standing. "He's trying to set fire to some of those black rocks—doesn't seem to be working."

Kittredge appeared undaunted as he remained focused upon the task at hand. Soon the observers lost patience and began leaving the building, which allowed John and Matthew adequate space to move closer. The black rocks were piled in an open grate, where Kittredge was doggedly attempting to set them on fire.

"You ain't never gonna get them things to burn," Henry Likens called from the back of the shop. "You shoulda never believed that lawyer from Salem."

Kittredge didn't acknowledge the remark. In fact, he acted as though he were alone in the room. Matthew strode back to where Henry stood. "Why's he trying to burn those rocks, Henry?"

"Some lawyer from up in Salem told him about black rocks from Pennsylvania that are supposed to burn. Said they could be used for fuel instead of wood. So ol' Jacob, he ordered two tons—forty dollars worth. Now he can't even get a spark going with 'em. He would have gotten more heat from setting his money afire."

When Matthew returned, Farnsworth was standing beside Jacob Kittredge, using a hammer to break up the black rocks. Jacob was now starting a fire with tinder and several larger pieces of wood. Once the fire was going, Farnsworth and Kittredge began placing the broken black rocks upon the fire until they'd covered the wood fire with two bushels of the small rocks. Matthew was amazed as he watched the rocks begin to take on a reddish-orange glow, the fire growing hotter by the minute. The horses, obviously sensing the fire and increasing heat, became skittish, kicking at their stalls, snorting, and neighing until several men rushed to get water to douse the hot coals. Still the fire continued. Finally Henry directed the men into a bucket brigade, and after several attempts they were able to exact enough water to calm the coals from a raging fire to glowing embers.

"What kind of rocks are those?" Matthew's voice was filled with amazement.

"Coal," Farnsworth simply replied. "Quite a fuel. My guess is that one day it will replace wood. Now, then, do you suppose Mr. Kittredge might be able to assist us with a horse since the excitement has died down a bit?"

"I'm certain he would be pleased to do so. After all, you certainly came to his rescue when the others were willing to stand back and laugh."

By the time Matthew and John Farnsworth left the livery stable, John was the proud owner of a fine black mare and a carriage that any man would be pleased to own. He was also the recipient of Jacob Kittredge's abiding loyalty.

"You can rest assured that your horse will receive the best of care, Mr. Farnsworth. Anytime you want your horse and carriage, you just send someone down here to tell me. I'll make sure it's ready at the appointed time. You've got my word on that, sir," Jacob said as he walked alongside his departing customers. "I can't thank you enough for helping me out. I was beginning to think I had been bamboozled out of my money. I fear the townsfolk wouldn't have permitted me to live down such an error."

"You are welcome, Mr. Kittredge, but I'm sure you would have finally compared the coal to tinder and wood, realizing that the smaller chunks might burn more easily. It appears as if you made a sound investment."

Kittredge nodded. "Thankfully so. And you've made a sound investment in that mare. She's a beauty."

Farnsworth shook Kittredge's outstretched hand and hoisted himself into the carriage while Matthew took up the reins. "I feel certain that by nightfall the good citizenry of Lowell will be well acquainted with the name of John Farnsworth," Matthew said as they moved down the street.

"Notoriety is the last thing I'm seeking," Farnsworth muttered. "Where are we off to now?"

"Number 7 Jackson Street. It's the boardinghouse operated by Miss Mintie Beecher. We selected Miss Beecher's house as she is reputed to operate the best boardinghouse in the city of Lowell. I'm told there are men who have offered to pay a handsome sum for room and board with Miss Mintie."

"In that case, how does it happen that there's a space available?" John inquired with a twinkle in his eye.

"One of the men was willing to give up his bed."

John's eyebrows arched and his lips gathered into a thoughtful pucker. "Really? In exchange for what?"

"A tidy sum of money, combined with the promise he would receive the next available opening at Miss Mintie's."

"I see. Well, then, let us hope that it won't take too long for my house to be completed. After all, I don't want to be the cause of a man being forced to give up his bed."

"There was no forcing involved, Mr. Farnsworth. The

gentleman understood it would most likely be a good span of time before he returned to Miss Mintie's. All of the men are aware that boarders just don't leave her house, and I was forthright in explaining that the Corporation had not yet begun construction of your house."

"All the same, we'll see if we can't rush things along. Right, my boy?"

There was no doubt that Farnsworth's figurative use of *we* was directed at Matthew. "Yes, sir, I'll do my level best."

"And call me John. 'Mr. Farnsworth' is a bit formal for the two of us, wouldn't you agree?"

"If that's your preference, Mister, uh, John," he quickly corrected.

Farnsworth grinned and nodded his head. "That's my preference. I've been thinking it might serve us well if I deposited my trunks at the boardinghouse, and then you and I could take a short tour of the area. You could point out land that might be suitable for my house."

Boott hadn't discussed the possibility of such a tour with either of the men. And, Matthew concluded, Farnsworth hadn't mentioned his idea of a tour with Boott before departing, either. He didn't want to overstep his boundaries with Boott, yet he didn't want to appear unwilling to assist Farnsworth. After all, Boott would be unhappy if Farnsworth conveyed any displeasure with his welcome to Lowell.

"It appears I've caused you a bit of a quandary," Farnsworth said as they arrived at Mintie Beecher's boardinghouse. "The tour can wait until you've had an opportunity to seek Mr. Boott's approval."

"I'll . . ."

Farnsworth held up his hand. "No need to apologize, my boy. Your first loyalty must be to Mr. Boott and his instructions. I understand. Now, let's see what the Beecher boardinghouse has to offer."

Each of the men lifted a trunk out of the carriage and placed them near the front step. Matthew rapped on the door and waited. Moments later he was greeted by Mintie Beecher. To say it was a warm welcome would have been untruthful, for the woman's welcome was meager and aloof. She stared in unabashed curiosity for several moments.

"Miss Mintie Beecher," Matthew introduced, unable to deal with the silence, "this is Mr. John Farnsworth."

"Well, at least you're prompt," she said, frowning. Her pinched expression led Matthew to believe she was less than pleased with this change to her orderly home.

"Well, bring your things," she said as she turned and headed for the stairs.

Matthew noted that she didn't even wait to see if they were following. He hurriedly lifted the trunk at his feet and threw an apologetic glance toward Farnsworth. "Guess we'd better get to it."

Farnsworth chuckled and hoisted the other trunk to his back. "It's clear she's the no-nonsense sort."

"To say the least," Matthew murmured, fighting to balance his load and clear the door.

Miss Beecher led the way to the upstairs bedrooms, pointed out Mr. Farnsworth's bed, chest, and allotted floor space for his trunks, then retreated back down the steps. The men placed the trunks along the wall and quickly followed behind. It seemed the expected thing to do.

"This is the parlor," Mintie announced. "You can have guests until ten o'clock in the evening, but no women on the second floor. Dining room," she said as she continued marching them through the house. "Dining chairs are not assigned. Pick whichever one is available. I expect my boarders to use proper manners, and I'll not tolerate any profanity in my house. No spitting on the floor. No boisterous talk or crude stories. No singing, unless of course we're having a musical night, and then you're allowed to sing in the parlor but nowhere else." She gave Farnsworth a stern, almost reprimanding look, as though the man had already sinned against the rules.

Matthew would have laughed out loud at the sight of this tiny but very determined old woman laying down the rules and regulations to a man twice her size, but he knew it would only serve to aggravate the situation.

Miss Beecher continued, "The house supplies clean sheets. If you want any other laundry done, you'll have to pay extra like the rest of my boarders. I'll expect you to take a bath at least once a week. I won't have smelly men stinking up my house."

"Yes, ma'am," Farnsworth replied. "Seems quite reasonable."

The older woman paused and assessed him momentarily. Again she eyed him, as if trying to ascertain some deep, mysterious truth. "The other house rules are posted by the door." She pointed a bony finger toward the front of the house, then proceeded to push up the wire-rim spectacles that now rested on the tip of her beaklike nose.

"If I didn't know better, Miss Mintie, I'd swear that you just got off the ship from England, too," Farnsworth said as he tried out one of the wooden dining room chairs before moving to another.

Mintie's eyes opened wide at the remark. "My name is Miss Beecher, and that's the most preposterous thing I've ever heard," she sputtered. "I've never set foot on the soil of England and shall never do so!"

"Really? You have that same disquieting aloofness so many of my countrymen hold dear. I thought you surely must have deep roots in the homeland."

Matthew watched as Mintie's cheeks flushed bright pink. He thought for a moment she might actually have a spell of apoplexy. She hesitated only a moment, however, before regaining her composure.

"In that case you should feel right at home, Mr. Farnsworth. I'll make every attempt to maintain my temperament so that you may continue to feel as though you're still in the bosom of your motherland," she replied, her features strained into a tight frown.

Farnsworth's face crinkled into a bright smile as he pulled a pipe from the pocket of his wool jacket. "Of that I have no doubt, Miss Mintie . . . excuse me, Miss Beecher."

CHAPTER 5

Mintie Beecher pulled back the heavy drapes that covered the dining room windows. There was just enough time to finish dusting the remainder of the downstairs rooms before preparing the noonday meal. Adjusting her spectacles, she peered across the street and smiled in satisfaction. Her sister hadn't pulled back the drapes in number 5. Mintie prided herself on being an efficient woman. It had served her well as her father's hostess in their Boston home, and although assuming the position of a boardinghouse keeper in Lowell wasn't to her liking, efficiency had continued to serve her well in this new post.

On the other hand, she seriously doubted whether Adelaide would ever develop any of the necessary skills to operate a smoothly run boardinghouse. Having carefully dusted the windowsills, Mintie began to move away from her vantage point. A blond-haired girl, bonnet askew and satchels in hand, was moving toward Adelaide's front door. *Another one!* How many chances would her sister receive? It was one thing when boardinghouse vacancies occurred due to circumstances beyond the control of the keepers. It was quite another when the tenants departed due to the ineptness of a keeper. And depart from

Adelaide's house they had, like mice fleeing a fire.

Mintie had warned her sister of the consequences of her lackadaisical attitude. Of course, Adelaide continually insisted she was doing her very best, but Mintie knew better. Adelaide had never attended to the important duties of running the Judge's household, always running off to a piano lesson or dress fitting. The work had always fallen to Mintie. The Beecher sisters had been the Martha and Mary of Lexington Street, at least from Mintie's martyred perspective.

Unfortunately, there wasn't time for her to both personally investigate the new boarder at Adelaide's house and have the noonday meal on the table as planned. Curiosity was one vice that Mintie had failed to overcome—that, along with giving unsolicited advice. Still, she thought, someone of wisdom and etiquette should be available to advise those who were less knowledgeable. Helping one's neighbor could hardly be seen as a vice.

Putting the matter behind her, Mintie called out, "Lucy, come here this minute."

The child came running on spindle-thin legs, jerking herself to an abrupt halt directly in front of Mintie's freshly starched white apron.

"How many times have I told you not to run in the house?" Mintie nodded with satisfaction when the child visibly shrunk back at her words. "It's beyond me how you manage to work as a doffer in the mill. It's a wonder you haven't been mangled by one of those machines. You absolutely *never* follow instructions."

"I'm supposed to run at the mill, Miss Mintie—the faster, the better. Then, when I come to help you serve meals, I have to remember to slow down. Sometimes I have trouble remembering."

"Well, that much is obvious. I want you to go across the street to my sister's boardinghouse. Tell Miss Beecher I need to borrow some darning thread."

"I saw some in your sewing basket just yesterday. I'll run and get it."

"Lucy, I said I *need to borrow some darning thread*. I don't give two whits what you saw yesterday. While you're there, you may discreetly inquire as to any new boarders. Now get yourself across the street!"

The child snapped out of her wide-eyed stare, turned on her heel, and rushed toward the door. The corners of Mintie's mouth turned up ever so slightly. *I'll get that girl trained if it's the last thing I do!*

The potatoes had been peeled and set to boil when the front door slammed, quickly followed by Lucy rushing into the kitchen. Leaning forward to catch her breath, the child extended her hand upward. A piece of limp thread dangled in midair.

An exasperated *hurrumph* escaped Mintie's lips. "She sent you back with that little piece of thread?"

Lucy nodded and extended her hand just a bit higher. "Miss Beecher said to tell you that she didn't bother to send more than a snippet because she knew you didn't really need the thread," Lucy panted.

Mintie could feel the heat rise in her cheeks. "What did you say, young lady? You told her I had thread in my basket, didn't you?"

"No, ma'am. Miss Beecher said you pride yourself on keeping stocked. She said she's never known you to run out of anything and that you just send me over there when you're snooping for information. She said to tell you that you're invited for a cup of tea this afternoon if you'd like to meet one of her new boarders."

"Boarders? How many new girls has the Corporation sent her?"

The child shrugged her shoulders. "Two or three, I think," she replied.

Mintie dismissed the child with a wave of her arm and turned back to her dinner preparations. How dare her sister pass such acerbic words through a mere serving girl? It was no wonder the Judge hadn't trusted Adelaide with the supervision of servants. Well, she would go to tea this afternoon—of that there was no doubt.

An hour later, the scraping of chairs and sound of footsteps announced that the men had finished their noon meal and were heading back to the mills. The older woman nodded at Lucy, and the two of them entered the dining room and began removing the dishes. Mintie glanced up from the table as John Farnsworth paused and turned her way.

"I was wondering if you might help me with a matter, Miss Mintie. I've been so busy since my arrival from England that I've not had time to go into town and visit the stationery shop. I promised to write my aging father back in the homeland, and I hoped that you might be willing to make such a purchase for me. I placed the money on my bureau. I would be most willing to reimburse you for your time and inconvenience."

Mintie frowned, drawing her brows together as she was known to do. She felt the tightness in her face and hoped her look relayed her displeasure. He'd called her by her first name, but instead of reprimanding him, she decided to let it pass. "I suppose I could put it on my list, but I won't be going shopping until tomorrow."

Mr. Farnsworth took a step backward and nodded. "Quite all right. I won't have sufficient time to write a proper letter until Sunday afternoon."

Lucy's eyes danced with anticipation as the door closed behind Mr. Farnsworth. "I'll go into town for you, Miss Beecher."

"I'll just bet you'd like to do that. I'm paying you to serve meals and clean up afterward, not go prattling off to town wasting valuable time on that Englishman. You best move along or it will be time for you to get back to the mill before you've finished your work here. You can be certain I'll not pay you for a shoddy performance of your duties. I'm going upstairs, but I'll be back down to check on your progress."

Mintie watched the child hasten into action and then hurried up the steps to the room occupied by John Farnsworth and five other men. Hesitating momentarily, she glanced up and down the hallway before silently chastising herself. Whom was she expecting to see lurking in the corners? There was nobody in the house except Lucy. Besides, Mr. Farnsworth himself had told her the money was on his bureau. She turned the knob and pushed open the door.

Entering the upstairs rooms on a Wednesday, she felt oddly out of place. Monday mornings and Thursday afternoons were the times she normally entered the rooms occupied by the men. Mondays for stripping the beds and gathering other laundry, Thursdays for dusting and scrubbing floors. Unlike the girls who worked in the mills, these men were more than willing to pay for cleaning chores that weren't included in their monthly rate for room and board—which was precisely why Mintie had taken the position as keeper of the men's boardinghouse. Across the street, Adelaide had enough difficulty maintaining some semblance of order with the few girls she had. How could she ever possibly manage a house that was completely full, plus the extra chores for the men?

Observing the coins, Mintie hesitated only a moment before sweeping them into her palm. Making a quick survey of the room, her gaze fell upon a tattered envelope lying atop Mr. Farnsworth's trunk. Instinctively, she reached for the missive but stopped herself. Instead, she leaned forward until her nose nearly touched the aging paper as she carefully read the name and address inscribed on the letter.

"Miss Beecher, are you still up there?"

Startled, Mintie jumped back, rushed out of the room, and hastened down the stairway. "What do you want?"

Lucy's upturned lips and sparkling eyes were quickly replaced with confusion. "Did I do something wrong, Miss Beecher? You said I'm to tell you when I complete my chores and to never leave without first telling you."

Mintie felt heat rising in her cheeks. "You did nothing wrong. Are you leaving now?" That was as much of an apology as Mintie would make to a servant.

"Yes, ma'am. I'll be back later."

Mintie nodded. Why did the child make that same remark every time she left the house? They both knew she would be back later. Lucy's family needed her earnings, and although it was a concession not easily made, Mintie needed Lucy's assistance. Still, it would do the child some good to learn proper manners and speech. Perhaps if time permitted, Mintie could further instruct the girl. There was no sense in allowing the child to turn into a hoyden.

Lilly tucked the porcelain teapot into a cozy and placed it on the dining room table beside a small silver tray of shortbread, teacups, and saucers. "I can complete the meal preparations, Miss Addie. I want you to enjoy your tea and have a nice visit with your sister."

"I never enjoy visits from my sister. She comes over here to snoop and feed her own ego, and that's a fact. Each time she spies a new boarder arriving or hears that one has departed, she shows up on my doorstep with her admonitions. After she's had her tea and enumerated my list of failures, she flies back across the street, leaving me to feel even more inadequate than when she arrived."

Lilly patted the plump woman's shoulder. She'd come to care about Addie in the few days since her arrival. There was something motherly in the woman, and it caused Lilly to miss her mother more than she realized. Though sometimes she remembered her mother doing little things—dusting the furniture, tucking a handkerchief in her sleeve, pouring tea—Lilly's favorite memories were of the times when she'd prepare for bed and her mother would come in and brush Lilly's long hair while they talked of the day.

"Sometimes," Addie confided, "I think sisters are merely a nuisance."

Her comment roused Lilly from her memories, and she shook off the sadness that threatened to ruin her day. "I always longed for a sister. But perhaps it wouldn't have been so much better than a brother."

Addie gave her a soulful smile. "Mintie is fifteen years my senior. She's always believed that age alone gave her the authority to manage my life," she replied. "But tell me more about your family. You have a brother? I'd like to hear about him—and the rest of your family. We have time before Mintie arrives."

Addie was difficult to refuse. The woman reminded her of a ray of sunshine, always lighting up the room, so Lilly heeded her request and sat down. "My brother, Lewis, is nine years older. We were never close. Oh, I attempted to win his affection as a little girl, but nothing seemed to work. Soon I learned to keep my distance. Lewis resented having another child enter the family circle. For some reason, which I fail to understand, he believes our parents ceased to love him when I was born."

" 'Tis true that some children can't seem to comprehend the fact that their parents have enough love to spread among all of their children."

"I suppose so, but I don't believe my parents could have been any more obvious in showing their love and affection for Lewis. Even after their deaths, he continues to despise me. He grasps at every opportunity to make my life miserable."

"Surely he's not quite that bad, my dear. You know, Mintie can sometimes make my life miserable with her callous remarks and rigid behavior, but deep down I know she loves me."

"Miss Addie, Lewis does not love me. From the time I could toddle, he took great pleasure in pulling my hair, pinching me, and even tripping me as I passed by him. When I was six years old, my dear brother held me upside down over the bank of the Merrimack River. Had Jonas and Matthew Cheever, neighbor boys who lived on the adjoining farm, not happened along that particular day, I'm certain Lewis would have dropped me over Pawtucket Falls and into the rushing waters of the Merrimack River."

"Now, now, don't think such a thing. Boys are prone to outrageous pranks—or so I've been told. Of course, that does seem a bit extreme. Perhaps he didn't realize the seriousness of his actions."

"He was fifteen years old, Miss Addie. And now that our parents are dead and he's made off with everything they ever owned, I suppose he doesn't care whether I'm alive or dead. He gave absolutely no thought to what would become of me after

Father died." Pain stabbed at Lilly's heart with the realization of how absolutely alone she felt.

Addie clucked her tongue and slowly shook her head back and forth. "I know it can be difficult to think good of someone who has hurt you so deeply, but I don't believe your brother wishes you dead. You're much too lovely a girl for anyone to wish you harm. I'm sorry to hear you've lost your parents, child. How long since their. . . ?"

"Mother's been gone five years, but my father was buried just last week," Lilly said with a tremble in her voice. She swallowed hard, hoping to hold back the tears that were forming and threatening to spill at the mention of her father's death.

The older woman leaned forward and wrapped Lilly in her embrace. "I had no idea. Why, you should still be allowed to mourn his passing. Seems just terrible that you should lose him and your home at the same time. But don't you worry. You're going to be just fine, Lilly," she whispered. "I can feel it in my bones. You have a home here now."

Lilly wiped at her eyes and tucked a stray curl behind her ear. "Thank you for being so kind. I didn't mean to become so emotional." Addie's kindness made it easy to give in to her sorrow and memories.

Lilly watched the older woman's face tighten into a grimace as the clock chimed. "Mintie." Addie breathed the word as if it held some mystical spell over them.

The forbidding announcement was followed by a sharp knock at the front door. Before Lilly had an opportunity to exit the dining room, Mintie Beecher swooped down the hallway, entered the room, and seated herself at the table. "Are you going to take my cape and bonnet, or must guests hang them up themselves, Adelaide?"

"I'd be pleased to take your cape and bonnet," Lilly offered.

"May I assume you are one of the new boarders?"

"She is," Addie replied. "What other questions have you come to ask me?"

Mintie's eyes grew dark as she wagged her finger up and down in front of Addie. "Watch your tone, young lady. You seem to forget whom you're speaking to."

"How could I forget when you constantly rush over here to remind me, Mintie?"

"I don't know what's gotten into you. I merely came by for a nice cup of tea. A brief respite in a week of drudgery. Now you've succeeded in ruining even that small ray of sunshine. Why must you be a torment to me when I only seek to maintain civility and unity for the sake of the Judge and our sisterhood?"

Lilly watched as Addie's face began to etch with concern at her sister's words. It was apparent that Mintie knew how to control Addie's every emotion. "I'll leave you ladies and be off to the kitchen," Lilly announced once she'd hung Mintie's cape and bonnet.

"No, I want you to join us."

Mintie Beecher's words were a command, not a request, and Lilly hesitated for a moment before speaking. "I thank you for the kind offer, Miss Beecher. However, I work for Miss Adelaide until I go to the mills, and she's instructed me to complete preparations for the evening meal. I can ill afford to take orders from another."

Addie patted the chair beside her. "Why don't you join us for a few minutes, Lilly? Then you can finish your work."

Lilly nodded and seated herself beside an obviously grateful Addie as Mintie poured the steaming tea. "How is it you're working for my sister?" Mintie's thin eyebrows rose in unison as she looked over her spectacles and awaited a reply.

Lilly studied the stern-faced woman momentarily. Her gray-brown hair had been pulled back into a tight and orderly bun. Not a single strand of hair dared to be out of place. Her gown was just as simple and no-nonsense. The dove gray cloth had been done up in a very plain fashion without benefit of trim or embellishment.

"Well? Are you tongue-tied?" Mintie questioned.

Lilly held back a sharp retort. "I don't begin my employment at the mills until next Monday, and we were able to reach a mutually satisfactory arrangement."

Mintie waited. An uncomfortable silence shrouded the room

as the older woman sat staring across the table, first at Lilly and then Addie.

Addie drew in a breath to speak but paused momentarily before proceeding. "I understand *you* have a new boarder, Mintie. I hadn't realized you had any vacancies until Mrs. Wilson gave me the news while she was measuring me some yard goods yesterday."

"Is that what she's telling folks? That I had a vacancy? How dare she? I had no vacancy. That young Mr. Cheever sent word, asking that I take on Mr. Farnsworth as a boarder."

The mention of the Cheever name caused a tightening in Lilly's chest. No doubt it was Matthew to whom Miss Mintie referred. He was a part of this nightmare that had been brought to Lowell by the Associates. His participation had forever put a wall between them. It had destroyed their love for each other— their plans.

Miss Mintie continued to ramble on. "He said he knew I had no openings, but Mr. Griggs agreed to move to another house so that I could take on Mr. Farnsworth."

"Seems odd to move one man out so another can have his place," Addie commented.

A look of pride washed over Mintie's face. Squaring her shoulders, she lifted her chin and elongated her neck until she resembled a matriarchal ostrich. "Well, Mr. Cheever's note said that he had been informed my boardinghouse was the best run in the city and that when he had questioned the men with regard to where they would live if given the opportunity, my house was the most highly recommended. He went on to explain that the Associates wanted Mr. Farnsworth to experience only the best that our boardinghouses had to offer."

"Cheever. That name sounds familiar," Addie remarked, glancing toward Lilly.

Lilly frowned. *Please don't ask me, Miss Addie. Please don't ask.* Lilly quickly turned her attention to Mintie. "What's so special about Mr. Farnsworth?"

"I'm not sure, but I can tell you that if I had known he was straight off a ship from England, I wouldn't have agreed to take him. He's probably a spy, and those Associates are too foolish to realize it."

Addie chuckled and leaned forward to pour another cup of tea. "Goodness, Mintie! Will you never get over thinking the English are continuing to plot against us? If the Associates were bright enough to stake out and build these mills and this community, I'm sure they're capable of choosing loyal employees."

"Spoken with a complacency the English would love to hear, dear sister. They've brought this Farnsworth over to help them with their calico prints, I've been told. Seems he brings with him the expertise to improve that fabric the mills are passing off as calicos at the present. Who is to say if that man is coming here to spy on us and send word back to England? If a man says he's willing to turn on his own country, he bears watching. Why, just today I saw a missive on his trunk bearing the imprint from a Lancashire factory. You'll not soon convince me he's come to aid this country in its bid toward industrialization."

"You were searching through Mr. Farnsworth's personal belongings?" Before she'd had time to think, the words had escaped Lilly's lips. She now had the full attention of both sisters. "I'm sorry, this is none of my concern. Please—disregard my question."

"I am not a snoop!" Mintie ignored her sister's raised eyebrows and turned her full attention to Lilly. "That letter was sitting out in plain sight. I was in Mr. Farnsworth's room at his direction. He asked me to purchase some stationery. He told me there were coins on his bureau to pay for the supplies. I did nothing improper."

"I'm sure you didn't, Miss Beecher. I didn't mean to question your propriety. In all likelihood, however, I doubt Mr. Farnsworth would send you into his room if he had anything to hide."

"I can see you'll do quite well with my sister. You two make a fine pair. Neither of you can see beyond the tip of your nose. Just remember how the Judge believed that there would never be an end to war with England until we put an end to them. The Judge was seldom wrong, Adelaide."

"He was wrong about his finances. If he had invested with the Associates, we'd still be living among Boston society. Instead, we're boardinghouse keepers in Lowell. I don't think there's any more to your Englishman than meets the eye," Addie replied.

"Well, Mr. Cheever certainly is interested in Mr. Farnsworth. He personally came to interview me and inspect my house before Mr. Farnsworth arrived."

Addie gave her sister a puzzled stare. "What does that have to do with your suspicions?"

"Nothing, I suppose. Well, except that Mr. Farnsworth must be important or Mr. Cheever wouldn't take such pains regarding his welfare. Mr. Cheever is an excellent young man—a man of quality, as the Judge would say. Quality and breeding always show. I trust that he would know if this Mr. Farnsworth were up to something. But then again, Mr. Cheever is very young."

Eventually, the sisters' conversation became nothing more than background noise to Lilly. The mention of Matthew Cheever and his involvement with the Associates sent her thoughts scurrying back to the summer after he'd completed his second year at Harvard. He'd returned to the family farm. For the remainder of that summer, she and Matthew had thoroughly enjoyed each other's company. Matthew's mother had even hinted to Jennie Armbruster that perhaps more than boundary lines would unite their adjoining farms. Lilly had blushed when her mother repeated the statement. And even though Matthew had gone off to Harvard University to further his education, he had pledged to maintain the family farm. He'd hinted at other pledges, as well. But those promises—those dreams—had been rapidly forgotten with the arrival of Kirk Boott.

"You hail from these parts?" Miss Mintie inquired, her shrill question breaking into Lilly's thoughts.

"Yes. East Chelmsford is my home." Mintie leaned in more closely to hear the voice that was barely a whisper.

"East Chelmsford? East Chelmsford no longer exists. This is Lowell," Mintie retorted, her voice carrying that same rebuking tone she had taken with Addie only a short time earlier. "Chelmsford was no doubt an English name."

Lilly shifted only slightly in her chair as she gazed back at Mintie with the same determination she had seen in the older woman's eyes. "This will always be East Chelmsford to me. Kirk Boott and his lords of the loom can name it whatever pleases them, but that doesn't mean it changes in my mind or heart."

"What has Kirk Boott ever done to you that you speak his name with such disdain?" Mintie inquired.

Lilly silently scolded herself. Confiding in Miss Addie was one thing—she was a person who could be trusted. But Miss Mintie was a woman to be reckoned with, one to whom you gave as little information as possible. "I'd best be getting to my chores, Miss Addie. Nice to make your acquaintance, Miss Beecher. Please excuse me," she replied, scurrying from the room before Miss Mintie could lodge her objections.

"Well, I never! Such rudeness—and she calls you by that awful alteration of your name."

Lilly heard the older woman's exclamation of surprise as she exited the room. She half expected Miss Mintie to follow behind, switching at her legs with a sapling branch. Lilly grinned at the thought, but her smile soon disappeared. Miss Mintie's harsh words were drifting into the room like storm clouds on a sunny day. She strained to hear Miss Addie's reply, surprised by the younger sister's lighthearted retorts. Amazingly, Miss Addie's cheerfulness was meeting with success; the conversation soon calmed to a normal level.

Almost an hour had passed when Addie bustled into the kitchen carrying the tea tray. "I thought she would never go back across the street. I apologize for my sister's rude behavior. She shouldn't have questioned you like that. Unfortunately, Mintie feels she has a right to ask anything she wants to know, but heaven help the poor soul who invades *her* privacy."

The two women laughed in unison. "She does have a way about her," Lilly remarked, sending them both into gales of laughter once again.

"I am glad you held your ground with her, Lilly. It didn't seem to affront her. As a matter of fact, she's invited the two of us for tea a week from Sunday. Perhaps more people need to confront her."

Lilly turned to face Miss Addie. "And what of *you,* Miss Addie? Have you ever confronted your sister?"

Addie furrowed her brow for a moment. "I have on one or two occasions. I remember one time in particular. It was probably five years ago. I had gone to the dressmaker's shop early in the day and picked up a new gown that I had specially ordered. It was a beautiful creation. That evening I donned my new dress for dinner. Mintie came downstairs and saw me. She accused me of being half-dressed, insisting I should wear a pelerine to cover my neck and shoulders. I refused."

Lilly stared wide-eyed at the rosy-cheeked woman. "What did she do?"

Addie frowned. "She continued on her tirade, saying the dressmaker had no sense of fashion placing such a tight band on my plump waist."

"That was a cruel remark."

Addie nodded her agreement. "She did say she would be praying that I would come to my senses before I died and ended up in the fiery caverns of hell. I told her I would appreciate any supplications she made to the Almighty on my behalf, but I still did not intend upon wearing dreary, ill-fitting garments. You see, my dear, I still held out hope that I would find a husband. In fact, I still do," she confided in a hushed whisper.

"There's nothing wrong with continuing to pursue your dream, Miss Addie. And finding a husband is an honorable dream. Certainly nothing you need to hide," Lilly replied.

Addie lifted a stack of plates from the shelf. "I know, but Mintie always chided me for such thoughts. She thought me ungrateful for wanting to leave the Judge's household. She said a husband would merely attempt to squander away the Judge's fortune. Fact is, he didn't need anyone else to help him do that. He managed to lose everything without any assistance whatsoever."

"And what of that new dress you wore? Was the Judge aghast at the sight of you sitting down to dinner without a cape about your neck?"

Addie giggled. "Mintie always discussed the business of the day with the Judge. That particular day he had been at a meeting with some business acquaintances concerning the growth of the textile industry and the fact that several of these men were going to invest in the creation of an entire community based upon the mill industry."

Lilly was mesmerized by the thought of it. A group of men sitting down to plot how they could purchase land with ample waterpower in order to make themselves wealthy. It was mind-boggling. The daughter of a man who had been privy to all of the information surrounding the plan to dupe the residents of East Chelmsford now stood before her.

"What else did the Judge tell you about the plan?" Lilly urged.

"He didn't support the idea."

"Why not?"

"The Judge was certain the British were somehow involved in it. The plans for the loom had been smuggled out of Britain, and he was sure there would be repercussions. The Judge became upset with me when I questioned the validity of his fears about the English and told me I was speaking like a Tory. Of course, I assured him I would never do such a thing. In any event, my dress—"

"So he thought the plan folly? Did he feel these business acquaintances were taking unfair advantage of the landowners?"

"He determined that the textile industry might prove to be a good investment—if, and only if, the British could be kept out. He intended to keep the matter under surveillance as a possible future investment. Of course, that never occurred. We would still be living among the society of Boston had he set aside his fears of the British and invested his money. As to the landowners, he never made mention of that, although he knew the purchase of land near Pawtucket Falls had already begun. Why all these questions about the landowners? I thought you wanted to hear about my dress."

"Oh, I do, Miss Addie. Please tell me what the Judge had to say about your dress."

"We had just begun eating our fresh strawberries. They were covered with sweet cream," she added, her eyes glazing over as though the sumptuous dessert might reappear with the telling.

Lilly waited as Addie licked her plump lips. "What happened?" She could wait no longer.

"Oh yes. Well, the Judge took a bite of his strawberries, then looked at me and said, 'Addie, that is a beautiful gown you're wearing this evening. It would make me proud if you would wear it when we go to dinner at the Whitneys' next week.' It was all Mintie could do to hold her tongue. Of course, I immediately told the Judge I would plan to do that very thing. When the Judge had taken his leave to go over some pressing paper work, Mintie told me I would gain an unseemly reputation if I entertained such a foolish notion. But I did it anyway," she said, her giggle once again returning.

Lilly laughed along with her. "It doesn't appear they ran you out of Boston."

"No. In fact, I had many compliments that evening, and Mintie in her brown frock received not one word about her attire. I don't believe I will ever forget that evening.

"Mercy! Look at the time. The girls will be home for supper in no time."

When six o'clock arrived, Lilly still hadn't made it upstairs to finish the unpacking she'd started days earlier, but Addie had successfully turned out four loaves of bread on her own. In between preparing fried potatoes, baked beans with pork, turnips, parsnips with horseradish sauce, and a sweet plum cake, they had managed to wash the dishes and once again set the table. It hadn't taken long for Lilly to realize that Miss Addie didn't comprehend the need to prepare in advance. With some menu and meal planning, the older woman could save valuable time. She had enjoyed their afternoon of visiting, but in the future they would need to devote such time to working on the basic skills of household organization.

Lilly enjoyed it when the girls returned home for the evening. They didn't rush into the house in one large cluster as they did for the noon meals. Instead, they entered in twos and threes, visiting with each other as they sat down for their meal at a more leisurely pace. Rather than the clamoring rush of the noonday meal, they seemed to actually enjoy the evening repast, savoring the smells and tastes of the culinary feast, as well as each other's company.

"I can't tell you how pleased we are you're teaching Miss Addie to cook," Prudence commented as Lilly placed another bowl of horseradish sauce on the table. She winked at Lilly as though they were great conspirators.

Addie smiled, not in the leastwise offended. "I'm trying hard to learn my lessons. After all, Lilly's going to work in the Appleton next Monday. She agreed to help me in the kitchen until then, but after that I'm on my own."

There were groans all around the table. "You mean we'll be going back to scorched stew and bread that's heavy as a rock?" Eva Medley soulfully inquired.

Lilly noticed Miss Addie's shoulders visibly slump and her bright smile disappear. "I think you're going to continue to be pleasantly surprised, even after I begin working at the mill. Miss Addie is doing a wonderful job in the kitchen. She's an exceptionally quick student. In fact, that bread you're eating is her creation. As is the plum cake," Lilly quickly replied. "And she also prepared those baked beans and pork you're so heartily eating. She simply needed a bit of guidance on seasoning and cooking time. By the time I start work at the mill she'll be more than capable."

"This bread is very good—and the beans, too, Miss Addie," Eva remarked. Several of the girls nodded their heads in agreement. "I haven't tried the cake yet, but it looks wonderful."

Nettie Smitson gave Addie a warm smile. "You keep this up, Miss Addie, and we may have the best boardinghouse in town by year's end."

A smile returned to Addie's lips, and her shoulders straightened a bit. "Thank you for your vote of confidence, girls. I'll do my best."

Lilly already felt a burgeoning affection for the plump boardinghouse mistress. Addie was kind and considerate—almost motherly in her attention toward her girls. However, as the evening wore on, Lilly noticed Addie's mood begin to change. She had been almost jovial as she clucked about the room, waiting on the girls and listening as they related the day's events and stories of home. But as the young ladies wandered off and settled into small clusters or drifted upstairs, she took on an air of dejection.

After watching Addie for several moments, Lilly took up a piece of writing paper. Lilly didn't know what sorrow had overcome the boardinghouse keeper, but perhaps a change of routine would help. "Shall we begin some menu planning, Addie?"

Addie nodded in agreement as the two of them walked into the kitchen. "Best squeeze in as much teaching as possible in the next couple of days," she commented.

"The girls seem like a friendly group. I've hardly had time to spend with any of them. Either I'm busy down here with you or they're well on their way to sleep by the time I get to our room."

"They're mostly a good lot. But they can be demanding— and unforgiving, too. Perhaps it comes from working in the mills and having to meet the demands that are placed upon them. They have very few hours of freedom from their work, and they expect to have their needs met when they come home. They'll take few excuses. The men over in my sister's house are more accommodating, especially when Mintie's ill. But the girls expect their meals on time, their laundry done, and the house in order, no matter what my circumstances may be. Oh, there are a few who understand, but the rest are quick to complain and tell me they'll soon move if I don't meet their expectations. They know how the Corporation works, and I realize their remarks are little more than veiled threats that they'll report me and I'll receive my discharge papers."

"Oh, Miss Addie, don't worry so needlessly. I promise I'm going to be here to help you. By the time I leave, you're going to have girls begging to get in this house."

Addie gave her a faint smile. "You're talking about leaving and you haven't even begun your work at the mill. You've got plans, haven't you?" Addie asked, the twinkle beginning to return to her eyes. "You'll most likely be taken for a wife before you've been with us even a year. Which reminds me, is the Mr. Cheever that Mintie mentioned earlier *your* Matthew Cheever?"

CHAPTER 6

Lilly sauntered back down Merrimack Street, her arms heavy with the groceries she had purchased for Miss Addie's girls. It was her first real outing since she'd arrived at the boarding-house—if one considered grocery shopping an outing. Addie had awakened that morning with a swollen foot, a flare-up of gout, she had explained while asking if Lilly would consider going to the market. It had been an apologetic entreaty, at least until Lilly assured the older woman she would enjoy a walk in the fresh air. And she had enjoyed every lighthearted step as she made her way to the market. A crispness of autumn hung in the September air, yet a vibrant golden sun shone down, vying for one last surge of summer's warmth.

Lilly relished the feeling. It took her back to happier times—days that seemed so long gone that they blurred in her memo-ries. With a sigh, she picked up her pace. Nothing could be gained by living in the past. Walking briskly, she made excellent time and, after finishing her marketing, decided she could allow herself a few extra moments to survey the array of new bonnets in Wellington's Millinery Shop. Perhaps with her first paycheck she would purchase a more grown-up creation.

Standing in front of the bonnet-filled window, Lilly felt a tap on her shoulder. Glancing around, she met Julia Cheever's warm smile. Julia, her deceased mother's dearest friend. Julia Cheever—Matthew's mother.

Julia pulled Lilly into a warm embrace. "I'm so sorry about your father, Lilly. We were out of the city when he passed away. Matthew mentioned that Lewis returned home for the funeral. I wondered if you had gone to New Hampshire with him. But now I see for myself that you're here."

"Actually, Lewis was a day late. He missed the funeral, but thank you for your concern," Lilly murmured. Pulling away, she offered Mrs. Cheever a weak smile. "I'm sorry. I must go."

"Nonsense, I've only just found you. You must tell me what is happening in your life. Where are you living? Am I amiss in my information regarding your brother living in New Hampshire?"

Lilly didn't want to tell the woman that she had no idea where her brother had taken himself. "I'm not sure about Lewis. I'm living on Jackson Street."

"Are you staying with friends?"

Lilly stiffened. "I really have to go. I have a great deal to do. I'm sorry." She made every attempt to hurry back to her secret hiding place at the boardinghouse. Of course, now it wasn't quite so secret.

"You'll not escape so easily, Lilly. I insist you come for supper this evening. And I'll not take anything but yes for an answer!" Julia insisted.

Fearing Matthew's participation in the meal, Lilly was loath to agree. "That could be rather uncomfortable for Matthew," she finally said.

Julia shook her head. "He won't be there. He's out of town on business."

Lilly made other protests. "I'm in mourning. It wouldn't do to have me partaking in dinner parties."

"Nonsense," Julia retorted. "We're practically family, and this would hardly be a party."

Lilly felt awash in defeat. Each of her arguments was met by

Julia's counterattack. No escape could be had, so she finally smiled as sweetly as possible. "Just tell me what time and I'll be there."

"Very good." Julia gave her the information, then added with a hint of amusement in her voice, "If you don't make your appearance, I'll send Mr. Cheever to fetch you."

Now, as Lilly watched Julia depart, she wished she had stood her ground and refused the invitation. Mrs. Cheever, the picture of refined elegance, glided down Merrimack Street, her skirt swaying like a bell. No doubt it was of the latest fashion and fabric. The Cheevers hadn't frittered their fortune away. Lilly swallowed hard. A dinner party at the Cheever home would bring nothing but discomfort and humiliation.

The older woman's parting words still echoed in Lilly's ears as she watched Julia disappear into one of the shops. *"If you don't make your appearance, I'll send Mr. Cheever to fetch you."* It sounded every bit a threat.

Lilly turned and hurried toward Jackson Street with un-welcome memories of the past invading her thoughts. It had been at Matthew's urging that the Cheevers sold their adjoining acreage some five years earlier and built a home in Lowell. Although Lewis had visited the Cheevers' new residence when he had made his occasional visits home, Lilly had never so much as seen their new house. Of course, Julia had invited her on many occasions when she'd come to the Armbruster farm for a visit, but Lilly had resisted. In fact, she'd gone out of her way to avoid even a glimpse of the new mansion. Seeing the Cheevers in another home would solidify their absence and force her to admit they were never coming back to tend their orchards or their flocks of woolly sheep.

"Of course, Father's death has assured that fact for me, so it truly doesn't matter anymore," Lilly told herself. She only wished it wouldn't hurt so very much.

———

Miss Addie was seated in the kitchen peeling potatoes and scraping vegetables for the potpies, her foot propped on a wooden stool. "You're back in no time at all. Did you run all the way?"

"No, of course not," Lilly replied, forcing herself to return the woman's jovial smile.

"I forget those young legs can carry you much more quickly than these worn-out old stubs. Did Mr. Lacy have everything we needed?"

Lilly nodded as she continued unpacking the basket, her back to the older woman. She continued searching her mind for some way she could avoid supper at the Cheever residence. A cheery Miss Addie tapping on her arm interrupted Lilly's solitary thoughts.

"I've been meaning to ask you again, Lilly, was the Matthew Cheever Mintie spoke of your long-lost beau? You went scampering out of the room like a mouse after cheese when I inquired about him earlier."

This time there was no escaping Miss Addie's question. "Yes. My, it appears you've made excellent progress on the potpies," she stated, hoping the change of subject would put an end to the investigation.

Her strategy, however, failed to work with Miss Addie. "And now he's Kirk Boott's protégé? It would appear you let a good thing get away from you, Lilly. If that young man has captured Mr. Boott's attention, he's sure to go far with the Corporation. Whatever caused the two of you to go your separate directions?"

"His affiliation with Mr. Boott and the Boston Associates."

"Why, that makes no sense, child. A man who loves you is establishing himself in the business world, and you find fault with him?"

"Perhaps it makes no sense to you, Miss Addie, but it's reason enough for me," Lilly replied as she crimped the dough she'd placed atop one of the chicken potpies that now lined the work-table.

"Well, are you going to explain it to me?" Addie inquired while scooting forward on her chair.

"It's a long story."

Addie gave her a broad smile. "I've got nothing but time to

listen while we're fixing dinner, and I love to hear a good story."

Lilly shook her head. There was no escaping this time. "It's not such a good story. Matthew and I were friends throughout our growing-up years. You may recall I mentioned he once saved me from drowning in the Merrimack River the day Lewis held me over Pawtucket Falls."

"That's right! I do remember," Addie agreed, her blue eyes sparkling at the realization.

"It wasn't until the year before Matthew went off to Harvard that we pledged our love. Matthew talked of the day when he would be in charge of his family's farm. Jonas, his older brother, had no interest in the land, but Matthew was like me—he had a desire to maintain his family's acreage. I cherished the idea of marrying a man who would work the land and keep me close to family.

"Anyway, it was his final year at Harvard when he began to change. He had been involved in discussions regarding the industrialization of our country in his classes at Harvard, and he began talking about proper utilization of the land and how it could serve more people—things that were completely foreign to his earlier beliefs.

"Then on one of his visits home, he told me he was no longer interested in farming, that he had convinced his parents to sell their acreage and hoped our family would do the same and that it would be best for us to do so. He said my father's health would soon prevent him from farming, and with Lewis's obvious lack of interest in the property, it only made sense to sell." Lilly looked away and tried to shake off the strangling sorrow that welled up in her heart.

"He had become a stranger to me. When my father resisted, someone wrote to Lewis telling him there was a good price to be had for our land. Needless to say, my brother returned home, and the land was sold. That was five years ago, in 1823."

Confusion imprinted Addie's plump face. "Five years ago? Where have you been since then?"

"On the farm, tending the orchards and caring for my father. The Associates knew they wouldn't need our land until the mills began to expand, so the contract contained a clause that we could continue to cultivate and live on the land for five years. As the day for our departure grew nearer, my father's health worsened. I believe he died of a broken heart. He had already lost my mother, and he couldn't face the possibility of beginning a new life away from everything he held dear. He died a week before we were to vacate our homestead.

"Lewis arrived the day after my father was buried—he was detained in a game of cards with some gentlemen in Nashua, New Hampshire. It seems he was on a winning streak and couldn't force himself away from the gaming table. Of course, he lost all of those winnings before he arrived back in East Chelmsford. Upon his appearance, he laid claim to the remaining gold pieces my father hadn't already given him. He then proceeded to sell everything of value that remained in the house before he rode away. In all likelihood, he gambled away his remaining inheritance before the week had ended."

Addie shook her head. "It appears that Lewis needs to be introduced to the Lord. Perhaps then he would change his ill-advised ways."

Lilly shrugged her shoulders. "The only way that will happen is if there's a revival in one of the taverns or brothels he frequents."

The color heightened in Miss Addie's cheeks as she shook her head again. "The Lord works in mysterious ways, Lilly. Don't sell Him short."

The corners of Lilly's mouth turned upward and formed a soft smile. "I would never do that, but I believe Lewis has already committed his soul. Unfortunately, not to God."

"I've seen some hardhearted characters change their ways. Perhaps we should pick a special time each day and pray for him," Addie offered with a sense of excitement filling her voice.

Lilly's smile faded as she finished preparing the last of the potpies and set them to bake. Wiping her floured hands on the white cotton apron, she turned toward Adelaide. "You are a truly kind woman, and I appreciate your offer, but I don't believe I could pray for Lewis—I'm not at all sure I care what happens to him."

Addie took hold of Lilly's hand. "Well, then, I'll just set aside some time each day and I'll be praying for the *both* of you. We'll see if God has something to say in the matter of Lewis and his evil ways."

"And *me,* Miss Addie? What are you looking for God to do with me?"

Addie gave her a wink and smiled. "Just a bit of softening on that heart of yours—I'm afraid it's beginning to harden at much too early an age. You're a good girl, and I just thank the Lord you've come into my life. I wish there was something more I could do for you, aside from your bed and board."

"There is one favor you could do for me."

"Anything. You just tell me what it is."

"I'm invited to a supper this evening—not until half past seven," she quickly added. "Would you give permission for me to attend?"

"Why, of course, Lilly. You don't need my permission to go out. The girls go out shopping and visiting every evening. However, it would be nice to know where you're going," Addie replied, giving her a grin. "Or am I being too meddlesome?"

Lilly couldn't help but laugh. Addie's deep blue eyes were alight with curiosity. "Julia Cheever, Matthew's mother, spotted me on Merrimack Street when I was shopping today. She insisted I come to supper this evening. I attempted to refuse her invitation, but she wouldn't hear of it. She threatened to send Mr. Cheever if I'm absent."

"It would be more interesting if she sent Matthew," Addie replied with a mischievous grin.

Lilly met Addie's lopsided grin with a stern frown. "Matthew won't be in attendance. Rest assured that I would never have accepted the invitation under any other circumstance. I'm certain Mrs. Cheever would never intentionally cause such an embarrassing situation for either of us."

"It is amazing what a mother will do for the well-being of her child," Addie whispered as she lifted her foot from the stool.

CHAPTER 7

Matthew smiled at his reflection in the large oval mirror that hung over the ornately carved mantel in his parents' parlor. He adjusted his cravat ever so slightly, then glanced out the front window. Pulling a gold watch from the pocket of his double-breasted waistcoat, he decided he could wait only five minutes longer. If his mother hadn't returned by then, he would ask Mary to deliver a message. But moments later, she entered the front door, a basket containing the morning's purchases hanging from her arm.

"Matthew, what a pleasant surprise," she greeted as he met her in the hallway. "I'll be with you as soon as I unpack these things. They had such fine produce at the market this morning, it was difficult to decide what to buy. Sit down," she urged.

"I can't stay, Mother. In fact, I'm already late."

"But since you're already here, I was hoping you'd stay for supper. I'm having guests."

"I couldn't possibly do that," Matthew replied.

"But, Matthew, this is the third time in recent weeks that we've invited you to join in our dinner party. I've already invited other guests and I am short one male escort. What is so important that you must create this last-minute disorder for me?"

Matthew squared his shoulders, his chest swelling as he spoke. "Mr. Boott wants me to accompany him to Boston for a meeting with Bishop Fenwick."

A startled look crossed Julia's face. "You've come at the last minute to tell me you are not attending my dinner party in order to go with Kirk Boott and meet with some Catholic priest? What's gotten into you, Matthew, that you think fraternizing with some papist is more important than attending my party?"

"Mother, I'm sorry if I've caused you inconvenience. However, this meeting is important to my future with the Boston Associates. Perhaps you could ask Jonas to bring along one of his acquaintances."

An exasperated sigh escaped Julia's lips. "Boston Associates," she remarked with a hint of disdain. "You have a Harvard education, Matthew. There are any number of businesses that would be pleased to employ you. Without, I might add, requiring you to travel so often that you can't partake in a supper engagement at your parents' home."

"At the moment, I don't have time to argue the benefits of working with Mr. Boott, but suffice it to say that I'm willing to make any necessary sacrifice in order to become a valued employee of the Associates."

"*Any* sacrifice, Matthew?" Julia pulled a lace handkerchief from her sleeve and began dabbing at her face. "I pray that remark isn't true."

"Please, Mother, you need not attempt to convince me you're going to faint over an offhand remark. I promise I won't sell my soul to the devil, but I am going to Boston with Mr. Boott."

"Well, do as you see fit. I'm sorry you'll miss my special guest. You'd better be on your way. I wouldn't want to detain you further," she replied as she began walking out of the parlor.

His mother's game playing was exasperating. She knew he wouldn't leave until the unnamed guest was revealed. When he had been a little boy, she could always entice him with a secret—

she still could. Julia enjoyed the game and he knew it. Yet, his curiosity forbade departing without knowing the name of her mysterious guest.

"You have my promise that I will be here for dinner a week from Sunday," he coaxed.

Julia stopped, turned toward him, and placed a finger against her pursed lips. "And that you'll be in attendance at Sunday services?"

"I'll be sitting alongside you and Father in the fourth pew," he answered.

"Now, don't take that peevish tone, or I'll be forced to require a greater sacrifice."

His mother held the trump card. They both knew it, and time was growing short. Accordingly, he gave her his most winsome smile. "I shall be pleased to attend church with you next week. Now, who is your surprise guest?"

"If you had more time, I would oblige you to guess," she coyly replied. "But since time is of the greatest import, I shall tell you. It is Lilly Armbruster."

Without thought, Matthew lowered himself onto the sewing chair behind him. "Lilly?" His voice was a hollow whisper. He stared up at his mother, feeling the blood drain from his face.

"Yes. I thought you would be pleased," she ventured. "Are you feeling ill, Matthew? You've lost your color."

"Where? How? Why did you do this?"

"I love Lilly. Just because the two of you are no longer—shall we say, betrothed—doesn't mean I don't want to spend time with her. Her parents are both dead. She has no family, unless you consider that scoundrel Lewis—which I don't. I wanted to reach out to her in some way but wasn't sure how. Then, as I was strolling down Merrimack Street this morning, I saw her in front of the millinery shop. I offered my condolences and explained that we had been out of town when her father passed away. I inquired about her welfare and asked if she would come to supper. She was as close to a daughter as—"

"But she *isn't* your daughter, Mother, and I am your son. You knew it would create an uncomfortable situation for me, but you went ahead and invited her. I can't believe you would do such a thing—or that she would accept."

Julia's attempt to appear composed fell short. She was wringing her hands, and tiny beads of perspiration had formed across her upper lip. "Don't think harshly of Lilly. She asked if you would be in attendance. I told her you were out of town on business. And you will be," she quickly added. "Although, I had hoped—"

Matthew rose from the chair. "Hoped what—that we'd renew our relationship? That we'd become engaged again? She's in mourning, Mother. Her father just passed on. How appropriate would it be for me to suddenly appear on her doorstep with ring in hand?"

"Well, granted, there are proprieties to be held to. However, if you feel the same way about her . . ."

"I don't want to discuss this further. It appears my trip to Boston will make an honest woman out of you, Mother. However, you will do nothing but cause pain for Lilly and me if you continue to interfere. Our relationship is over. And please remember it was Lilly who terminated our liaison. I didn't drive her off."

"If you hadn't taken up with Kirk Boott and that group of Bostonians, she'd still be at your side."

"You and Father didn't object to my association with them when it fetched you a better price for your land than that of the other East Chelmsford residents," he retaliated.

Julia shook her head in denial, her cheeks growing flushed. "That was *your* doing, Matthew. You convinced your father to sell the acreage."

"Your life has never been better than here in Lowell."

"There is no doubt my life is easier, but don't try to disguise the truth with that argument. You wanted to impress those men with the fact that you were an East Chelmsford resident who could give them an advantage dealing with the locals as they attempted to purchase the land. You started with your own family in order to impress them. Now, I'm not saying what you did was in any way improper. And I would venture to say that most of the original landowners are doing well, even though they feel misrepresentations were made to them. Unfortunately, Lilly Armbruster is *not* one of those people who has benefited. And it breaks my heart."

"The fault lies with her brother, not the Boston Associates. The Armbrusters received more than most."

Julia nodded her head. "Perhaps. But the coins that line Lewis Armbruster's pockets do nothing to help his sister. This discussion will do nothing to change Lilly's circumstances.

"You best be going, Matthew, for I'm sure Mr. Boott is anxiously awaiting your arrival."

He wished now that he had merely sent his regrets. The conversation with his mother had completely ruined the excitement of traveling to Boston and meeting with Bishop Fenwick.

"Give my regards to Father," he said as he opened the front door.

"You may do that yourself next Sunday. I haven't forgotten your promise. I'll expect to see you promptly at ten o'clock. And don't think I haven't noticed your absence in church the past two weeks, young man."

Matthew could only nod in agreement as he bounded down the front steps. His mother had succeeded in ruining his journey into Boston, yet there she stood on the wide front porch, waving her lace handkerchief after him as though she were bestowing some unspecified blessing upon him.

He rushed down the street, turned the corner, and hastened toward the Boott residence. A sigh of relief escaped his lips when he saw the carriage had not yet departed. As Matthew drew closer, he observed the legendary tyrant-in-residence pacing back and forth along the pillared entryway to his mansion, a look of annoyance etched upon his face. Quickening his step, he rushed onward, his pounding heart threatening to explode within his chest. Sights fixed on Boott, Matthew watched as his mentor turned toward the street and headed for the awaiting carriage. Matthew raised his arm, waving it back and forth above his head. He didn't have breath enough to call out a greeting.

"You are seventeen minutes late," Boott stated in a measured voice. "I loathe tardiness, Matthew. You should remember that in the future."

Matthew gasped for air. "Yes, sir. I apologize. I stopped to say hello to my mother—"

Boott held up his hand. "Please—don't give me an excuse. As far as I'm concerned, there is no excuse for tardiness. If you're finally prepared, let's be on our way."

A deafening silence permeated the carriage. Matthew determined he would await Mr. Boott's opening comment. He certainly wasn't going to cause himself further embarrassment—at least not if he could help it. The pastoral countryside prepared for autumn, a hint of rustic color beginning to tinge the green landscape, and Matthew settled his gaze out the carriage window. Passing the farms and orchards, his thoughts returned to the conversation with his mother. Somewhere deep inside him, he longed to be sitting at the supper table this evening, filling his senses with Lilly and her charming laughter, touching her chestnut curls, and gazing into her golden-flecked brown eyes.

The warmth of the sun beating upon the carriage coupled with the beauty of the countryside served as reminders of times spent with Lilly. He missed their long walks and the simplicity of plucking an apple from a tree in the orchard or reading poetry by the river. But most of all, he missed sharing his dreams with Lilly. Why did she have to be so unyielding? They could have shared a wonderful life together, if only she would have opened her eyes to reality. No matter that he had presented valid, intelligent arguments for selling the farmland. She could not be convinced that East Chelmsford's future lay in manufacturing, not farming. His thoughts were entirely focused upon Lilly when Boott's words broke the silence.

"Since our supper at Nathan's earlier this week, I've given further thought to your ideas regarding the Irish. Although there is merit to meeting with the bishop, I don't want to appear overly zealous about the possible role of the bishop or the Catholic Church in Lowell. When we meet with Bishop Fenwick, I will do the talking. Unless I specifically direct a question to you,

you will say nothing other than proper formalities. Is that understood?"

Matthew nodded his head in agreement. "Absolutely."

"I can only hope you'll perform this task more efficiently than your late arrival this morning." The comment was laced with sarcasm. Boott's sardonic grin followed the biting remark.

"You can depend on me, Mr. Boott," Matthew reiterated, his palms growing moist.

Boott ignored the assurance. "Let me give you a bit of background about Bishop Fenwick. Before his assignment to Boston, he held an appointment in New York. Fenwick's not as popular as his predecessor, at least not among the Protestant elite of Boston. However, he does understand his need for assistance from them if the Catholic Church is to continue prospering in his diocese. Right now they're struggling, with Holy Cross being their only strong parish."

"Then you think he'll be pleased with the prospect of offering religious instruction to the Irish in Lowell?"

"I'm told he has only five priests for the entire diocese. I don't know what will or will not please him, but I do know he's a shrewd man. The last thing I want to do is appear vulnerable. He would consider us easy prey."

Matthew stared across the coach and met Boott's steely gaze. "Prey? How could a man of the cloth victimize the Corporation? And why would Bishop Fenwick even entertain such a notion?"

"Don't underestimate the clergy, Matthew—especially the papists! There's nothing they covet more highly than a nice piece of acreage. Always in the name of the church, of course. I'm willing to donate to their cause when a favor is needed, but the amount and kind of donation will be on *my* terms, not those of Bishop Fenwick. Or any other clergyman, for that matter."

The messages were clear. Keep your mouth shut, keep your ears open, keep your mind sharp, and be careful where you place your trust.

And by all means, be punctual.

Impressed with Boott's knowledge of Bishop Fenwick and

the Catholic Church, Matthew, at the same time, was thankful that Boott hadn't inquired if he had gathered any information for their meeting with the bishop. Leaning back against the leather-upholstered carriage seat, Matthew wondered if Bishop Fenwick had been carefully preparing for their arrival, scrutinizing Kirk Boott's heritage and business acumen. If so, this meeting could prove even more interesting than he had anticipated.

CHAPTER 8

Several carriages lined the drive in front of the Cheever house on Pawtucket Street. Lilly determined it fitting that there should be a street named after Pawtucket Falls and that the Cheever home should be located on that particular street. Of course, the Cheever family truly belonged on their acreage adjacent to Pawtucket Falls, just as she belonged on the Armbruster farmstead. *If only the Boston Associates had begun their fancy manufacturing dreams in some other place—New Hampshire or perhaps Vermont,* she thought as she approached the house.

There was still time to turn and go back to her room on Jackson Street, and she hesitated a moment. Would Matthew be in attendance after all? Surely not—she could trust Julia Cheever's statement that he was out of town. Besides, the thought of Randolph Cheever appearing at the front door of the boardinghouse to fetch her would give rise to questions from the other girls.

Straightening her back and taking a deep breath, Lilly walked up the front steps and knocked. Her heart began to race when the door opened and a man stood beside Mrs. Cheever, his back toward her as he talked with a group of guests. When he turned, she felt a rush of relief—or was it disappointment? Before her, extending his hand in greeting, stood Matthew's older brother, Jonas.

"Well, if this isn't quite the surprise," Jonas exclaimed. "How good to see you, Lilly. So this is our surprise guest. Mother has been taunting us all afternoon."

"Us?" It was all Lilly could manage for the moment. All eyes were turned in her direction.

"Father and me," Jonas replied. "We've suffered an afternoon of pure torment, both of us guessing until we'd exhausted everyone we could possibly think of. Won't Matthew regret that he couldn't attend this evening?"

"Didn't I say you would be surprised? I was right, wasn't I?" Julia questioned. Her eyes were dancing with delight as she pulled at her husband's arm.

"Absolutely correct," Mr. Cheever replied.

"How nice to see you again, Lilly," greeted Sarah, Jonas's wife.

"Lilly, it's been too long," continued Mr. Cheever. "Hopefully your arrival means my wife will now serve supper." He grasped her hands in greeting and bent down to whisper, "I'm famished."

Lilly smiled at the remark. She remembered that Mr. Cheever's favorite greeting when coming home from the fields had been, "I'm famished—when do we eat?"

"You couldn't possibly be famished, Randolph. You've been in the kitchen sampling food all afternoon," Julia countered. "Come along, Lilly. I'm going to seat you next to Jonas and Sarah."

The meal consisted of a multitude of courses, beginning with a delectable lobster bisque, and all were served with an expert ease and graciousness that caused Lilly to marvel. Julia Cheever was no longer the farm wife serving dozens of workers during harvest season; she was now the accomplished society hostess entertaining refined guests. How had the transition been exacted in such a short time, she wondered.

"Do tell us what's going on in your life since moving from

the farm, Lilly. Where are you living?" Jonas inquired as a server offered Lilly a heaping platter of mutton.

Prying questions. She had known they would be asked. Why had she placed herself in this prickly situation? "On Jackson Street," she replied, offering nothing further.

"Jackson? I thought Jackson was nothing but boardinghouses for the mills," Sarah stated. She grimaced ever so slightly and shuddered.

"So it is," Jonas remarked. "Are you certain it's Jackson Street?" he asked, turning back toward Lilly.

Had the question not been so insulting, Lilly would have laughed aloud. She wasn't sure what bothered her more, the fact that Jonas was actually questioning if she knew her own address or that she was being confronted with the realization that working in the mills diminished her social acceptability. She remained silent. All eyes were turned in her direction, a sense of discomfort suddenly permeating the room.

"Sometimes Jonas doesn't think before he speaks," Julia finally said, breaking the silence. "Nor does Sarah," she quickly added. "But they meant no harm, dearest Lilly. Hasn't the weather been unseasonably warm for this time of the year?"

With the expert ease of a perfect hostess, Julia had changed the conversation and set her guests at ease. Once again the room was abuzz with meaningless small talk as Lilly attempted to devise some plan of escape.

"Come along, everyone," Julia instructed. "We're going to play charades, and I don't want any of you men sneaking off to smoke cigars or talk business."

Randolph laughed as he and two of his colleagues turned in their tracks and returned to the parlor. "We wouldn't think of running out on a game of charades," he teased.

"I really must be leaving," Lilly whispered to her hostess. "We have a curfew."

"Nonsense. Randolph will escort you home and explain that you were with us. I'll not hear of you running off this early in the evening," Julia replied, her voice growing louder and more insistent when Lilly began to shake her head in disagreement. "I absolutely refuse to permit your departure!"

Lilly winced as the other guests began to look in their direction. "Fine. I'll stay for a little while. But I really must leave within the hour."

"We'll see," the unrelenting woman replied, giving her a smile. "All right, let's number off into teams. You begin, Randolph. You're team one," she instructed as she continued around the room assigning each guest a number.

In spite of her misgivings, Lilly joined the others, shouting out possible answers as guests performed their antics, laughing and cheering for several hours, forgetting the drudgery of her life and the tiny, airless bedroom she shared with seven other girls.

The Cheevers were standing at the doorway bidding their guests farewell as Lilly approached. "Ready, my dear?" Randolph inquired as he offered his arm.

"I can walk home alone. I don't want to take you away from your remaining guests," Lilly replied.

Randolph shook his head. "I'll hear of no such thing. It's a beautiful night, and the fresh air will do me good. Besides, I'll be back home before Julia has an opportunity to miss me," he quipped as he winked at his wife.

Lilly didn't argue. It would be wasted breath and she knew it. "Thank you once again for a lovely evening," she said, kissing Julia's cheek.

"You must promise you'll return to see us soon."

Lilly merely nodded, knowing she wouldn't soon return to socialize among the elite of Lowell.

"I've missed you, Lilly," Randolph stated. "I'm genuinely sorry things didn't work out between you and Matthew."

"And I've missed you and Mrs. Cheever, but time goes on and our lives change," she replied in a feeble attempt to appear philosophical about her station in life.

Mr. Cheever patted the hand she had tucked inside his crooked arm. "It's true our lives change, Lilly, but sometimes I think we do better to look at life in smaller slices, a change at a time, perhaps. Sweeping generalities sometimes tend to diminish those minor changes. We need to take time and realize that sometimes good comes along with bad."

"I'm not sure I understand what you mean, Mr. Cheever. My life has been turned upside down—nothing is the same. East Chelmsford no longer exists. Lowell has overpowered and smothered the life out of East Chelmsford."

He smiled and shook his head. "I disagree. The name has changed and the town has grown, but East Chelmsford and her people are still alive and vibrant. Lowell didn't smother us. We've been cultivated and nurtured so that we could change and grow into a larger, more productive community. Sometimes I think we humans just don't want to give in and think that any good can come from change. Could you agree with me on that?"

"I suppose. But it's difficult to find good that has come from all of this so-called industrialization. Our beautiful farmlands are now ugly brick buildings and canals. I miss the tranquility of the countryside, the pride of orchards producing bountiful crops, and the pleasure of seeing herds of woolly sheep roaming about."

"I see. And do you miss the years of drought when we broke our backs attempting to eke out a living on the few crops we could produce? Don't forget the bad as you remember the good, child. Otherwise, you paint yourself a false picture. There were good things about those days, but there were just as many hard times. One must keep events in perspective. Change is always going to be a part of our lives. If we don't grow and change, we stagnate and die. Perhaps you should attempt to see Lowell with the unbridled enthusiasm of a newcomer. I believe you would find it exciting and, dare I say, quite lovely."

Lilly looked up at Mr. Cheever and was instantly reminded of Matthew. Although Jonas was marginally handsome and well spoken, it was Matthew who had inherited not only his father's good looks but his gift of persuasion. It was indeed a formidable combination. She feared she still hadn't succeeded in obliterating Matthew from her memory after all.

CHAPTER *9*

Boston, Massachusetts

Matthew tugged at his waistcoat as he and Kirk Boott followed closely behind a tranquil, black-clad priest. After traversing several hallways, the cleric rapped on a carved oak door, waited for a response, then opened the door to Bishop Benedict Fenwick's private office.

The rotund man rose from a cushioned red velvet chair and came out from behind his desk, his dark-eyed gaze fixed on Boott. His upturned lips and the dark curly locks that surrounded his forehead and cheeks gave the bishop a youthful appearance. A stiff gold braid trim surrounded the edge of his unbuttoned collar, thus permitting his sizable double chin to rest upon a layer of soft white fabric. Matthew noted that the row of black buttons aligned down the front of the bishop's jacket strained against the man's expansive bulk.

"Good to see you once again, Mr. Boott," Bishop Fenwick greeted, stretching his arm in welcome.

Kirk grasped the proffered hand and then turned to Matthew. "May I introduce Matthew Cheever, Your Excellency. He has recently been hired by the Boston Associates to assist me with my duties in Lowell. I decided to reward his hard work with a trip to Boston."

"A pleasure," the bishop replied, extending his ring-adorned hand to Matthew. "Always good to meet with men who have the best interests of our citizenry at heart. Sit down, sit down," he offered, gesturing toward two dark blue brocade chairs opposite the large walnut desk.

Matthew and Kirk seated themselves, remaining silent as the bishop circled the desk and lowered his expansive body into the velvet-upholstered chair. The walls behind the desk were lined with matching walnut bookcases, each shelf crowded with volumes of leather-bound books. Across the room, an ornate silver tea service rested upon a marble-topped serving table. At the ring of a small gold handbell, a priest entered the room. He carried a tray of small cakes that he placed on the table before silently pouring tea into three china cups and exiting the room as noiselessly as he had entered.

"Tea, gentlemen?" The words were formed as a question, but both men knew what was expected.

They drank the spiced tea with lemon and ate the layered cakes Bishop Fenwick offered. They exchanged pleasantries, discussed the weather, and inquired into one another's health. It was the way of genteel, well-bred people. It was also the way of far-reaching men hoping to gain advantage and power.

When Bishop Fenwick had finally eaten his fill, he leaned back in his chair, reaching his arms across the expansive girth of his belly. His thick fingers barely met. Boott leaned forward ever so slightly, obviously awaiting some signal that the cleric was ready to move their conversation into a more serious vein.

"I assume you gentlemen haven't made an appointment to see me merely to inquire about my health," the bishop stated. He leaned deeper into the chair, his eyes hooded by thick black lashes.

Matthew remained silent as Boott leaned forward, a look of concern now crossing his face. "Indeed, we do have a matter of importance to bring before you, Your Excellency. Not a matter that will be easily resolved, but a problem I believe we can eventually solve if we work together. Reasonable men can always benefit each other. Don't you agree?"

The bishop's eyelids opened wider. Matthew noticed an obvious spark of interest in the cleric's dark eyes. "Unreasonable men have been known to become quite reasonable when the stakes are high enough, Mr. Boott. Just what is it that you perceive as our mutual problem?"

"Simply stated, the growing Irish population in Lowell," Kirk replied. "Not that the Irish themselves are a problem," he quickly added when the bishop unfolded his hands and gave him a look of obvious displeasure. "I take responsibility for this whole situation. It's my lack of planning—not giving thought to the permanency of our Irish brothers in the community. To be honest with you, Bishop, I didn't expect they would want to remain in Lowell. I always assumed they'd want to return to Boston and live among—"

"Their own?"

"Well, yes, if you want to put it that way. However, we have an ever-increasing number of Irish in Lowell who appear to be setting down roots. I don't want to sound disparaging, but the Irish tend to be a clannish sort of people. You'd agree with that, wouldn't you?"

The bishop nodded and stroked his plump red cheek. "They find comfort in that which is familiar. Not unlike most of us, Mr. Boott. However, the Irish do bring with them a deep sense of loyalty to the clans of their homeland and align themselves accordingly. In that regard they are somewhat different from other immigrants."

"Right," Boott chimed in, vigorously nodding his head up and down. "Well stated, Your Excellency." He hesitated for a moment before continuing. "Another thing that I've observed about the Irish is their deep regard for the church."

"For a moment there, I thought you were going to say their deep regard for a pitcher of ale." The bishop gave Kirk a serious stare but then snorted as he attempted to hold back his own laughter. "It was a joke, good fellow—you're permitted to laugh."

Kirk's nervous laughter mingled with Bishop Fenwick's snorting noises for what seemed several minutes. Matthew sat quietly, observing the interchange, a smile emerging on his lips when the bishop finally gazed in his direction. "And what do *you* think of our Irish brothers, Mr. Cheever?" The bishop's question brought the laughter to a startling halt.

Matthew glanced toward Boott, who nodded his head ever so slightly. "I agree with Mr. Boott's assessment, sir."

"Not much of an independent thinker? I'm surprised Mr. Boott would hold you in such high esteem," the bishop rebutted.

Matthew knew he was being baited. His words must be carefully chosen. He dared not fail a second test in one day. "I don't believe the fact that I agree with Mr. Boott's assessment gives credence to your judgment of my ability to evaluate a given situation. It merely affirms the intelligence of my employer's evaluation of this particular circumstance. I, too, believe the Irish hold the church in deep regard," he replied in a measured voice.

The bishop laughed aloud. "Well put, my boy. Don't know if I could have done better myself in such formidable circumstances. Isn't that right, Mr. Boott?"

A forced smile formed upon his mentor's lips. "That's exactly right, Excellency."

"Well, then, we all agree the Irish hold the church in high regard. So what is your problem?"

"They have no church in Lowell, no place to worship, no church leader to marry or bury them, no priest to hear their problems or direct them down the path of righteousness," Boott replied.

The bishop's face was stoic, unreadable. "I'm going to guess that since you've determined there is a problem, you've also devised some type of solution."

"I've given thought to several ideas, but nothing concrete just yet," he lied. "That's what I want to discuss with you. Surely you have some knowledge of the increasing problems the Irish face in Lowell. After all, they are your people," Boott said, obviously hoping to lead the matter into a discussion where he could further ascertain the cleric's stance.

"You're right that they are Catholics, and in that regard, they are my people. I would agree that all Catholics need spiritual leadership. However, Mr. Boott, they are your people also. They are in Lowell because you could find no others willing to perform the grueling labor of digging your canals and building your factories. Now that they have decided to remain in Lowell, you have a dilemma. You find them difficult to control, yet you need them close at hand to continue constructing your growing community. It is truly a troublesome situation."

Bishop Fenwick was obviously enjoying himself as he rose from the chair and moved aimlessly about the room, stopping directly in front of Boott and forcing him to look up into the bishop's face as he continued the assessment. "As I see it, you need the Irish—at least the men. However, you don't want them living in Lowell, mucking up the tidiness of your well-thought-out progressive community. So now you've decided the Catholic Church should come to your rescue. Would that be what prompts your visit to Boston?"

Matthew had become increasingly uncomfortable as Bishop Fenwick spoke. The cleric had painted the Boston Associates, and particularly Kirk Boott, as tyrannical, abusive men who had shamelessly abused the Irish population of Lowell. It was ludicrous. Yet Boott seemed undaunted by the turn of events. Instead, he smiled at the bishop and helped himself to one of the remaining cakes sitting on the marble-topped table. Seeming not the least disquieted by the silence, he finished the cake, carefully wiped his mouth with a linen napkin, and waited until Bishop Fenwick had finally seated himself in the velvet chair.

"Now, then, let me see if I can adequately respond to your summation. First of all, I didn't go rousting about hunting for Irishmen to work in Lowell. It was Hugh Cummiskey that led a group of his fellow clansmen from the Boston docks to Lowell seeking me and asking for work. I doubt you will have any difficulty verifying that fact. Once Cummiskey and his men were working, word spread that there was work available in Lowell. I never advertised, encouraged, or lured any immigrants, Irish or otherwise, into the community. Those who chose to come and work have been paid a fair wage. I have no control over how they spend their money or where they place their values. However, I believe the church should have a vested interest in their eternal souls, and I'm sure you could find use for a bit of their earnings if they cared to give a portion to the church."

The bishop gave a hearty laugh. "I always enjoy a good sparring event with you, Mr. Boott. Now, let's get to the heart of the matter. We both know the Irish are beginning to form settlements in Lowell, and we both know they get out of control from time to time. What is it you want from me?"

"Short term, I'd like to have you assign a priest to serve the Catholics. Long term, I'd like to see you build a Catholic church that would serve to unify the Irish who settle in Lowell."

The bishop once again stroked his flushed cheek. "To a man unfamiliar with you and the goals of the Boston Associates, that would appear to be a plan cultivated to fulfill the needs of your fellow citizens. However, we both know that this proposal is made more for your benefit than that of the Irish people of Lowell, and I'm sure you also know I have a shortage of priests. Simply put, I don't have a priest I can send to Lowell, much less the funds to purchase land and build a church."

Matthew watched the unfolding scene. It was a methodical exchange, a game of chess played with words rather than pawns and kings. Both men retained their composure. It was Kirk's move, and Bishop Fenwick waited patiently.

"Would additional funding assist you in securing another cleric for the diocese?" Kirk ventured.

"Perhaps. But I would need to present a long-term plan, something of substance, to my superiors if I were going to assign a priest to Lowell. After all, we have a more urgent need for priests in larger cities."

Kirk nodded, acknowledging it was his move. Matthew was enjoying the discourse. It was obvious his employer would need to raise the stakes if they were going to make any progress.

"There is a piece of land, large enough for a good-sized church. It lies directly between the two Irish settlements.

Possibly it could draw them together, become a source of unity. I think I could convince the Associates to sell it at a very reasonable price, perhaps even donate it to the church. I feel certain your parishioners would be more than willing to donate their labor once you've enough funds to begin building."

Bishop Fenwick's lips turned upward, and he rubbed his large hands together. "I believe I could take this information to my superiors with the expectation of a satisfactory result for all concerned. Why don't you write a figure on this piece of paper that we could expect to receive if another priest were assigned to the diocese? Oh, yes, and why don't you jot down the address of the property you're going to assign to the church. It would make my discussion with the church more, shall be say, *profitable* to all concerned."

Kirk accepted the outstretched pen and dipped it into the ink before writing the requested information and returning the pen. The bishop slid the paper back across the desk and placed a pair of spectacles across the bridge of his nose before reading the inscribed words. After reading, Bishop Fenwick nodded his head, rose from his chair, and extended his hand to Kirk.

"I'll be in touch with you once I have something definite to pass along."

"Always a pleasure visiting with you, Your Excellency," Kirk responded.

"If not a pleasure, at least profitable," Bishop Fenwick replied as he rose from his chair to dismiss them.

The same priest who had earlier admitted them now escorted the two men down the maze of hallways and out the front doors. There was a note of finality to their visit as the cleric pushed the heavy doors closed behind them.

"The meeting went well, don't you think?" Boott inquired as the two of them stood waiting in the lobby of the Brackman Hotel a short time later. "Hope you don't mind mixing a bit of pleasure with our business," he continued, without waiting for an answer to his first question.

"No, of course not," Matthew replied. "I thought the meeting—"

"Ah, here they are now," Kirk interrupted as he walked off toward the two women entering the front door.

Matthew watched the exchange from a distance. Both ladies had the same aquiline nose, wide-set eyes, and broad shoulders of their male relative. Unfortunately, the features that created a rather striking appearance in Kirk Boott failed to have the same effect on the female members of the Boott family.

"This is the young man I've been telling you about," Kirk announced as he pulled Matthew forward. "Matthew, this is my sister, Neva Locklear. And this," he said, wrapping his arm around the younger woman, "is my lovely niece, Isabelle. I know you'll find it difficult to believe, but she's every bit as bright as she is comely."

Matthew felt the heat rise in his cheeks. He had assumed they would dine with some of the Boston Associates for supper. What was it that Kirk had said as they'd followed the priest down the hallway? Something to the effect that he had made reservations for supper and hoped the evening's discourse would prove as fruitful as their meeting with Bishop Fenwick. Yes, those were his words. There had been nothing about dining with his relatives. Matthew silently chided himself. While he had been looking forward to supper and a lively discussion with the Associates, Boott had been anticipating a reunion with his sister and niece. A liaison that, for some unknown reason, caused a prickling sensation to course down his spine.

"I hope you don't mind, Matthew, but I took the liberty of posting a letter to my sister setting forth all of your many virtues. He's everything I promised, isn't he, Neva?"

Matthew watched the shrewd glance that passed between Kirk and Neva. This was more than meaningless chitchat. No matter that Boott was lively and engaging, that he appeared the carefree host entertaining guests for the evening; there was purpose to every word being uttered.

"He is absolutely delightful. Don't you agree, Isabelle?" Neva inquired, placing her hand atop Isabelle's unadorned left hand.

Eyes cast downward, Isabelle nodded her head in agreement.

"Speak up, Isabelle. We can't hear you with your head down," Neva persisted.

"Yes, he is everything you promised, Uncle Kirk."

Matthew's head jerked up and he looked at his employer. Boott's comment several days earlier echoed in his mind. *A wife must be chosen with no less intelligence and cunning than one chooses a lawyer or business partner.* Was this then the intelligent, cunning choice that Boott had in mind for him?

"Look at this," Nadene said, jabbing Lilly with her elbow. "The book of John has Jesus saying, " 'I am the way, the truth, and the life: no man cometh unto the Father, but by me.' " She pointed to the verse in the fourteenth chapter. "Then look here," she added, "My granny has written a note that says, " 'God will make thee provision. He will make a way even when it seems impossible.' " She turned and looked at Lilly. "Jesus said that He's the way. Do you suppose that's what my granny was talking about?"

Lilly was chilled and wanted only to slip under the covers and go to sleep. The sole reason the candles were still burning was the fact that Pru and Sarah had taken a last-minute trip to the necessary. "I suppose it could mean that," Lilly finally answered. "Although the Bible is full of examples where God used people to fulfill His plan." She thought of her own mission. Surely God had put her plans in motion as surely as He had sent Jonah to warn the people of Nineveh.

Lilly wanted only to change the subject and scooted down in the covers. "Did your grandmother always write notes about Bible verses?"

"Oh my, yes." Nadene replied. "It's one of the reasons I cherish this Bible so much. It was the one thing Granny left me when she died. Just look here. Sometimes she wrote her thoughts alongside the verse—right on the same page. A great many times, however, she wrote on a scrap of paper and just stuck it in between the pages. When I need to understand a particular passage, I often find Granny's words help."

Nadene closed the Bible and put it aside. She blew out the candle and then settled back on her pillow. Only the candle from Pru's bedside still shone. The other girls seemed to have fallen asleep, mindless of Lilly and Nadene's discussion.

"I take my Bible with me to the mill," Nadene told Lilly in confidence. "I like to pull it out and read it when I have a moment."

"I've heard some of the other girls say they tape up bits and pieces of articles and books. Seems a shame to tear something apart just in order to read while you work."

Nadene sighed. "I could never tear up Granny's Bible, though I've seen some girls do just that. I suppose it gives them comfort in the midst of their trials, so I cannot fault them."

Lilly knew it had been some time since she'd concerned herself with reading the Bible. Even the small portion shared by Nadene pierced her heart and conscience. *I am the way,* Jesus had said. Lilly had heard that verse even as a child. It was a convicting statement—one on which she didn't want to dwell at the moment.

I know God has brought me here with a special purpose, Lilly reasoned. The turmoil in her heart churned while her mind mocked her for the traitor she was. How could she be certain of anything God wanted? She wasn't exactly listening to Him these days.

CHAPTER *10*

Lowell, Massachusetts

Lilly's trembling fingers fumbled with the strings of her bonnet. More than anything, she wanted to awaken to discover that this was nothing more than a bad dream. She wanted to be back in her cozy room at the farm, where she could smell the scent of burning wood in the fireplace and feel the coolness of an autumn morning on her windowpane. Rather than join the ranks as an anonymous mill girl rushing off in the early morning darkness to toil in the Appleton, she wanted to escape to the peaceful countryside of East Chelmsford—even more, she wanted her identity back.

"You're going to do fine today. There's no doubt that once you've mastered your tasks in the spinning room, the overseer is going to wonder how the mill operated without you," Addie encouraged.

"I wish I shared your confidence," Lilly replied, still groping with her bonnet strings.

"You'll be back here in no time, eating your breakfast and telling me your fears were misplaced. Just remember that I have your name on the top of my prayer list today. Now off with you—you dare not be tardy on your first day."

Lilly attempted to smile. It proved impossible. "I can use as many prayers as you can squeeze into your schedule."

Miss Addie's words echoed in Lilly's mind—at least temporarily. It was more likely the overseer would rue the day he hired her, she decided. Once outside the door, the other girls surrounded her, and as they made their way to the mill, girls from the other boardinghouses joined them. Lilly was swept along with the momentum, no longer in control of her destiny, the force of the bustling girls now carrying her along toward a worrisome future.

A short time later two of the girls abruptly broke off and hurried toward No. 1 of the Appleton, their void quickly filled by others, all rushing toward No. 2. They hurried through the gate, across the yard, and up the winding staircase. Lilly stopped short and turned into the counting room. She breathed a long sigh of relief. Thaddeus Arnold was nowhere in sight. Instead, a rotund middle-aged man with a balding pate and cherry red cheeks occupied the chair. He smiled in her direction. Lilly glanced over her shoulder expecting to find someone behind her. There was no one, yet she was somewhat surprised to see the man still sporting a smile when she turned back in his direction. He crooked his finger, beckoning her closer. Taking a hesitant step forward, Lilly was buoyed by his broadening smile, so she continued onward until she was standing directly in front of him.

"You must be Lilly Armbruster." His tone was deep and resonant, much like her father's voice.

"Yes, I was to report to Mr. Arnold—Thaddeus Arnold—but I don't see him."

He motioned her toward a wooden chair. "I am Lawrence Gault, and I've replaced Mr. Arnold. He has been promoted to another position with the mill." Mr. Gault gave her another broad smile, his cheeks puffing into the shape of two rosy apples. "I fear you'll be forced to complete your employment papers with me."

Lilly issued a silent prayer of thanks. At least she didn't have to begin her day dealing with that pompous, beady-eyed Mr.

Arnold. Returning the man's smile, she dropped into the empty chair beside his desk. "It will be a pleasure, Mr. Gault."

She sat quietly as Mr. Gault slid a neatly stacked pile of papers toward her then pushed his wire-rimmed spectacles onto the bridge of his nose. "Now, then, this is your employment agreement. You should read the terms, and if you have any questions, we can discuss them. While you're reading the agreement, I have some other papers I must complete, but please interrupt me if you find something that you don't understand."

Lilly nodded and returned his smile. This man was certainly a refreshing change from her initial interview with Mr. Arnold. After scanning the first paragraph relating to duties of the overseer, she slowed down and began reading more carefully. She found the rule one of the girls had mentioned. It stated that she must agree to stay for a minimum of one year, and all employees intending to leave employment of the company must give two weeks' notice of such intention to the overseer or their contract would not be considered fulfilled. She scanned the paragraph requiring she be at work unless the overseer determined her unable to attend due to illness.

The rule regarding church attendance, the one Nadene had mentioned, was next. It stated that regular attendance at public worship on the Sabbath was necessary for the preservation of good order and that the Company would not employ any person who was habitually absent. Did the Boston Associates truly feel it necessary to include church attendance as one of their rules? Perhaps she should ask Mr. Gault. On second thought, perhaps she should not. It would be foolhardy of her to be labeled as a troublemaker on her first day. Yet she wondered about such personal matters being regulated by an employer.

"I trust you read the last paragraph regarding your wages—you'll be paid the last Friday of each month. Any questions?" Mr. Gault inquired when she glanced in his direction.

Heeding her better judgment, Lilly moved her head back and forth. "No, the contract appears to address much more than I could have ever imagined."

If Mr. Gault noticed the sarcasm in her voice, he gave no

indication. Instead, he dipped his pen into an inkwell and thrust it toward her while pointing at an empty line at the bottom of the page. Lilly wavered for only a moment before carefully affixing her neat signature to the page. Her fate was sealed. She knew it, Mr. Gault knew it, and God knew it—and of course, following the Lord's plan was the primary reason she was here. She was now positioned to become the instrument of God—ready to mete out rightful retribution upon Kirk Boott and his wealthy associates for the many wrongs they had inflicted upon the farm families of East Chelmsford. Her mission had just begun.

Her stomach churned. *I am doing the right thing,* she assured herself. *This has to be what God has required of me.* A momentary confusion swept over her. What if she'd misunderstood? What if God wasn't bringing her here to rid East Chelmsford of the mills? She handed the papers back to Mr. Gault then pressed her hands against her temples. *This has to be the right thing to do—there simply aren't any other options.*

Mr. Gault finished reviewing the papers and removed his spectacles. "Follow me. I'll show you where you'll be working," he said, rising from his chair.

Together they walked from the agent's office and crossed the mill yard, Mr. Gault waving and calling out hellos to several of the men pushing carts of cotton that would soon be devoured by the carding machines.

The white tower with its huge clock cast a shadow across one of the brick-lined flower gardens that centered the yard. The bright, colorful blooms of spring and summer were gone, replaced by fading, dried stalks, providing evidence of the changing season. Lilly followed Mr. Gault to the narrow winding stairway that ascended one end of the mill. The enclosure covering the stairway jutted out from the structure, giving the appearance of a misguided afterthought.

They entered the stairwell and began their upward climb, the clamoring of the pulsing machinery growing louder with each turn. Lilly instinctively wrinkled her nose at the stale, fetid air. By the time they had passed the second-floor landing, Mr. Gault had slowed his pace, and when they finally stopped outside the third-floor doorway, his breathing had turned shallow and labored. Lilly balanced herself on the narrow top step as he hesitated and grasped the doorknob with his right hand.

"Fortunately, we need climb no farther," he said, his words bursting forth in short gasps. He gulped another breath of air. "I'll take you in and introduce you to your supervisor." The words were barely out of his mouth before he stopped with a look of recognition on his face. He gulped two more breaths. "Thaddeus Arnold is the supervisor of the spinning room," he said in an apologetic tone before pushing open the door.

The blood drained from Lilly's face, leaving her pale and shaken. This must be a cruel joke—the thought of facing toady little Thaddeus Arnold every day. Being forced to tolerate his infuriating pomposity was surely more than she could bear.

Mr. Gault waved to someone across the room. Lilly fixed her attention on the room, allowing the scene to tug her back to the present. She was greeted with Mr. Arnold's leering gaze. Despite the intense heat and humidity that hung in the room, a shiver ran up her spine, and she quickly glanced downward. Lint was already clinging to her dark chambray dress. *I should have listened to Miss Addie and worn my faded old work dress,* she silently chastised herself. Had it not needed laundering, she would have taken the older woman's advice. Instead, she had gone to bed. Now she would pay for her laziness.

Mr. Gault mouthed his good-bye before making a hasty departure out of the room and back down the stairway.

Lilly stood mute before Mr. Arnold, the humidity and his leering stare dampening her hair and her spirits in synchronized accord. He slithered off the stool and motioned for her to follow. They walked past Mary Albertson, who had a room across the hall at Miss Addie's boardinghouse. None of the other operators looked familiar, but several of them extended a welcoming smile as she followed Mr. Arnold down a narrow aisle, attempting to keep her distance from the machinery that was spinning thick white ropes of cotton onto tall bobbins.

Lilly placed a finger to her ear. How could anyone be expected to spend her waking hours in these horrendous conditions? And yet, the other girls seemed oblivious to the thundering noise that surrounded them. They moved on cue, shifting to and fro in time with the machines, carefully unknotting any errant thread that dared tangle before gliding back in place to continue their vigil. Silent sentries, they guarded over the metal monsters that thundered and pounded as they produced the thread-laden bobbins.

Without warning, Mr. Arnold's fingers closed around her wrist, startling Lilly to attention. She pulled free and met his beady-eyed glare. Mouth turned upward in a half smile, his touch lingered on her arm while his defiant look dared her to say a word. Finally he stepped aside.

"This way," he shouted, pointing toward several frames that stood idle at the end of the row. She followed, relief flooding her soul as she spied Nadene. Mr. Arnold motioned Nadene to join them. "Nadene Eckhoff," he screamed into the lint-filled air.

Lilly nodded. "We board in the same house," she screamed back.

"Get to work!" he commanded before walking away. Lilly tried to hide her relief as she turned to face Nadene.

Nadene rewarded her with a bright smile as she pointed toward the handle. She grasped Lilly's hand in her own and together they pulled the handle, sending the machine into motion, adding yet another level of noise to the already deafening racket. The two of them watched the machine momentarily, and then Nadene pulled Lilly toward another frame.

"This one is yours, also. It's not difficult; just watch that the roving doesn't twist or snarl. Mr. Arnold comes around every hour to assure himself our work is satisfactory, so be mindful your bobbins are filling evenly. He always looks at the bobbins. The other day he threatened to reduce Mary's pay because he said she was daydreaming and her bobbins weren't filling uniformly. He's new to his position, and several of us think he's hoping to impress his superiors by increasing our workload. We don't like him much," she added, pulling the handle and causing the second machine to move into frenzied gyrations. "If the roving goes awry, I'll come help you if need be," she promised as she moved back to her own frames.

Lilly nodded and mouthed a thank-you before beginning her wearisome vigil over the metal beasts. It was mindless work, with nothing to break the monotony except the occasional skewed roving or unevenly wound bobbins. The clamor of the machinery was deafening, but the other girls seemed unaware. Curiously, they appeared to be in a trancelike state, each having escaped to some unknown place—somewhere far beyond the walls that surrounded and held them prisoner. She wished that *she* could escape into their dream world, but the noise prevented her departure. It held her captive, a slave to the torturous din.

She startled at Mr. Arnold's touch. He had come up behind her, placing his hand on the small of her back. Stepping away from the machine, she backed into his awaiting arms. He held her in a viselike grip, his acrid breath assailing her nostrils as he leaned in close to her ear, his fingers squeezing her flesh. "Your bobbins are not winding properly," he said, slowly releasing his hold. He held up a bobbin in front of her face. "Unacceptable!" he screamed. His beady eyes gleamed grotesquely as he grabbed her by the arm. "Watch after those machines," he screamed as they passed Nadene. Lilly turned to look back at Nadene as Mr. Arnold pulled her along, back out the door and into the stair-well, then pushed her into the corner. "Do you want to maintain your position in this mill?" he snarled. His yellow teeth were bared like an animal attacking its prey.

Lilly turned her head as he moved in closer. His arms pinned her on either side. She ducked beneath his arm and then held up a warning finger. "Don't touch me, Mr. Arnold, or you'll live to regret it," she shouted. Quickly, she turned the doorknob then rushed back into the room, down the aisle, and to her position at the machines. She didn't look up until she heard the faint sound of the breakfast bell. It grew louder as the girls quickly slammed their machines to a halt and began rushing toward the doorway. Nadene shoved the handle back on one of Lilly's frames and motioned for her to quiet the other one.

"Hurry or you won't have enough time to eat breakfast and

get back here on time," Nadene said as she headed toward the door.

The other girls were already moving into the stairwell as she made her way down the row of machines. A strange noise caused Lilly to look over her shoulder. She swallowed hard. Thaddeus Arnold had another girl backed into a corner. She appeared to be smiling and nodding in agreement, although Lilly couldn't be sure. Edging closer to the door, Lilly continued watching, unable to tear herself away from the unfolding scene. Arnold's hands were around the girl and his head was bent forward. It was impossible to see if they were talking or if he was kissing the girl. The thought was repugnant. His head came up as he stepped back and allowed the girl to move away. Lilly shivered as she watched Thaddeus pat the girl's backside. Silently, Lilly slipped into the stairwell, her hands quivering as she wondered just what liberties Thaddeus Arnold might be taking with the girls employed at the Appleton.

At each level, additional operatives poured into the stairwell, each group seemingly more harried than the last, until they finally reached the bottom. Rushing forward to greet the crisp, bright morning, Lilly inhaled deeply. Her dress was damp with perspiration, and suddenly the cool air was more enemy than friend. She drew her cloak tight around her body, looking neither to her right nor left as she hurried down Jackson Street. She couldn't drive from her mind the scene of Thaddeus Arnold with the girl. What if he approached her again?

Suddenly someone took hold of her arm and Lilly whirled about. "I'm sorry. I didn't mean to startle you," Nadene apologized. "I wanted to tell you that you did a grand job this morning. You've nothing to worry about." Nadene matched her step to Lilly's.

"Thank you. I didn't expect you to wait on me. You're wasting precious time when you could be eating your meal."

"Some things are more important than food. I was concerned about you. Did Mr. Arnold give you a difficult time this morning?"

Lilly hesitated. "He told me if I didn't do a better job he'd be required to terminate me."

Nadene didn't seem overly surprised. "He did that with the other girl who just started yesterday. I think Mr. Arnold's afraid *he'll* be terminated if he doesn't do well in his new position. After he's more secure, perhaps he'll stop his bullying behavior."

"Has he said anything to you?" Lilly inquired.

Nadene gave a small giggle. "I don't think he would dare. Mr. Boott himself transferred me to the Appleton because of my abilities in the spinning room at the Merrimack. I doubt Mr. Thaddeus Arnold would say one word to me. And don't you worry; he won't fire you, not with me for a teacher."

"Why should you care whether I succeed?"

Nadene smiled. "That's easy. I care because you're my friend."

Four or five girls were already eating breakfast when they arrived at the boardinghouse, and several others were reaching for bowls of food as they seated themselves. Lilly had been at work for only two hours, yet it seemed an eternity. Dropping onto one of the dining room chairs, she sat idle as the ravenous girls around her continued their feeding frenzy. Josephine nudged her with an elbow. "Pass the potatoes," she sputtered, her mouth still filled with half-eaten food. She grabbed the potatoes from Lilly's hand and swallowed. "You had better get some food on your plate, or you're going to go hungry."

Lilly nodded and put a mound of the potatoes on her dish when Josephine returned the bowl to her. It was the first time since her arrival that Lilly had been seated at the dining room table. It didn't feel proper, Miss Addie serving breakfast without any assistance, but the older woman appeared to be doing very well on her own. The meal was hearty and on time, which was no small task for someone who only a week ago had served her boarders bread that would sink a ship.

In spite of a throbbing headache and upset stomach, Lilly poured a dollop of cream on a small bowl of pumpkin mush and forced a spoonful into her mouth. She swallowed hard, forcing the protesting lump downward, then clutched her midsection as the orange glob settled heavily in her stomach. Had Miss Addie not been watching, Lilly would have avoided breakfast altogether. Instead, she added a portion of fried cod, a biscuit, and a small wedge of cheese to the potatoes already congealing in grease on her plate. What was she thinking? It would be impossible to force another bite into her mouth, yet she didn't want to offend Miss Addie. Using her fork, she pushed the food around her plate, occasionally feigning a bite or two. Busy with their own plates, the other boarders didn't seem to notice. Within fifteen minutes, the girls began scurrying away from the table, some of them grabbing a biscuit to eat as they rushed back to the mill. Hoping she would go undetected, Lilly cautiously scraped her remaining food back onto the large serving platters and issued a silent thank-you when no one seemed to notice.

"Breakfast was splendid," Lilly whispered to the older woman as she prepared to leave.

Addie blushed at the praise. "I know you haven't time to visit, but did everything go well this morning?"

Lilly nodded. "As well as could be expected in such a place. I'll tell you more this evening," she promised.

"Yes, of course. Hurry along. I'll see you at dinnertime. By then, you'll be an old hand at operating your machinery."

Lilly didn't respond. She tied her bonnet, walked out the door, and joined the group rushing off toward the mill—all seemingly happy they had this opportunity to support themselves. Lilly cringed at the thought of spending years inside the walls of the towering brick fortress. Already she longed to return to a life where she could walk outdoors whenever she pleased. Thankfully, she told herself, she would be here only long enough to carry out God's plan of retribution.

CHAPTER 11

Matthew bounded up the steps to the Cheevers' front porch. He had left work an hour early, so his mother would undoubtedly be surprised at his arrival. The thought pleased him. After all, he had promised to come to dinner on Sunday, but that visit would be bound by duty rather than choice. Arriving unexpectedly at a time when the two of them could relax and enjoy their time together would be like old times, he decided.

Entering the front door, he called out, "Mother, where are you?"

"You needn't yell. I'm right here," Julia replied. She was seated in her tapestry-covered sewing rocker, her fingers deftly pushing and pulling a thread-laden needle in and out of a delicate piece of embroidery.

Matthew smiled, walked to where she sat, and kissed her cheek. "You don't act surprised to see me," he remarked, seating himself opposite her chair.

"You forget I have a clear view of the front street. I saw you coming long before you reached the door. I've even had several moments to contemplate why my son would be paying me an unexpected visit."

There was a lilt to her voice. She no doubt already suspected why he had come. He might succeed in fooling himself but never his mother. She continued her sewing while he settled into the chair, contemplating his reply. Should he come right out with it, or should he attempt to convince her there was no ulterior reason for his visit? Matthew settled into the chair, elongating his body as far as possible, then propped his feet on the matching footstool.

"Do sit up correctly, Matthew. You're going to crush your tailbone or pinch a nerve in your back sitting in that ungentlemanly position. You're just borrowing future medical problems when you don't use proper posture. Ask Dr. Barnard. He'll confirm the truth of what I'm telling you."

"I don't want to talk to Dr. Barnard about crushed tailbones or pinched nerves, Mother. I've come to hear all about your supper party," he said.

"Truly? That's a bit odd, since you generally tell me that all supper gatherings are dull and unimaginative." She gave him a wry grin before continuing. "Well, it goes without saying that the meal was delightful. I served the most delectable lobster bisque, and the mutton was beyond description—so tender it nearly melted in my mouth. And then there were baby peas with caramelized onions and parsleyed potatoes. Oh yes, and cherries jubilee, one of your favorite desserts. See what you missed? Positively a gastronomical delight, as your father would say," Julia gloated.

Matthew watched his mother's animated face as she delightedly recounted the details of each culinary offering. He remained patient as she explained the placement of her centerpiece and stemware, knowing she was baiting him to interrupt her once again. He would not. She would only prolong the agony by detailing each of the gowns worn by her female guests, or worse yet, the details of some latest piece of stitchery the women had discussed in the music room.

He pushed his chair back onto its rear legs and then quickly let it back down when his mother snapped her fingers. Obviously his mother was going to force him to ask questions.

Perhaps if he told her about his trip to Boston, she would give him the information he truly sought. Might as well wade in and test the waters, he decided. "I had an interesting time in Boston. Mr. Boott and I met with the bishop and then had supper with some of Boott's relatives. His niece, Isabelle, joined us for supper. She's quite lovely. Boott seems to think she'd be a good match for me." He hesitated only a moment and then added, "I trust you enjoyed delightful conversation during supper?"

Too late he realized he had said more than his mother could tolerate. Mentioning Isabelle was a mistake. Julia's posture had turned rigid at the remark. She appeared ready to do battle as she placed her sewing in the basket beside her chair and turned to give him her full attention.

"So Kirk Boott has entered the matchmaking business? Well, you can give him a message from your mother. Tell him that when we find ourselves in need of a matchmaker's assistance, I will personally come calling."

"Now, Mother, don't get upset. He knows I'm not seeing anyone at the moment and made a casual suggestion. I'm certainly not obligated to call upon his niece in order to maintain my position with the Corporation."

She leveled a stare directly toward him. "Are you *absolutely* sure about that?"

"Preposterous! How could you even think such nonsense?"

Julia stood up and stared into the mirror above the mantel. Pulling a small decorative comb from her hair, she tugged at several strands before tucking the comb back into her coif. She turned and looked down at her son. "Matthew, you would be surprised at how cunning people can be. Don't deceive yourself. You would make a fine catch for Boott's niece—a nice addition to his family, and having you as a member of the family could do nothing but help his cause as he ascends upward in the Corporation. You could be the son he never had. I'm sure he wishes his daughter were old enough to marry; then he could truly take you on as a son. Don't you see what he'll do?"

"I'm sorry I mentioned the supper. And that's all it was, Mother—supper."

Julia's lips turned upward in a sardonic smile. "You think that's all it was? Just remember that I've warned you. His niece will soon appear in Lowell, and you will be expected to be her escort. Mark my words."

"I was hoping for a pleasant afternoon of visiting, Mother. Would it be possible to change the subject? I'd wager the women were begging to know the secret ingredients for your cherries jubilee."

Julia picked up her embroidery and once again began to stitch. "The supper party was delightful, and lest you think you've succeeded in changing the subject without my realization, be aware that I know what you're doing."

Matthew responded with a hearty laugh. "Yes, Mother, I'm well aware that we'll not change topics unless you choose to do so." He took a deep breath before proceeding. "Did all of your guests attend?"

She graced him with a demure smile. "All except you. Why don't you ask what you really want to know, Matthew?"

He shook his head in resignation. "All right, Mother. Did Lilly attend?"

Julia nodded in satisfaction. "I knew that was why you came to visit. Yes, Lilly attended and she looked stunning. I dare say, that girl becomes more beautiful with each passing minute. She inherited both her mother's charm and her father's intelligence. You let a good thing slip away, Matthew. In my heart, however, I do believe you could win her back if you would set your mind to the task."

Matthew tugged at his collar as he rose from his chair. He didn't want to speak in haste. No need to intentionally become the target of his mother's ire. He would speak calmly, rationally. He cleared his throat and turned. "Please try to remember, Mother, that it was Lilly who terminated our relationship. As you may recall, I was planning to ask Mr. Armbruster for Lilly's hand when she became consumed with anger regarding the Boston Associates purchasing the farmland."

Julia waved her lace handkerchief in his direction. "Don't make excuses, Matthew."

"I'm not making excuses. I'm reminding you of what occurred. Lilly said she wouldn't consider continuing our relationship unless I promised to remain a farmer and disengage myself from the Boston Associates."

His mother shrugged her shoulders. "Did you even consider her wishes?"

Matthew stared at her in disbelief. His mother was talking utter nonsense, yet he dared not confront her with such a remark. "You realize we are discussing the choice I made for my life's work? Lilly wanted me to bend to her will. Think about what a precedent that would have set for our married life. I didn't want to begin married life having my wife dictate my professional choices. Think how Father would have rebuffed such an idea when you two were contemplating marriage. What if you had told him you wouldn't marry him unless he gave up farming and became a banker? I think he would have reconsidered marriage. Even God's word substantiates my position—a wife is to be subject to her husband."

"Don't begin quoting the Bible to me, Matthew, for it also says a man will love his wife above himself. Lilly is a fine girl. Your Mr. Boott will find none that will even begin to compare. You can't imagine the sorrow I felt for that child, knowing she's lost every member of her family, and now she's relegated to working in the mills."

"She's working at the mills?" he asked without thinking.

His mother gave a self-satisfied smile. "Yes. Poor child. There was nothing left to do."

Matthew tried to compose himself. He didn't want the matter to get out of hand any more than it already had. "You exaggerate, Mother. Lilly has not lost every member of her family. Lewis is still alive, and if she's working in the mills . . . well, it's because she chose to work in the mills. I didn't force her to take a position in the mills. And please don't forget the fact that there are girls who come from all over the countryside, anxious for such an opportunity."

"Don't even mention Lewis Armbruster in the same breath with his sister. Lewis was a mean child, and he's grown into a despicable man. I'm told he left Lilly penniless, gambling away all of the family's money. It would have been better for Lilly had she been left without Lewis. He's served only to make her life more miserable. As for working in the mills, we both know how distasteful that must be for Lilly."

"I agree Lewis is a poor excuse for a brother. He is, however, a living member of Lilly's family. And although Lilly may find working in the mills distasteful, it was apparently her choice to seek employment with the Associates. I might also remind you that Lilly is no stranger to physical labor. She grew up working on the family farm, which is certainly more taxing than operating machinery in the mills."

His mother was looking past him, staring out the front window toward the dusk-filled skies, a smile beginning to form upon her lips. He would say nothing further. Obviously he had made his point.

"I believe your father is home," Julia remarked, the front door opening as she spoke.

"Look who I've brought home for supper, Julia," Randolph called out from the entryway. His broad smile faded, however, as he walked into the room with Lilly. "Son, I didn't realize you would be . . ." His voice faltered as he looked toward Julia, obviously hoping she would rescue him.

Julia rushed toward Lilly, pulling her into a warm embrace. "What a delightful surprise—two of my favorite people for supper. Let me take your cape, dear."

Matthew watched in awe as his mother released Lilly, unfastened her cape, and removed it from the girl's shoulders before there was time for any objection. It was difficult to ascertain whether Lilly was angry or merely perplexed to find herself in his presence. He watched the color rise in her cheeks as she reached for her cape.

"I told Mr. Cheever I should go back to the boardinghouse, but he insisted. I really must be leaving," Lilly said.

"Nonsense. Of course you'll stay. Supper will be ready in no time at all. Let me go see how things are progressing," Julia stated while moving toward the kitchen. "Randolph, you bar the door if she attempts to escape."

Matthew stood transfixed. His mother was right. Lilly appeared to grow more beautiful each time he set eyes upon her. He struggled for a moment to gain his voice. "Don't leave on my account, Lilly. I'll go," Matthew croaked, his voice suddenly foreign to his ears.

Julia whirled about. "Nobody is going anywhere. We are going to have supper—all of us—together, like the civilized people we are. Now sit down and visit while I see about the preparations," she commanded.

Julia marched out of the room as they seated themselves. Lilly folded her hands and stared at the floor; Matthew leaned back and cupped his folded hands around his knee. Randolph pulled his pipe from his pocket, tapping it gently in his hand. Silence reigned.

"How was your trip to Boston, Matthew?" Randolph finally asked.

"It went very well. Thank you for asking, Father. How was your day, Lilly?" Matthew ventured.

"Hot and tiresome," she replied without looking up.

"Hot? I've been in Lowell all day and the weather has been beautiful. Where have you been that you consider it so hot?"

"In the Appleton Mill, where the windows are nailed down. Unlike you, I didn't have the opportunity to walk about town enjoying the beauty of the day. You should pay a visit to one of the weaving or spinning rooms. Perhaps then you would understand my reply," Lilly stated, her gaze now riveted in his direction.

"Supper is ready," Julia announced, a bright smile on her face as she came back into the room. "I can't begin to tell you what a joy it is to have servants preparing meals, Lilly. It is such a change for me. Come along now and tell me what you three have been discussing."

As the evening wore on, it seemed that Matthew irritated Lilly at every turn. It wasn't his intent. In fact, he had valiantly endeavored to find neutral topics of discussion throughout supper. However, with each attempt, the conversation returned to the mills and Lilly's discontent. To his amazement, Julia appeared to navigate the conversation toward Lilly's circumstances at every opportunity.

"Matthew!"

Julia's voice brought him back to the present. "Yes?"

"Lilly must return to the boardinghouse. I've insisted you escort her. Of course, she objected, but I told her I would brook no argument—from either of you. Hurry. She's in the hallway with your father," Julia insisted in a hoarse whisper.

He met his mother's steely stare. There was no use arguing, for it would only result in additional embarrassment for all of them. "Ready?" he inquired, nearing the front hallway.

Lilly nodded in his direction. It appeared, however, that Julia was intent on prolonging the farewell. Matthew waited patiently as Julia hugged Lilly several times while attempting to elicit the girl's promise to return soon. He noted Lilly's careful choice of words as she sidestepped the issue and made her way down the front steps.

"Mother hasn't lost her knack for manipulating people's lives," Matthew remarked as they walked down the street.

"So it would seem. I am truly amazed by her transition from farm wife to fashionable hostess. Her party last Saturday evening was exquisite."

"No doubt. You probably were never told that my mother's family was both influential and wealthy. She grew up accustomed to elegant parties and expensive belongings. Her parents were aghast when she married my father. Needless to say, her life changed dramatically. The transition to farm wife was much more difficult than what she has experienced returning to a life of advantage."

"I would have never suspected, but it certainly explains her ability to entertain in fine fashion. I must admit that I'm surprised. I always thought your mother was content as the wife of a farmer."

"She was very content with her life on the farm. However, she was delighted to return to a more leisurely lifestyle. Given the opportunity, I believe most women would do the same."

Lilly stopped and looked up at him. "But not all. There are still women who prefer farm life."

"Yes, Lilly, I am well aware of your opinion," Matthew replied as he took her elbow and began to lead her across the street.

She tugged her arm from his grasp. "I can find my way back to the boardinghouse, Matthew. We're out of your mother's vantage point, and I promise she'll never hear from my lips that you didn't escort me all the way home."

"I'm afraid you'll have to put up with me a while longer, Lilly. There's no way I dare leave you. My mother will subject me to a multitude of questions at her first opportunity. Moreover, I would suffer her wrath should she discover I left your side before reaching the door of the boardinghouse."

"You can tell her—"

Matthew placed his finger on her lips. "Please don't encourage me to tell her a lie. It's impossible. From the time I was a little boy, she always knew when I was lying."

Lilly backed away. Matthew couldn't quite figure her mood, but she seemed almost fearful of him. "You're an adult now, Matthew. You've become an expert at deceit. I'm sure that once you set your mind to the task, your mother won't suspect a thing. And, as I said, I certainly wouldn't tell her that we parted company before reaching the boardinghouse."

Her words stung. While he considered himself truthful and straightforward, she thought him cunning and deceitful. He had never lied to her, never hidden his desire to succeed in the business world. Surely she didn't think he should hold to a childish promise to farm the rest of his life. Those words had been spoken long before he entered college and realized the scope of what the world had to offer. He had explained all of this to her, but she had closed her ears, unwilling to plan a future unless it was solely on her terms. "I didn't realize your hatred ran so deep," he finally replied.

She didn't respond, so they continued onward, an uncomfortable silence threatening to smother them, until they finally arrived outside number 5 Jackson Street.

"Hello, Lilly," Josephine Regan greeted as she and Jenny Dunn approached from the opposite direction.

Lilly nodded her head. "Hello."

The two girls waited. "Aren't you going to introduce us to your *friend*?" Jenny finally asked.

Lilly's teeth were clenched together, her jaw forming a hard line. "He is *not* my friend; he is Matthew Cheever. Matthew, these are two more of your employees, Josephine Regan and Jenny Dunn. Good night, ladies. Good night, Mr. Cheever."

Matthew watched as she turned, walked inside, and left him staring after her. *"He is not my friend,"* she had said emphatically. The words rang true, and the emptiness left in their wake devastated Matthew's sense of well-being.

"Where have you been, Lilly? Nadene wouldn't tell us anything except that you'd been invited to supper," Marmi squealed as Lilly walked in the bedroom door.

"Shhh. You'll waken the others," Lilly cautioned.

Marmi and Prudence sat up in bed, their attention focused on Lilly. "Tell us, then, or we'll continue to get louder until you do," Prudence warned.

"You have no shame, either of you! I have nothing exciting to report. I had supper at the Cheever household and came home."

The girls' disappointment was evident, but they quickly recovered. "We spent most of the evening deciding on dresses for the Lighting Up Ball. I think we're going to trade dresses this year. Pru is going to put new lace on my dress, and I'm going to refashion hers just a bit. We're hoping no one will realize. Do you have something special you plan to wear?"

The color had heightened in both girls' cheeks. Just talking about the dance had obviously given them great pleasure. Lilly wasn't sure how they could become excited over something as trivial as a dance, but she would never tell them her true feelings. "I don't plan to go," she replied simply.

Their gasps echoed through the room. "Not going? But you must. We all go—it's . . . well, it's expected. The ball is one of the nice things that the Corporation does for us," Marmi explained while Prudence bobbed her head up and down in affirmation.

"If it's one of the *nice* things the Associates do for us, surely they won't mind if I don't take advantage of their kindness. I think what they want are hours of drudgery in the mills, not the opportunity to hold us on the dance floor."

The two girls giggled. "That's true for most of the men, but there are a few who find it enjoyable to pull a girl or two close," Prudence replied. Once again the girls began their chortling.

Lilly glared at them. "You find that kind of repugnant behavior humorous?"

Immediately the girls sobered, Marmi appearing on the verge of tears. "Several of the girls have managed to find husbands at the mills," Marmi whimpered. "Is it wrong to giggle about that? We all want to find a husband. The Lighting Up Ball is a good opportunity to meet some of the men."

Lilly silently chided herself. Prudence and Marmi didn't know about Thaddeus Arnold and his disgusting activities; they were merely excited about having an evening of fun squeezed into their monotonous existence. She was spoiling the small ray of sunshine in their lives. "You're right, Marmi—the ball is an excellent place to meet some of the men. Please accept my apology. I'm tired and didn't think before speaking."

Immediately Marmi's mood lightened and she bounced across the bed. "That's all right, Lilly. Do you have a special dress you can wear?"

There was a soft knock. Prudence climbed across the bed and stood whispering through the door, "Who is it?"

Instead of a reply, Josephine and Jenny pushed open the door. Josephine folded her arms and plopped down on the bed opposite Lilly. "Just *who* are you, and how is it you know the likes of Matthew Cheever?" she demanded.

Lilly was silent. How could she answer Josephine's questions? Matthew Cheever was from another time and place. A time and place that no longer existed, that had slipped away and would never return.

CHAPTER *12*

Restlessness plagued Lilly's sleep. Images of her father and Lewis arguing were mingled with a woman's screams. Lewis was counting coins at a table in front of the fire while her father mumbled indecipherable words.

The scream again. Lilly's eyelids fluttered and then closed. Lewis was riding off at full gallop on a chestnut mare.

Another scream.

Lilly bolted upright in her bed. A loud crash followed by a piercing cry and a man's muffled voice filled what should have been a silent night. She looked about the darkened room, her heart pounding. The other girls slept soundly; even Nadene's cough was silent tonight. Something crashed against the wall, followed by a heavy thud.

"Please don't," a woman begged, her voice shrill.

Lilly grasped Nadene's arm. "Wake up, Nadene," she whispered. "Please wake up!"

"I didn't hear the bell," Nadene muttered.

Lilly leaned close to Nadene's ear. "The bell hasn't sounded yet. There's something going on next door. Listen!" The man's voice grew louder. A dull thud reverberated, then sobbing followed a woman's shriek. "Did you hear that?"

Nadene nodded. "These row house walls are not very thick. I hear it almost every night."

"You do? Why haven't you mentioned it?"

Nadene wriggled upward in the bed, leaning her back against the headboard. Lilly sat beside her, both of them staring toward the wall separating them from the sickening sounds.

"I decided there was nothing we could do. Losing sleep isn't going to benefit Mrs. Arnold, and it certainly isn't going to do us any good, either."

Lilly's mind reeled at Nadene's words. She turned in the darkness and looked toward Nadene. She could barely make out her friend's features. "Mrs. Arnold? Mrs. *Thaddeus* Arnold? Is that who lives there?"

"The Arnolds moved in last week after he became supervisor of the spinning room. That's when the noises began. We never had any of these disturbances when Mr. Hester and his family lived next door in the supervisor's quarters."

"Do you think Thaddeus Arnold is beating his wife?"

"Think about it, Lilly. Who else could it be?"

Lilly heard the words, but her mind raced, thinking of the times she'd seen Mrs. Arnold outdoors. On those occasions when Lilly had walked nearby, Mrs. Arnold had turned her back or rushed indoors. Surprised by the older woman's reactions, Lilly had decided Mr. Arnold didn't want his wife associating with the hired girls. Now Lilly feared that Mrs. Arnold had become reclusive in order to hide her bruises. An involuntary shiver coursed through her body. How could that poor woman endure living with Thaddeus Arnold? she wondered.

"We must do something, Nadene. I can't bear to sit here and listen to her suffer."

"What do you suggest?"

Lilly remained silent for several minutes, just long enough for the noises to resume. "I'm going to knock on the wall so he knows we can hear them," she finally replied. "If Mr. Arnold knows someone can hear them and that we know what he's doing, surely he will stop."

"I don't know if that's wise. Sometimes it's best to stay out of other people's business."

"Wouldn't you want someone to help *you,* Nadene?"

Nadene began coughing raspy, croaking sounds from deep in her chest. Finally able to get her breath, Nadene wiped her nose and once again leaned back. "Of course I would. But Mr. Arnold's our supervisor. If we get into the midst of his family problems, it could lead to more trouble than you or I could ever imagine."

At that moment Mrs. Arnold's voice pealed out in a desperate cry for help. Lilly bounded off the bed, grabbed her heavy work shoe, and began pounding on the wall. Again and again she beat against the wall, all the while praying that her feeble effort would somehow rescue poor Mrs. Arnold. Her hand and arm ached when finally she ceased her efforts. She dropped the shoe and turned back toward the bed. All was silent. Prudence and Marmi were huddled beside Nadene, where a candle now flickered on the bedside table. Katie, Sarah, Beth, and Franny had all joined together on one bed. Their faces were etched with apprehension and fear.

Prudence finally broke the silence that hung in the room. "Have you gone mad?"

"I don't think so," Lilly replied with a nervous giggle. "I think Mr. Arnold may have gotten the message."

"What message?" Marmi's wide-eyed innocence reminded Lilly of a small child.

"That we can hear through the walls, Marmi. That we know he's beating his wife. I'm hoping Mr. Arnold realizes that if he doesn't stop his ugly behavior, there will be repercussions."

Prudence folded her arms across her chest and shook her head. "You may find that the repercussions are directed at us rather than Mr. Arnold. That man could cause more problems than any of us can conceive."

"If Mr. Arnold takes steps to persecute any of you, I'll take the blame. What occurred is my doing. I'll absolve you of any involvement," Lilly promised.

Katie motioned to Sarah. "Come on, we need to get to

sleep." Sarah slipped into bed first since she slept against the wall. Katie joined her while Beth and Franny went to their own bed.

Prudence squirmed between the beds and plopped down beside Lilly. "It's not that we disagree with you, Lilly. But we all need our jobs. He has the power to make things happen. We don't."

Lilly nodded. "We may have more power than you think, Prudence. Either way, I can't ignore his behavior. He's a vile man who apparently has no respect for women, even his own wife. But for now I believe we had better try to get some sleep. I've kept everyone awake long enough," Lilly said as she snuffed the candle and settled back into bed.

"What you did was a good thing," Marmi whispered into the darkness.

"Thanks," Lilly replied. She closed her eyes and tried to pray. Instead she found herself questioning God, wondering why such horrible things happen to people. Why, she wondered, didn't God make life any easier?

The events of her own life flooded her thoughts. God had allowed her to suffer at the hands of her brother. God had taken her parents just when she needed them most. It all seemed so unfair. *I tried to live as a good Christian girl,* Lilly reasoned. *Did I do something so very wrong that God had to punish me?* She pushed the thought aside. God was good and loving, just and fair. She had to believe that.

But if God was good and fair, then why had she come to this place in her life?

You have a mission, she reminded herself. *God was even harsh with Jonah when he avoided the job God had given him to do. When I complete my mission, God will smooth the way for me. He will be pleased with me then and make things right again.*

Perhaps she had become privy to Thaddeus Arnold's behavior in order for God to reinforce the need for retribution against the Boston Associates. Tonight's incident was one more reason that she must remain strong in her determination to mete out justice against the greedy men and their selfish motivations. Once again sleep came, this time filling her mind with dreams of an idyllic countryside filled with bountiful fruit trees and sheep drinking from streams of crystal clear water.

Thaddeus Arnold's icy stare had remained fixed upon Lilly for several days. At first she hoped it was merely her imagination. But when he slithered off his chair and began walking near her machines several times each day, she realized he was playing a game, stalking his quarry as he watched and waited. His beady eyes appeared to dance with pleasure when he noted her discomfort.

Lilly could only assume Mr. Arnold was hoping to find fault with her work as he strutted back and forth checking her bobbins. He would draw close, his breath hot on her neck as he stood behind her, and then silently he would retreat. That is, until yesterday when he approached from behind, leaned in, and allowed his body to come up against her while he pretended to examine her roving, telling her he expected her to be present at the Lighting Up Ball.

She had remained silent, giving no indication of the repulsion that raged within her. The incident, however, was catalogued among Lilly's memories, now added to her mounting list of grievances against the Associates. By week's end, Thaddeus had apparently grown bored of the game and was once again settled on his perch, a vulture carefully eyeing his prey.

Lilly knew deep thankfulness when Saturday finally arrived. As she and Nadene left the mill yard at the end of another long day, she took satisfaction in knowing she need not face Thaddeus Arnold the next day. "He knows it was me," Lilly said, locking arms with Nadene as they walked down the street.

"No he doesn't. There is no way he can know for sure. He can't see through the walls. He doesn't even know where you sleep—only that you board with Miss Addie."

Lilly stopped in her tracks and pulled Nadene to a halt. "Haven't you been watching him this week? The way he's been coming around me? And those evil beady eyes, always watching me. He knows. One day he'll say something. I'm sure of it."

Nadene giggled. "I'm sorry, but you sound so dramatic. You need to put this whole thing out of your mind."

Anger welled up inside Lilly. "You would think it was serious, too, if he constantly watched you." She hesitated a moment. "Yesterday he leaned up against me. Do you think I should overlook that, also?"

Nadene's mouth dropped open, and her eyes widened in astonishment.

"I don't know why you would be surprised by his actions; he's always handling other girls. He said I'd best be in attendance at the Lighting Up Ball. I'm sure he will find some way to humiliate me if I do attend the ball. If I don't make an appearance, I'm certain he'll find a reason to have me terminated."

Nadene looped her arm back through Lilly's as they began walking once again. "I'm so sorry. I shouldn't have laughed at you. I didn't think Mr. Arnold would take things so far. Why don't you talk to Matthew Cheever and see if you can be transferred to the Merrimack? Surely he would help you."

"Ask Matthew to bestow a favor upon me? I think not." Lilly cringed inwardly at the thought. She'd told Nadene a little about her past with Matthew. Nadene thought there should be a reconciliation between them, and no doubt she thought this would be a good way to rekindle their communication.

"You can ill afford to become filled with pride right now," Nadene cautioned. "If Mr. Arnold has become bold enough to—"

Lilly stood squarely in front of Nadene, blocking her entry into the boardinghouse. "I don't want anyone else to know about what's happened at the mill. Promise you won't tell."

"I promise, but I think you're making a big mistake," Nadene replied. "Why not talk to Miss Addie at least? She would keep your confidence, and perhaps she'd have some ideas."

Lilly shook her head as they entered the house. "No, I don't want her to think I'm depending on her to resolve the problem with Mr. Arnold, because I'm not. Besides, she'd worry herself sick."

"Well, who are you relying on?" Nadene whispered.

Lilly placed her bonnet and cape on one of the hooks beside the front door. "God, Nadene. I'm relying on God."

CHAPTER *13*

Making her way down the steps and into the kitchen, Lilly smiled at Miss Addie, who was carefully assembling a plate of cookies.

"I thought it might be a nice gesture if I took some cookies to Mintie when we join her for tea," Addie remarked. "Did you enjoy the church services this morning?"

"The church services were fine," Lilly replied without much enthusiasm. "Taking cookies is a lovely idea, Miss Addie. I'm sure your sister will beg for the recipe once she's tasted them."

Addie beamed at the praise. "I know you'd prefer to spend your afternoon visiting with the girls or going for a walk. You're always so kind and generous."

Lilly blushed. If only Miss Addie knew her private thoughts regarding Thaddeus Arnold and the Boston Associates, she'd not think her either kind or generous. "Taking tea with Miss Mintie won't consume my whole afternoon. Besides, there will be ample time for a walk or other frivolity later in the day. Let me carry the plate," Lilly offered.

Mintie greeted them at the door, her smile fading somewhat as she glanced toward the plate of cookies. "Did you think I wouldn't provide you with a proper tea?"

Before Addie had an opportunity to reply, Lilly thrust the plate forward. "Addie was certain you would prepare a sumptuous tea tray, but I insisted we bring the cookies. My mother taught me it was good manners to take a small hostess gift when visiting friends and relatives. Since you are both a friend *and* relative . . ."

Taking the extended plate, Mintie led them into the parlor. "Oh, tut, tut, we don't need to make an issue over a few cookies. I'm sure they'll make a nice addition to our tea," Mintie conceded, gracing Lilly with a tentative smile. She directed them toward the settee before fluttering into the kitchen.

"Thank you, Lilly, but you shouldn't have told a falsehood," Addie whispered. She hesitated a moment. "Of course, I should have corrected your falsehood, so I'm as guilty as you. I believe we're both in need of forgiveness—and over something as simple as a plate of cookies!"

"I didn't tell a total falsehood. My mother *did* teach me that it was proper etiquette to take a gift when visiting," Lilly whispered with a smile.

Mintie returned with the teapot and cups. Lucy, the little ten-year-old doffer who assisted as Miss Mintie's part-time servant, followed close behind carrying a tray laden with tiny sandwiches and delicacies. Lucy placed the tray on a small serving cart, then backed against the wall, although she continued to stare at the food with ravenous eyes.

"All of the men except for that Englishman have gone out for the afternoon," Mintie commented in a hushed tone while pouring hot tea into three cups. She handed each of them a small china plate. "Try these sandwiches, Adelaide," Mintie instructed her sister. "Go on. Get out of here, Lucy," she continued, waving at the child as though she were shooing away an insect.

"I believe this would be an excellent opportunity to teach Lucy how to conduct herself among genteel women. My mother insisted it was best to learn proper etiquette at an early age," Lilly put in.

Mintie stared at Lilly, mouth agape. "I don't think a serving girl need know how to conduct herself at tea. What earthly purpose would be served? Lucy is certainly never going to marry into proper society."

"If she knows how tea is to be conducted, it will teach her how to properly serve at those times when you wish to merely enjoy your guests," Lilly countered. "Come here, Lucy. We'd like you to join us for tea. That way you can better serve Miss Beecher's guests in the future." Lilly patted the empty cushion beside her.

The child looked back and forth between the two women and then quickly darted to where Lilly was sitting. The temptation of the food had won out, as Lilly knew it would. "You must pay heed to Miss Beecher's training as you take tea," Lilly instructed, looking toward Mintie for affirmation.

Mintie's spectacles slipped down the bridge of her nose as her head dipped up and down in agreement. "Take a plate and watch," Mintie said to the child.

Once they had filled their plates, Mintie began pouring Lucy's tea into a matching china cup. She turned toward the child, her eyes steely pinpoints. "Conversation at a tea is not to be repeated. That is your second lesson. Do you understand?"

The child's head bobbed up and down in agreement. "Yes, ma'am. I won't hear a thing you ladies say."

Mintie gave an affirming nod before directing her attention back toward Addie and Lilly. She leaned forward with her long nose almost dipping into the teacup that was resting in her hand. "I'm growing more concerned by the minute," she confided in a hoarse whisper. "That Farnsworth fellow has received several letters from Lancashire, and there have been strange men at the front door on three different occasions. I have no doubt he is a spy determined to assist in the downfall of this country."

Lilly stifled a giggle. "I think you're being a bit dramatic, Miss Beecher. I'm sure Mr. Farnsworth is merely becoming acquainted with some of his fellow Englishmen. His visitors are probably men who work at the mills and live on the English Row."

Mintie straightened her shoulders and pursed her lips into a circle. "I suppose that is why they speak in hushed tones and grow silent when I approach?"

"Perhaps they merely want their privacy," Addie suggested.

"I can see you two are cut from the same cloth, neither one of you willing to open your eyes to the—"

"Good afternoon, ladies."

They all looked toward the doorway at the sound of a man's voice. "We're taking tea, Mr. Farnsworth," Mintie declared.

He walked into the room and stood near the settee. "I can see that, Miss Mintie."

Mintie's lips tightened into a straight line. She curled the corner of her linen napkin and then watched as it rolled back into place. Finally she cleared her throat and looked up at the man. "John Farnsworth, one of my boarders," she said, looking toward Addie and Lilly. "Mr. Farnsworth, this is my sister, Miss Adelaide Beecher, and one of her boarders, Miss Lilly Armbruster."

He bowed his head and extended his hand. "It is a pleasure to make your acquaintance, Miss Beecher and Miss Armbruster."

The color heightened in Addie's cheeks. "Would you care to join us, Mr. Farnsworth?" She appeared besotted with the tall stranger. Mintie, however, was momentarily speechless, obviously shocked at her sister's behavior.

Mr. Farnsworth folded his large frame into the chair beside Addie. "I would be delighted," he replied.

Mintie leveled an icy glare at her sister before turning toward Mr. Farnsworth. "You need not feel obligated to accept my sister's invitation, Mr. Farnsworth. I'm sure you have more important things to do this afternoon."

He picked up a teacup and extended it toward Mintie. "Not at all. Tea on a Sunday afternoon is more than I had hoped for."

"More than I had hoped for, also," Mintie mumbled under her breath. She poured his tea and sent Lucy scampering off to the kitchen to set another kettle of water to boil. The child returned to the parlor as a knock sounded at the front door. "See to the door, Lucy. Most likely it's one of Mr. Farnsworth's acquaintances."

Lucy nodded her head and rushed from the room, returning moments later with Matthew Cheever in tow. "Mr. Cheever said he came to call on Mr. Farnsworth. I told him Mr. Farnsworth was taking tea with us, so he could come have tea with us, too," the child proudly announced.

Mintie expelled an extended breath from between pursed lips and crooked her finger. Lucy moved directly in front of her mistress. "Lucy, for some reason I believed that *I* was the hostess of this gathering."

Lucy looked down at the floor, her thick brown hair falling forward and covering her oval face. "You are, ma'am. I'm sorry," she muttered.

Addie strained forward and touched Lucy's arm. "Well, I, for one, am very proud of your behavior, Lucy. You exhibited excellent manners by inviting Mr. Cheever to join us for tea. One must never make a guest feel unwelcome. Isn't that correct, Mintie?" Without waiting for a reply, Addie shifted her gaze toward Matthew. "You have the rare opportunity of joining us for Lucy's etiquette lesson, Mr. Cheever. Do sit down."

Lilly was pleased Addie had rescued the child from Mintie's clutches. However, she wished Addie had stopped short before inviting Matthew to take a seat. There was no way to gracefully escape the group, which was increasing by the minute. Mr. Farnsworth and Addie were now in a discussion. Mintie was busy instructing Lucy how to properly pour Matthew's tea, and Lilly was fidgeting with the pleats of her skirt.

"Lovely day," Matthew ventured.

"Yes, but I must soon return to the boardinghouse. I have several matters that need my attention this afternoon. I must say it was quite a surprise to see you enter the room. Do you often visit your employees at their boardinghouses?" Lilly inquired.

"Not often, but I consider John a friend as well as an employee. I stopped by to offer him an invitation to dinner next Sunday. I've expressed such admiration for John that my parents are both anxious to meet him, Father in particular."

Lilly finished her tea and handed the empty cup to Lucy, whose cheeks now resembled those of a squirrel preparing to store food for the winter. "You like the cookies?" Lilly asked with a warm smile.

"Yes, ma'am," the child mumbled, a few crumbs slipping through her lips.

"I do, too. Which are your favorites?" Lilly inquired.

Mintie watched as Lucy pointed to the cherry-flavored shortbread cookies. "It's impolite to point *or* to talk with your mouth full," Mintie corrected in a stern tone.

"I don't believe she offended any of us," Lilly commented. "She liked your cookies, Miss Addie. You'll have to give your sister your recipe. I'm sure she'll want to make some soon."

"Those were my favorite, also," John Farnsworth commented. "In fact, I think I'll have another."

"You have as many as you'd like. In fact, I'll leave the plate, and you can have some this evening," Addie replied.

"Only if he promises to share them with Lucy and me," Matthew chimed in, helping himself to another of the buttery cookies. He turned toward Lilly and in a hoarse whisper added, "Unless you'd like to bake a special batch just for me some day soon."

"I don't think so," Lilly whispered in return. Her heart skipped a beat as she met Matthew's gaze.

"You used to like to bake me cookies."

Lucy tugged on Lilly's arm and smiled. "Miss Beecher says it's rude to whisper."

"And she's absolutely correct," Lilly replied. "I really must return to the boardinghouse." The two men jumped to their feet as she stood up. "Thank you for the invitation. It's been most enjoyable, Miss Beecher. Miss Addie, you need not rush home on my account. Please stay and enjoy yourself."

"Why don't Matthew and I escort you ladies home?" John offered.

The flutter of activity appeared more than Mintie could bear. Lilly wasn't sure if Mintie was angry they were leaving or relieved that she would be absolved of continuing Lucy's etiquette training. Either way, she was obviously unhappy.

"Grand idea," Matthew agreed. "I could use a bit of fresh air."

"They live only across the street," Lucy offered. "Maybe you should take a walk into town or out toward the falls if you want fresh air."

Matthew laughed and then leaned down to whisper into Lucy's ear. He stood up and glanced at the other guests. "I know whispering is rude, but I wanted to share a secret with Lucy. Please forgive my impolite behavior."

Lilly gave every plausible excuse in the hope of escaping by herself. She was, however, unsuccessful. By the time she reached the front door, Matthew was clinging to her elbow while John and Addie were deep in conversation, oblivious to everyone except each other. Lucy was behind her, tugging at her other arm.

There was an urgency in the child's appearance. "Miss Lilly, could I talk to you for a moment?"

Lilly separated herself from Mintie and the other guests. "What is it, Lucy? Is something wrong?"

"First, I want to thank you for helping me today. The tea was such fun, even if Miss Beecher will scold me once you've all gone home." She rocked from foot to foot momentarily and with widened eyes looked up toward Lilly. "I know I shouldn't ask, but Mr. Cheever said that if I could convince you to take a walk with him, he would pay me a week's wages. That would be most helpful to my family. We're very poor." Her voice was warbling, and tears threatened to spill over at any moment as she ended her plea.

Lilly stooped down and embraced the child. "You go collect your coins, Lucy. I'll take a walk with Mr. Cheever." Lucy's face immediately transformed. Her wide smile caused her sunken cheeks to become walnut-sized puffs. "Thank you, Miss Lilly, thank you!" the child called over her shoulder as she rushed toward Matthew.

Lilly remained several steps away, observing the exchange between Matthew and Lucy while feeling angry that he had involved the child in such a scheme. How had a simple afternoon tea turned into this farce?

Matthew approached looking quite pleased. Lilly couldn't help but remember back to a time when the very sight of him had set her heart to racing. Of course, it wasn't exactly beating a funeral dirge at the moment.

"That was hardly called for," Lilly said as he took hold of her arm.

"Would you have walked with me otherwise? Answer honestly."

Lilly looked away, afraid of the way he made her feel. "No, I don't suppose I would have."

"Then it was completely called for," he whispered against her ear.

CHAPTER *14*

The walk with Matthew wasn't nearly as unbearable as Lilly believed it would be. Addie and John Farnsworth decided to accompany them, and with the two of them carrying on a lively conversation, Lilly and Matthew scarcely had to speak two words.

Still, she was greatly relieved when they turned back toward the boardinghouse. Lilly had a long list of reasons already formulated as to why she couldn't linger once they arrived. Seeing Addie was about to invite the men inside, Lilly opened her mouth to excuse herself.

"Well, look who's here," Matthew said before she could speak.

Lilly couldn't believe her eyes. She had finally arrived home, prepared to escape Matthew's company, when Julia and Randolph Cheever pulled their carriage to a halt in front of the boardinghouse.

"What a pleasant surprise!" Julia exclaimed. She was leaning across Randolph's legs, her head poking out of the carriage. "We were going to stop and invite you to join us for a picnic in Belvedere, Lilly. This is going to be especially nice. You can *both* join us. Come along, children; get in the carriage," she ordered.

Lilly stepped back, tugging free of Matthew's grasp on her arm. "I really cannot accept your invitation. I have laundry to complete this afternoon."

Julia gasped. "Have you forgotten it's Sunday, Lilly? Your poor mother would be appalled at the thought of her daughter doing laundry on the Lord's Day."

"Since I work long hours all week, Mrs. Cheever, I have little choice," Lilly replied.

"Nonsense, child. I'll see to that little dab of laundry tomorrow," Addie offered as she and John drew closer to the carriage. "You go and have fun this afternoon."

Matthew grinned and folded his arms. "Now what will you do?" he questioned under his breath.

Lilly wanted to scream at him. Even more, she wanted to wipe the smug grin off his face. But with everyone's attention focused in her direction, she could do neither. "I haven't been home all day, Mrs. Cheever. With church services this morning, tea this afternoon, and a short walk with these gentlemen," she extended her arm in a sweeping gesture, "I truly must beg to be excused."

"I absolutely will not hear of it," Julia insisted. "You're too young to hole up in your room on such a beautiful fall day. Besides, you must eat. You get settled in the carriage this minute, young lady. I'll not take any excuses."

"May I assist you?" Matthew inquired, his grin growing wider.

Lilly ignored his offer. She climbed into the carriage and positioned herself as far into one corner of the seat as possible. Matthew settled in beside her, taking full advantage of the available space.

The carriage had begun on the road out of town when Julia turned and looked over her shoulder. "You look uncomfortable, Lilly. Move over and give her some room, Matthew."

"By all means, do move over, Lilly," Matthew whispered, amusement dancing in his eyes. Before she could protest, Matthew placed his arm around her shoulder and physically pulled her closer. "There. Isn't that better?"

She glanced down at his leg. His knee was leaning heavily against her own. Lilly gave his leg a hefty nudge and forced a smile upon her lips. Matthew's face registered surprise at her action. Good! He need not think she would idly sit by and permit him to make a mockery of her or their previous relationship. For the remainder of the ride, her hands were folded in her lap, her spine rigid and aching by the time they arrived in Belvedere.

"I wanted to surprise you," Julia began as she began to unpack the picnic supper.

"I don't know if I can manage another surprise," Lilly replied. There was more truth than humor in the statement, but obviously Julia found it a charming reply as she giggled at Lilly's remark. "You've always had a way with words, Lilly. It's part of your allure. Isn't it, Matthew?"

Matthew glanced toward his mother, then at Lilly. "That's true, Mother," he said with his brow wrinkled in thought. "However, Lilly has other *strengths* that would amaze you. Why, just today in the carriage, the strength of her—"

"What was your surprise, Mrs. Cheever?" Lilly interrupted. "You never told me."

"What? Oh, yes, the surprise. In just a little over an hour," she said while looking at the timepiece pinned to her bodice, "there will be a magic show. A talented magician from Europe is touring the country, and he's performing here. That's why we came to Belvedere for our picnic. We were told the young magician is quite talented. It's said he can pull a coin from your ear—imagine that!"

"Amazing!" Matthew replied in mock surprise. "Actually, truth be told, I was supposed to join Kirk Boott and his family for this very show. Anyway, I'm starving, Mother. Would you like some assistance with the food?"

"Lilly will help me. You men go take a walk. By the time you return, we should be ready."

She shooed the men away and began unpacking embroidered linen napkins, plates, and silverware, along with fried chicken, biscuits, and homemade preserves. Lilly grouped the items together as Julia instructed, the two of them completing the task in quick order.

"You see? Things go much more smoothly when the men aren't here to interrupt," Julia remarked. "Now we have time to relax and visit until they return. You've been on my mind since you visited us last week, Lilly. I know you can't be planning to spend the rest of your life working in the mills. Have you had time to make some solid plans for your future, child?"

Lilly hesitated. "You're right about the mills. I don't plan to work there my entire life, but it's difficult to judge how long I'll need to remain. I buried my dreams the day I buried my father. My future had always included living on our farm in East Chelmsford, being a wife, raising children, and working alongside . . ."

"Matthew," Julia said, completing the sentence. "I can understand that you long to have things as they were, Lilly. I know that it is more comfortable when things remain constant. You must remember, however, that if we don't embrace new adventures in life, we are left behind with nothing but monotony. You would soon bore of such a life, child. There comes a time when we must accept change and make it work for us—move on. Unfortunately, most of the changes you've experienced were beyond your control."

Lilly nodded her head. "Perhaps they were beyond my control, but that doesn't change anything. The future I had hoped for went to the grave with my father."

"Lilly, you need a fresh perspective, new goals for your future. We need to develop a plan." Julia's voice took on a tone of excitement. "I think you need to take one step at a time and focus on one major area. We've established that you don't want to remain in the mills and you do want to marry. I think the first step should be a reevaluation of your relationship with Matthew. He still cares for you—a mother knows these things. And deep down, I believe you still love him."

Her heart hammering, Lilly gave a sigh of relief as Matthew and Randolph reappeared and dropped onto the ground beside them.

"You two appeared to be deep in conversation. What was the topic of interest today? Mrs. Brodmeyer's hat or your new piece of stitchery?" Randolph asked, fondly patting his wife's cheek.

"Neither, Randolph! You men act as though a woman can't have a thought in her head that goes beyond fashion or house-keeping."

Randolph's eyes widened at the retort. "I'm sorry, my dear. It wasn't my intent to offend you. What world event were you discussing? Perhaps the summer launching of the Baltimore and Ohio Railroad. Or maybe that rascal Andrew Jackson's vie for the presidency. Matthew and I would be pleased to converse with you on any such topic."

"We were having a private conversation that doesn't require a male perspective," Julia replied. "But thank you for your apology," she added, handing him a plate.

Lilly glanced at Mr. Cheever from beneath thick brown eye-lashes. The poor man appeared totally baffled but filled his plate and began eating without further comment. Matthew, however, continued to bait his mother, obviously enjoying the fact that each of his questions caused her further discomposure.

"Come now, Mother, do tell. I could argue that you and Lilly are being rude, and we all know that proper ladies are never impolite. What about *you*, Lilly? Wouldn't you like to share with Father and me? After all, earlier this very afternoon you taught a little girl about the rules of etiquette."

Julia's cheeks flushed. She stabbed a piece of chicken and flopped it onto Matthew's plate. "*You*, Matthew. I was discussing you and the fact that you're still in love with Lilly. Tell me, son, what would you like to share with the rest of us in regard to that matter?"

His plate dropped to the ground, his discomfort evident. "That was uncalled for, Mother."

Lilly would have laughed out loud had she not been equally embarrassed by the topic. Matthew looked positively mortified.

"No, Matthew, it wasn't," Julia replied in a steady voice. "You would not allow the matter to rest. I answered your ques-tion only because you prodded me until I did so. I spoke the truth. Now let's eat our supper. We want to be finished before the show begins."

Throughout their meal, carriages continued arriving from Lowell and the surrounding countryside. Word of the magician and his supernatural abilities had obviously extended well beyond the immediate vicinity. There was an air of excitement as folks strolled about, visiting as they waited outside the old yellow house that had become the favorite spot for visiting entertainment in the surrounding countryside. Julia and Lilly packed the remains of their picnic into the basket and waited with Randolph while Matthew took the basket back to the carriage.

Lilly tried not to think of Matthew or the comments made by his mother, but it was rather like telling someone not to look in the cookie jar. The more she thought of not thinking about Matthew, the more she did think of him.

Julia muttered under her breath and stiffened. Lilly immediately glanced up and saw the object of the older woman's concern. Matthew was striding toward them, accompanied by Kirk Boott and three women.

"Look who I found," Matthew exclaimed. "Mother, Father, Lilly, you know Kirk Boott. I'd like to introduce you to his wife, Anne. And this is Kirk's sister, Neva Locklear, and his niece, Isabelle Locklear. I believe I mentioned having supper with them while I was in Boston." He looked at Lilly as if to ascertain her reaction.

Mr. Cheever extended his hand to Mr. Boott, and the ladies nodded toward each other.

"We've heard the magician is quite talented," Isabelle remarked.

The silence was momentarily deafening. "That's what my parents have said, also," Matthew finally replied.

Isabelle smiled at Lilly. "You are Matthew's sister?"

"No. I'm one of your uncle's hired hands, Miss Locklear, a mill girl. At one time, however, my family's farm adjoined the Cheevers'. That was before the Boston Associates redesigned the landscape and turned East Chelmsford into what is now known as Lowell."

The group stared at her as though she were some lunatic who had escaped from an asylum. Lilly wasn't sure why they appeared shocked at her reply. She would have continued her discourse, but Julia took hold of her wrist in a viselike grip that sent a searing pain up her arm.

Kirk smiled broadly at Julia. "I hope you won't mind, Mrs. Cheever, but I'd like to steal your son away for a while. Isabelle was sorely disappointed when I was unable to locate Matthew before leaving Lowell—he was to have joined us for our outing today. But it appears that fate is with us, Isabelle," he said, now looking at his niece. "We have ample room in our carriage. He can accompany us back to Lowell."

Julia leveled a foreboding stare at her son. "Matthew?"

Matthew avoided making eye contact with his mother. Instead, he looked at his father. "I'm going to join the Bootts and Locklears for the show." He kissed his mother's cheek. Turning away, he added, "Good-bye, Lilly. I'm sure you're pleased to be free of me."

Lilly stared after the group, angry at the longing that invaded her spirit as she watched them leave. Isabelle's laughter floated back where Lilly stood, reminding her that Matthew was no longer a part of her world. He, too, had changed. And not for the better—at least not in her opinion. One minute he acted attentive, almost affectionate, and the next minute he performed in a roguish manner.

The remainder of the day was a haze. The magician appeared; the people cheered and clapped; laughter surrounded her—but Lilly was unaware of it all. She was watching Matthew and Isabelle, unable to focus on anything except the two of them as they whispered and laughed, obviously enjoying each other.

Darkness was beginning to fall and long shadows overtook the roadway as they returned to Lowell. Lilly leaned back against the carriage seat and closed her eyes, anxious to get back to her room. She had planned to spend some time with Nadene today, but there would be little opportunity for much visiting this evening. The thought that she must once again arise before dawn and voluntarily commit herself to a prisonlike existence inside

155

the walls of the Appleton Mill caused her to shudder.

Julia turned sideways in her seat. "I do hope you enjoyed yourself in spite of Matthew's rude behavior. I thought the magician was delightful."

"Now, now," Randolph chided. "It's not as though we had planned for Matthew to join us. He had every right to join Mr. Boott and his family."

The horses slowed as Mr. Cheever directed them down Merrimack Street, then on toward Jackson. He pulled to a stop in front of number 5 and assisted Lilly from the carriage. It was then that she spied three men huddled together. It sounded as though they were having an argument, their voices ringing loud in the crisp autumn air.

She stepped behind the carriage and squinted her eyes to see them in the shadows. The men raised their heads and looked in her direction. Two of them were men she had never seen. She strained to distinguish the features of the third man, the taller one, who had pulled his jacket collar tight about his neck. He looked directly toward her, then hurried off. Lilly had a sudden rush of recognition. It was Miss Addie's escort from earlier that afternoon; it was Miss Mintie's imaginary English spy; it was *John Farnsworth*.

Matthew knew he had angered his mother, and he'd had every intention of stopping at his parents' house upon his return to Lowell. Boott, however, had other plans, insisting there were matters he wished to discuss with Matthew tonight. And so he acquiesced without further argument, accompanying the group back to the Boott mansion. The only bright spot since their return to Lowell had been the fact that Kirk had rejected the ladies' invitation to join them for lemonade. He had insisted there was pressing business that required their attention.

"I trust you found the magic show enjoyable," Kirk said as they entered his office. He poured himself a glass of port and nodded toward another glass. "Care for something a bit stronger than lemonade?"

Matthew shook his head. "No, nothing, thank you. I'm anxious to know what urgent matter you need to discuss before morning."

Kirk seated himself in his leather chair and pulled a fat cigar from the humidor sitting atop his desk. Giving the cigar his undivided attention, he moved it back and forth beneath his nose several times, inhaling the pungent aroma before carefully snipping off the end. "I think we may have the beginning of some problems at the Appleton. I want you to investigate—secretly, of course. A number of incidents have occurred in the spinning room since Thaddeus Arnold became supervisor. Apparently he believes that an operative has intentionally caused a couple of mishaps within the last few weeks. Personally, I doubt his suspicions, but I have an obligation to investigate."

"Was there any major damage?"

Boott lit the end of his cigar and puffed several times until the ash turned bright red. "No. They were minor mishaps. You know we have frequent accidents."

Matthew leaned forward, resting his arms across his thighs. "I guess I don't understand why Mr. Arnold would even think one of the girls was involved, unless he had some reason for his suspicion. It makes no sense. The girls don't get paid if they miss work. Why would they want to do anything to jeopardize the operation of the spinning room?"

"Exactly! I agree with you, Matthew, but I need to show the Associates I'm on top of things. I wouldn't want it to be said that I'm not checking out information that comes to me. Perform a minimal investigation; talk to a few people. I told Arnold's supervisor I'd get back with them in a few days. If I tell him it's my opinion there's no need for alarm, he'll let it rest, and I can report that the matter has been investigated and has no merit. Fair enough?"

Matthew rose from his chair, "I suppose so. I'll get to it first thing in the morning. However, I don't see how I can be too discreet about the matter. It's going to require talking to some of the people working in the spinning room, isn't it?"

Boott nodded. "Try to find someone you can trust, someone

that won't tell the other girls about the investigation. Perhaps Arnold can advise you if there's a girl who can be trusted. I doubt you'll have difficulty. None of them want to lose their position. After all, they've become dependent upon their monthly pay."

Matthew began to move toward to the door. "Was there anything else we needed to discuss?"

Kirk leaned back in his chair and took another draw on his cigar. "There's no need to rush off, Matthew. If nothing else, we can discuss your future with Isabelle."

CHAPTER *15*

The morning dawned cool and gray, much like Matthew's spirits. He bent his head against the early morning chill and walked toward the Appleton Mill. Lawrence Gault was in the counting room writing in a leather-bound ledger when he entered. Matthew liked the older man; he had a firm handshake, honest eyes, and a quick smile.

"Morning, Mr. Cheever," Lawrence said, pushing away from the desk. "Dreary morning out there, but the sun's shining in here," the older man continued, pointing to his heart.

Matthew smiled. "What's making it shine?"

"Jesus, of course. A man can't have the doldrums too long when he thinks about having a Savior who was willing to die for him. Make sense?"

Matthew nodded. "Couldn't argue that point, Mr. Gault. I was hoping you could help me. I need to speak to Thaddeus Arnold."

"You want me to go get him for you? Be glad to do that."

"No need. Directions will be fine."

Mr. Gault appeared relieved when Matthew didn't take him up on the offer to fetch Thaddeus. Matthew now understood why. The walk across the yard and up the winding stairway would have been difficult for a man of Gault's size and age. Matthew hesitated a moment and took several short breaths before entering the spinning room. The humidity in the mills never ceased to overwhelm him. Kirk had explained that the operatives became accustomed to the heavier air, their lungs adjusting to the moisture after a few weeks. Matthew wasn't sure if Boott's assessment was correct, but it made sense that the body could adjust.

Thaddeus Arnold was near the rear of the room talking with one of the operatives. Matthew moved toward where they stood, the machinery pounding out a vibrating cadence that deadened the sound of his footsteps.

Arnold jumped away from the girl at the touch of Matthew's hand upon his shoulder. The supervisor's face reddened, and he stammered a quick welcome into the deafening noise that permeated the room. Matthew pointed toward the door, and Thaddeus began threading his way toward the entrance as Matthew followed behind. When he looked up, Lilly was staring at him. Damp ringlets clung to her forehead. He smiled, but she didn't acknowledge him. Thaddeus stood anxiously waiting by the door and moved into the stairwell at Matthew's nod. The level of noise diminished only slightly, so Matthew pointed toward the steps.

When they reached the mill yard, Thaddeus quickly turned and looked up at Matthew. "I wasn't doing anything to that girl. She gives me trouble from time to time, and I'm required to reprimand her," he sputtered.

Matthew rubbed his forehead; his head was throbbing. "I'm here to inquire about a couple of accidents. You made some accusations regarding those incidents."

Thaddeus dipped his head up and down several times. "Yes, I'm glad Mr. Boott took my allegations seriously. We've had a number of accidents of late. I have reason to believe one, or perhaps several, of the operatives may be causing these problems."

Now that Mr. Arnold was on the offensive, he appeared more relaxed. Matthew noted that Arnold's stammering had ceased as he made his declarations against the girls. Completing his account, Thaddeus squared his shoulders, obviously proud of himself.

"Can you give me any reason why it would be beneficial for one of these girls to cause problems with the machinery, Mr. Arnold?"

Thaddeus appeared perplexed by the question.

Matthew took him by the arm and began to walk back toward the stairwell. "You see, Mr. Arnold, it is to the girls' *disadvantage* to have machinery inoperative. They don't get paid unless they are working. That is why I've asked if you can furnish some plausible reason why you think an operative would create such mischief. Otherwise, it would seem that the incidents are purely accidental. There are occasional accidents on all of the floors, both here and at the Merrimack. Unfortunate as it is, people sometimes don't pay attention, and accidents soon follow that inattentiveness. Perhaps there is some problem on your floor, among the girls themselves—or with you?" Matthew ventured.

Thaddeus paled at the remark. "The operatives might have a problem among themselves—I'm not sure," he stammered. "I have no problem with the girls. Well, I am obligated to reprimand them when they're not working up to the requirements—like today when you came into the room," he hastily added. "You may be correct. I may have been borrowing trouble, assuming there was a problem where there is none."

"I can continue to investigate the matter." Matthew left the offer dangling, wondering if Thaddeus would snatch the bone or run off with his tail between his legs.

"You're probably right, Mr. Cheever. I'm new at this position and want to do well. Most likely I've overreacted. I was only trying to look out for the Corporation. I don't want anything to interfere with your profit."

Matthew had guessed correctly. He had suspected Arnold would let the matter drop. He was sure the man was hiding something. Perhaps Lilly knew what it was. "Should you decide that you want me to investigate further, you can tell Mr. Gault to contact me personally. No need to bother Mr. Boott with these matters, Mr. Arnold. I had best not keep you away from your work any longer."

"Thank you, Mr. Cheever. I appreciate your time. I'll do as you said."

Matthew watched as Arnold scampered away, his shoulders stooped over as he rushed back to the stairwell. Something about Thaddeus Arnold bothered him.

CHAPTER *16*

Prudence twirled about the room in her forest green silk. "I knew you'd change your mind and come. What made you decide? Was it Marmi's description of all the fun or the anticipation of dancing with Kirk Boott?"

Marmi giggled at the remark. "He is quite an excellent dance partner. I had the privilege of two dances with him at the Blowing Out Ball last spring."

Lilly smiled at the girls. She dared not tell them that Thaddeus Arnold had promised he would find a reason for her termination if she didn't attend this evening. Instead she replied, "I think it might be unwise to remain at home and permit you to have all the fun, Prudence. Besides, I don't think Nadene would forgive me if I didn't go along."

Nadene offered a smile. "That's true. I dislike these required functions. They make me uncomfortable, while Pru and Marmi have loads of fun."

"I wager I'll have more fun than Pru," Marmi replied. "She's too picky about her dance partners. Not me. If someone invites me to dance, I'm going out on the floor and having a whirl."

The four of them made their way downstairs, where Miss

Addie stood waiting in a sapphire blue creation. Lilly knew the gown had come from the collection of things Addie brought from Boston. Lilly had helped her touch up the gown, refreshing the style with a bit of lace and trim. She'd also taken out the waistline when Addie wasn't looking. Lilly's reward was her choice of gowns from Miss Addie's collection. Of course, the dress had to be completely remade to accommodate Lilly's slender frame, but it was better than having to wear one of her childish, well-worn pieces from the past. Besides, nothing that Lilly owned was worthy of a ball.

"Oh, just look at you girls. I can't decide which one of you is the prettiest," Addie exclaimed as they paraded single file through the hallway for her approval. "The other girls left a few minutes ago, and we must stop for Mintie. Hurry, now—we don't want to be late."

"Just wait until John Farnsworth sees you in that dress. He'll be coming to call every evening," Lilly whispered as they walked out the front door.

Addie blushed. "I've been so excited by the prospect that I've hardly been able to eat. Why, just look, the waist on this gown is much looser."

Lilly smiled and nodded. "Indeed, I was going to comment that you looked quite trim." No sense bursting the woman's bubble of enthusiasm.

"Oh, thank you for helping me with this dress. I don't know what I would have done without you."

"Nor I without you," Lilly commented, gently lifting the edge of her silk skirt for emphasis.

"That burgundy really is your color," Addie replied. "And you've made it over in such a delightful manner. The way you've cut the neckline is modest yet completely youthful. And your waist, why, it's so very tiny, and that black cording only emphasizes it."

Lilly felt her cheeks grow hot. She hadn't worn anything this lovely in a very long time. Memories rushed in of a time when her mother had waived the rules and allowed her to accompany her parents to a party at the Cheevers. Lilly had worn a very grown-up gown of pale pink. Her mother had even helped her to arrange her hair, pinning part of it up and leaving the rest to hang in ringlets around her face and shoulders. Lilly had felt very special that night, and Matthew's reaction to her had left her feeling weak in the knees.

As if reading her mind, Addie whispered, "I'll bet Mr. Cheever won't be able to even look at another woman tonight. You'll simply take his breath away."

Glancing up, Lilly caught sight of Mintie peering out the front window. The moment the group began to walk across the street, the door flew open, and she marched out the door to meet them. "It's obvious you've been absent from polite society much too long," Mintie greeted. "We are going to be late! Apparently you've forgotten that *proper* ladies do not enjoy making a spectacle of themselves. You are supposed to be setting a proper example for your young charges, Adelaide. Tsk, tsk," she chastised through pursed lips while casting a look of disdain in Addie's direction.

"And your gown is once again inappropriate. The style is much too youthful. You're a woman of forty and five and should dress in accordance."

"Speaking of gowns, I thought you had discarded that dress several years ago, sister. Isn't that the frock the Judge described as frumpy?" Addie inquired.

The girls giggled and Mintie gasped, smoothing down the dull brown gown. "For a woman of my years, this dress is most assuredly better than that which you've chosen for yourself."

Lilly could see that Addie hadn't meant to make her sister feel bad. Unfortunately, Miss Mintie just seemed to bring out the worst in people.

"I'm sorry, Mintie. That was a most insensitive remark," Addie said. Mintie failed to accept or reject the apology. Neither did she offer an apology for her own biting remark only minutes earlier.

If Addie noticed, she gave no evidence. Instead, she joined in with Prudence and Marmi's infectious laughter, forgetting the caustic beginning to their evening. Even Mintie began adding to the animated conversation as they approached the Old Stone House on Pawtucket Street.

"The balls are not nearly as grand as what we held in Boston, but they do their best to charm the Lowell society," Mintie stated rather casually.

Lilly found it amusing that Mintie would actually allow herself to be momentarily caught up in the revelry. Lilly had never seen her this way. It made Mintie more accessible—more human.

"I've never gone to a ball in Boston," Marmi commented, "but I simply adore the parties we have. I shall dance all night."

"No doubt you'll need a hefty supply of salts for soaking tired feet," Mintie told Addie. "If you need extra, I might have some to share."

Lilly found Mintie's generosity out of character. Perhaps the party spirit had found its way into the old woman's heart after all.

"Right this way, ladies," Phineas Whiting welcomed as their small group entered the slate stone edifice. He appeared to enjoy nothing more than having his establishment filled with patrons determined to have a good time. He tugged at his graying beard and smiled at the near-capacity crowd. "There's punch if you've a thirst and food if you've a hunger, courtesy of the Associates, of course," he announced, waving his arm in a welcoming gesture, "and music for your entertainment."

"Indeed there is." Someone pressed his hand into the small of Lilly's back. "After searching the room and not seeing you, I was afraid you hadn't taken me at my word," Thaddeus Arnold whispered in her ear. "I believe this is my dance." His fusty warm breath caused her to shiver. His hand clenched around her waist. "Don't refuse me," he hissed from between his yellowed teeth.

Mr. Arnold's fingers dug deeply into the flesh around her waist. "I wouldn't want to deny your wife the privilege of being your partner," Lilly replied, searching the crowd, hoping to see his wife's familiar face. Yet she could not escape his grip. Even worse, John Farnsworth was escorting Miss Addie toward the dance floor, leaving Lilly alone to fend off Arnold's advances. There was no escape as he pulled her forward onto the dance floor and pushed firmly against her. Lilly wished the orchestra was playing anything but a waltz.

Bracing her hand against his left shoulder, Lilly pushed until there was a small space between them. "You need not hold me so tightly. I'm sure your superiors would find such behavior unseemly, especially for a married man."

"You'll learn to enjoy having me close to you," he replied, his eyes now alight with wickedness.

Lilly glared in return. "I don't know how any women could bear to have you close at hand, but hear me well, Mr. Arnold. I will *never* permit you to take advantage of me."

He tightened his grasp and twirled her around. "You may change your mind. There are certain advantages to be gained when you're nice to me, Miss Armbruster." The words slid from his mouth with practiced ease. "You should talk to Mary Caruff. She can tell you the privileges that flow to those who enjoy spending a little extra time in my company."

He had Lilly's attention. She had assumed all of his advances toward the girls were unwelcome. Was she to believe there were girls who were willing to permit his advances in exchange for favors? That concept was even more disturbing than the thought that he would take unfair advantage of an employee.

"Talk to Mary Caruff and Rachel Filmore," he said, apparently observing the confusion etched upon her face. "They'll tell you how, shall we say, *profitable,* their extra time with me has been."

Lilly was incredulous. "Am I to understand that you actually pay Mary and Rachel for their company?"

"I didn't say that I pay them," he said, tugging her closer. His mouth was against her ear. "They grant me certain privileges, and I do the same thing for them. Understand?"

Pulling her head away, she looked into his beady eyes. "You give them special favors at work, is that what you mean?"

He looked at her as though she didn't have sense enough to come in out of the rain. "Of *course* that's what I mean—for those who willingly cooperate. I overlook the fact that they come in late on occasion, and I make sure they have the best machinery. It's good that you are beautiful. If you were required to depend upon your intelligence or wit to figure things out, you'd die a certain death."

Lilly didn't acknowledge his comment. "What about the girls who don't cooperate? What do you do for *them*?"

His eyes glistened and his fingers moved up her back. "If you must know, they have a great deal of difficulty accomplishing their work to meet specifications, and within a few weeks they find themselves out of work. And without their good conduct discharge, they are unable to work in any other mill. Most are required to return home. I'm told one of them was so distraught that she jumped from Pawtucket Falls to her death, although I assured Mr. Boott it was most likely an accident, that the girl surely wouldn't have taken her life over losing her job. Wouldn't you agree?"

"I find it difficult to believe such a vile man as you is able to sleep at night. Do you ever wonder what the elders of the church would think of your behavior? I seem to recall that you are among the leadership at St. Anne's."

His look of surprise was worth every ounce of fear in her heart. It was obvious Thaddeus Arnold was not accustomed to being confronted. Their conversation lapsed at the same time as the music.

"There you are," a voice boomed from behind them. Both Lilly and Thaddeus turned to see John Farnsworth striding toward them. "I've come to claim a dance," he said. "I'm sure you won't object." The Englishman dwarfed Thaddeus, who was visibly irritated by the intrusion. He finally acquiesced, releasing Lilly's hand and walking toward the door.

Lilly breathed a sigh of relief, hoping that she had seen the last of Thaddeus Arnold for the evening. "I hope you don't mind the intrusion, but Miss Addie said she thought you would enjoy a new partner," Farnsworth said as they began to circle the floor.

"Miss Addie is a very perceptive lady. I am extremely pleased to have you as my partner, Mr. Farnsworth. Have the two of you been enjoying yourselves?"

"Yes, indeed. Miss Addie is excellent company."

Lilly considered the morsels of information she had been fed by Miss Mintie concerning Farnsworth. Surely they weren't enough to consider him a man set upon treason. He was kind and generous, a true gentleman who would be a fine match for Miss Addie. Yet seeing him secreted in the shadows with those men the other night gave her concern. She wanted to encourage him to call upon Miss Addie, yet if there was a question of character . . .

"I've been giving thought to asking Miss Addie if I could call on her. Do you think she would accept an invitation?" John asked, breaking into her thoughts.

"Yes, well—I imagine she would consider such an invitation," Lilly stammered.

John gave a hearty laugh. "You don't sound overly convincing. Perhaps I should rethink my plan."

"No, don't do that—I'm sure she would be very pleased to have you call on her," Lilly quickly replied. She wasn't going to stand in the way of a possible suitor for Miss Addie.

"I thought I saw you with some other men last Sunday night when I was returning from Belvedere," Lilly continued as Mr. Farnsworth twirled her about the floor in a surprisingly agile manner.

Farnsworth gave no sign of recognition. His brows furrowed, as if he were thinking where he might have been that night. "What time?" he asked.

"It was getting dark, around seven-fifteen, perhaps. Our carriage came down Jackson Street. When we approached the corner, I saw three men having a loud discussion. Two of them ran off. I didn't recognize either of them, but the third bore a striking resemblance to you, Mr. Farnsworth."

He appeared to be sifting through her words. "It may have been me. I believe I was out with several other gentlemen on Sunday evening. I can't say that I recall them running off when we parted company, however. Was there some reason you were concerned about my whereabouts?"

Lilly felt the heat rise in her cheeks. "No, not at all. I was merely surprised to see you. I didn't realize you had already developed friendships here in Lowell."

He smiled down at her. "With the number of Englishmen working at the Merrimack, I've had little difficulty becoming acquainted. Thank you for the dance," he replied as the music came to a halt. "I'll trust your advice in regard to Miss Addie and hope she doesn't disappoint me when I seek permission to call."

Lilly quickly surveyed the room, hoping she could slip out the side door without being noticed. There hadn't been any stipulation as to how long she was to remain at the party, merely that she attend. Weaving her way through the crowd, she passed the punch table and was only steps from the door when someone boldly grabbed her by the waist.

"Not planning to run away, are you? We weren't finished with our little talk." Mr. Arnold had pushed her against the stone wall, the cold slate cutting into her shoulders as she backed away from him. "I believe you were commenting that the arrangement shared between several of the girls and me might be of interest to others. I would strongly suggest that you refrain from such remarks." His face was taut, his jaws clenched as he continued to block her movement.

Trembling, Lilly tried to bolster her courage. She twisted her hands together, hoping he wouldn't see how badly they were shaking.

"Is this some new dance where you block your partner's movement, Mr. Arnold?" Matthew asked as he neared where they stood.

Thaddeus quickly dropped his hold and stepped away. "No. We were merely having a discussion about the excellent working conditions in the spinning room. Miss Armbruster is learning how to adapt to her new surroundings."

"I'm sure you don't mind if I interrupt your conversation. Miss Armbruster owes me a dance," Matthew replied, never taking his gaze off of Lilly.

Acting the proper gentleman, Mr. Arnold bowed from the waist and uttered his consent. Lilly avoided looking in his direction, but she could feel his gaze upon her even after Matthew led her onto the dance floor.

"Charming fellow. I didn't realize you cared for his type. And isn't he married?"

"You're not amusing."

"Ah, dear Lilly, you used to think I was quite amusing," he replied, pulling her a bit closer as the orchestra began a waltz. "Remember this song?" he whispered. "Remember how some of the matrons thought us mad to allow waltzing in our gatherings?"

The music, the dance, and his arms all blended together, transporting her back to a time when she was safe and when life made sense. Without thinking of how it might look, she rested her head on his shoulder, desperately wishing her life could return to those happier days. Her fear of Arnold had left her feeling quite weak, and Matthew's supportive embrace renewed her strength.

"It pleases me that you're finally able to show you still have feelings for me, Lilly," Matthew said as he gently pressed her fingers to his lips.

"What? Because I agreed to one waltz you think I'm still in love with you?"

"No, not just the dance—your head on my shoulder, the look in your eyes. I'd have to be blind not to see your devotion, and it pleases me very much."

Mortified, Lilly couldn't believe what he was saying. How dare he assume such utter nonsense? Had she not been cornered by that lecherous Thaddeus Arnold, she wouldn't have even considered dancing with Matthew. "You're completely wrong, Matthew. In fact, you would be astounded if you knew just how loathsome I consider you and the life you've chosen."

Matthew glanced down at her. His gaze was piercing. "Lilly, it's time you stop lying to yourself and to me."

"Really? Is that what you suggest?" She smiled sweetly, lifted her foot, and stomped down on Matthew's foot as hard as she could. "Consider that a token of my love, Matthew," she said as he groaned and lifted his foot slowly.

"*There* you are, Matthew. I have a young lady here who's anxious to dance with you," Kirk Boott said as he and Isabelle walked onto the dance floor. "Good evening, Miss Armbruster," he added.

Lilly nodded at Kirk and Isabelle. "I'm sure Matthew will be delighted to dance with you, Isabelle. He seems to be in fine form tonight. Aren't you, Matthew?" Without waiting for an answer, she rushed from the dance floor.

CHAPTER *17*

Matthew fussed with his shirt collar, wondering if he would ever feel comfortable when Kirk Boott summoned him. He had no reason to be concerned—at least no reason of which he was aware. Yet the delivery of Kirk's engraved stationery emblazoned with his handwritten scrawl filled Matthew with trepidation. *Come to my office now. Boott.* Minimal phraseology was all that Boott needed to bring any employee running, but most especially one who aspired to become a member of the elite Associates.

Ten minutes later, Matthew knocked on the door of Boott's office. "What kept you?" Boott inquired without looking up from the paper work scattered across his desk. Glancing up, he emitted a loud guffaw. "You needn't look terrified, Matthew. It was my feeble attempt at humor." Kirk pointed toward one of the chairs sitting opposite his desk. "Do be seated, my boy. Can I get you something to drink?"

"No, nothing. How can I be of assistance?"

Kirk leaned back in his chair and propped his lanky legs across the desk. "Isabelle tells me she thoroughly enjoyed spending time with you at the Lighting Up Ball. I believe she was hoping you would extend an invitation for dinner or perhaps the theatre in the near future. Since it's been nearly a month since the ball, I thought I would inquire as to the problem."

Matthew squirmed in the chair, wondering if Isabelle's social calendar was the sole purpose Boott had summoned him. "The distance between Boston and Lowell makes it difficult for me to keep company with your niece and stay abreast of my duties for the Corporation. However, I'm pleased to hear she enjoyed the ball," Matthew hedged.

"Isabelle speculated that you might be interested in the Armbruster girl. I'm certain Isabelle has drawn that conclusion based upon seeing you in Miss Armbruster's company each time she has visited Lowell. I told my niece it was mere happenstance." Kirk's forehead furrowed into deep creases as he lifted his eyebrows and looked at Matthew. "I know you'll be pleased to hear that my sister and Isabelle will be visiting next weekend. I was hoping you could join us for dinner on Saturday evening, shall we say around seven o'clock?"

Matthew longed for the courage to tell Boott he wouldn't be available. Instead, he nodded his agreement. "Was that all you wished to discuss?"

Kirk rose from his chair and moved toward the window looking out on his gardens at the back of the house. "No, no, of course not. There are several matters that need our attention. Did you have an opportunity to investigate the accidents at the Appleton?"

Kirk continued staring out the window with his back toward Matthew. "Yes, and I believe your assessment was correct. After spending some time talking with Mr. Arnold, he agreed that he may have overreacted to the incidents. As you know, he's new to his position and is anxious to make a good impression."

"That's not a bad thing—wanting to impress me. Wouldn't you agree?" Kirk inquired, turning the unwavering gaze of his steel-blue eyes on Matthew.

They both knew there was only one acceptable answer to Kirk's question. Matthew hedged momentarily, not certain where Kirk was headed. "I would agree as long as it doesn't compromise one's personal beliefs," he finally replied.

A wry grin wrapped itself around Kirk's lips. "Not willing to sell your soul for a position with the Associates? Is that what you're telling me, Matthew?"

"Is that what the Associates require?" Matthew questioned in return.

Kirk ran his hand across the stubble of his jaw. "Let us hope not, for I fear you would fail to meet the prerequisites, my boy," he said, his voice laced with a hint of sarcasm. "I've asked Hugh Cummiskey to join us. He should be arriving momentarily. The Associates agree we should begin working out the arrangements we've made with Bishop Fenwick. Cummiskey is our starting point. I've decided to assign this project to you since you were instrumental in presenting the church as a solution to the increasing Irish problem."

Leaning back in his chair, Matthew considered the consequences of Boott's assignment. If the project were a failure and the Irish continued with their infighting, Matthew would be held accountable. He wondered, however, if the project proved successful, who would receive the accolades. A knock sounded at the front door. Moments later a mobcapped servant escorted Hugh Cummiskey into Boott's office.

"Hugh, good to see you. You remember Matthew Cheever, don't you?"

"Afternoon, gentlemen." The burly Irishman nodded at both men as he made his way into the room. Pulling a flattened cap from his head, he ran broad fingers through a mass of disheveled black curls before seating himself beside Matthew.

"I know you're busy with the canal, Hugh, but I think I have some interesting information for you," Kirk began. Over the next hour, he laid out the Associates' decision to bring a priest to Lowell on a somewhat regular basis and commence building a Catholic church. "You don't appear overly pleased," Kirk said as he completed his explanation.

Hugh leaned forward and rested his brawny arms atop the highly polished desk. "Oh, I'm pleased by the idea of having a church for the men and their families, but here's my concern—

where are you gonna put it? We're already divided. I fear a church in one camp or the other will only add to the turmoil."

Kirk gave him a knowing smile and nodded. "We suspected the division of the clans could be problematic. Matthew made a suggestion that appears to have some merit with Bishop Fenwick as well as the Associates."

"What's that?" Hugh inquired.

Kirk pointed to Matthew, and Hugh immediately turned his attention toward the younger man.

"If we build the church directly between the camps, it could serve as a point of unity," Matthew explained. "There's a parcel of land the Associates have agreed they will deed to the Catholic diocese for that purpose. The agreement, however, is hinged upon a labor force consisting of your fellow Irishmen. While the land and materials will be furnished at no cost, labor would be the responsibility of the men living in the camps. We're insisting upon your men supplying the labor for several reasons. One, the cost of the project would be prohibitive from the Associates' point of view if they were required to furnish labor; second, working together on a joint project could aid in bringing the Irish community together; and third, your men are skilled laborers, as well as being the ones who will benefit from the structure." Matthew turned toward Boott for affirmation, but Kirk's gaze was riveted on Hugh Cummiskey.

"What do you think, Hugh?" Kirk asked.

"Quite an undertaking for my men. They'd have to do the work on their off hours, and we both know they don't have many of those—leastwise not during daylight or good weather. These men have got families to feed, and whether those mouths are in Lowell or Boston or Ireland, their families look to them for provision. Don't get me wrong—I think the idea of a church is a good one, but how do I ask them to give up their wages and donate time to build a church?"

"*You* don't. We'll designate that privilege to good Bishop Fenwick. I'll make arrangements to have the bishop come and speak a week from Sunday if he's available. I doubt he'll have difficulty convincing the men that it's a privilege rather than a sacrifice to give their time."

Hugh gave a low laugh. "I don't know if I'd go quite that far, but the bishop's influence will go further than mine."

Kirk rose from behind the desk. "I've assigned Matthew to oversee this matter. In fact, I may send him to Boston to talk with the bishop. I'm sure he could find time to make at least one other call while he's in the city." Kirk cast a sidelong glance at Matthew. "What do you think, Matthew? Are you up to a trip to Boston in the next few days? It will give you an opportunity to set Isabelle's concerns to rest."

Matthew was pleased at the prospect of visiting the bishop on his own. The fact that Kirk considered him capable of conducting a high-level meeting without accompaniment was flattering. *If* it was his ability Kirk truly believed in. Kirk's caveat that he pay Isabelle a visit gave him pause to wonder. "I'll leave in the morning," Matthew agreed.

"Why don't we walk over to the Acre and take a look about," Kirk suggested as he moved around the desk. Matthew and Hugh rose in unison. There was no doubt in either of their minds that if Kirk wanted to visit the Acre, they would visit the Acre.

Cummiskey's Irish brogue filled the air as the three men made their way to the acre or more of land that contained a ramshackle collection of board, tin, and sod cabins and shanties. The pungent smell of cooking cabbage and potatoes mingled with the odor of human bodies permeating the air. Kirk pulled a crisp, neatly folded handkerchief from his pocket and placed it to his nose.

Cummiskey grinned. "Smell of cabbage bother ya?"

Kirk immediately tucked the handkerchief back into his pocket and gave a strained laugh. "Let's say that cabbage is not among my favorite foods. Now, this camp is primarily Corkonians from the southwest of Ireland, and they occupy the original acre. The Connachts, from west-central Ireland, are on the other piece of land, the half-acre site. Is that correct?" he inquired, smoothly changing the topic of conversation.

Matthew was impressed with Boott's knowledge of the camps. Perhaps Kirk hadn't taken time to visit the squatted land in some time, but he had certainly secured enough information to be well versed in a discussion of the area with Cummiskey.

Cummiskey nodded. "Of course, in Ireland the clans are much more divided. Fortunately we've divided into only two factions in Lowell. Which works in your favor, my friend. You've only two clans to pull together instead of hundreds." His dark eyes sparkled with merriment. "It's a grown man's job you'll have attempting to pull these men together."

"Well, I have you and Bishop Fenwick to aid me in that regard," Boott countered, his laughter matching Cummiskey's.

A natural-born builder, Hugh began measuring the area, obviously beginning to picture the edifice and its placement on the piece of land Kirk had shown him. "Are you planning on using slate like at St. Anne's?" Hugh inquired, the sparkle still in his eye.

"If we have a stockpile of slate, we may decide to do that, Hugh. I was planning on a Gothic style, with a tall central tower topped by a gilded cross. Smaller spires surrounding the central tower would be visually pleasing, don't you think, Matthew?"

Matthew had been following along behind Hugh and now came into a circle with the other two men. "Yes, Gothic for a church is quite beautiful," he replied. "You may want to consider . . ."

His words died away as a woman's shouts echoed down the muddy street, causing the three men to look toward a tin-roofed hovel. Matthew strained to see the man who was rushing away from the shanty. Had the fellow not looked so out of place among the filth and poverty, Matthew wouldn't have been intrigued. Squinting against the sun, Matthew stared at the male figure wearing an expensive-looking coat. The man turned, glanced over his shoulder, and headed off down a side street. A shock ran through Matthew. William Thurston!

"You were saying, Matthew?" Kirk inquired, pulling him back to the present.

Matthew rubbed his forehead. "What? Oh yes, I was saying

you might want to consider small spires at each corner of the building to give it a sense of balance."

"Yes, I like that idea. What about you, Cummiskey? Think a spired church building, say about forty feet by seventy, would improve the appearance of the Acre?"

"It certainly can't hurt it," Cummiskey replied. "Just having Matthew convince the bishop to get a priest to Lowell on a regular visiting schedule would be helpful."

"I'm sure Matthew will be successful in his visit with the bishop, Hugh. In the meantime, let's not discuss this project among the people. Don't want to get their hopes built up too high and then have something go amiss."

Cummiskey nodded his agreement. "If we're through here, I think it best if I head back to work. Not that my men can't handle the job without me." Once again he filled the air with his rowdy laughter.

The bulky Irishman waved his arm high in the air as he sauntered off toward the canal. Kirk and Matthew waved in return and then moved off in the opposite direction. The two men walked along in silence for a short distance. Finally Matthew could stand it no longer. "That was William Thurston back there."

"Yes, it was," Kirk replied.

"Is that all you have to say? Don't you find it strange that he would be in the Acre after hearing his disparaging remarks at the Appletons' dinner party?"

Kirk shook his head. "Yes, but I also remember William didn't hide the fact that he spends time in the Acre. In fact, I wondered at the time if he wasn't anticipating just such a circumstance as this. He didn't want questions raised if he were to be seen around the Paddy camps."

"Didn't you hear what that woman shouted?"

"There are some things that should be forgotten, Matthew. This is one of them."

Lilly smiled as she entered the kitchen. Addie was bustling about the warm kitchen, her cheeks flushed a bright pink as she placed the last of the supper dishes on a shelf along the wall. A wisp of her graying hair had escaped and was now firmly clinging to her perspiring forehead. She appeared startled when she finally noticed Lilly. "Am I late? I was trying to hurry," she apologized.

"We have ample time. Please don't hurry so. In fact, why don't you go to your room and get your hat. I'll finish up in here. It's not as though I don't know where these pots and pans belong." The older woman hesitated a moment. "Go on," Lilly encouraged. "I wouldn't have offered if I didn't want to help."

"You're a sweetheart, Lilly Armbruster," Addie called over her shoulder as she rushed from the kitchen, leaving Lilly to complete her few remaining chores.

In no time at all, the two of them were sauntering outside in the cool, moonlit evening. Lilly was bone tired, but she had promised Addie she would go shopping with her. Besides, being with Addie was a joy, for her easy laughter and kind ways never failed to touch Lilly's heart and refresh her spirit. This evening, she was sure, would be no different. She would come home feeling more invigorated than when she left.

"Evening, Mrs. Arnold," Addie called out in her ever-cheerful voice. "Are you out enjoying this fine weather? If you're walking into town, you're welcome to join us."

Mrs. Arnold glanced in their direction as they approached where she stood with an empty basket hanging from her arm. "No, I've changed my mind. I'm not going this evening," she said, raising her head a bit as she spoke. Quickly she turned and rushed back into the house.

"Strange woman, that Mrs. Arnold. Looked like her face was dirty," Addie remarked. "And why would she go to the trouble of donning her shawl and basket without going to do her shopping? She's a rather unfriendly woman, although I've tried to be neighborly in the little time I have for visiting."

"It wasn't dirt on her face, Miss Addie. And she went back in the house because she didn't want us to see she's got bruises all over herself. Her husband beats her."

A look of horror spread across Miss Addie's face. "Oh, child, such terrible accusations you're making. Where would you get such a notion?"

As they continued into town, Lilly explained in detail the first night she'd heard the screams from next door. "Nadene and I made a pact. Whenever either one of us hears Mrs. Arnold screaming, we beat on the wall. He knows that we hear him, and he stops. He still hasn't stopped completely, but at least it doesn't happen *every* night anymore."

"Have you told anyone else? Someone in authority that could possibly help the poor woman?"

Lilly's look of disgust was all the answer Addie needed. "To whom would we go, Miss Addie? Who would listen to us? Nadene can't afford to lose her job."

"Nor can you, my dear," Miss Addie replied as the two of them walked into Markham's General Store, which like the other shops in Lowell, extended shopping hours into the evening to accommodate the full schedules of the mill girls.

"Women are the property of the men they marry," Lilly said softly. "Sometimes a woman marries well, and sometimes she doesn't. Beatings come along with those poorer matches."

"My, but you're cynical for one so young."

"Maybe," Lilly replied, "but I speak the truth and you know it. Mrs. Arnold would be at a loss without her husband, and he clearly abuses her."

"Still, it seems there should be someone who would care, doesn't it?"

Nodding her agreement, Lilly led the way as the two women made their way down the center of the store.

"Now, there's a sight to make a man's eyes sparkle."

Lilly and Addie turned to see John Farnsworth standing behind them. "Good evening, ladies. Out for a bit of shopping and fresh air on this lovely evening?"

"Indeed we are, Mr. Farnsworth," Addie replied with an infectious smile. "And what might you be looking for this evening?"

"Nothing in particular. I just felt the urge to walk into town and get a bit of fresh air. Now I know why. It was to escort you two lovely ladies for a slice of cake and a cup of tea over at Clawson's."

"Why don't the two of you go ahead and have dessert," Lilly suggested, but Addie's look of dismay quickly caused her to reconsider. "On second thought, a cup of tea sounds wonderful." If Miss Addie didn't mind returning to town tomorrow to complete her shopping, why should she object to sitting in the quiet of Clawson's Tea and Pastry Shop? Besides, both Addie and Farnsworth wore expressions of delight.

Mrs. Clawson seated them at a small table near the rear of the shop, where Farnsworth regaled them with tales of the English countryside. He had just begun to tell Addie of his father's debilitating illness when Mrs. Clawson delivered three slices of buttery pound cake covered with a rich, smooth lemon sauce. She placed a sturdy glazed teapot in the center of the table and then surrounded it with china cups and saucers. "Enjoy your cake and tea," she encouraged. Smiling, she hastened off as the small bell over the front door chimed.

Farnsworth extended his arm and waved. "Mind if I join you?" Matthew Cheever inquired as he approached their table.

"Sit down, sit down," Farnsworth encouraged amicably. "I'll have Mrs. Clawson deliver another cup. Would you like a slice of cake?"

Matthew seated himself between John and Lilly. "Are you enjoying your cake, Lilly?" he asked.

"It's very good. Thank you," she replied, keeping her tone formal and uninviting.

"On Miss Armbruster's recommendation, I believe I'll have to try some," Matthew replied, giving Lilly a grin. Farnsworth signaled Mrs. Clawson, who quickly brought another serving of cake along with a cup and saucer.

When Lilly wouldn't banter with him, Matthew turned his attention to Farnsworth and attempted to engage him in a business discussion. Lilly gave Matthew a triumphant grin when John appeared uninterested and turned his attention back toward

Addie. "I don't think Mr. Farnsworth finds you particularly interesting this evening," Lilly whispered.

"Then perhaps *you'd* be willing to talk to me," he suggested. "Consider it a gesture of goodwill toward Miss Addie."

Lilly took a sip of tea. "As long as I may choose what we talk about," she said, waiting until Matthew nodded his agreement.

"What delightful thing would you like to speak of?" he questioned. Cutting into his cake, Matthew took a bite and smiled. "This is good but not quite as good as the treats you used to serve me."

Lilly stiffened and murmured, "I wonder if you could tell me what the good Boston Associates think of men who beat their wives."

Matthew stared at her in obvious disbelief. He took a long sip of tea then eyed her as if to regard how serious she was about the matter. "This is ridiculous, Lilly. What are you talking about?" His voice held an edge that conveyed she was speaking nonsense.

"Don't take that tone with me, Matthew Cheever. You know me too well to believe I'd lie about such a thing. There is nothing ridiculous about Thaddeus Arnold beating his wife until she's black and blue." She shook her head as hideous images came to mind. "Poor woman. I'm regularly awakened by her screams begging him to stop. Now, if you'll excuse me, I've finished my tea and cake. I believe I'll walk home."

Matthew looked to where John and Addie sat engrossed in their conversation. Turning back to Lilly, he pressed close and whispered, "Surely you realize we'd need proof of such allegations. You can't just make unfounded accusations."

Lilly tolerated his nearness in order to continue her discussion. "I've seen her bruises, and so has Miss Addie. She avoids all contact with other people—a prisoner in her own home—no doubt to keep anyone from asking questions. She's likely suffering unimaginable horrors. I doubt Mr. Arnold is going to come forward and admit to his despicable behavior." Lilly pulled away from him and got to her feet.

"Just a moment, Lilly," Addie said. "John and I are leaving, also."

John pushed himself away from the table and then assisted Addie. "I asked Addie's permission to escort you ladies back home, and she has graciously agreed," Mr. Farnsworth said.

"I was hoping to have a bit of time to discuss a couple of matters, John," Matthew said, rising from his chair. "I'm sure the ladies would excuse you."

John gave Matthew a look of obvious disbelief. "This may come as a surprise to you, Matthew, but I much prefer the company of these ladies to yours." Miss Addie gave a nervous giggle while Lilly leveled a smug look in Matthew's direction. "You're welcome to join us, however."

"It appears I'll be required to do so if I'm going to have any time with you," Matthew conceded as the group walked out the door. "I suppose I can force myself to remain in Lilly's company a bit longer," he said as he and Lilly walked ahead of the older couple.

Lilly glared at him. "I imagine you will have to force yourself since it appears you can't stand to hear the truth about your employees. I'm sure you'd be much more comfortable with Isabelle and her fawning behavior."

Matthew looked rather surprised. "You're jealous, Lilly. You see, you do still care," he said in a hoarse whisper.

Lilly felt a momentary rush of embarrassment as his words hit home. She pushed her feelings aside and kept walking. "This has nothing to do with Isabelle; it has to do with Mrs. Arnold," Lilly retaliated.

"If it will make you feel better, I promise I'll check into Mr. Arnold's behavior."

"Will you truly?" She looked back to ascertain his sincerity.

Matthew's expression revealed his concern. "Lilly, you know how I feel about such matters. I could never abide a man hitting his wife. I promise I'll check into it."

Lilly nodded. "It's just that she's . . . she's . . . all alone." The words were as much a reflection of her own heart as they were concern for Mrs. Arnold. "If we don't come to her aid, who will?"

"I understand, Lilly," Matthew said softly. For a moment their gazes were fixed on each other.

They continued to walk, but their steps were slowed considerably. Matthew held tightly to her arm and added, "Lilly, why are you jealous of Isabelle?"

For a moment Lilly thought of sharing her heart. She opened her mouth to speak but fell short when Addie called out, the spell broken. She pulled away.

"You appear to be limping, Mr. Cheever. Did you hurt your foot?"

Matthew stopped, allowing the older couple to move alongside them. "As a matter of fact, I did—at the Lighting Up Ball. A clumsy dancer stepped on my foot and bruised it rather badly. But I'm sure it will heal."

"And it's still sore after all this time? That must have been painful. I'm so sorry," Addie replied, a look of genuine concern on her face. "You should try using a cane. It would help take the weight off your injured foot. The Judge used a cane most of the time—gout, you know. He said it helped immensely," she continued in a motherly tone.

"Thank you for your concern, Miss Addie," Matthew said as the older couple moved ahead of them. Pulling Lilly close, Matthew bent down to whisper in her ear. "You can't deny your feelings forever. I know you care about me."

Lilly didn't want to make a scene in Miss Addie's presence, but neither did she want to give Matthew the upper hand. Turning to speak to him, however, she found his lips only inches away from her own. Unnerved by his nearness, she forced herself to speak. "You'd best watch yourself, Matthew Cheever, or that same clumsy dancer may step on your other foot, and I doubt a cane will do you much good then!"

CHAPTER 18

Autumn leaves crunched beneath his feet as William Thurston walked down Merrimack Street. Bending his head against a brisk gust of wind, he pulled a watch from his pocket and then quickened his pace. He certainly didn't want Lewis Armbruster standing around the Acre waiting for him. Worse yet, he didn't want Lewis, a much younger man with an insatiable appetite for women, spending time with Kathryn O'Hanrahan. She'd sell her soul for a crust of bread. In William's mind, that was true of all the Irish; they had no morals, no interest in rising above their circumstances. Instead of working to remove themselves from their plight, they banded together and reveled in their misery. Why he couldn't get Boott and the other Associates to see the Irish for what they truly were was beyond him. The Irish, with their dirty ways and constant brawling, were going to eventually ruin all that was good and pure in Lowell.

William spied Lewis coming from the opposite direction down Adams Street and breathed a sigh of relief. "Hello, Lewis," William said as they drew closer together. Lewis nodded in greeting and matched William's stride as the two of them walked through the mud and muck that filled the crooked paths leading into the Acre. Without knocking, William led the way into one of the hovels.

A young woman with auburn curls and a creamy white complexion sat before the waning fire. She was wrapped in a blanket, a young child asleep on her lap. "I don't like meeting in this place," Lewis whispered as Thurston walked deeper inside the room.

William turned, gave him a look of disgust, and pointed toward the only chair in the room. "Sit down. We agreed our meetings needed to be in a place where we wouldn't be seen together, and we have that safety here. Don't we, Kathryn?" The woman nodded her head but said nothing. "Take him and go outside. We won't be long," Thurston ordered.

"The boy isn't feeling well. 'Tis cold and damp outdoors." There was a pleading in her voice as she looked into William's steely eyes.

He despised the way she was always attempting to manipulate him. "Do as I say, Kathryn," he said from between clenched teeth. He glared down at her until she finally lifted the sleeping child into her arms and carried him out of the shack. When she had finally cleared the doorway, William turned to Lewis. "There have been six accidents at the Merrimack and ten at the Appleton in the last month. Why isn't Boott alarmed? Have you been getting word out that the Irish are to blame for these incidents? Because if you have, Lewis, I certainly haven't heard the rumors. What am I paying you for?"

"No need to take your personal problems out on me, Thurston," Lewis replied as he looked toward the doorway. "As for why Boott isn't concerned about the Irish, you'd need to ask him yourself. I'm afraid I don't have access to Boott or any of your other powerful friends, for that matter. I've done what you requested, but you need to remember that the Irish couldn't possibly have caused some of those incidents. The people of Lowell are not stupid. I'm not going to spread rumors that are unbelievable. I've made accusations against the Irish when there was a possibility they could have been involved, but people haven't put much stock in the idea."

In spite of the coolness of the room, William's face had flushed beet red, and the veins in his neck were throbbing. "Why is it that I'm the only person who can see what a menace these people are? You need to explain that the Irish are angry because of their wages, their living conditions . . . Use some imagination, Lewis! Surely you can do that much!"

Lewis looked up and met Thurston's hardened stare. "I've already tried that. To be honest, I believe the Irish may be involved to a certain extent because *I* certainly haven't been the cause of all the recent accidents. There were two mishaps at the canals, one at the Appleton, and three at the Merrimack that were not my doing. If the Irish didn't cause those particular accidents, there may be others set on the ruination of the mills—unless you have somebody else working for you. Do you, Thurston? Have you hired someone besides me to assist with your accidents?"

"How dare you question me! You're nothing more than a lackey—a henchman paid to do my bidding. Whether I've hired others to assist in my plans is none of your concern. You just follow my instructions."

"I thought we were more than that. I thought we were friends. After all, we spent a fair amount of time at the gaming tables together—shared quite a few suppers together."

William smirked. "You sound like a jealous wife, Lewis. I trust you to carry out my orders; that should be enough. We were companions on equal footing at one point, but that has changed, hasn't it? You've no fortune to your name. You're not even a propertied man anymore."

Defeat registered on Lewis's face, and Thurston pressed the matter to eliminate any further confusion. "I've hired you to do a job. Our business association makes it necessary for you to recognize my authority. I tolerate your calling me by my given name, but I will not abide your questions of how I conduct my business. Do you understand?"

"Yes, I believe I do," Lewis stated rather flatly.

"Good. Now, tell me, when you make accusations against the Irish, what kind of remarks are you hearing in return?"

Lewis's air of superiority had diminished. His gaze was cast downward as he dug the toe of his boot back and forth into the dirt floor. "People believe the Irish are happy with their way of life here in Lowell. My remarks about their living conditions have recently been countered with a rumor that Boott may be assisting the Irish in securing regular visits by a priest, and although I'm loath to believe it, some say the Associates have donated land for a Catholic church. Do you know if that rumor is correct?"

"What? I've no knowledge of such a donation. That's preposterous! The whole idea is to rid Lowell of this Irish vermin. Why would the Associates even consider such nonsense?" William spewed. Surely such insanity was merely fodder for the rumor mill.

Lewis leaned against the slats of the wobbly wooden chair. "I don't know, William. I'm merely telling you what I've heard. Have you attended recent meetings where anything of this nature was discussed? Do any of the Associates hold individual title to property around the Acre, or is the land jointly held by the Corporation?"

"Da," a tiny voice announced. The little boy who had been sleeping on Kathryn's lap toddled into the room, his eyes still matted with sleep. He raised his arms to William, obviously wanting to be picked up. "Da."

"Go out with your mother," William sternly replied to the child. Hadn't he told Kathryn time and again that the child was not to refer to him as his father?

Just then Kathryn came in, obviously frantic to know where the child was. "Sorry, I was talkin' to me sister and he got away." She grabbed the boy up and headed for the door. "It's awfully cold outside."

"You can come in soon. Go on!" he commanded. The child's lip quivered as though he might cry. Kathryn wrapped him in her shawl and quickly left.

"What was it you were asking me, Lewis?" William inquired, his thoughts having been scattered by the child's intrusion.

Lewis gave him a pensive look before replying. "About the

donation of land for a church. Do you have any knowledge of such a transaction?" he reiterated.

"No, of course not. There's been no discussion. . . ." He hesitated and turned toward the small, flickering fire. He hadn't attended the last meeting of the Associates. Nathan had asked him to complete some meaningless business in Nashua; he'd been unable to return to Boston in time for the meeting, and he'd given Nathan his proxy.

The Associates had contrived against him—of that he was now certain. It was obvious Boott had won the allegiance of the Corporation. He turned around and faced Lewis. "I spoke in haste, Lewis. At the time of the last meeting, I was in Nashua at Nathan Appleton's request. It appears as if my colleagues may have conducted some business to which I'm not yet privy. We may have to explore another tactic."

"Like what? I don't see what else we can do."

"Cummiskey may be the key. The Irish listen to anything he says. If he's out of the picture, perhaps . . ."

Lewis rose from the chair. "Now, wait a minute, William. I'm not going after Cummiskey. I'd end up with every Irishman in Lowell after my hide. Besides, even if they didn't have Cummiskey, they'd follow another. O'Malley's his second; he'd step in and take over."

"I was thinking more along the lines of buying him off, Lewis, not killing him," William replied, attempting to hold his temper in check. He needed to find some way to play a pivotal role in turning things around. Why was it so easy for the likes of Boott and Cummiskey to gain power and devotees, he wondered. "For enough money, Cummiskey might be willing to exert his power and veto the idea of a Catholic church. That would surely enrage the Irish; they'd think Boott had gone back on his word." He remained silent, his mind racing. "I need time to think this out, Lewis, develop a plan. I've not decided if we should direct our efforts toward Cummiskey or Boott. In the meantime, you continue in your attempts to foster negative feelings toward these heathens."

"Might I ask a personal question?" Lewis tentatively ventured.

William was absently staring into the fire and nodded his head.

"If you dislike the Irish so intensely, why is it you've fathered a child by an Irish woman?"

William wheeled around and pointed a thick, stubby finger in Lewis's face. "Why, you impudent—! That woman, and what I do with her, is none of your business. As for the boy, he's not your concern. Do you understand me?" Lewis's contrite appearance was enough to convince William he'd made his point. "Go on home. And tell the woman and boy to come in as you leave," Thurston said with a dismissive wave of his hand.

Matthew walked into the small office in the counting room of the Appleton. The space had only recently been assigned to him and bore little evidence that he worked here. It was diminutive compared to Boott's office at the Merrimack, but Matthew found it to his liking. He viewed Boott's willingness to assign him to a different mill as a vote of confidence, and he liked the people who worked in the offices of the Appleton, particularly Lawrence Gault.

"I thought I would stop by and see how you're doing here at the Appleton, Matthew. All settled into your new surroundings?" Kirk asked as he strode into the room and seated himself on one of the two straight-backed oak chairs.

Matthew nodded and smiled. "Yes, it's more than adequate. I'm only just getting settled in, but I'm quite comfortable."

Kirk returned his smile. "Good. I'm anxious to hear about your trip to Boston. You did get my message upon your return?"

"Yes. My condolences to Mrs. Boott on the loss of her mother."

"Thank you. We were required to remain in New Hampshire longer than I'd anticipated. But one must allow women their time to grieve. Quite frankly, Mrs. Boott was so distraught I was beginning to think we'd never get back to Lowell. Ah, well, I digress. Now, tell me about your meeting with the good bishop. It went well, I hope."

Matthew knew the time of reckoning had come. Boott smiled and nodded his head, seemingly pleased with Matthew's report. At least until Matthew related that the bishop couldn't possibly visit until November or possibly December.

"What? That means we can't break ground before next spring at the earliest," Boott said, jumping up from his chair. "I thought he was interested in this project!"

Matthew hoped he could have a calming effect upon Boott, but he doubted whether the remainder of his report was going to accomplish such a feat. "He *is* interested. However, he believes there will need to be a good deal of groundwork done in order to support the church. The bishop tells me that the diocese expects church funding to come from parishioners. If the parishioners are going to support the church, the bishop believes a more affluent Catholic base of middle-class citizens is needed in Lowell."

Boott was pacing back and forth across the small office. "Why didn't he say these things when we first met with him? Does he expect me to find affluent Irishmen who wish to immigrate to Lowell? They don't exist! I thought you said your meeting went well. I'd hate to think what I'd be hearing if you thought it went poorly."

Matthew bowed his head momentarily. The words stung, yet there was more to report. "Bishop Fenwick believes that within the next year or two, the Irish population of Lowell will swell. The increasing numbers will encourage more affluent Irishmen from Boston—shopkeepers and the like—to open businesses in Lowell. In turn, those men will provide a broader income base to support the church," Matthew explained. "Bishop Fenwick believes that as long as the Irish know the Associates have made a commitment to give the land, they won't be unduly averse to waiting a year or two for the church."

Kirk continued to pace back and forth. "And what about his promise for regular visits by a priest?"

Matthew didn't want to answer. He knew Boott's ire would

only increase. "Why don't we take a walk? You're obviously in need of more space than my office affords." When Boott offered no resistance, Matthew rose from his desk and rushed to open the door.

When they had reached the street, Boott looked both directions, then turned to Matthew. "Which way?"

"Toward the Acre."

"Ah—good idea. Let's take a look at the land we're setting aside to give to the diocese. By the way, how was Isabelle? I trust you two enjoyed your time together?"

Matthew gave his mentor a tentative glance. "As it turned out, Isabelle had a previous commitment. By the time I arrived at your sister's home, Isabelle had already departed for dinner. I fear the entire journey could be viewed as a failure."

Kirk slapped Matthew on the back. "Not entirely. At least we know the bishop has talked to his superiors. We know exactly what is required in order to make a final decision. Any problems arise during my journey to New Hampshire?"

"Nothing outside of the usual—only a small accident at the Merrimack. Other than that, operations have been running smoothly. There is, however, a matter I wanted to discuss with you. I'm not sure my timing is the best," he hesitantly replied.

Kirk laughed. "It doesn't sound like anything I'm going to enjoy hearing. You may as well go ahead and give me all the bad news at once. Is production down?"

"No, nothing like that. It's a matter of a more personal nature. There are some concerns regarding Thaddeus Arnold, the super—"

"I know who he is. What kind of concerns? Is he unable to manage the spinning room?"

"There are reports he's abusive to his wife—that he beats her. Some of the operatives who live in the adjoining house have heard them. It seems it's an almost nightly occurrence."

Boott ran a hand across his forehead. "Is there any proof? Has the wife come forward to complain?"

Matthew shook his head. "Mrs. Arnold has been seen bearing bruises, but there's no proof they were caused by her husband, and she hasn't lodged any complaint."

"Ah, Matthew, what goes on in a man's home is his business. Moreover, we need actual proof of such allegations. After all, Thaddeus is an elder in the church, and we wouldn't want to tarnish his reputation based on unfounded remarks. Such talk could be devastating to his future with the company. Perhaps his wife is the type who needs a heavy hand. She may even realize it herself since she doesn't come forward."

"I beg to disagree, Mr. Boott. I don't think a man needs to beat his wife into submission, and I certainly don't believe that any woman wants to be beaten by her husband."

Boott shrugged. "You're young, Matthew, with much to learn. It's the way things are. Women's opinions and ideas don't count; they need to remember their place. It merely takes some women longer than others to learn to accept their station in life."

Matthew walked along silently, wondering how Lilly might respond if she were to hear Boott's comments. He was certain she wouldn't remain silent.

"Well, there's also the matter of keeping your employees awake throughout the night. We can't have the girls so exhausted by the tirades of Arnold and his wife that they can't perform their duties." Matthew figured if Boott wouldn't see the seriousness of the situation for Mrs. Arnold, perhaps he would care about the well-being of his workers.

"I suppose that does bear some consideration," Boott replied. "Say, isn't that Lewis Armbruster up there? I thought he was in Nashua." Kirk waved his arm, indicating a man who had exited the Acre and was walking toward them. "I haven't seen him since he helped us finalize the purchase of his father's farm."

The man looked in their direction as Matthew was about to answer. "If it isn't Lewis, it's his double. I didn't know he was back in Lowell, either. Apparently he didn't want to be seen," Matthew remarked as Lewis turned and rushed off in the opposite direction.

Kirk nodded in agreement. "It appears there are any number of people interested in visiting the Acre nowadays—and most have little desire to be seen there."

CHAPTER *19*

An insistent rapping on the front door brought Addie to her feet. She had hoped for a half hour of peace and quiet before beginning the evening meal. For a moment she considered ignoring the interruption. Instead, curiosity won out, and she hobbled to the front door, the aching bunion on her right foot slowing her gait.

"For heaven's sake, Adelaide, what took you so long? I could catch my death of cold standing out here waiting for you," Mintie scolded as a cold November breeze whipped its way inside the door Addie opened. Without invitation, Mintie pushed onward toward the parlor. "No tea?" she called out before Addie had managed to limp back to the room.

"No, sister, I didn't take time to make tea. I was hoping to spend a half hour studying the Bible. Unfortunately, I had managed to read only a few verses before your unexpected arrival."

Mintie ran a gloved finger over the decorative teacart sitting near her chair and then pursed her lips in disapproval. "It appears you need to be dusting your furniture rather than relaxing," Mintie replied, waving her finger in the air as though she were checking for wind currents.

Addie lowered herself into a chair and gingerly elevated her foot on a small upholstered stool. "I'm thinking that the Lord would prefer I read His word than worry about a smattering of dust. But if it bothers you immeasurably, you have my permission to dust everything in sight," Addie said with a sweet smile.

Mintie appeared dumbstruck by the remark but recovered quickly. "I didn't come to do your housework. I came to talk," Mintie retorted.

"Then talk, Mintie. You're the one distressed by my housekeeping. I was only making an offer."

Mintie's face screwed into a look of consternation. "You've changed since we moved to Lowell, Adelaide. And not for the better, I fear. However, that's not what I've come to discuss." She leaned forward, folding her body in half. "It's that John Farnsworth. I know you've taken a fancy to him," Mintie said before raising her open palm toward Addie. "Don't try to deny it. You wear your heart on your sleeve. You always have. However, you must nip these feelings in the bud. There's no doubt he's a traitor—a spy. I tried to warn you, but you wouldn't listen. If you have a broken heart, you have no one to blame but yourself," Mintie triumphantly announced.

Addie tucked a wisp of hair under her white mobcap and stared at her sister in disbelief. "I'm beginning to worry about your mental condition, Mintie. You must get over this fixation with traitors and spies—it's not healthy."

Mintie gasped and turned pale. "Adelaide Beecher! It's difficult to believe we were reared in the same family. Now you listen to me. That Farnsworth is up to no good. He leaves at all times of the night, probably off to meet with other spies or visit those adulterous Irish women—or both. And that's not all." She paused as if to ascertain whether she'd be overheard. Casting a glance over her shoulder, Mintie leaned forward. "He receives missives from England—*all the time*."

Addie giggled. "You do have a flair for the dramatic, Mintie. I always thought *I* was the gifted child when it came to such matters."

Mintie let out a snort and wagged her finger at Addie. "This is not a matter to be taken lightly. There are men who come to the house at all hours—they don't even leave a calling card. Any man worth his salt wouldn't come calling without a card. What does that tell you?"

Without waiting for an answer, she continued. "They're spies! Just like him, intent on keeping their identity a secret. I tell you, the Judge would have sent them packing. If a man isn't refined enough to carry a calling card, he isn't worth receiving. Why, any such caller to the Beecher house would have been out on his ear!"

Addie set her rocker into motion, careful not to disturb her propped foot. "You need to settle yourself, Mintie. You're overwrought for no reason whatsoever. Our circumstances here in Lowell aren't comparable to those in Boston, and you can't expect people to present calling cards. These are working-class people. And so are we! Our days of receiving calling cards are over."

Mintie was shaking her head in disgust. "Good manners don't begin and end with circumstances, Adelaide. Civility is a necessity for all classes of people."

"I agree. Civility and good manners transcend circumstances. But calling cards are not a necessity among—"

"Posh! They're not leaving calling cards because they are spies. Honestly, Adelaide, you remind me of a mule wearing blinders. It's obvious to *most* people that spies don't leave calling cards because it's their *modus operandi*." She paused and took on an exasperated expression. "You'll remember that term from the Judge—it means how they operate."

"I remember the term well. I simply do not see how it has anything to do with anything."

"They don't want anyone to know who they are or where they've been," Mintie argued. "And you need to stay away from that John Farnsworth!"

"John Farnsworth is a fine man who loves it here in Lowell. The men who come to the house are probably some of the Englishmen from work who need special instructions or some such thing."

"You go ahead and make excuses for him, but when he and the British blow this place to smithereens, you'll know I was right. People no doubt hesitated to believe the British would burn the president's home in Washington."

Addie couldn't stifle another chuckle. She knew her laughter served only to anger Mintie further, but her sister's allegations were preposterous.

"That's right, you keep sniggering, but I know there's a plot underway. I heard Farnsworth talking to some of those men about ordering more blasting powder for the canals. They're not pulling the wool over my eyes! They're stockpiling that blasting powder until the British arrive to take back the country, and your John Farnsworth will supply them with ample explosives to complete their treacherous plans."

Addie realized there was no convincing her sister she was wrong, yet she wished she could find some words that would assuage Mintie's concerns. "Can't you see, Mintie, that there is truly a need for additional blasting powder for the new canals that are planned? They're expanding all the time."

"Your naïveté never ceases to amaze me, Adelaide. Can't *you* see they have those strong-backed Irish brutes to dig out the canals? Why would the Corporation spend money on blasting powder when they have those beasts of burden? You mark my words, Adelaide Beecher, you've set yourself up for heartbreak. I would think you'd have learned that the first time when that Charles went off with another woman." Mintie sat back in her chair with a smug smile on her face.

"Charles did not leave me for another woman, and you know it. We agreed to end our courtship when the Judge insisted I could not marry until some eligible bachelor was willing to wed you. We both knew that would not soon occur."

A small gasp escaped Mintie's lips. She jumped up and rushed toward the front door without so much as a good-bye.

"I'm sorry, Mintie. I shouldn't have spoken such cruel words," Addie apologetically called after her sister. "Oh, Father, why did I let my tongue get the best of me yet again?" she wistfully prayed as she rose from the chair. Her peaceful half hour was nothing more than a memory, and dinner preparations awaited her in the kitchen.

By the time the girls began arriving home, Addie had analyzed her conversation with Mintie so many times she was now convinced her older sister's accusations against John might have merit. The longer she tried to persuade herself Mintie's arguments were nonsensical, the more concerned she became. Perhaps John was a traitor. Yet how could she believe such a thing? He spoke of his fondness for Massachusetts and desire to bring his father from England. And he professed to love the Lord—and certainly acted like a God-fearing Christian man. It was all too difficult to sort out right now, for dinner wouldn't serve itself.

———

"You sit down right now," Lilly ordered. "I'm going to do these dishes, and you sit there and keep me company. Take your shoe off and put your foot up. Then tell me what's wrong."

Addie's eyebrows arched. "What makes you think anything is wrong? Besides my bunion and gout, of course."

"I know you too well, Miss Addie. You snapped at Prudence when she asked for more apple butter, and when Mary Alice said her meat was a bit tough, you were not very pleasant. I've never seen you like this. I insist you tell me what's happened."

Addie looked down at the floor and placed her hands on her cheeks. "It's Mintie. She came over here this afternoon offering proof that John Farnsworth is a spy. And, Lilly, I'm not so sure she's wrong. I've mulled it over for the past several hours, and what she says makes sense."

"Preposterous! Tell me what evidence she's produced." Lilly completed washing the dishes as Addie recounted the afternoon of tragedy wrought by Miss Mintie.

"I don't want to believe ill of anyone, especially not of John."

"Then don't," Lilly said, wiping her hands on a towel before sitting down beside her friend. Taking Addie's hand into her own, Lilly gazed directly into the older woman's eyes. "Now that you've repeated all of Miss Mintie's allegations aloud, don't you see how foolish they are? John Farnsworth has no more interest in overthrowing the country than you or I. Your sister is saying these things because John has begun calling upon you. Mintie doesn't like the idea of you having a suitor. In a word, Miss Addie, your sister is jealous."

"Do you really think that's all it is? I keep remembering that she was suspicious of him when he first arrived."

Lilly giggled. "Only because he had a letter from England, which doesn't prove anything except that he keeps in communication with his father. I think he should be commended for writing home—not treated like a criminal. The only thing Miss Mintie has proved is that she's a jealous snoop. I think what Miss Mintie needs is a suitor of her own, someone to keep her mind and time occupied—and I think I may know just the person!" Lilly smiled to herself even imagining the stiff-necked spinster on the arm of a beau.

Addie placed a hand over her mouth to stifle her laughter. "I don't think Mintie would consider taking a suitor."

"We'll see. I have a very convincing gentleman in mind. Given a chance, I think he may be able to soften her up a bit." Lilly saw a glimmer of hope return to Addie's expression.

"Thank you for your help, Lilly. Speaking of help, I forgot to mention I've gone next door the past several mornings hoping to visit with Mrs. Arnold. She came to the door the first day but didn't let me in. She said she didn't have time to visit. After that, she didn't even answer the door, but I knew she was in there."

Lilly nodded. "I'm sure she's afraid to talk to anyone. That husband of hers has her frightened to death. And Matthew Cheever was proven to be no better." Lilly tried to keep her emotions under control. Frankly, she was just as mixed up over Matthew as Miss Addie was over Mr. Farnsworth.

"He hasn't done one thing to help," she continued. "I'm certain he's afraid the reputation of the wonderful Corporation might be tarnished if word got out that one of their fine supervisors beats his wife. But there must be some way to help her. We'll figure something out—with or without Matthew Cheever."

"Now, now, dear, Matthew is a fine young man. I'm sure he's

looking into the matter. Things don't always move as rapidly as we think they should. He's a busy man."

Lilly folded the dish towel and turned toward Addie. "Sometimes we can't depend on busy men, Miss Addie. Sometimes we must take—"

"Lilly, come quick," Prudence insisted as she burst into the kitchen, her face flushed with excitement. She bounced from foot to foot, obviously wanting immediate attention. When Lilly didn't quickly move, Prudence began tugging at her roommate's arm. "Come on—you have a visitor."

"Hurry! It may be Matthew," Addie urged.

Addie's words caused Lilly to halt midstep and pull her arm away from Prudence. "Is it Matthew Cheever?"

Prudence shook her head. "No. I've never seen this man before, and he wouldn't give his name. He said he wanted to surprise you. He's quite handsome and *very* sophisticated—probably from Boston. If you're not interested in him, promise you'll introduce me? Please?" Prudence begged, folding her hands in prayerlike fashion.

"Stop it, Prudence," Lilly replied with a giggle as she followed Prudence toward the parlor. "I don't know any handsome, sophisticated man who would be calling on me. It's probably a mistake." Lilly stopped in the doorway, unable to believe her eyes. Across the room sat an elegantly clad Lewis, surrounded by at least five fawning mill girls.

The moment he spied her in the entrance, he jumped to his feet and motioned her forward. "Don't stand there staring at me as though you've seen a ghost. Come give your big brother a hug, dear Lilly."

Her roommates sat watching the unfolding scene, envy etched upon each of their faces as she walked toward Lewis. She allowed him to embrace her only for the sake of issuing her edict. "I want you to leave here immediately," Lilly whispered in his ear before pushing away from him.

"Why don't we take a short stroll? I've been anxious to see you since my return from Nashua. We have much to talk about," he said, giving her a piercing stare. "Get your cloak, Lilly," he hissed, taking hold of her arm.

"Oh, don't leave us so soon," Prudence cooed. "Lilly hasn't even had an opportunity to make proper introductions."

Lewis bowed and kissed Prudence's hand. "I'll be returning often, dear girl, and I'm sure we'll have the opportunity to become better acquainted. Trust me." With a self-satisfied smile, he tipped his hat at Prudence and grasped Lilly's arm.

Lilly thought Pru might actually swoon. She held her hand to her face with an expression of complete adulation. The other girls were no better. Lilly looked to her brother and had to admit he was quite stylish and well-groomed. No doubt the gaming tables had smiled favorably upon him.

"Until we meet again, ladies," Lewis said, bowing low. He pressed Lilly toward the door, pausing only long enough to pop a top hat onto his head.

"What do you want, Lewis?" Lilly asked as soon as they exited the door. "I'm not going for a stroll. We can talk right here."

"Truly? Your little friends are watching out the window. If we stand here much longer, I'm sure at least one or two of them will be out here to join us."

Lilly pulled her arm away from his grasp and began walking. "What is it you're after, Lewis? Why have you returned to Massachusetts?" A million thoughts raced through her head. If he was here for money, he'd be out of luck. She wasn't about to part with any of her hard-earned wages to support his lifestyle. Christian charity only extended so far.

"I could tell you I was concerned for your welfare, but we both know that isn't true. Tell me, dear sister, how does it feel to be working for the Corporation you hold in such contempt? Do you ever revel in the thought of somehow usurping their power?" He emitted a callous laugh. "No, that would never happen to my little sister, would it? She's the perfect child who never does wrong. Dear Lilly would never consider doing anything unchristian—she doesn't have wicked thoughts."

His words stung her conscience. If he knew how many

people had been the victims of her unkind thoughts and deeds in recent months, he would certainly question her Christianity. The idea was frightening. "I'm not perfect, and we both know that, Lewis. I dislike working for the Corporation, but you left me penniless; I had no choice. Quit avoiding my question. It's cold out here. Tell me what it is you want so I can go home and you can go back to wherever it is you came from."

"I'm not going anywhere, Lilly. I plan to be in Lowell for quite some time. As a matter of fact, that's one of the reasons I've come to see you. I understand that most of the mill girls are quite frugal with their money and some of them have accumulated rather large sums. If you're one of those girls, I could use your help. I'm broke and need money, and you are the only family I have."

"I have no intention of helping you, Lewis. I can't believe you have the audacity to come to me for money."

He shrugged. "If you aren't one of those girls who has plenty of money, then introduce me to one. I'm not interested in the ones who are sending their wages back home to their poverty-stricken families. My inheritance is gone, and I can't be wasting time."

Lilly gaped at him, astonished at his request. "I'll do no such thing. I'm not going to assist you in duping any of these girls out of their hard-earned wages. Surely you can find some other more profitable scheme."

"Poor Lilly. You don't understand much, do you? These girls are vulnerable, unscathed little flowers waiting to be plucked. I can move from one to the other, permitting them the pleasure of keeping company with an educated, handsome man as well as assisting them with the proper investment of their wages."

Lilly was aghast at his proposal. "Investment of their wages into your pocket! So this is how you now intend to support yourself?"

"Don't be ridiculous. Those girls don't have enough money to support my needs, but their funds would be a nice addition to my income. You need not concern yourself with my welfare. I've entered into a business venture with a gentleman of considerable means. However, I'm sure your little friends would be thrilled to purchase an expensive gift or two for a handsome beau," he said with a smirk. "I find that for the right amount of affection, propriety is often overlooked."

Lilly turned and briskly headed back toward the boarding-house. "You sicken me, Lewis. Do you stay awake at night think-ing of vile ways to hurt people?" She gave him a look of disgust. "I will not be a part of your schemes."

"As you choose, but I'll succeed with or without your help. It will merely take a bit longer to weed out the girls who are penniless. Incidentally, did I mention the fact that I saw Matthew and Kirk Boott today? Matthew has certainly managed to endear himself to the Corporation, hasn't he?"

She knew Lewis; his words were intended to cause pain. "If you're interested in Matthew's position in the Corporation, you'll need to talk to him."

"I believe I hit a sore spot. I'm so sorry, Lilly. You know I would never want to open old wounds," he said, sarcasm drip-ping from each word. "Well, here we are, back to your humble dwelling. Tell me, is it true? Do you really sleep four girls to a bed?"

Lilly turned, fixing him with what she hoped was a scathing expression. "Get away from me, Lewis. Go away and don't ever return. I have no desire to be associated with you or your schem-ing."

Without saying a word, Lewis leaned around her, opened the door, and made his way inside the house before she could object. Lilly watched in amazement as Lewis boldly strode into the par-lor and immediately took command of the group. "Ladies, I wanted to once again tell you what a pleasure it was spending time with you earlier this evening. I will be returning tomorrow evening if any of you happen to be available for a visit." He smiled broadly. "One more thing," he added, "don't believe a thing my sister has to say about me. She's a teeny bit jealous—fearful of losing my attention. In fact, she sometimes tells horrid tales regarding my behavior, hoping to dissuade young ladies from keeping company with me. Don't you let her convince you with those exaggerated stories. We must join forces and conspire against her if I'm to have the pleasure of calling upon you fair maidens." Lewis directed an exaggerated wink at the group, then bowed and bade them good-night. The girls giggled in delight.

Lilly couldn't believe her ears. Her brother had completely outmaneuvered her.

CHAPTER 20

Lilly had given Matthew ample time. It was now blatantly obvi-ous the Associates were not going to hold Thaddeus Arnold accountable for his barbaric behavior. Having weighed the mer-its of the company's indecisiveness, Lilly prayed with fervor and then decided the Corporation must suffer the consequences of God's disapproval—using her, of course, as the instrument of His displeasure. Arnold's behavior was merely the catalyst God was using to move her forward. She was ashamed she had wavered in her earlier beliefs, but it was now abundantly clear she must move forward and bring the Corporation to ruin before further expansion could be completed.

Developing a plan, however, was much more difficult. Quick, decisive action was needed. However, the feat must be destructive enough to bring business to a halt—damaging enough to insure the Associates would rethink their earlier deci-sion to blemish the Massachusetts countryside with brick and mortar factories. Yet her plan must remain safe enough to keep the operatives from harm. She had learned from her earlier plots that stopping one machine, or even several, was not detrimental to the Corporation. Those incidents had merely succeeded in reprisals being meted out to the operatives by Thaddeus Arnold.

"No, I must figure a way to bring production completely to a halt," Lilly murmured as she strolled through the small but growing town. When the plan first began to grow in her mind, she had never figured it would be so difficult to sabotage the Corporation and their mills.

The wind whipped at her thin cloak, causing Lilly to pull it tight. No one would ever suspect that a worthless mill girl could have such an agenda against the Associates, and that was just as Lilly would have it. As God would have it, too. After all, Lilly felt quite confident that her mission had come from the Almighty himself. God had given her the desire to see the land returned to its original beauty—to see the Associates refund the monies and farms they had so greedily consumed. True, it would be difficult at this stage to see the mills destroyed and the land returned to pastures and farms, but Lilly knew that with God all things were possible.

Days passed as she attempted to devise her method. Finally, in the middle of the night an idea wove itself in and out of her sleep-induced haze. When Lilly awakened, the plan was clear.

"You seem a million miles away," Nadene said as the two finished making their bed.

"Hmm?" Lilly heard the words but scarcely registered them.

"Did you have a romantic dream?" Pru teased. "I did, and it was about that brother of yours."

Those words snapped Lilly to attention. "Lewis is bad news. He lives only for himself. Mark my words, you'll rue the day you met him."

Pru danced away toward the door. "He said you'd be like this, but honestly, Lilly, you don't have to worry about losing a brother." She winked and added, "Maybe instead, you'll gain a sister." She didn't wait for Lilly's reply but instead glided out the door as though she were skating on a pond of ice.

"Silly girl," Nadene remarked.

"More than silly. She's truly daft if she thinks Lewis can bring her anything but pain."

Pulling a brush through her crown of curls, Lilly returned to thoughts of her scheme. She made every attempt to find fault with the plan. She found none. Picking up Pru's tortoiseshell mirror, Lilly momentarily stared at her reflection. Her hair, she decided, was acceptable and so was her idea.

Nadene and Lilly rushed down the stairs, grabbed their cloaks from the row of pegs near the entrance, and rushed out the front door toward the Appleton. By the time the breakfast bell rang two hours later, Lilly's anticipation was rising to new heights. Feigning a problem with her machine, she urged Nadene to return home without her. Lagging behind until the room had emptied, Lilly picked up a piece of roving and held it to the flame of a whale-oil lamp hanging on the wall, then quickly threw the burning rope into a cart of roving that stood near the center of the room. Casting a glance over her shoulder as she left the room, Lilly nodded in satisfaction. The roving was beginning to smolder, and random flames were starting to lick along the edge of the cart.

Lilly hurried from the mill yard and down Jackson Street, finding herself out of breath when she finally arrived at the boardinghouse. The familiar smells of fried ham and biscuits greeted her as she pushed open the front door.

"Hurry, Lilly. I filled a plate for you," Nadene called out.

Lilly seated herself and slowly began cutting the piece of ham. Chewing slowly, she broke apart one of the thick biscuits and began to slather it with butter. "Would you pass the jam, please?"

Nadene stared open-mouthed at her friend. "You don't have time for jam. We need to leave in less than a minute, Lilly."

A tiny smile played at the corner of Lilly's lips. "If you insist," she replied, rising from the chair as she continued nibbling at the biscuit. "I think I'll finish this as we walk."

Nadene scurried out of the room and was waiting at the front door, holding Lilly's cloak. They were nearing the mill when they heard men and women screaming. Suddenly the tower bell began ringing. Nadene and Lilly glanced at each other, then began running toward the mill.

"Fire on an upper floor," one of the men yelled.

Nadene seized the man's arm. "Which floor?"

"Third—spinning room," he replied without hesitation.

"N-o-o-o!" Nadene cried as she began running toward the mill.

Lilly stared after her friend in disbelief. "Nadene, where are you going?" she screamed. "Come back here!" Lilly broke into a run. Why was Nadene rushing toward the building? What could she be thinking? Nadene had already made her way through the crowd of operatives who had gathered closer to the mill. Lilly glanced up. Flames were evident through the glass windows. As she grew closer to the building, Lilly saw Nadene arguing with one of the men. He was shaking his head and had grasped her friend's arm. Lilly watched in horror as Nadene broke loose from the man's grip and raced into the stairwell. With wooden legs she moved onward until she reached the man. "Where is she? Why didn't you stop her?" Lilly screamed.

The man looked at her, his face etched in disbelief. "I tried to stop her. I couldn't follow her—I was ordered to stay here and prevent anyone else from entering the building."

"Well, you didn't do your job very well, did you?" Lilly condemned as she attempted to push past him.

He pulled her back. "Maybe not with your friend, but I won't fail again. Now get back," he ordered.

"She'll die. I have to go after her," Lilly argued, pushing at his arm as she attempted to go around him.

He grasped her shoulder and turned her away from the building. "No! Now get back."

"Lilly! What are you doing? Get back from the building."

Lilly turned to see Matthew running in her direction. "Nadene's up there—she's gone to the third floor. I must get her out. Please help me!" Lilly pleaded.

Matthew placed his arms around her. "If you'll move away from the building, I'll see what I can do. Give me your word that you won't attempt to follow me."

"I promise. Just please hurry," she begged, moving away from the entryway.

She watched until Matthew was out of sight. What if he

found Nadene . . . dead? What if he couldn't find her at all? "Matthew will find her—he must. Surely the fire hasn't spread enough to cause Nadene immense harm," she murmured. The hollow words did little to calm the growing uneasiness that was seeping into her consciousness.

She strained forward, watching the stairwell. Two men exited the building and issued orders before rushing off toward some unknown destination. Lilly paced back and forth while maintaining a steadfast gaze toward the entryway. Would Matthew never return? Perhaps she should break through the guards and go search for Nadene herself. Head raised high and shoulders straight, Lilly approached the Appleton.

One of the men stood resolutely, with elbows bent as he rested his beefy hands on his hips. His lips tightened into a straight, determined line as she grew closer. "Where do you think you're going?" he asked, moving directly in front of her.

Lilly attempted to ignore the man's question and push her way through. Too soon she found it impossible to break his grasp. Shaking her arm, she gave him a frosty glare. "Turn me loose!"

"Not a chance," he replied. "I was ordered to keep spectators out—you, in particular," he added with a grin.

Lilly stomped her foot. "You turn me loose or you'll answer to Matthew Cheever!"

"Really? Well, he's the one who told me to keep you out of there," the man replied while turning toward the burning building. "Besides, there's Mr. Cheever now."

Lilly swung her head toward the stairwell. Matthew was carrying Nadene's lifeless body in his arms. "Lilly, come quickly," he called out, never breaking his stride.

Lilly pushed past the men and ran at breakneck speed, her cape billowing open in the crisp breeze until she was finally alongside Matthew. "Is she . . ." The words stuck in her throat.

"No, but her breathing is shallow—there was a lot of smoke in the room. She's unconscious and burned in several places. Let's get her back to the boardinghouse. I'm hopeful she'll come around, but I'm afraid she's going to have some terrible scars.

Would you carry that?" he asked, nodding toward the Bible lying atop Nadene's soot-covered dress.

Lilly reached up and gathered the book into her hands. "It was her grandmother's Bible. Her mother gave it to Nadene when she moved to Lowell," Lilly explained as she attempted to clean the stained leather cover with her dress. Words of wisdom and insight to the Scriptures were inscribed upon the pages— Nadene's only link with her beloved grandmother. Of course she would walk through fire to retrieve it.

"I had to pry it from her hand. What was it doing in the spinning room, anyway? There are rules against reading at work," Matthew challenged before breaking into a fit of coughing.

Lilly glared in response. "Rules? My friend is dying and you're telling me about rules?"

Matthew glanced down at her. "Don't overstate the situation in order to change the subject, Lilly. Nadene is injured, but she's not going to die. We don't permit reading or other activities at work because we want to prevent you girls from injury. And although her reading didn't cause the fire, the fact that she ran back in the building was based solely upon the fact that she wanted to retrieve her Bible. Had the Bible been at home where it belonged, Nadene would be safe."

"Or if the fire had never started," Lilly murmured.

"The fire was an accident over which we had no control. Fires and textile mills are constant companions. The Bible, however, should not have been there. Nadene *had* control of that situation. If she had followed the rules, this accident could have been prevented. Do you understand what I'm saying?"

Lilly nodded in acknowledgment. She longed to tell him he was the one who didn't understand—that she alone was responsible for Nadene's perilous situation. Yet she remained silent, lacking the courage it would take to speak the truth. Guilt wound around her heart like roving to a spindle.

"I sent one of the men to fetch Dr. Barnard. Try not to worry. The damage is minimal, and we should be back in operation by morning."

He was obviously attempting to cheer her, but his words only made it more difficult for Lilly to bear. Nadene was injured, and she had failed in her mission. *I should have waited until evening to start the fire,* she thought. But having evaluated the prospect of remaining behind after the final bell, Lilly knew such a feat would have been impossible. Thaddeus Arnold was always the last one out of the room each evening, making sure the lamps were snuffed and the room was in proper order for the next morning's work. He would never permit an operative in the spinning room after his own final departure. But at the breakfast and dinner bells, the man wasn't nearly so cautious. Like the rest of them, he was anxious to rush home for his meal. Knowing she must protect the lives of those working in the mills, Lilly had hoped that the half-hour break would permit the fire adequate time to do its damage. She had been wrong.

She touched Matthew's arm as they reached the front door of the boardinghouse. "If there was so little damage to the Appleton, how is it Nadene's condition is so dreadful?" she inquired with her voice trembling.

"From all appearances, her cloak caught on fire, which caused the burns to her hands and arms. Smoke caused the remainder of her health problems. I'm guessing she became disoriented in the haze and couldn't find her way out of the building."

The front door opened. It was obvious Miss Addie had been watching for them, no doubt informed by some of the girls who had run ahead to explain the situation.

"Follow me, Matthew. We'll put her in my bedroom. Dr. Barnard is waiting," Addie instructed as she led the way to her room. "Put her on the bed—carefully, we don't want to cause her undue pain."

Matthew nodded his agreement before lowering Nadene onto the crisp white sheet. "I'll leave her in your hands, Dr. Barnard. I must get back to the mill and then report to Mr. Boott."

"Absolutely, Matthew. You've done all you can for the girl. Miss Addie and I will see to her care," Dr. Barnard replied.

Lilly could no longer hold her emotions in check. Tears rolled down her cheeks as she viewed Nadene's condition. Along one of Nadene's arms angry red flesh appeared to be blistering, while the other was interspersed with purplish black wounds. Both hands were charred and blistered. The smell was unlike anything Lilly had ever known. She felt her stomach churn and knew she might very well lose the contents of her stomach.

Backing out of the room, Lilly fought the sensation of dizziness that threatened to send her to the floor. *What have I done? Dear God, what have I done?*

———

Matthew rushed back to the Appleton, relieved when he was met by a calm-looking Hugh Cummiskey. "We've got things here under control, Mr. Cheever," Hugh reported. "The fire is out and once the smoke has cleared, work can begin."

"How much damage?" Matthew inquired.

"None to the machinery or the building itself. A cart of roving is ruined. Other than that, nothing of consequence."

Matthew breathed a sigh of relief. He didn't want to carry a report of extensive damage to his boss. "I'll feel better if I take a look for myself before reporting to Mr. Boott. He may ask if I've seen the damage for myself."

Hugh nodded in agreement. "No need to explain, Mr. Cheever. I understand."

Matthew ascended the stairway and surveyed the room. Cummiskey was correct. There was little damage, and work could certainly resume by morning if not sooner. Already the unpleasant smell of smoke had subsided, and several men were cleaning soot from the machinery and floor. Satisfied there was nothing further needing his attention, he returned to the mill yard, where Cummiskey awaited him.

He gave Cummiskey a slap on the shoulder. "You were right, Hugh. Thank you for your valuable assistance," Matthew said. Turning to the supervisor, he added, "Mr. Arnold, I'll leave it to your discretion to determine when work can commence." He then headed off toward Mr. Boott's home. He disliked being the bearer of bad news, especially when it entailed production at one of the mills. But he doubted whether anyone else had rushed to inform Boott. After all, it wasn't a pleasant task. He sounded the doorknocker, surprised when Boott himself answered the door.

"None of the help is around when you need them," Kirk said as he ushered Matthew into his office. "What brings you here this time of day, Matthew?"

At Kirk's invitation, Matthew seated himself. "I wanted to personally advise you there's been a fire in the spinning room at the Appleton." Kirk jumped up from his chair at the report. "Very little damage. We'll be operational by morning. Perhaps earlier," Matthew quickly added.

"Details—give me details, my boy," Kirk insisted.

Matthew reported what little he could and awaited Kirk's instructions.

"Of course, I'd like to know *how* the fire got started, but I doubt we'll ever gain that piece of information. However, it appears we may need to take further safety precautions. Why don't you and the supervisors meet and discuss future prevention. You can report your ideas to me, and then we can make a final decision on implementation."

Matthew agreed, pleased that their meeting had been brief and Mr. Boott had remained calm. "I'll report back to you by Friday," Matthew said as they walked onto the expansive front porch.

"Friday will be fine. I almost forgot—Isabelle, Neva, and several other relatives are arriving on Friday. I promised them a tour of the Appleton. They find this industrialization process difficult to fathom without actually seeing for themselves. Once they get inside, I'm certain they won't want to remain for long. I told Isabelle I would have you take charge of the tour. I hope you don't mind. There's no hurry, for I think I've convinced Neva to remain in Lowell until after the holidays. And, of course, we'll expect you to join us for dinner Saturday evening."

"Certainly. I'll be pleased to escort them through the mill," Matthew replied. He knew there was no other acceptable answer.

Soon after Matthew had placed Nadene upon the bed, the cool, fresh air from Addie's bedroom window, along with the vinegar Dr. Barnard had placed under her nose, rendered Nadene conscious. With Nadene's awakening, her pain was clearly evident. Lilly couldn't bear to watch the ministrations as Addie and Dr. Barnard separated Nadene's fingers. Her friend's hands resembled two giant spiderwebs by the time Dr. Barnard secured the splints and bandages. Lilly had followed Dr. Barnard's directions and mixed a salve of linseed oil and lime-water and then quickly exited the room, offering to complete Addie's household chores.

While Lilly began paring potatoes for the evening meal, Nadene's moans cut through the afternoon silence of the boardinghouse. Lilly began humming, then singing aloud, hoping she could drown out the sounds of her friend's misery, along with her own guilt. When that didn't work, she began to pray—first for Nadene's healing, then for her own forgiveness. She wasn't sure if it was answered prayer or the fact that Dr. Barnard had completed his treatment, but Nadene's moans finally ceased. Although her own feelings of guilt had not completely diminished, Lilly knew she was forgiven for the part she had played in Nadene's injuries. Along with that forgiveness came the awakening realization that her behavior had been for the fulfillment of her own selfish desires rather than at God's direction.

Your sinful behavior is not from God, a small voice seemed to whisper to her consciousness.

"I know, Lord," she whispered. "Look what I've done in the name of righteous justice." She closed her eyes, hoping she wouldn't cry. But she was unsuccessful, and giant tears wet her thick dark lashes before tumbling down her cheeks. *How could I have been so wrong—so blind to the pain I might cause? I thought you'd given me a mission, but I've messed things up so badly.*

"Are you salting the potatoes with those tears?" Addie asked as she placed her arm comfortingly around Lilly's shoulder.

Lilly sniffed and attempted a smile. "How's Nadene?"

"She's resting. Dr. Barnard gave her some paregoric. You better get back over to the mill. If they've started up production, Mr. Arnold will expect you to be there no matter what Nadene's condition. Don't you worry. I'll be able to hear Nadene if she awakens."

"I know you're right, but going back into that mill is the last thing I want to do, Miss Addie."

Once again Addie pulled Lilly into a comforting embrace. "I know, dearie, but there's nothing to fear. I'm sure the fire was just one of those rare occurrences that won't ever happen again. As the Judge used to say, you can't let fear rule your life—you've got to get back up on a horse when it throws you."

Lilly nodded. The lump in her throat prevented a reply. *If Miss Addie knew the cause of the fire, she wouldn't be so quick to offer kind reassurances,* Lilly thought as she walked toward the Appleton. Wrapping her cape tightly against a bracing current of cold air that whipped down the street, Lilly tucked her head down and moved resolutely toward the mill yard. She must find Mr. Arnold and ask if he would permit her to operate Nadene's frames. Locating Thaddeus Arnold was not difficult. He was rushing about the mill yard with his chest swelled out like a banty rooster as he issued orders to the clustered girls and pointed them toward the stairwell.

Hurrying toward the distasteful little man, Lilly called out, "Mr. Arnold! May I have a word with you?"

He peered over the top of his spectacles, his gaze roaming over Lilly's body in a manner that caused her acute discomfort. He beckoned her forward.

Keeping her eyes focused downward, Lilly approached him. It required all the humility she could muster to stand before the pompous little man. "Would you permit me to operate Nadene's frames until she is able to return?"

His lips formed a malevolent grin. "And my consent would be worth *what* to you?"

Lilly could feel the blood pumping, pulsing and coursing its way through her body, pounding upward into her temples. If she didn't hold her temper in check, she knew she would explode at the pompous excuse of a man standing before her. She lifted her head and met his beady-eyed stare. "Why, Mr. Arnold, I was merely hoping to keep production at full rate—hoping to be of some assistance to you in this difficult time. With Sarah gone home for several months and now Nadene unable to tend her frames, I was certain you would be distraught over their vacancies." Her voice was sweet and melodious, the very essence of a spring breeze floating through a brisk November morn. Even she was surprised by the gentleness of her reply.

Mr. Arnold appeared to be overwhelmed by her response. There was a momentary appearance of trust in his gaze. Ever so slightly, she lifted her eyebrows—waiting, anticipating his agreement. His lips turned upward into a smile that revealed his yellowed teeth. "You're a difficult girl to figure out, Miss Armbruster. I never presumed you would be concerned about production in the spinning room. So you're offering to operate Nadene's frames while she's recovering? Just because you want to help me keep production at full rate?"

Lilly's gaze was fixed on his bony fingers as they moved across the growth of stubble along his jaw. "And because I want Nadene to receive her pay. She has her family to support."

A spark of recognition shone in his eyes. "Ah, so it isn't that you want to help *me,* is it, Miss Armbruster? What you really want to do is help your friend remain on the pay ledger, even though she won't be working. Isn't that correct?"

He was on the attack. "Technically, I wish to help you both, Mr. Arnold," she replied, her voice resonating with all of the meekness she could muster.

He folded his arms across his sunken chest. "You realize I can order you to operate Nadene's frames without additional pay. Operation of the machinery is at my discretion. So once again, Miss Armbruster, I would ask this: what is my agreement worth to you?"

Lilly met his lustful gaze with an icy glare. "My silence. At least for the present time."

Thaddeus's mask of confusion was quickly replaced by a scowl of recognition. "I'll permit you to work Nadene's frames, and you may sign the ledger and collect payment on her behalf. If you betray our agreement, you'll suffer dearly. Speak to no one of this arrangement," he added. She remained transfixed, amazed he had so willingly agreed to her request. "Why are you standing there gaping at me? Get back to work!" he hissed before stalking off toward the counting room.

Lilly rushed toward the steps before he could recant his decision. The disgusting odor of smoke filled her nostrils as she moved up the stairs, but the smell was nothing compared to the vile odor of burnt flesh. For as long as she lived, Lilly would never forget that smell.

The spinning frames remained silent while the girls scrubbed soot from the floors and equipment. One of the mechanics had managed to unseal several of the windows, and cold, fresh air was beginning to waft through the room. Lilly inhaled deeply, grabbed a pail of water, and began cleaning Nadene's frames. She didn't know how she could possibly manage four frames, but somehow she would—she must.

Penance was required, and penance would be given.

CHAPTER 21

The next morning, work in the spinning room returned to normal. For everyone except Lilly and Nadene, that is. Nadene was now ensconced in Addie's bedroom having her bandages frequently changed, while Lilly was furiously attempting to operate four spinning frames instead of two.

Shortly after lunch, Kirk Boott came on the floor accompanied by several men. When he recognized Lilly, he paused long enough to inquire as to her health and well-being, then briefly introduced her to William Thurston and Nathan Appleton before moving down the line with Mr. Arnold. Lilly thought Boott scrutinized her for a rather long time, given the situation. He seemed as though he wanted to ask her something but instead turned his attention back to his companions. Lilly felt awash in guilt. Surely he didn't have some idea of her responsibility for the fire.

By the time the evening bell rang, announcing the day's end, Lilly was exhausted. For twelve hours she'd moved back and forth among the frames, dampening her fingers before quickly reaching in and mending the broken strands of roving, replacing empty spindles of roving with full ones, and pulling off each of the full spindles of thread to be replaced by an empty spindle. However, it seemed as if she always had the incorrect spindle in her hand at the improper moment.

"Managing to keep up with your frames?" Thaddeus snidely inquired as she brushed past him on her way through the narrow doorway.

"Yes, thank you." She didn't want to smile sweetly, but she did.

His fingers wrapped around her wrist. "If you decide you'd like to make some other arrangements, I'll try to accommodate. You look quite weary," he whispered, releasing the hold on her wrist and then patting her backside.

She slapped at his hand. He winked and gave her a lewd grin that made her shudder as she ran down the winding staircase, out through the mill yard, and down Jackson Street. Pushing open the front door, she pulled off her cape, hung it on the peg, and hurried in to see Nadene. "How are you feeling this evening?" she inquired, her breath coming in short sputters as she leaned against the doorjamb.

Nadene gave her a smile. "Better than you, it would appear," Nadene remarked in a cheerful voice. "You look as though you've had the longest workday of your life. What's wrong?"

Lilly was making excuses about not sleeping well when Prudence pushed open the front door. "Did you hear there's been another accident?" she called out while slamming the door behind her. "This time at No. 2."

Nadene reached out for Prudence as she entered Addie's bedroom, then stopped when the pain refused to allow her fingers to work. "What kind of accident? Was anyone injured?"

"Nope, no one injured, praise be to God," Pru added almost as an afterthought. "Appears work will be at a standstill unless they get things fixed this evening."

"What happened?" Lilly persisted. She couldn't halt the feeling of adulation that swept through her. An accident had occurred; no one was injured; and she hadn't been involved. It appeared God was taking care of matters on His own. After Nadene's injury, Lilly had prayed for forgiveness. She had even promised to bow out of the retribution business, telling God she now realized He could handle matters without her intervention. And so He had. This latest accident was affirmation at its finest, she decided.

"There's a jam in the waterwheel, or maybe one of the cogs is broken. I'm not sure. But from what I heard, Mr. Moody is mad as a wet hen. He says the men weren't being careful or some such thing. Anyway, we're not to report for work tomorrow unless they send someone to fetch us," she finished with a smile.

"No work, no pay. Let's hope things are fixed soon," Miss Addie remarked, a twinkle in her eye. "If they keep you off work too long, you'll be forced to make it through the week without buying a new hair ribbon or two."

Lilly then fetched a plate of food and brought it to Nadene. "Can you manage to feed yourself?" she asked, looking at her friend's splayed fingers.

Nadene gave a deep, racking cough. "No, but I'm not hungry. Why don't you sit with me and you can eat it," she said when the coughing finally subsided. "Miss Addie fed me earlier."

Lilly plopped down on the small sewing rocker and began forking the food into her mouth. She was ravenous. Although there was little time for manners when eating her breakfast and noonday meals, she usually attempted to eat her evening meal more slowly. However, it seemed impossible to do so this evening.

"Prudence says your brother has been courting her. They've met after dinner twice this week. She tells me Lewis is quite the gentleman. I think she's smitten with him. I do wish I could find a man who would take an interest in me. That would certainly take care of my worries," Nadene lamented as Lilly took another bite of lamb stew.

"Or add to them," Lilly replied in between bites of ham and green beans. "I wouldn't wish my brother's attentions on anyone. Believe me, he's not the kind of man who treats a woman with any respect. His interest is in money, not Prudence. Money is the only thing that has ever held Lewis's interest. Perhaps I should talk with Prudence."

"Please don't. She'll know I've told you and never forgive me. Lewis told her you would discourage the relationship. In fact, he said you'd accuse him of being after her money."

"And she prefers to believe him? Has he inquired about her funds?"

Nadene giggled. "Yes, but she fibbed to him. She told Lewis her family is quite wealthy but her father thought working in the mills would give her a better appreciation of money."

Lilly sputtered on the piece of biscuit she had shoved in her mouth. "She didn't!"

Nadene nodded her head in affirmation. "Prudence said he appeared to believe her. I did mention that lying was a sin, but Pru merely smiled and said it was an ungentlemanly question that didn't deserve a proper answer."

"It would appear as if Lewis has met his match—at least for the time being. I hope Pru doesn't get hurt. Lewis can be cruel and vindictive, but I'll not betray your confidence," Lilly replied as she rose from the rocking chair.

Nadene struggled to sit up. "Where are you going? I wanted to visit."

Lilly gave her a feeble smile. "I'd like nothing better. However, I promised John Farnsworth I'd accompany him into town. He said he needed some help choosing a birthday present for Miss Addie. Don't breathe a word."

"So Mr. Farnsworth is courting Miss Addie. They'll make a wonderful twosome, don't you think?"

Lilly nodded. "If I get back early, I'll stop in again."

"Oh yes, please do. I'll want to hear what you pick out."

Lilly glanced at the clock in the hallway, ran her fingers along each side of her head, hoping the loose strands were tucked into place, then hurried out the door. John Farnsworth was waiting when she arrived at the corner. "I hope I didn't keep you waiting long," she greeted.

"I just arrived," he said as he came alongside her and they walked toward town. "I hope you have an idea where we might find a gift. Until now, I've only visited the livery stable, the wheelwright, the general store, and Mrs. Clawson's pastry shop. I've not visited any of the other establishments here in Lowell."

Lilly turned and gave him a bright smile. "Prudence tells me that Mr. Whidden and Mr. Childs have both recently received new shipments in their stores, everything from crockery to fabrics and lace. Did you have something particular in mind?"

He gave a hearty laugh. "Well, I certainly *don't* want to purchase any crockery or kettles. That would only serve to remind Miss Addie of her daily chores. I think I'd prefer to give her something a bit more personal, though nothing that would cause eyebrows to rise. I had given consideration to some pretty combs for her hair. She has these few wisps of hair on each side that appear to escape and cause her bother. But perhaps a pretty shawl might be a better choice."

Lilly pictured the short flying strands of hair that Miss Addie was constantly pushing behind her ears. "I think the combs are a wonderful idea, Mr. Farnsworth. But I'm sure she would be delighted with either item." Lilly couldn't contain her enthusiasm. "I believe we could find the combs or a shawl at Mr. Whidden's store; it's located on Gorham Street," she advised as they rounded the corner.

Mintie was glad she had chosen to wear her woolen cape. A cold north wind was attacking the few leaves that remained attached to their trees. Those that had already fallen now rustled beneath her feet as she clipped along at a steady pace toward Mrs. Hirman's house. She didn't want to be late.

"Tardiness is an excuse for laziness"—at least that is what the Judge had always told his daughters. Not that Adelaide had listened to half of what the Judge had dutifully attempted to teach them in their formative years. "I don't know what's gotten into her," Mintie muttered, still upset that Adelaide had refused to attend the formation meeting of the Ladies' Temperance Society. After all, what would Mrs. Hirman and the other good women of Lowell think of her sister's absence? No doubt she would be forced into making excuses for Adelaide. And what would she say? That her sister had little interest in fighting for temperance?

Mintie slowed her pace a bit, allowing herself to remain behind a group of girls who were obviously walking to the shops in town, anxious to spend their earnings. "Just like Adelaide! Off to purchase a piece of silk or lace, not frugal enough to save for a rainy day," she mused, watching as the girls crossed Gorham Street and entered Mr. Whidden's store. She stopped momentarily when she heard a man's familiar voice as a couple left the store. She squinted her eyes and peered across the street. The two were laughing as the man handed a brown-paper-wrapped package to the girl he was with. Mintie's lips screwed into a tight little pucker and her eyes widened. *John Farnsworth and Lilly Armbruster.* She moved behind the trunk of a giant maple tree, even though they would probably not notice her in the dark, unable to tear her gaze away from the sight. Farnsworth extended his arm, and Mintie watched in horror as Lilly leaned in, said something, then looped her arm through John's. She continued staring after them as they sauntered down the street, slowing in front of the shop windows, pointing at one item or another, their laughter echoing through the thin night air.

When they were finally out of sight, Mintie peeled herself away from the tree and stood staring after them as they continued arm in arm down the street. "I wonder what Adelaide will think about this!" she muttered before turning on her heel and proceeding toward Mrs. Hirman's house on John Street.

The turnout for the meeting was greater than anticipated, and Mintie found herself squeezed into a tiny space at the rear of the parlor, where it was difficult both to see and hear what was being said. Her mind continued to wander back to earlier events of the evening. Perhaps it was a good thing Adelaide had chosen to remain home tonight. What if she had been forced to deal with the sight of John and Lilly? Mintie immediately decided she would stop and visit with Adelaide on her way home.

Mrs. Hirman interrupted Mintie's thoughts when introducing Mr. Thorndyke, who promptly passed pamphlets out, enumerating the necessary steps for organizing an effective temperance union. The illustrious speaker, as Mrs. Hirman had described him, proceeded to discuss each step in minute detail. Just when Mintie thought the meeting could go on no longer, Mr. Thorndyke opened the meeting for questions.

Mintie squirmed in her seat until Mrs. Hirman finally announced that refreshments were being served in the dining room. Making her excuses for an early exit, Mintie offered perfunctory thanks, rushed out the door, and headed toward home.

She was on a mission to save her sister from the English scoundrel who was undoubtedly seeking favors from the young Miss Armbruster. Mintie's feet couldn't carry her quickly enough. Adelaide needed to accept the fact that John Farnsworth was a scallywag through and through. And as for Lilly— well, she was obviously intent on finding a way out of the mills, and John Farnsworth was her answer! "That young woman is getting more than she bargained for. Just wait until she discovers John Farnsworth is a traitor. I'd say that Lilly Armbruster and John Farnsworth are quite a match," Mintie muttered as she scurried toward Jackson Street. Yes indeed, the sooner Adelaide knew of this liaison, the better.

———

An insistent rapping at the front door caused Addie to shift uncomfortably in order to get to her feet.

Lilly scurried from Addie's bedroom calling over her shoulder, "You sit still, Miss Addie. I'll find out who it is."

The knocking continued nonstop, and Addie couldn't imagine what must be wrong. She looked to Nadene and shrugged. "Someone certainly sounds urgent."

Before Nadene could reply they heard Lilly question, "Miss Beecher, is something wrong?"

Mintie's determined voice demanded answers. "Where's my sister?"

Nadene began to cough, causing Addie to reach for a glass of water. "I wish she'd stayed home," Addie whispered as she offered Nadene the drink.

"Is she in there with that girl—the one that was burned?" Mintie again demanded.

Addie sighed and replaced the glass on the stand. "So much for our enjoyable time."

"Yes. We were visiting in the bedroom—keeping Nadene company," Lilly announced as Mintie entered the doorway.

"Adelaide! Come here—we need to talk," Mintie commanded from the doorway.

"Why don't you join us in here? My foot is causing me pain," Addie said, pointing toward the footstool.

Mintie crooked her finger. "Out here now. We need privacy. It's important."

Addie rose from the chair and limped after her sister. "I'll be back shortly," she whispered to Nadene and Lilly.

Mintie turned toward her sister as soon as she had crossed into the kitchen, which was the only room that proved vacant. "You'd better sit down. I have some news—some unpleasant news—about your Englishman."

"John Farnsworth? Oh, Mintie, I don't want to have that 'he's a spy' conversation again. I've listened to all your stories, and I still don't believe John is disloyal to this country." There was a hint of irritation in Addie's voice.

Mintie pointed toward a chair. "Sit down, Adelaide. It's worse than that. You've been betrayed. Not only is that Farnsworth fellow a traitor and a spy, he's a womanizer."

"A *what*? Oh, Mintie, would you please stop this nonsense."

"It's not nonsense. You may recall that the temperance meeting was this evening." Mintie didn't wait for an answer. "I, of course, attended by myself since you elected to stay home. I was walking down Gorham Street minding my own business when something caused me to look over toward Whidden's Mercantile. And who do you think I saw walking out of the store, arm in arm, laughing and talking like two lovebirds?"

Addie gave her sister a blank stare. "I have absolutely no idea, Mintie, but I'm sure you are going to tell me." Why couldn't her sister just leave her to enjoy the evening?

Mintie pursed her lips and pushed her spectacles onto the

bridge of her long, narrow nose. "John Farnsworth and," she paused momentarily, "your little boarder, Lilly Armbruster."

Addie was silent.

"Did you hear me, Adelaide? John Farnsworth is courting Lilly Armbruster. I saw them with my own eyes. I'm sure you'd have to admit that Lilly was gone from the house earlier this evening. Well? She left the house, didn't she?"

Addie nodded her head. "She was gone for a short time this evening."

"There you have it. You can't trust anyone. I told you that Farnsworth was up to no good, but did you believe me? And that Armbruster girl, I didn't like her from the day she arrived. But did you listen to me? No. You took her in, treated her well, and now she's turned on you. I'd wager she even knows you've taken a liking to Farnsworth, but that didn't stop her."

Addie placed her hands over her ears. "Stop it, Mintie. I don't want to hear any more of this nonsense. I can't believe Lilly is interested in John Farnsworth."

Mintie gave her a disgusted look before wagging her finger back and forth in front of Addie's face. "You think Lilly wants to remain a mill girl the rest of her life? Farnsworth may not be wealthy, but I've heard he's paid a handsome wage, and the Corporation is building him that fine house. It's enough to turn a girl's head."

"You'll not convince me any of this is true, so you may as well quit trying," Addie declared. "If you'd like to visit about something pleasant, you're welcome to join us in the bedroom. If not, I suggest you return home," Addie announced as she rose from her chair.

"After what I've seen this evening, I have no intention of exchanging pleasantries with Lilly Armbruster. I'll bid you good-night, Adelaide." Head raised high, Mintie marched out the front door without further comment.

As soon as the front door had closed, Addie sat back down, her mind reeling with the accusations she'd just heard from her sister's lips. Could it possibly be true? Lilly was a beautiful girl, capable of turning any man's head. But wouldn't she choose a handsome young man such as Matthew Cheever over a man old enough to be her father? Not that some girls didn't prefer older men, Addie argued with herself. But it was Lilly who had encouraged the relationship with John Farnsworth. Why would she do such a thing if she were interested in him herself? None of this was making any sense. Perhaps the best thing was to confront Lilly.

Addie hobbled down the hallway, surprised that the throbbing sensation had disappeared from her foot. She could hear Lilly's muffled voice and then listened as both girls said a quiet amen.

"Did Miss Mintie leave?" Nadene inquired as Addie entered the room.

Addie nodded and took her seat opposite Lilly. "My foot isn't hurting as much."

Nadene and Lilly smiled at each other. "We've been praying for you," they uttered in unison.

"Thank you. It appears your prayers are being answered," Addie responded. "It's chilly outdoors tonight, isn't it?" she inquired, her gaze focused upon Lilly.

Lilly gave an enthusiastic nod. "Oh yes, the wind is as blustery and cold as a frosty January morning. It took a good five minutes in front of the fire to ward off the chill when I returned home."

Addie picked up her needle and began darning a hole in one of her woolen stockings. "I was surprised you went out on such a cold night. Did you have a meeting to attend?" she asked without looking up from her sewing.

Addie watched from under hooded lids as Lilly fidgeted and then glanced toward Nadene. "No. One of the girls mentioned a new shipment had been delivered to the bookstore. I was anxious to see what new titles had arrived."

"I see. And did any of the other girls go with you?"

"No, none of the other girls."

Addie couldn't look at her young boarder. Obviously Mintie was correct. If there nothing to hide, Lilly would have merely told the truth and explained why she and John had gone into town. Unfortunately, there appeared to be no other explanation for Lilly's behavior.

That night before blowing out her candle, Lilly took up her Bible. *Oh, Father,* she began to pray, *thank you for the wonderful day. I'm excited to know that you have the ability to control the fate of the mills, without using me to do something dangerous or harmful. Soon the enemy will fall, and I couldn't be happier. Once they see what they're up against, that you stand between them and their fortune, they'll hightail it out of here once and for all. Please, just keep my friends from harm.*

She opened her Bible and found herself staring down at the twenty-fourth chapter of Proverbs. It seemed as good a place as any to read. Her heart fairly soared, and the idea of bolstering herself further with Scripture was pure delight.

Verse ten caught her attention. " 'If thou faint in the day of adversity, thy strength is small.' " Her voice was barely audible as she mouthed the words. Lilly nodded in agreement. The need was great to stand firm when problems arose. She wanted her strength to be very evident.

She continued to scan the verses, hardly giving them much true attention. Her joy over the problems sustained by the mill that day kept drawing her back to thoughts on the matter. It wasn't until Lilly reached the seventeenth verse that she took notice.

"Rejoice not when thine enemy falleth, and let not thine heart be glad when he stumbleth: Lest the Lord see it, and it displease him, and he turn away his wrath from him."

Lilly read the verse over and over again. Rejoice not. It hardly seemed fair that a person was not to take joy in the defeat of her enemies. Lilly thought perhaps she'd misunderstood the meaning. She tried analyzing the verse in a different way, but there didn't seem to be another way to look at it.

She flipped the page to the twenty-fifth chapter. Perhaps Solomon was simply feeling generous that day. Maybe she'd find further proof of her own feelings in the next passages.

Verse twenty-one loomed out at her. *"If thine enemy be hungry, give him bread to eat; and if he be thirsty, give him water to drink."*

She slammed the book shut. Maybe God would prefer she just go to sleep and not worry about it. After all, she wasn't called to cause further harm, so perhaps she could avoid dealing with her enemies completely. She sighed. *But of course I have to deal with them. They're all around me—maybe not here in my room, but the very room I share has been provided by them.*

She snuffed out the candle and snuggled down into the bed. Sometimes God's Word made no sense at all.

CHAPTER 22

Matthew approached the front door of the Boott home at seven o'clock sharp with feelings of both equanimity and trepidation. While he wanted to be counted among Boott's confidants, a member of the elite inner circle, he disliked being thrust into the role of Isabelle's suitor. Other than their connection through Kirk Boott and the fact that they were both single, Isabelle and Matthew shared few interests. Perhaps during this visit they would find some common ground, and Matthew would view her in a new light. Thus far he'd seen a selfish, self-indulgent young woman who cared for little except the latest fashions and traveling abroad.

The front door opened, and Kirk greeted him with a genial smile. "Pleased you could make it, Matthew. I believe there's someone in the parlor anxiously awaiting your arrival," he said as he gave him a friendly slap on the shoulder. "Shall we join the others?"

Matthew nodded, though he had a growing distaste for social gatherings of any type. They made him uncomfortable, yet he had learned long ago that dinner parties were a necessary evil in the business world—invented by a woman in order to spend a bit of time with her husband, he had decided.

The parlor was filled with chattering men and women dressed in their finery, each attempting to impress the others with a bit of gossip or talk of the latest social event. Paul Moody was standing near the fireplace, and Matthew began working his way through the crowd toward the man who capably headed up the mechanics of the mills while supervising the operation of the locks and canals.

"Mr. Moody," he called out as he edged a bit closer. Continuing to weave his way through the crowd, he finally reached Moody's side. "Glad to see you. I had hoped to get over and visit with you today but ran short of time. Any progress to report on that broken cog?"

Paul accepted Matthew's proffered hand, giving it a hearty shake. "Good to see you, Matthew. To be honest, I didn't know if I'd be here tonight. In some respects I had hoped for an excuse to stay away. I detest these required dinner parties," he said under his breath. "However, we managed to repair the waterwheel over at No. 2, and the mill is in full operation once again."

"That's great news. The last I had heard, it appeared we'd be nonoperational for at least the full day tomorrow. Any idea what caused the problem?"

Paul rubbed a weatherworn hand across his forehead. "I dislike reporting this, but it appears there's been some foul play."

"What?" Matthew couldn't believe his ears. "You think someone wants the mill shut down?"

"I don't know what the actual intent might have been, but from our investigation it appears someone spent a great deal of time and effort under the darkness of night in order to damage the waterwheel. That cog couldn't have possibly broken under normal conditions."

"It's not that I don't believe your assessment, but the whole concept is difficult to believe. What purpose would it serve?"

Paul shrugged his shoulders and met Matthew's gaze. "Perhaps someone bears a grudge against one of us or harbors jealousy over the return of profits we've begun to realize. And, of course, there are still those anti-Federalists who believe an agrarian society is the salvation of this country. Who knows how far they would go to make a point."

Matthew stared into the fire, his thoughts whirling with the prospect that the Corporation might be dealing with deliberate criminal activity. If that were the case, there would most likely be future attacks. Any stoppage of the mills would mean a short-fall in profits, a dreadful prospect for the Associates. No doubt the Bostonians' anger would initially be directed toward the Lowell management. And once their anger subsided, they would expect a quick and certain solution. It would be best to have the situation in control before any further trouble erupted. But how?

"How are things progressing with the Catholic church? Kirk mentioned Bishop Fenwick was to make a visit by the end of the year. Any word in that regard? It would appear that a church could be a stabilizing factor with the Irish," Paul commented.

Matthew's body snapped to attention. "You think the Irish are involved in this waterwheel incident?"

"Whoa! I didn't say any such thing—the thought hadn't even crossed my mind. I was making an inquiry regarding a totally different topic, Matthew."

"So you *don't* think the Irish are involved?"

Paul grasped Matthew's shoulder and gave him a broad smile. "If I knew who was responsible, I'd have already taken care of matters. I have no more reason to suspect the Irish than anyone else in this town."

Matthew nodded. "I'm sorry. It appears as if I jumped to conclusions, Mr. Moody. To answer your question, Bishop Fenwick has sent word he'd rather wait until spring for his journey to Lowell. It seems he dislikes traveling in cold weather. He did say he would be able to make an announcement to his Catholic believers in Lowell upon his arrival."

"I assume that means the bishop has received approval from higher authority to bless the project?"

"So it would seem," Matthew agreed. "Mr. Boott was pleased by the message although a bit irritated the bishop was delaying his visit to Lowell."

"*There* you are, you naughty boy."

The syrupy words pulled Matthew's attention away from Moody. He turned, his face now warm from the heat of the blazing fire. Isabelle stood beside him in a pale blue gown, the square neckline and sleeves embroidered with a shimmering gold thread, and her lips formed into a tiny pout. The voluminous sleeves, so popular of late, were held out by some manner, causing it to be almost impossible to stand very close to Isabelle from the side.

"Isabelle! What a lovely gown." Trite, but he could think of nothing else to say at the moment. It broke with etiquette that she should seek out a man who was not a relative. It also went against the rules that she should interrupt two men who were in the middle of a conversation.

"I couldn't believe my ears when Uncle Kirk told me you had arrived nearly half an hour ago. Just why haven't you been able to locate me during that expanse of time?" She gave him a coquettish smile and fluttered her long brown lashes.

"You'd best come up with an excellent reply, my young friend, or I dare say you'll pay dearly," Paul remarked as he slapped Matthew on the shoulder and walked off toward the center of the room.

"You'll have to admit the room is extremely crowded, Isabelle. I spied Mr. Moody, and there was a matter I needed to discuss with him. Please accept my apologies," he dutifully requested.

She gave him a sidelong glance and once again puckered her lips. Her brow creased into what Matthew assumed was intended to be a thoughtful pose. "I don't suppose I have any choice but to forgive you. However, there will be no talk of business while you're with me this evening," she cautioned. "You didn't mention my hair. Do you like it fashioned this way?"

Matthew nodded. "It's lovely, very becoming." For the life of him, he couldn't remember how she had worn her hair the last time he'd seen her, but he'd told the truth. It was a becoming style, even if he couldn't be considered an authority on such matters.

"You look quite stunning in that frock coat," Isabelle gushed.

"That shade of brown is quite perfect, and the fawn color trousers are absolutely the height of fashion. I'm pleased to see that you take such care with your appearance."

Matthew tried not to appear amused, but the conversation seemed absolutely ludicrous. "I'm afraid I cannot take overdue credit for my attire. I simply grabbed the first available coat."

"Oh, Matthew, you're such a tease. Now come along," Isabelle ordered, taking his arm as she pulled him into the line of guests that was beginning to form. "Aunt Anne has seated us together, but I'm sure you expected she would."

"Of course," he replied as they found their places at the table. "I would have been shocked by any other arrangement. Your uncle Kirk tells me you're interested in taking a tour of the mills during your visit," he continued as he helped her into her chair. Conversation with Isabelle was difficult. She didn't want him to discuss his work, and he didn't want to hear about the latest fashions or the social activities in Boston.

"Every year since my father's death, his sister has come from England to visit. She's the one who wants to view the operation of the mills here in Lowell. I think Uncle Kirk has failed to convince her that working conditions are dissimilar to those in English textile mills. Mother, of course, insisted that I accompany them. She thinks it will prove to be an excellent educational experience." There was an evident note of disdain in her final remark. Obviously Isabelle was certain there was nothing to be learned anywhere but in Boston or abroad.

"I must agree with your mother. I think you will learn a great deal. At a minimum, it should make you thankful you're not required to work in order to support yourself."

Her head tipped upward and her back stiffened. "What a preposterous comment. The thought of such a concept is ludicrous, and I certainly don't need to visit a mill in order to realize that such a fate is not a part of my future." That said, she turned and directed a question to Jasmine Appleton, who was seated at her right hand.

"I'm sure there are others who have believed exactly the same thing," Matthew softly replied. She didn't hear him. He didn't care. His thoughts were upon Lilly and the long days she now labored in the mills. Certainly she had never entertained the slightest notion that she would be working twelve hours a day at a spinning frame.

A smiled formed on his lips. Lilly not only managed under such circumstances, she actually seemed to thrive. He'd never known her to look more beautiful. He thought back on his mother's remark at breakfast several days ago.

"Lilly won't remain single for long, Matthew," she had told him. *"You must come to your senses and establish yourself in her life. You must give her a reason to believe you still care."*

But what of her giving me a reason to believe she cares? Matthew mused. Although he was quite confident Lilly cared more for him than she let on. The crux of the matter was that he wanted her back in his life. He wanted to rescue her from her life at the mills and see her happy again. That didn't seem like too much to ask for—but apparently it was. Lilly wanted no part of him. He represented the mills every bit as much as Kirk Boott did. No doubt Lilly hated them both.

────────

The sound of the morning bell disrupted Lilly's dream. She had been running through the orchard with Matthew waiting in the distance, beckoning her toward him. The continual clanging of the bell was a wretched affirmation the apple-filled orchard had only been a dream; reality was this small, cold room on Jackson Street. Her body longed for additional sleep, but she knew such an idea was no more than a dream—an unfulfilled wish for something that would not occur. She threw back the heavy quilt and was assaulted by the frigid morning air. The November chill had formed an icy crust on the two small bedroom windows, and her breath was creating tiny vapor puffs with each exhale. With a shiver, she longed for the warmth of her family's hearth.

"You'd better hurry, Lilly. Nadene told me you were going to change her bandages before leaving for work this morning," Marmi mumbled through the faded brown dress she was pulling over her head.

The words caused Lilly's feet to hit the floor. She quickly dressed and rushed downstairs, anxious to keep her promise to assist with Nadene's care. Miss Addie had barely acknowledged Lilly's offer to assist with the nursing duties when she had presented the idea. In fact, Miss Addie had been very quiet, almost aloof, since Mintie's departure and the brief interrogation as to Lilly's whereabouts a few nights earlier.

"Good morning," Lilly greeted as she skidded to a halt inside the downstairs bedroom. Her gaze was immediately drawn toward the dirty bandages lying on the table beside Nadene's bed. "I came down to help with your dressings. Has Miss Addie already changed them?"

Nadene nodded and coughed. "I told her you would be here to do it, but she said she didn't need your help. She's not acting like herself. It appears something is bothering her, but when I asked, she said she was fine."

Lilly gathered the dirty bandages and tucked them under her arm. "I was late. I should have been here on time. I'll wash out the bandages and get them into some boiling water before I leave. I'll stop in for a minute when I return for breakfast," she promised, rushing from the room.

Addie was in the kitchen, already setting bread to rise and making preparations for the morning meal. She was silent until Lilly filled a small basin with water and began to scrub the bandages. "Leave those dressings and go on to work. I can manage just fine without your help."

The words sliced through the air like shards of sleet on a winter day. "Are you upset with me, Miss Addie? Have I done something?" Lilly timidly inquired.

"I guess you know better than I whether you've done something improper," Addie replied, keeping her back turned toward Lilly.

Lilly attempted to still the tremor that was rising in her throat. "I don't think I've done anything, but if I have, would you please accept my apology? You've appeared angry with me of late, and the last thing I would ever want to do is hurt you, Miss Addie."

241

"Is that so? Well, if you don't think you've done anything wrong, then I suppose you have nothing to apologize for—or to worry about for that matter. Final bell's ringing. You best get down the street before they close the gate," Addie replied without a glance in Lilly's direction.

Tears welled in Lilly's eyes as she rushed from the room. The other girls were already gone. She grasped her cape and ran out the door, still tugging the woolen fabric around her body as she raced toward the mill. She scooted into the mill yard as Mr. Gault was closing the gate. "Best hurry, young lady," he called, giving her a broad smile.

Lilly gave him a quick wave as she continued onward. One or two other girls joined her in a sprint toward the stairwell. By the time she reached her floor, Mr. Arnold was perched on his stool waiting to command the machinery into operation. Lilly wound her way down one of the aisles and came to a halt behind her machines just as he lowered his arm, signaling work to begin. Lilly pulled the lever on the four spinning frames and attempted to catch her breath. She glanced toward Mr. Arnold; he was watching her every move.

When the breakfast bell finally rang, Lilly quickly pulled the handles on her frames and scurried toward the door. "See that you're back on time, Miss Armbruster. Let's don't forget I'm doing you a favor permitting you to operate those extra machines," Mr. Arnold stated as she passed him.

She didn't have the energy to argue. "Yes, sir," she replied. The smirk that immediately crossed his lips annoyed her, but Thaddeus Arnold was forgotten by the time she entered the boardinghouse again. Quickly filling a plate with food, she made her way to the bedroom. "I've brought you some breakfast," she informed Nadene.

Nadene gave her a bright smile. "Sit down and eat it yourself. Miss Addie brought me my breakfast before you got here, but I'd love your company."

Lilly attempted to hide her disappointment. It was becoming obvious that Miss Addie wasn't going to accept her offer of assistance. Lowering herself into a chair positioned near the bed, she took a bite of ham. "I think Miss Addie is angry with me, but I'm not sure why. Has she said anything to you?" Lilly asked.

Nadene gave her a thoughtful look. "She hasn't said anything, but I can try to find out if you like. She *has* been unusually quiet."

Lilly swallowed a mouthful of food and wiped the corners of her mouth. "I've already asked her. She didn't give me a straight answer, but I honestly can't think of anything I've done to upset her."

"Try not to worry, and I'll see if I can get her to talk to me while she's doing her mending this afternoon," Nadene said. "Are you having a good morning?" A cough wracked her frail frame.

Lilly grimaced as Nadene's breathing came in ragged gasps. Had her lungs been further damaged by the fire? "I'm not sure there's much else that can go wrong today. I'd better take my plate to the kitchen and get back to work. I don't dare rush in at the last moment again. Please rest easy," she said, turning back to her friend. "You must get well."

Matthew pulled the carriage to a halt and then assisted Isabelle and her mother and aunt toward the front gate of the Appleton Mill. "Here we are," he announced as they neared No. 2. "It's a bit noisy inside," he absently warned the women, his thoughts wandering back to the sight of William Thurston and Lewis Armbruster entering one of the newer hostelries known as the Wareham House as he had passed down Merrimack Street only minutes earlier. Seeing Lewis and William deep in conversation caused Matthew to recall the day he and Kirk had observed both of them slinking about the Acre. Those two men were cut from the same cloth—both self-serving, angry tyrants willing to hurt anyone who might get in their way. He wondered why they might be keeping company.

Isabelle tugged at Matthew's arm, a look of disgust crossing her face. "It's beginning to snow. Are we going to stand out here in the cold, or are you intending to take us inside?"

Matthew started to attention. "My apologies, ladies. This way, please," he said as he led them to the front gate and rang the bell. Mr. Gault came outside and gave them a hearty wave. "Good afternoon, Mr. Gault. I plan to take the ladies through No. 2. I thought we would stop here for a moment before getting started."

"Pleased to have you," he said as he opened the gate and led the group across the yard and into the building. "In this building we have girls who trim, fold, and prepare the cloth for shipment," he explained, pointing across the room. "We also have an office where we maintain the time cards, pay records, and accounts of the Corporation," he advised as he led the group into the counting room.

Isabelle glanced about the room. "Why do you keep the employees locked in here?" she inquired, nodding toward the gate they'd entered.

"The bells ring announcing the time schedule of the mills— when to rise, when to arrive, when to leave for meals, when to return from meals. The gates are closed once the final bells ring. If an employee is late, it's noted on the pay and attendance records," he replied. "Surely you've heard the bells ringing since your arrival in Lowell."

Isabelle nodded. "A person would have to be totally deaf not to hear those annoying bells ringing all the time," Isabelle replied, looping her hand through the crook in Matthew's arm and stepping closer.

Matthew glanced at her fingers that were grasping his arm in a possessive grip. "Thanks for your assistance, Mr. Gault. I think we'll go over and let the ladies have a look at the carding machines. Shall we, ladies?" he asked while leading the three women out the door. "The Corporation has what we refer to as a bale-to-bolt operation. The cotton arrives in bales, then it's opened, picked, and then cleaned on the machinery over on that side of the room. And these machines," he hollered above the noise, "are the carding machines—very dangerous. These machines comb and strain the cotton fibers into slivers."

Isabelle tugged on his arm. Matthew knew she wanted to

leave, but Neva and Mrs. Danbury appeared to have an interest in the operation, asking questions as they slowly moved about the room. Matthew leaned down to Isabelle's ear and said, "Go and wait by the stairs. We'll be out shortly."

When they finally joined Isabelle, she was pacing back and forth in the tiny stairwell. "I'm freezing out here."

"I doubt that, dear," Neva replied. "The stairway is enclosed."

Isabelle stomped her foot. "Well, it may be enclosed, but it's not heated, and my feet feel as though they turned into icicles."

"Would you like to remain in the counting room until we've finished?" Matthew offered.

Neva moved forward and took hold of her daughter's arm. "I don't think an hour of discomfort will do you any harm, Isabelle. Come along," she said while giving Isabelle a gentle push toward the steps.

Matthew led them onward until they stood in front of the door to the third floor. "We have drawing and spinning machines in separate areas on this floor. As you can already hear, it's very noisy. There are drawing machines, where the long slivers from the carding machine are stretched until the ropes are about two inches thick. Those fragile ropes go to the roving machine, where they are drawn out and lengthened still further and given a slight twist, although the fiber is still very weak and breaks easily at this point," he explained, looking among the three women as he spoke. "Let's go in and have a look," he said before pulling open the door and escorting them inside.

Isabelle immediately thrust a finger in each ear. Matthew grimaced while watching her attempt to zigzag through the aisle of machinery, her elbows flapping in midair. Reaching from behind, he grasped her arms and pulled them down. "You need to keep your arms down, or your clothing may get caught in the machinery," he said while leaning over her shoulder and speaking into her ear.

It seemed the afternoon would never end. Lilly turned off one of the frames, bent over, and removed a row of thread-laden spindles, placing them into a box that one of the young bobbin girls was awaiting. Lilly gave the child a quick smile and began refilling her frame with empty spindles. Her back aching, she finished the chore and stood up, poised to slap the lever into action. Her raised arm, however, stopped in midair. Matthew was a few feet away, leaning toward Isabelle and whispering into her ear. Lilly watched a demure smile play at the corner of Isabelle's perfectly shaped lips as she glanced over her shoulder toward Matthew. An unexpected knot formed in Lilly's stomach as she viewed the two of them—Matthew, Kirk Boott's favored protégé, arm-in-arm with Isabelle Locklear, Boott's very available niece. Why was the sight of them almost more than Lilly could bear? After all, she no longer cared one whit about Matthew Cheever. She attempted to turn her gaze, but the sight of them held her captive until she realized Matthew was returning her stare. He smiled and began moving toward her with Isabelle following quickly behind. *Exactly what she didn't want!*

"Lilly!" Matthew mouthed her name.

She nodded while reaching into one of the frames to fasten a broken thread. He moved to her side and yelled above the din, "We're touring the mill. Could we observe you working at your machines?"

Shrugging her shoulders, Lilly pointed toward Thaddeus Arnold. She wanted to scream at him to take his lady friends away from this place—away from her. Instead, with Mr. Arnold's permission, they gathered around, watching each movement as Lilly tended the frames, their finery a stark reminder of her disheveled hair and shabby dress. Thankfully, they attempted to ask few questions. The older women appeared entranced at the sight of the machinery; Lilly felt entranced with Matthew.

Lilly breathed a sigh of relief when the group finally exited the floor. Matthew had touched her arm and mouthed his thanks before escorting them toward the door. Lilly had continued working, ignoring his overture—angry he had singled her out as an example to his *respectable* friends. The final bell rang, and she hit the four levers and hurried toward the door. Her head throbbed, her arms and legs ached, and Lilly longed for peace and quiet. But there was no place of solitude in the boarding-house. Perhaps Miss Addie would be happier this evening. The strain of Miss Addie's cool behavior toward her these past few days had taken its toll. A hint of misery seeped into her step; she missed the older woman and her cheery camaraderie.

CHAPTER 23

Kirk kissed the cheek his sister offered as the driver completed loading trunks onto the awaiting coach in front of his home. "I really would prefer you wait until after the Christmas holiday for your return to Boston, Neva. You did promise you'd stay with us at least six weeks," Kirk said while eyeing his niece, who had already seated herself inside the carriage.

Neva held Kirk's hand momentarily. "I know, and we truly appreciate your hospitality, but under the circumstances . . ."

Kirk nodded his understanding while assisting Neva into the coach. "I'll be in Boston after the first of the year. I'll call on you at that time, but please send word immediately if you should need anything before then."

"You know I will, and please don't worry. Isabelle will be fine once she's back in Boston. There will be a flurry of parties for her to attend. You and Anne have a wonderful holiday."

Kirk motioned to the driver, who immediately flicked the reins and set the horses into motion. Neva waved a gloved hand as they pulled away from the house. Watching until the coach was out of sight, Kirk placed his beaver hat firmly upon his head and headed off toward the Appleton. It was cold, but he decided the brisk air would do him good. Wondering how much of the information Isabelle had related was truth and how much was exaggerated rhetoric due to a deflated ego, he determined a visit with Matthew should set the record straight.

Stomping the mud from his boots before opening the door, Kirk entered the counting room of the Appleton. The ever-watchful Mr. Gault had seen him coming and rushed out to have the gate open for his arrival. *Good man, Gault,* he thought. *Wonder if Matthew's considered him for a promotion.*

"Ah, there you are, Matthew. I was hoping you'd be in here," Kirk said as he entered Matthew's small office and seated himself in the one available chair for guests.

Matthew glanced up from his desk. "What brings you out in this cold, damp weather? Is there a problem at one of the mills?"

"No, nothing so dreadful. Our Boston visitors left a short time ago, and I thought you and I might discuss what happened between you and Isabelle. I don't mean to appear obtuse, but I'm not sure if she was completely forthright with me. Would you consider telling me exactly what occurred? She seemed positively adamant about returning to Boston immediately."

Matthew rubbed his forehead and met Kirk's gaze. "We had a disagreement after she toured the mill. She told me she would never consider living in a small city such as Lowell and that she finds the whole concept of the mills disgusting. She was planning to have you arrange work for me in Boston, and when I told her I had no desire to leave Lowell, she became angry, saying I was attempting to manipulate her. Quite frankly, I think she believed our relationship had developed to a much more serious level than I had yet considered, sir."

Kirk rose from his chair and walked to the window. He stood with his back toward Matthew. "I suspected as much, although I will tell you that I'm disappointed. I had hoped you and Isabelle would find a common ground, but I know she's a determined, self-centered young woman. She led me to believe that you had, well, how shall I say it? Treated her with less than proper respect."

Matthew could feel his heart begin to race. "What? I did no

such thing, and I'm shocked that Isabelle would stoop to such tactics. Granted, she was angry when I told her I had no intention of making my home in Boston or of an imminent marriage, but I thought we parted with a mutual understanding that we weren't compatible. She even spoke of a man in Boston who had recently proposed to her," Matthew explained. "I hope you believe that I would never do anything to compromise any woman. It's not who I am nor what I believe in."

Kirk turned around and faced Matthew. "I suspected Isabelle hoped you would be the recipient of my wrath. Isabelle doesn't take rejection easily."

The subject of Isabelle was soon discarded for talk of production and expansion, with Kirk spending the greater share of the afternoon in Matthew's office. By the time Kirk started toward home, he knew hiring Matthew had been an excellent decision. There was no doubt the Associates needed Matthew more than Isabelle did. And besides, they would appreciate him more.

———————

Rather than sit with the other girls, Lilly prepared a plate of food and carried it into Addie's bedroom. "Have you eaten?" she asked Nadene, who was propped up in bed reading a book.

"Yes. And I've talked to Miss Addie, too. I know why she's upset with you."

Lilly moved to the edge of her chair. "Why?"

"It seems that Miss Mintie was on her way to a meeting the night you and John Farnsworth met to shop for Miss Addie's birthday present."

"What difference does *that* make?"

Nadene gave her a look of exasperation. "I'm going to tell you, if you'll give me a minute. Miss Mintie saw you two together, and she couldn't wait to tell Miss Addie. Mintie has convinced her sister that Mr. Farnsworth is romantically interested in you and that you've betrayed her by alienating Mr. Farnsworth's affections."

"Oh my! How could Miss Addie believe such nonsense? Mr. Farnsworth is old enough to be my father."

Nadene scooched up a little farther and leaned against her pillow. "I know, but I think Miss Mintie has succeeded in winning her over. Why don't you go and talk to her after supper when she's alone in the kitchen?"

Lilly agreed that a private discussion with Miss Addie would be best. "Will you pray with me?" she asked Nadene. "I want to be able to tell Miss Addie the truth without ruining her birthday surprise, but most of all I want to restore our friendship. I can't do that unless she trusts me. I fear I won't find the right words."

"Let's pray that God will give you the perfect words to set things right. I'm certain God wants your relationship restored, too."

Lilly gave her friend a smile. "Thank you, Nadene. I think you're right—the words do need to come from the Lord."

An hour later, bolstered by the time she and Nadene had spent in prayer, Lilly walked into the kitchen and offered to help with the supper dishes.

"I would think you have other things of more importance, perhaps a gentleman caller to go shopping with in town," Miss Addie replied as she picked up a worn dish towel and began drying a plate.

"We need to talk about gentlemen callers, Miss Addie. Nadene told me what you believe—about John Farnsworth and me—and none of it is true."

Miss Addie wheeled around and glowered. "You expect me to believe my sister *didn't* see you in town with John Farnsworth? Mintie is many things, but a liar isn't one of them."

Lilly wanted to pull back her words. After all that prayer, she'd still said the wrong thing. "I misspoke. The part about there being any romantic involvement is totally false. We were in town together. I was assisting him with a purchase—for a friend. We stopped in several shops and then came back home." Lilly paused before continuing. "Miss Addie, John Farnsworth is old enough to be my father. Surely you don't think I could have feelings for him. He's a kind and generous man—a wonderful suitor for you. But certainly not for me. And even if Mr. Farnsworth were a man who captivated my interest, I would never seek his affections when I know that you find him . . ."

"The most wonderful man on earth?" Addie concluded, a blush rising to her cheeks.

Lilly smiled. "Exactly! Miss Addie, I would never intentionally do anything to hurt you or destroy our friendship. I love you," Lilly said, the words fighting their way around the lump that had risen in her throat.

"Come here, child," Addie said, beckoning Lilly into a warm embrace. "I've missed you, too, more than you can imagine. I must tell you that Mintie's words were very convincing. I had hoped that young Matthew Cheever would come calling and assuage my fears. When that didn't occur, I thought you were probably meeting John on the sly so I wouldn't suspect."

As if on cue, Prudence rushed into the kitchen. "You have a caller in the parlor, Lilly—a gentleman," she announced with a broad grin.

"Not John Farnsworth?" Addie inquired, then quickly placed a hand over her mouth. "I'm merely jesting, Lilly."

"No, much younger and much more handsome," Prudence replied. "Guess!"

"I certainly hope it isn't my brother," Lilly replied. "Lewis is the *last* person I want to deal with this evening."

Prudence crossed her arms and gave Lilly a scowl. "Well, personally, I'd love to see Lewis, but I've not seen him for several days. It's Matthew Cheever."

"Speak of the devil," Lilly muttered. "Please tell Matthew I'm busy this evening," she said to Prudence, then turned to pick up the dish towel. Miss Addie was staring at her with a question in her eyes. If Addie's suspicions about John Farnsworth and Lilly were going to be laid to rest, Lilly knew she must see Matthew. "Pay me no mind, Prudence. I'll be into the parlor momentarily. I'm tired and didn't want Matthew to see me looking so disheveled, but I doubt he'll even notice."

"Don't keep him waiting, or one of the other girls will soon have his attention," Prudence warned as she left the kitchen.

Lilly forced her lips into a bright smile and tucked a loose curl behind one ear. "You see, Miss Addie? Matthew has been quite busy. Mr. Boott has had relatives in town, and Matthew has been required to spend his evening hours at the Boott residence. Otherwise, I'm sure he would have been here."

"I do apologize, dear. I allowed my mind to conjure up all sorts of wild ideas. Do forgive me," she asked, placing her plump arm around Lilly's waist.

"Of course you're forgiven."

"You need to give your cheeks a pinch. You need a little more color," Addie instructed as Lilly walked out of the room.

Matthew was standing in the doorway, holding her cape. "I thought we could walk into town," he said as she neared him.

"Do you have Isabelle's permission?" she asked, immediately scolding herself once the words were out. She sounded like a jealous lover worried about competition for her beau.

Matthew grinned as he held out her cape and escorted her out the door. "You have nothing to fear from Isabelle. Isabelle and I have nothing in common; we're totally unsuited."

Lilly stopped in her tracks. "Is there some reason you came calling upon me tonight, or were you merely hoping to heap more misery on what has been a wretched week?"

He pulled her hand into his arm and tugged her along toward town. "Wretched because I came to the mill with Isabelle? Because if that's the case, I've come to set your mind at ease," he said with a smile.

She moved onward, intrigued by his statement. "How so?"

"Isabelle has returned to Boston to find a man she considers more suitable. She wants to live among her privileged friends in Boston, and of course I have no interest in living anywhere but Lowell. When I made it clear we were not of like minds, she insisted on immediately returning to Boston."

The moonlight shone upon Matthew's finely chiseled profile. As he turned and smiled, Lilly's heart began to melt—his gaze warm upon her icy heart. Quickly she turned away, forcing herself to remember the pain he had caused in the past. Matthew Cheever would not hurt her again. "And you think that because Isabelle has rushed off to Boston, you'll begin calling on me.

After all, I should fall at your feet in thankfulness for the privilege. Is that correct?"

Matthew stared at her in obvious disbelief. "What has gotten into you, Lilly? You sound angry and bitter."

"Perhaps because I *am* angry and bitter. And it's you that's helped to turn me into what I am, Matthew," she fired, her hands curled into fists.

Matthew looked down at her. "Take charge of your own life, Lilly. I'm not the cause of your happiness or your sadness. You're the girl who once told me your joy was in the Lord. Is it not still so? Because you've fallen upon hard times, have you forgotten where true happiness lies?"

She knew he was right, but that only served to increase her anger. "How dare you talk to me about bitterness or happiness, Matthew. You've experienced nothing but prosperity and good times. Come and talk to me when you've had to suffer losses, and we'll see where *your* joy lies," she spat.

"I'm sorry," he offered in a voice that suggested true sympathy. "I know your losses have been great. Perhaps we should change the subject to something more neutral," he suggested as they sat down in the Wareham restaurant.

"Coffee, tea, hot cider?" said the young man who stood poised to wait upon them.

"Tea," Lilly replied.

"I'll have tea, also," Matthew said, then turned back toward Lilly. Before he could speak, however, several other patrons entered the room, their voices loud and excited.

"The mills are truly giving life to this community," an older man said to the group. "I would have been in the poorhouse by now, but the mills brought prosperity to my business."

"You don't have to sell me on it, Benjamin," another man said. "I couldn't be more delighted. I was ready to take a loss on the farm and move south with my sister. I watched my father die trying to work the land, and I wasn't going to follow suit."

The words hit Lilly hard. She'd never heard any of the locals, with exception to the Cheevers, sing the praises of the mills. How could they be so delighted to see the land torn up and scarred with huge brick monstrosities?

"Without this industrialization, my boy would have had to leave the area to find work. He was certainly no farmer and no storekeeper," the first man continued. "I know at first I was against the mills, but in the past five years they've definitely convinced me. I don't know when I've enjoyed a better life."

Lilly looked up to find Matthew watching her. He knew she'd overheard the conversation. It was hard not to as the men had taken the table next to theirs. Without taking his gaze from her face, Matthew reached out and took hold of her hand.

"I'm not the devil, and neither is Kirk Boott."

Lilly swallowed hard. Matthew's touch was doing things to her that she'd just as soon ignore. But she couldn't. She tried to fight it, but the memories came rushing back. Memories of his tender touch, his sweet, soft words, his gentleness.

Matthew's voice was low, almost husky, as he added, "When you look at the overall scheme of things, more people have prospered from this than suffered."

Lilly pushed aside the memories and replaced them with anger, for it was her only defense. "So my suffering and that of my family's is unimportant because more people have prospered than endured what we have?"

"The mills didn't rob you. Lewis did," Matthew said matter-of-factly. "Sooner or later, you're going to have to understand that."

"Lewis may have squandered the money given him by the Associates, but he would never have had the money to begin with if it hadn't been for their greediness to buy up all the land."

"Lilly, be fair."

She pulled her hand away. "Like the Corporation has been fair to me—to my father?"

"Your family received more than most," Matthew countered. "Your father didn't have to sell, but it was prosperous to do so."

"Lewis connived him into doing it."

"Lewis didn't want to be a farmer. Your father knew that—knew, too, that he was getting too old to run the place alone."

"He had me!" Lilly exclaimed, her voice raising an octave.

Matthew shook his head. "No, Lilly, he thought you belonged to me."

Lilly felt the age-old tightness in her chest. The misery of the past few years and the bitterness that had taken root in her heart caused her no end of pain. She lowered her gaze to the table, fighting the urge to cry. It would do no good. It couldn't take back the years of sorrow.

The waiter came with their tea, but Lilly could hardly drink it. She wanted to return home, to hide away in her bed and never get up again. She wanted to forget about bells and roving and loud machines that she seemed to hear long after they'd been turned off.

"I didn't ask you out to fight with you, Lilly." Matthew's words were soft and soothing. "I want to find a way to get beyond your anger with me."

The men at the table beside her were laughing and discussing plans for the holidays. One man confided that the extra money his business had made would allow him to take his wife to see her mother in New York. Lilly felt ill.

"Your tea is getting cold," Matthew offered after several minutes had passed in silence.

Still Lilly said nothing. As her emotions tumbled over each other, she tried desperately to think of a way to dismiss herself from the table without creating a scene.

Matthew picked up the conversation again as if nothing had ever happened. "Speaking of your brother, I've seen Lewis several times over the past few weeks. I didn't realize he was back in Lowell. The last I knew he was in Nashua. What brings him back?"

Thinking of Lewis was the trick she needed to steep herself in protective anger. Looking up, she met Matthew's gaze. "I have no idea. Lewis and his whereabouts aren't a topic I care to discuss," she said in what she hoped was her most dismissive tone.

Matthew reached across the table and took hold of her hand once again. "Lilly, this is important. I'm concerned that Lewis may be involved in some unsavory activity. I'm concerned that he and a man named William Thurston are up to no good. I want you to be honest with me," he said, his voice sounding urgent.

"You're hurting me," Lilly said, pulling from his grasp. She pushed back her chair and stood up. Everyone turned to look, but Lilly didn't care. "If you want to know, I suggest you invite Lewis to join you for tea," she said as the waiter came to check on them, "because I certainly don't want the tea—or your company." Pulling her cloak around her shoulders, Lilly turned to leave. "Please don't follow me, Matthew."

Although Lilly truly expected him to come running after her as she stormed down the block, it appeared he had taken her words to heart. She glanced over her shoulder one last time. Matthew was nowhere to be seen.

Her thoughts turned to Lewis. *What is he up to?* she wondered. And what of that Thurston man? She remembered the name from when Kirk Boott had brought him and Nathan Appleton to the mill. Lilly knew nothing about William Thurston, but if there were underhanded deeds to be done, she had no doubt Lewis was involved.

Against Lilly's wishes, he had occasionally called upon Prudence and probably several other girls who lived in different boardinghouses. Most likely he was garnering as much attention and money from the girls as his charm would permit. The thought of her brother preying upon girls who spent long, tedious hours in the mills sickened her.

Slowing her pace, Lilly tilted her head ever so slightly and listened. Footsteps. Perhaps Matthew was following her. In spite of her anger, she smiled and slowed her stride. A hand reached out to take hold of her, the arm coming around her shoulder.

"What are you doing out alone on this cold night?"

Lilly turned and looked up. Instead of Matthew, however, she looked into her brother's face. "Lewis. How strange that you should suddenly appear."

"Not so strange. I'm coming to call on your dear friend, Prudence. She promised to have a special gift for me this evening," he said. "You do need to purchase something a little warmer than this cloak for winter, Lilly. And in case you haven't noticed, it's really quite shabby. They've been receiving new shipments of some very fine clothing in town."

"I don't have money for a new cloak, so there's no need for me to go shopping. Obviously you have both time and money, Lewis. How is it that you can afford that new beaver hat?"

"Ah, not just the hat, but all of my clothing—even the boots and an expensive engraved pocket watch," he replied. "Your little friends are most generous. Pru, Mary, and even little Franny make marvelous companions. So sweet and so giving. I'm going to have to redirect them soon, however. They truly enjoy buying me gifts, but now that my wardrobe is complete, I'd rather have their money."

"Young ladies shouldn't be buying articles of clothing for a man to whom they aren't related. Nothing so personal should ever pass between you and those girls."

"Ah, but they adore me."

Lilly's teeth were clenched so tightly that her jaw began to hurt. "You have no conscience, Lewis." She wanted to hurt him, just as he was hurting the girls who worked in the mills—just as he had hurt her for years. "By the way, Lewis, exactly what *is* your relationship with William Thurston?"

He grabbed her arm, his fingers digging into her flesh. "How do you know about William Thurston?" His face was etched in both anger and fear.

Lilly met his gaze and pulled loose of his grasp. "So you *have* formed some kind of alliance with Mr. Thurston. You're planning something terrible, aren't you, Lewis?" she asked as they reached the boardinghouse.

He pushed her against the cold, hard bricks of the house and pinned her there, his hands on either side of her shoulders. "I want to know who has been making inquiries. How have you come by this information, Lilly? I trust you remember how cruel I can be when you're not cooperative," he threatened.

"I'm not a little girl anymore, Lewis. You no longer frighten me, and I'll not tell you what I know. Suffice it to say that you have been seen in Thurston's company, and people are wondering about such a liaison. Perhaps you and Thurston should consider setting aside any plans you might have—unless they be for good," she said, ducking under his arm and hurrying inside.

Lilly leaned against the front door and listened to the sound of her brother's footsteps as he walked away from the house. Prudence would have no gentleman caller this night.

CHAPTER 24

Matthew and Kirk pulled on their gloves and mounted their horses, one a bay gelding, the other a chestnut mare. "I want to ride out toward the falls," Kirk said as the horses began to trot away from the livery. Matthew nodded as both men urged their horses into a gallop and moved toward the outskirts of town. It was an unseasonably warm December Sunday, perfect for a ride in the country and talk of the Associates' expansion projects.

"The funding has been arranged for additional mills," Kirk said as they neared Pawtucket Falls. "We're going to begin work on another canal this spring, as soon as the ground has thawed sufficiently. Which means additional work for Hugh and his Irishmen. There's certainly been no lack of work for them when the weather cooperates. I worry about problems through the winter, though. Idle hands can breed problems. Speaking of which, you know how disappointed I was with the bishop's decision to delay his visit."

Matthew moved his horse ahead of Boott's, leading the way through a thick stand of leafless trees. "I understand, but we can't move forward with building a church during the dead of winter, either. There are plans to send a priest for Christmas mass. That should help."

Shots rang out in the distance, and Matthew tightened the hold on his reins. "Someone hunting for dinner, I suspect," he said, glancing over his shoulder and then shifting in his saddle to gain a better view.

Boott fought to control his gelding, but the horse reared and dumped Kirk off the back. After hitting the ground, Boott didn't so much as try to get out of the way of the stomping horse.

"Whoa there, boy," Matthew called out to the horse in a reassuring tone. Turning his own horse, Matthew approached slowly, not wanting to startle Boott's horse, and grabbed the reins. Another shot echoed in the distance, followed by the sound of pounding hooves. Somebody was hunting, but not for dinner. Matthew jumped down from his horse, holding fast to both sets of reins. Trying to take shelter among the trees, he looked off into the distance, hoping to catch a glimpse of someone, wanting to make sense of what was happening. He looked to where Boott lay on the ground. There was no movement, no sign of life. "Mr. Boott, can you hear me?" he called.

There was no answer. Crawling closer, Matthew could see that there was blood along Boott's temple. Apparently he'd hit his head when the horse had thrown him. Another cursory glance revealed a telltale reddish stain on Kirk's pant leg. He'd been shot! Matthew had to get Kirk to a doctor. Struggling under Boott's weight, he lifted the man into his arms and then hoisted him onto the horse. Then Matthew held the older man in the saddle while mounting up behind him. He pulled his own horse along by the reins. Every muscle in his body was stretched taut, anxiously awaiting the next shot, expecting to feel his flesh torn open by the searing pain of a lead ball. He urged the horse onward, praying they would be safe.

The ride into town seemed endless, the heaviness of Kirk's body constantly shifting to and fro. The horse was unaccustomed to carrying two riders and was now pulling against the reins. The horse's skittishness and the blood that now stained Kirk's breeches and coat caused Matthew to wonder if they would arrive before his boss was dead.

A short time later, he dismounted in front of Dr. Fontaine's office and carefully pulled Kirk off the horse. "Give me a hand," he called to a group of Irishmen ambling down the street. "Mr. Boott's been shot."

Once Kirk was in the office, Dr. Fontaine took charge. He insisted Matthew immediately inform Mrs. Boott of Kirk's condition. "And don't bring her back here to the office. I don't need to perform surgery with a weepy wife looking over my shoulder," he warned. No doubt Mrs. Boott would be distraught, and Matthew had no idea how to handle such a situation. He thought of Lilly but immediately rejected that thought. A mill girl calling upon Anne Boott, relating ill-fated news of her husband? *Never.* But then he thought of his mother. It would be only a short distance farther to stop by home and ask that she accompany him.

Julia Cheever was delighted Matthew had sought her council and assistance, and once they arrived at the Boott residence, she quickly shooed him away, insisting that he could be of little help. "We'll prepare things here at the house. You go back to Dr. Fontaine's office and make yourself available to transport Mr. Boott home once his wounds are tended," Julia instructed.

Matthew wasn't sure Dr. Fontaine would be sending Kirk home any too quickly. In fact, he wasn't sure if Kirk was still alive—but he wasn't about to inform the two women of his fears.

A beaming Addie sat surrounded by all of her young boarders as well as Mintie and John Farnsworth. "What a perfect birthday this has been," she said.

"And it's not over yet," Prudence said, placing a forkful of birthday cake in her mouth. "We're pleased your birthday is on Sunday; that way we can celebrate all afternoon, can't we?"

There was a declaration of agreement among the girls. Mintie, however, appeared a bit nonplussed at the amount of attention being showered upon her sister. "The Judge didn't approve of birthday parties," Mintie commented unpleasantly.

"But he always bought us a special gift for our birthday," Addie replied. "It was Mother who disliked birthdays."

John drew a bit closer to where Addie sat. "Speaking of presents," he said, holding out a package, "I hope you'll accept this along with my very best wishes for your special day."

Addie gave him a smile. "Why, John, you shouldn't have bought me anything."

Mintie's lips shriveled up tighter than a prune. She crossed her arms across her bosom and glared in Addie's direction. "You're right—he *shouldn't* have purchased a gift. It's inappropriate."

However, her comment went unheeded. The girls gathered around, watching as Addie's plump fingers untied the brown cord and peeled away the paper. Nestled inside the wrapping were two tortoiseshell combs.

"They're beautiful, John," she said, her cheeks flushed as she held out the combs for the girls to see.

"I can't take all the credit for choosing them," he said. "Lilly accompanied me into town a couple weeks ago and assisted with my choice."

A spark of recognition shone in Addie's eyes. "She went with you one evening after dinner, didn't she? Probably the night of the temperance meeting," Addie said, turning her gaze toward Mintie.

"I don't know about the temperance meeting, but we did go after dinner," John replied. "We managed to keep our secret from you, however. I swore Lilly to secrecy, and she was true to her word."

Addie met Lilly's gaze. "She certainly was. I never suspected she had gone with you to purchase a birthday gift. *You* would never have suspected such a thing, either, would you, Mintie?" Addie inquired, turning toward her sister.

Mintie glowered and shifted in her chair. "You're not going to accept those combs, are you? What would the Judge think of a man purchasing such a gift for you? It's improper, that's what it is," Mintie retorted, adjusting her shawl more tightly around her neck.

"I *am* going to accept them, Mintie. And quite happily, I might add. As for the Judge, I don't know what he would say, and quite frankly, I don't care."

Mintie's eyebrows arched high on her forehead, and her mouth opened to form a large oval. A loud knocking at the front door interrupted whatever retort may have been upon her lips.

Lawrence Gault entered the room, his gentle composure visibly shaken. "John, come quick. I've received word that Kirk Boott and Matthew Cheever were riding near Pawtucket Falls, and they've been shot. They're at Dr. Fontaine's office. I was told it might have been an ambush."

John quickly donned his coat and hat. "Someone intentionally shot Mr. Boott and Matthew? Why would anyone do such a thing?"

Lilly hurried along behind the two men, her hand at her throat. "Wait, Mr. Farnsworth, I want to accompany you," she called after him. He turned and gave her a questioning look. "I've known Matthew since we were children."

He nodded. "Come along, then," he said, taking hold of her arm.

Lilly felt her heart begin to race. What if Matthew were dead? The very thought brought her more pain than she could have imagined. He couldn't be dead. He just couldn't be.

Her feelings didn't so much surprise her as worry her. She did still have feelings for Matthew Cheever. Feelings that went far beyond that of merely caring for his well-being. She hoped neither man would die from such an attack but felt honest grief at the thought of Matthew being wounded.

They arrived at Dr. Fontaine's office in record time, the three of them breathing heavily when they finally entered the doctor's office. Lilly's eyes widened at the sight of Matthew pacing about the doctor's front door. He wasn't hurt. She didn't know whether to hug him or scream at him for worrying her.

John quickly extended his hand toward Matthew. "We heard you'd been shot. I'm pleased to see that we received a false report. What about Mr. Boott? Was he injured?"

Matthew gave them a grim look. "I'm afraid that report is true. Dr. Fontaine is with him. He was shot while we were out riding. His horse reared, and Boott fell and hit his head. He didn't regain consciousness. It appeared serious, but I'm not an authority on such things. Mrs. Boott is expecting me to transport him home once the doctor has finished with him."

"I could use some assistance in here," Dr. Fontaine called out from the other room.

Lilly watched as the men exchanged glances. Matthew seemed to pale at the request. "I'll go," John replied. "Lawrence, why don't you get word to the other Associates. They'll want to know."

"I could do that," Matthew offered.

John furrowed his brow and gave a negative nod. "Mrs. Boott will be expecting to hear from you. It's best you remain here."

The moment both men were out of earshot, Lilly turned on her heel and faced Matthew. "You don't even bear a scratch," she remarked with relief.

"I didn't know you cared so much," Matthew said, his voice bearing a hint of amusement.

Lilly's anger flared to mask her embarrassment. She hadn't known that little fact, either, but she wasn't about to let Matthew believe she cared.

"Were you hoping for sympathy? Is that why I received a message you'd been shot? Do you realize how frightening it is to hear such a report?"

Matthew gave her a smile. "I didn't send out *any* report, Lilly, but if I had realized it would bring you running to me, I might have done so. Your appearance serves to prove what I've already told you."

She glared in his direction and folded her arms. "And what might that be?"

"That you're still in love with me."

"I am *not* in love with you. Right at this moment, I don't even like you," she sputtered. "The fact that you would flatter yourself with such a notion is . . . is . . ."

"Marvelous? Enchanting? Wonderful? We're meant to be together, Lilly. You know it and so do I," he said, reaching out to draw her into his arms.

"I suggest you stop right there, Matthew Cheever, or the story going about town that you've sustained an injury *will* be true," Lilly said, pulling out of his grasp. Confusion made reasonable thought impossible. *I'm not in love. I'm not.*

Lilly hurried from the house and walked back to the boardinghouse, angry that she'd once again given Matthew reason to believe she still cared for him. Even if she did.

But I don't, she told herself, desperate to push aside any doubt. *I reacted that way only because we've known each other forever. I don't care for him. I could never . . . love . . . him.*

Such a possibility was out of the question, for she could never align herself with a man who was intent on forcing industrialization upon the farmlands of New England. It seemed as though no matter how much she prayed about her life and the miserable takeover by the Associates, God was continually confronting and challenging her to accept the changes. She didn't want to, yet within her heart she knew she must.

After all, others had. Some people were quite happy with the change, as she'd heard that night at tea. Some people were thriving, excited, joyous even at the prosperity that had come their way. The girls she lived with were grateful for the opportunity to come in from their farms and poorer country life. They thrived on earning money for themselves and while some sent home most of their pay, others were living quite nicely, dining out and buying new clothes.

Lilly looked down the street, seeing the mills in the distance. The mills had given this community new life. Lowell wasn't her beloved farm community. Instead the simple country maiden had grown into a sassy, citified woman of the world. And to Lilly's sorrow, it appeared people were beginning to accept— even embrace—the change.

"Things will never be the same," she murmured.

"All things change in time—some for the good, some for the bad.

But change they will." The words had been spoken to Lilly by her mother. She sighed. "Oh, Mama, things have changed, and I don't know how to change with them. It hurts so much to know you're gone—that Father and the farm are gone." Wiping a tear from her eye, Lilly bolstered her courage and approached the boardinghouse. *I have to be strong,* she told herself. But inside, she found little strength to draw on.

Prudence and Marmi hastened into the hallway upon her return. "How badly are they injured? Is Matthew . . ." Marmi hesitantly inquired.

"Matthew is fine. He wasn't injured. Mr. Boott was shot, but the wound wasn't fatal. The doctor was operating when I left." Lilly pulled off her bonnet and set it aside.

"That's certainly good news," a familiar voice commented.

Lilly turned. "What are *you* doing here, Lewis? Did you have anything to do with this?" she whispered as she pretended to draw him into an affectionate embrace.

"Dear sister. Why would I be involved in such an incident? How can you think such a thing of your brother?" he whispered in return.

"Quite easily," Lilly responded as she moved away from him and turned toward Prudence. "Don't give him any of your money, Prudence. He's been calling on at least two other girls who have been buying him gifts, also. If you don't believe me, I'll give you their names, and you can verify what I'm saying. Lewis is a cad who will do nothing but hurt you. It pains me to tell you this, Pru. If you continue keeping company with him, he'll take every cent you have, and then you'll never hear from him again. Please heed my words," she begged her friend before leaving the hallway and making her way upstairs.

That night, Lilly again tried to find solace in her Bible reading. A troubling thought flittered through her mind. *If I'm going to rejoice in Kirk Boott's downfall, I would have to rejoice in the possibility of Matthew's, as well.* The thought of him bloodied and dying actually brought tears to her eyes.

I don't want anything bad to happen to Matthew. Whether or not there exists hope for us to remain friends, I don't want him hurt. But the destruction of the mill and all that he's worked for would hurt him, she thought.

Fearfully, like a child about to be reprimanded, she opened the Bible. She flipped through the pages, heading for the back of the book. There was no way she wanted to get stuck in Proverbs again.

Colossians seemed a safe distance away, so she focused her attention on the third chapter. The second and third verses went straight to her heart.

"Set your affection on things above, not on things on the earth. For ye are dead, and your life is hid with Christ in God."

God, Lilly prayed, *I don't fully know what this verse means. In some ways, I've placed my affection on the earth—on the way things used to be. I'm mourning the past, the loss of my loved ones, the hope of things remaining the same. I want to understand your Word, but it seems every time I open it, I'm just that much more confused. Please help me.*

———

Shortly after breakfast the next morning, a knock sounded at the front door. Addie knew it was Mintie coming to further chastise her about the combs she'd accepted from John Farnsworth. For a moment she considered not answering the door, but experience had taught her Mintie would persist. "I don't have time to sit and visit, Mintie," Addie said as she pulled open the door.

"What kind of greeting is that? Living in this hamlet has caused you to lose all sense of proper etiquette," Mintie chided after pushing her way through the door and stomping snow off her feet. "It's difficult to believe it could snow through the night after that beautiful day we had yesterday."

"I'm surprised you'd be out in such weather," Addie replied as she headed off toward the kitchen.

"Where are you going? I don't want to sit out in the kitchen," Mintie said.

Addie glanced over her shoulder. "I told you I was busy. I'm paring apples, and I can't do that in the parlor." She heard

Mintie's *hurrump* and sigh of exasperation but chose to ignore both.

"I have news," Mintie said, seating herself in one of the straight-backed wooden chairs.

Addie didn't comment.

"Did you hear me? I have news," Mintie repeated.

"I heard you. And I have no doubt you're going to tell me every word of it."

It was obvious Mintie chose to ignore her sister's sarcasm. "I sent Lucy to pick up a few supplies this morning. There's word about town that the Irish are responsible for shooting Kirk Boott. Folks are saying the Irish are upset over their living conditions in the Paddy camps. I think that's a bunch of nonsense. The Irish have always appeared to enjoy living in squalor."

"And I'm sure you'd be an authority on what the Irish enjoy," Addie muttered.

"Speak up! I couldn't hear you," Mintie admonished.

"Nothing, Mintie, I didn't say a thing."

Mintie nodded and moved her chair closer to the fire. "I'll tell you what I think. I'm convinced it's the English. They're trying to find a way to stop the production of cloth here in New England. They fear a decline of our imports from them."

"Goodness, Mintie, the Tariff of Abominations has already dealt imports a heavy blow. The English goods are taxed very high and . . ."

"Exactly my point. The English have reason to hate us and to put an end to our mills. I know you don't want to hear this, Adelaide, but there is no doubt in my mind that John Farnsworth is at the very root of this. In fact, I believe he hired someone to kill Kirk Boott and made his appearance at your birthday party in order to cover his involvement in the deed. He is a covert, traitorous man, sent here to aid in the ruination of this country."

Addie gasped in disbelief. "I cannot believe you would say such things about a fine man like John Farnsworth. When you arrived, I thought you had come to berate me for accepting his gift. Now I find you've come to accuse him of attempted murder and treason against this country. Since you're intent upon defaming John Farnsworth, I must ask you to leave this house. I'll not tolerate such talk, Mintie."

Mintie jumped up, her chair toppling to the floor. "You would choose that British spy over your own flesh and blood? I can't believe what has happened to you, Adelaide Beecher. No doubt the Judge is rolling over in his grave at this very moment," she harangued while darting toward the front door.

"Mintie," Addie said, following her. "I want to say something, and I want you to hear me out."

The older woman turned, her face fixed in a pinched expression. "Go ahead, you could hardly shock me further."

Addie drew a deep breath and let it out slowly. "I don't understand why you feel you must hurt me. For as long as I remember, you've seemed to go out of your way to cause me pain. You berate me at every turn, never offering a single word of kindness or praise. You disdain my choices in clothes and friends, and you bring up hurtful things from the past to emphasize my shortcomings." Tears filled Addie's eyes. "I don't understand how you can hate me so much."

Mintie's expression fell. She appeared to be genuinely stunned by Addie's words. "I . . . You can't believe that I hate you."

"Then why do you do these things? Are you afraid I'll embarrass you? If John happened to be a spy, and I had made a terrible mistake in caring for him, it would be my mistake—not yours. Don't you see? Your fearfulness of the English and your bitterness over whatever it is you hold against me is tearing apart any affection we might have between us. I am your sister, Mintie, flesh and blood just as you said. Yet I've seen you treat stray dogs better than you do me." Tears streamed down Addie's cheeks, much to her dismay. She didn't want Mintie to think her weak, but her pain was so deep there was no way to contain her emotions.

"Please go now," she told Mintie and opened the door for her. "I want to be alone."

CHAPTER 25

Lilly slipped into her gown of layered yellow muslin and shivered. It was hardly warm enough for the winter, but her choices were few, and this was one of the last of her gowns acceptable to wear to Sunday services.

While doing up the buttons, she silently chastised herself for agreeing to accompany Miss Addie to St. Anne's for Sunday services. The ritual at the Episcopal church made her uncomfortable, for she hadn't attended often enough to learn the order of service. She much preferred attending the Methodist church with Nadene, where she knew exactly what to expect. But Miss Addie had asked if she would attend St. Anne's with her during the Advent season. The older woman said it would be her Christmas gift from Lilly since she disliked attending services alone. Lilly had hastened to point out that Mr. Farnsworth and Miss Mintie both attended St. Anne's, but Miss Addie had quickly retorted that it was Lilly's presence she desired.

Addie was waiting at the foot of the stairs in her fur-trimmed coat, a relic of the prosperous days when she, Mintie, and the Judge had resided among Boston society. "You look lovely," she greeted as Lilly descended the staircase, "except for that frown you're wearing."

Lilly smiled at the remark. "It's not a frown; I was merely deep in thought."

Peeking from beneath her matching fur-trimmed bonnet, Addie gave a bemused look. "Then you must be thinking *terrible* thoughts."

"I was contemplating the fact that I don't want to see Matthew Cheever. And Matthew attends St. Anne's," Lilly remarked as they left the house. She fussed with the ribbons of a bonnet she'd borrowed from Miss Addie, hoping the woman would just let the matter drop.

"Your feelings for him run deep."

"No, they don't," Lilly said in protest. "It's just that our past makes me uncomfortable."

Addie smiled. "Not near as much as your future."

"Don't say that. I don't have a future with Matthew."

"Say what you will, my dear. I won't nag at you to be honest with me, but I think sooner or later you'll have to be honest with yourself. Have you prayed about it—asked God what He desires for your life?"

Lilly refused to even contemplate her friend's question, confusion washing over her. First Julia Cheever had worked to put Lilly back in Matthew's life. Then Matthew himself, in that smug, self-confident way of his, had made certain Lilly knew he still considered a future for them. And now Miss Addie. It was just too much.

"Oh, here comes John," Addie whispered.

At that moment, the older woman reminded Lilly of a blushing young girl excited at the sight of her first beau. Lilly felt a twinge of envy. She remembered feeling that way.

John pointed toward the western horizon. "Looks like snow clouds over there. Perhaps you'd like to join me for a sleigh ride one day soon, Addie." It was more a comment than a question.

Lilly glanced toward the older woman, curious how she might react to John's offer. The fact that God had blessed Addie with a modicum of joy in the midst of a humdrum daily life gave

Lilly hope. Hope for herself and all the other girls that they, too, might find some respite from the monotony of the mills.

"A sleigh ride would be lovely, John. Perhaps Lilly and Matthew could join us."

Lilly couldn't believe her ears. She jabbed an elbow in Miss Addie's direction but missed the mark. "I don't want to go on a sleigh ride with Matthew," she hissed in Addie's direction.

Addie turned and gave Lilly a gentle smile. "Of *course* you do, dear. You just haven't accepted the fact that you and Matthew still care for each other," she answered sweetly.

Lilly would have rendered a protest, but it was no use. The church bells would drown out anything she might say. Besides, it was obvious her denial would fall upon deaf ears. She remained silent as the three of them approached the gray slate church building. The vestibule was filled with churchgoers not yet ready to enter the sanctuary. Lilly nervously glanced about, but Matthew was nowhere to be seen. She breathed a sigh of relief.

"Are you ready to go in and be seated?" Addie inquired. "John is going to sit in our pew. Mintie will have a fit," she said with a nervous giggle.

"I'll go in last. That way Miss Mintie will be seated next to me," Lilly replied, knowing that Mintie's attendance would dramatically diminish Addie's ability to enjoy John's presence.

"Thank you, Lilly," Addie said as John held open one of the heavy wooden doors leading into the sanctuary.

A firm grasp on Lilly's shoulder caused her to stop and turn. A smiling Randolph Cheever met her gaze. "What a pleasant surprise. Look who's here, Julia," he said as he turned toward his wife.

Julia Cheever was in her Sunday finery, her drawn bonnet of navy blue silk impeccably matching her empire dress. "Lilly! I didn't realize you'd begun attending St. Anne's. I insist you come and sit in our pew."

"Thank you for the invitation, but I'm attending with Miss Addie. I fear it would hurt Miss Addie's feelings if I were to sit with you," Lilly explained.

Julia nodded in obvious understanding. "I'll not argue. I

certainly wouldn't want anyone to think I would encourage bad manners. However, I doubt you can find an excuse to turn down a dinner invitation. We're going to take you home with us after church, aren't we, Randolph?" There was a note of triumph in her voice.

There had to be some way Lilly could offer her regrets and escape dinner at the Cheever residence. Matthew hadn't yet made an appearance, but there was no doubt he would attend Sunday dinner at his parents' home. "My friend Nadene sustained severe burns at work several weeks ago, and I really must return home to help tend her bandages and keep her company," Lilly replied. She had spoken the truth—she did want to visit Nadene, and sometimes she helped change her bandages.

Mintie Beecher scurried into the vestibule and then stopped momentarily to clear the fog from her glasses. Lilly tensed at the sight of the older woman, thankful Mr. Cheever was now urging his wife forward. "Services are going to begin," he said.

Julia stepped alongside him. "We'll discuss this after church," she promised.

Pretending she didn't hear, Lilly made her way down the aisle and opened the small door that permitted entry into the pew. Scooting in close beside Miss Addie, she folded her hands and waited. The swishing sound of Miss Mintie's dress was drawing nearer. The pew door clicked. Lilly flinched but kept her gaze focused upon the floor.

Mintie sat down and gave Lilly a poke with her needle-sharp elbow. "What is everybody doing in our pew?" she inquired in an irritated whisper.

Lilly sat still, her head bowed. "Worshiping God. And I'm certain that He's glad you've joined us," she whispered in return. She forced herself to swallow hard as a giggle bubbled up and threatened to spill out.

"You be careful with your sass, young lady," Mintie warned as she leaned forward in an obvious attempt to gain Addie's attention. Fortunately for Addie, she had chosen a bonnet that successfully kept Mintie out of view.

Once again the pointy elbow stabbed into Lilly's side. "Tell

Adelaide to look this way. I want to tell her something," Mintie ordered in an authoritative whisper.

Lilly placed a finger to her lips, hushing Miss Mintie as if she were a small child. "Miss Addie is praying," she replied, then bowed her own head. She could feel Mintie's unyielding gaze throughout the remainder of the service. The moment the organ sounded the last chords of the final hymn, John and Addie quickly exited out the opposite pew door.

Lilly attempted to follow them, but Mintie's fingers dug into her arm. "I wanted to sit next to my sister. You should have stepped out and permitted me entry beside her. You should be sitting in your own pew or with one of the other girls. Do you pay pew rent here?"

"No, I don't."

"Then you should go where you pay your own pew rent and let me sit where I pay mine," Mintie snarled.

Lilly looked deep into the older woman's eyes. There was no doubt she was irate, yet behind the angry facade there was something else. Fear? Isolation? "I'm sorry you're unhappy, Miss Beecher. I know you miss your sister. Perhaps if you would reconsider your feelings toward John Farnsworth, the two of you could set things aright. I'm sure it would please Miss Addie as much as it would you."

There was a faint softening of Mintie's frown as she peered down her nose at Lilly. "The impertinence of youth."

"Who, me? Or were you meaning Miss Addie?" Lilly questioned.

"Never mind," Mintie said, stiffening. For a moment her expression seemed quite sad, and Lilly actually felt sorry for the older woman.

They said nothing further, and Lilly stood silently watching as Mintie marched out of the church with her shoulders squared, head high, and back straight as an arrow. No doubt she let anger and irritation be her companions—it kept people from getting too close. Close enough to hurt you. Lilly had learned this very well for herself.

In a flash, she saw herself growing old—old as Mintie

Beecher. Just as old and just as lonely and cantankerous. *Do you really want that for yourself?* a voice seemed to question. *Do you really want to lose your chance at real happiness?* Lilly shook the penetrating thoughts away.

The aisles were crowded but Lilly could see Julia Cheever wending her way through the congestion, heading directly toward her. She felt a twinge of guilt as she left the pew and pushed her way through to catch up with Addie and John.

Moments later a horse halted a short distance ahead of where the three were walking, and Randolph Cheever jumped down. "Lilly! We want you to join us for dinner. Let me help you into the carriage."

She could hardly turn and run. Smiling, she permitted him to assist her, thankful that Matthew was not present.

Matthew unlocked the front gate to the Appleton and went directly to his office. He would be glad when Kirk was finally able to return to work. Not that he had any aversion to the additional responsibility. In fact, he found it flattering that Kirk now relied upon him even more. But when Kirk was present there seemed to be an air of authority that permeated the mills. Of course, Mrs. Boott was disinclined to have her husband return for at least another six weeks, saying he could comfortably work from his office at home. Matthew doubted his boss would stay away that long!

He wasn't sure if it was the unsettling silence of the mill on a Sunday or the fact that he was meeting William Thurston and Lewis Armbruster for a secret discussion that was causing his anxiety. He read through several ledgers Mr. Gault had placed on his desk Saturday afternoon and reviewed the paper work Kirk had given him. He was finishing his notes when the gate bell rang. He startled to attention.

The two men stood waiting, talking in quiet tones, Thurston wringing his leather-gloved hands as Matthew approached. "Gentlemen. Come in," Matthew said while holding open the gate.

Matthew couldn't shake his feeling of uneasiness as they walked in silence to his office. He now wished he had insisted on waiting until Monday morning. "I'm expected somewhere within the hour, so perhaps we should get to our business. Tell me, what's so important that we need to meet in secret on a Sunday afternoon?" Matthew asked, looking back and forth between the two men.

Armbruster turned toward Thurston, who was obviously the delegated spokesman. "Lewis and I have become privy to some information. We've weighed the merits of coming forward and with whom we should discuss this matter. After a great deal of thought, we determined you were the best choice."

Matthew leaned back in his chair and met the man's gaze. "And why am I the best choice?"

Thurston leaned forward, arms resting upon his thighs. "You live here in Lowell, you work closely with Kirk and, I dare say, you have almost a father-son relationship with him. I know how devastated you've surely been over his harrowing experience— the thought that he could have been killed! Well, it's more than I even care to think about! I'm certain we would all be extraordinarily delighted to mete out punishment to the culprit who shot him."

Matthew listened intently, careful to hide his excitement at the prospect of finally discovering who had ambushed Boott. "Do I understand that you're prepared to give me the name of the person responsible for Mr. Boott's injury?"

Thurston shifted in his chair. "We have information."

Matthew attempted to hide his irritation. "What does that mean? Either you know who's responsible or you don't."

"We know who's responsible, but we don't have a name. We know it's a young Irishman."

Matthew stared at the duo in disbelief. "Well, *that* certainly narrows it down."

"Sarcasm doesn't suit you," Lewis retorted. "And, quite frankly, telling you it was a young Irishman certainly *does* narrow the possible suspects."

William held his hand up and silenced Lewis. "If you'll

permit me to continue, I will more fully explain. There is an informant, also an Irishman. I need not tell you what a tenuous situation it would place him in if word leaked out regarding his willingness to cooperate in the investigation. He wants assurance his name will not be involved in any way. And, of course, he would expect a reward for the risk he would be taking."

Matthew stood and began pacing in front of the window along the south wall of his small office. "So this unnamed informant doesn't want anyone but you and Lewis to know his identity. Does he have any proof to substantiate his accusations?"

"He has a piece of cloth that was torn from the coat of the person he says committed the act; the cloth was found out in the woods near where Boott was shot. My informant also told me that once he names the person, you could check with Hugh Cummiskey about the culprit. It appears this fellow and Boott had an argument, and Cummiskey witnessed their disagreement."

Returning to his chair, Matthew sat down. His head hurt. He rubbed the back of his neck and then met William's piercing gaze. "It sounds convincing, but I want names before I talk to Mr. Boott. Your man will have to wait upon any possible reward until we're certain the name he gives you is the actual offender. I'm certain you realize the ramifications if these accusations are correct," Matthew said, once again rubbing his neck.

Thurston nodded. "I've said it before and I'll say it again. The Irish are a blight on this community. They're an unruly, uneducated bunch of rabble-rousers who are spreading like the plague throughout the town. Their tempers often lead them to take matters into their own hands. If this incident with Boott doesn't prove my point, I don't know what it's going to take to convince the rest of you."

"I'm not sure everyone shares your views on the Irish, William. In any case, I'll need to have *all* the evidence—names, the piece of fabric, exact location where your man retrieved the cloth, and any other information he's got that will substantiate his accusations against this as yet unnamed Irishman. Once I have that information, I'll go to Mr. Boott. Tell your man that he'll have to furnish the name of the culprit and his proof before we'll move forward and investigate his claim. No reward until we're certain his information is correct. Get back with me after you've talked with him."

"Investigate? I've already done that for you. You're expecting a lot from this man, and yet you're doing nothing to show your good faith," Thurston argued.

Matthew shrugged. "Any reward would come from Mr. Boott. Surely you can convince your informant that he's dealing with a man who will do right by him."

William rose from his chair and moved toward the door. "He was hoping for a speedy resolution. As you can understand, he wants to leave Lowell as soon as possible. He'll need money."

"I understand. As soon as you fulfill my requests, I'll go directly to Boott. You have my word. We both know he is a generous man and one who is willing to make a quick decision. If he's convinced by the evidence, I'm sure a reward will be immediately forthcoming."

William nudged Lewis on the shoulder. "Come on, Lewis. I want to get this resolved. I should be back with you in the morning, Matthew. You'll be here at your office?"

Matthew nodded and then walked out with the two men and unlocked the gate. "Until tomorrow."

A blast of cold air whipped down the street, and Matthew bent his head against the chill. He watched the twosome walk off in the direction of the Paddy camp. He wanted to discuss Thurston's proposal with Boott, but he would wait. Perhaps William would be unable to secure the information and wouldn't return. He walked back to his office and retrieved his coat and hat. Why would anyone choose Lewis Armbruster or William Thurston as confidants to carry an offer? Especially an Irishman!

Matthew glanced at the clock atop the tower in the center of the mill yard. He was famished. If he hurried, perhaps he could make it home before all the food was cleared from his mother's table.

The Cheever home had been modestly decorated for the Christmas holidays. Evergreen boughs trimmed with red ribbons lined the banister and fireplace, making the place quite festive. Lilly thought it homey and very beautiful. She thought of her childhood and the special way her parents used to make her feel on Christmas morning.

Not that they didn't make me feel special throughout the year, she chided. But Christmas was always special. They had wonderful times of singing and laughing. They would share gifts, most handmade but all very precious, and they would dine on wonderful delicacies. Lilly had almost forgotten how wonderful it had all been. The last five years with her father had been meager and less than festive. In part because of the impending realization that soon the farm would be lost to them forever. And partly because that's the way Lilly chose it to be.

For a moment she felt overcome with guilt. She could have made it far more special for her father. His last years shouldn't have been spent dealing with someone so steeped in anger and hatred as Lilly had been.

"I hope you've saved room for dessert," Julia Cheever told Lilly.

Lilly silently chastised herself for having attempted to avoid Mr. and Mrs. Cheever's dinner invitation. The food was delicious, and the quietude of three people around the table was refreshing. She had almost forgotten the pleasure a family meal afforded.

"We have cherry pie," Julia said. "Matthew's favorite. It's a shame he isn't here to enjoy it."

Lilly withheld any comment regarding Matthew. "Let me help you remove the dishes," she offered while pushing back her chair.

The two women cleared the table while Randolph enjoyed a cup of coffee and awaited his dessert. They were preparing to cut the pie when the front door opened and the sound of stomping feet could be heard in the hallway. "It's me, Mother. Have I missed dinner?"

Matthew! She had relaxed too soon. At least dinner was over, and she could make her excuses for an early return to the boardinghouse. After all, she had told the Cheevers she wanted to spend time with Nadene.

"Would you mind fixing Matthew a plate while I cut the pie, Lilly?" Julia asked.

How could she refuse? "Certainly," she replied as she started to heap a plate with food.

Julia beamed. "There! I told you that you'd be surprised, didn't I?" she chortled at Matthew as Lilly entered the dining room.

Matthew gave Lilly a broad smile. "Why, thank you. I can't remember when I've been served by a lovelier hostess," he said as she set his plate before him.

Lilly didn't fail to note that, in her absence, Julia had seated Matthew directly beside her at the table, where a piece of pie now awaited her return. She pulled her chair out and moved it as far away from Matthew as possible without appearing overly obvious. "I must leave shortly," Lilly said as she forked a piece of the flaky pastry toward her mouth.

Julia jerked to attention. "Nonsense! I'll hear nothing of you leaving so soon."

"Nor I," Matthew agreed. "We have several things to discuss," he quickly added.

"In that case, your father and I will retire to the parlor and give you two a bit of privacy while you finish eating, Matthew. Come along, Randolph," she ordered, turning her attention toward her husband, who was shoveling his last bite of pie into his mouth while nodding his head.

Lilly glanced back and forth between the couple, wishing she could jump up and rush into the other room with them. She didn't want to be alone with Matthew, for it would serve no purpose. Their conversations always culminated in harsh words and disagreement. She finished her pie and prepared for the worst.

"It's good to see you, Lilly. I've been wanting to talk with you ever since our last . . ." he hesitated for a moment.

"Disagreement?" she asked, finishing his sentence.

He gave a comfortable laugh and nodded his head. "I hope we'll do a little better."

"We always fight. Even when I don't plan to, you say something that brings out the worst in me."

"Like when I questioned you about Lewis?" Matthew asked softly. "I apologize for that. I know he's hurt you greatly. Still, I would like to know what brought him back here."

While his questioning at the restaurant had seemed forceful and imperious, his simple retiring statement had the opposite effect. She found herself now wanting to share her own concerns regarding Lewis. "Then it may be best to discuss Lewis first. You wondered why he's in Lowell, and the only answer I can give is that he generally comes home when he has no money and nowhere else to go. I do know he's short on funds. All of his inheritance has been gambled away, and as usual, he's looking for some way to support himself that doesn't require work on his part."

Matthew finished eating and pushed his plate toward the center of the table. "Did he actually tell you his money is gone, or is that supposition based upon his return home?"

"He asked me for money when he arrived, saying his inheritance was gone. I don't doubt his word, especially since he told me he planned to begin escorting some of the mill girls. He assumed they would be easy prey. Obviously he was right. I know he's been accepting gifts and money from several different girls."

Matthew smacked his palm on the table. "Despicable behavior. How could he do such a thing?"

"He appears to have no conscience. He did mention some time back that he had entered into an alliance with a man of means. When we were last together you mentioned he was keeping company with William Thurston. I saw Lewis that very night and asked about his relationship with Mr. Thurston."

Matthew leaned forward and met her gaze. "What did he have to say?"

Lilly thought for a moment. She wasn't sure she wanted to

take Matthew into her confidence. And yet Lewis had threatened her—surely she should tell someone. "He appeared extremely upset that anyone knew of the liaison, though I'm not certain why, and he wanted to know who had made inquiry regarding their association."

"And what did you tell him?"

Lilly gave him a thoughtful look. "I told him if there was an evil plan afoot he should set it aside. He firmly asserted I should stay out of his business."

"So he may be working for Thurston, but we know he's being at least partially supported by his lady friends."

"Oh yes. He appears to accept gifts regularly from the girls. I've attempted to convince the girls he's a scoundrel. They don't believe me, but once he's taken their money and run off, it's *me* they'll be angry with," she lamented.

He stood up from the table and then assisted Lilly with her chair. "Unfortunately that's probably true, but if you've warned them, I don't know what else you can do. Why don't we move into the parlor? It's much more comfortable."

Randolph was reading, and Julia was embroidering on a piece of linen that she immediately placed in her sewing basket. "I gave Cook the rest of the day off. I'm just going to go to the kitchen and clean up. And your father is going to help me. Aren't you, Randolph?" Julia added quickly.

Randolph glanced up from his book with a puzzled look on his face. "I'm not certain. If you're merely arranging for the children to be alone, Julia, I think I would prefer to take my book and sit in the dining room."

"Randolph!" Julia chided as her husband followed along behind her, chuckling.

Matthew settled onto the settee and patted the cushion beside him. "Please sit down," he said, glancing up at Lilly. "I have something else I want to ask you," he said as she settled beside him and then turned, giving him her full attention. "About your appearance at Dr. Fontaine's office," he began.

Lilly could feel herself stiffen. He was going to confront her again. "I don't think there's anything to discuss."

"I want to thank you for your concern. My behavior was arrogant and unseemly. I hope you'll forgive me. Instead of acknowledging your act of friendship, I made assumptions that were obviously incorrect and made you uncomfortable. Can you forgive me?"

Lilly relaxed into the settee's padded cushion. She didn't know how or why Matthew had changed his opinion. "I forgive you," she murmured, feeling a trembling start somewhere deep inside her.

"Lilly, we've known each other too long to play games with one another. I know your heart is wounded from the things that have transpired. Things you believe me responsible for. I'm sorry for any part I've had in hurting you."

She looked into his eyes. Instantly she realized the mistake. She looked away just as quickly, but Matthew took hold of her chin and drew her back to face him. "Please believe me. I know your feelings for me have changed, but I would like very much for us to be friends."

Friends.

The word stuck in Lilly's mind. Why was he saying this now? Perhaps another woman had gained his attention; perhaps he finally believed she no longer loved him. For whatever reason, the word felt empty and void of any real meaning.

CHAPTER 26

Thurston arrived at the Appleton shortly after eight o'clock the next morning. "I thought I'd get an early start, before Mr. Cheever is caught up in the day's work," William told Lawrence Gault, who was escorting him in through the gate.

Lawrence gave a hearty laugh. "If you're going to get an early start around here, you'd best be here by five-thirty," Gault replied with a grin. "We've already gone home for breakfast and returned."

"Mr. Thurston to see you," Lawrence announced as William brushed past him and walked into Matthew's office.

"Morning, Matthew," William said, closing the door. "I have what you've requested with one exception."

Matthew looked up from his desk.

"The informant prefers to remain anonymous, but he's given me the information and the piece of cloth. He's directed me to continue as his liaison. I hope you will find that arrangement satisfactory."

Matthew shrugged. "It's not up to me to decide, Mr. Thurston. I'll take Mr. Boott whatever information and evidence you give me. He can evaluate it and make a determination."

287

"Johnny O'Malley's the one who shot Kirk. Here's the piece of cloth that was torn from his coat."

Matthew took the piece of fabric as William explained exactly where O'Malley had been situated when the shots were fired and offered to ride with Matthew to the very spot. "Excellent idea. That way there can be no confusion."

"Exactly," Thurston agreed, leading the way.

They mounted and rode in silence.

"Over there," Thurston said, pointing toward a wooded area. "My informant said he found the piece of cloth over in those trees."

"You're sure?" Matthew inquired while riding up alongside William's horse.

Thurston nodded. "Absolutely."

Matthew rode into the wooded area with Thurston following close behind. "So O'Malley was on his horse in this grove of pines, and the informant found that scrap from his coat somewhere right in here?"

William sat astride his horse and held his arms as if aiming a musket toward the clearing. "That's right," Thurston replied. "And O'Malley shot Kirk right over there. That *is* where Kirk went down, isn't it?"

"Yes, exactly," Matthew replied. "Don't think there's anything else for us to see out here. I'll go directly to Boott's house and talk to him."

They returned in silence.

William gave Matthew a satisfied nod as they rode down Merrimack Street. "I'm staying at the Wareham House. You'll get word to me?"

"Yes," Matthew replied as he tugged on the reins and directed his horse toward the Boott residence. He was glad to be free of William's company. Merely being with the man made him uncomfortable and filled Matthew with a hundred questions.

Anne Boott led Matthew into Kirk's office. "He won't stay in bed. I doubt his leg will ever properly heal," she reported.

"Nonsense! My leg is healing just fine. What brings you here this morning, Matthew?"

"A few developments concerning that wound to your leg, sir."

———————

"I want to speak with you, Miss Armbruster," Thaddeus Arnold said, grasping her arm as the other girls exited the building.

Lilly's heart began to pound in her chest as the last of the girls rushed out the door. She wanted to rush along with them.

"I've been permitting you to operate Nadene's frames, and she's been receiving full pay," he said, his fingers now relaxing their grasp and slowly moving up her arm. "Any word from the doctor when she'll be returning to work?"

Lilly flinched away. "He says she won't be able to return until February or possibly March. Her hands were badly burned. The doctor doesn't want her to return until he's certain she can operate the machinery without causing herself further harm." Lilly didn't bother to add that the doctor had serious doubts of Nadene being able to return at all—and not entirely because of the fire. Nadene's lungs were badly damaged by consumption. Truth be told, she probably wasn't going to recover.

"I've decided I need additional *encouragement* if you're to collect Nadene's pay."

"I told you I would remain silent about your behavior with the other girls here at the mill, and I've done so—I'll do no more."

"And I've decided that without someone to substantiate your silly accusations, no one will believe you," he said, grabbing her around the waist and pulling her close.

"Let go of me," Lilly screamed, twisting loose of his hold. "I'll never agree to what you're asking." She raced from the room and didn't stop running until she was inside the boardinghouse.

That night Thaddeus Arnold beat his wife. Lilly knocked on

the wall with her shoe, but he didn't stop. She covered her ears as the screams continued. It was obvious. He wanted her to hear.

"I'll meet you around the corner from your house tomorrow evening at eight o'clock," Lilly whispered to Thaddeus Arnold as she left work the next day.

He smiled an evil, yellow-toothed smile. "Why not just stay here after work?"

"There would be questions at home," she quickly replied. "I change Nadene's bandages after work, and I have plans for this evening." She hurried out the door and down the steps before he could say anything further. Her gaze was drawn toward the flickering light in Matthew's office.

Matthew!

Perhaps he could help her out of this dilemma she had just created for herself. *But he didn't help when you first told him of Mr. Arnold's behavior,* a small voice whispered into her thoughts. She shoved the negative thought to the back of her mind. Matthew said he wanted to put the past behind them—that he wanted to be friends. Perhaps he would feel this was one way he could prove his friendship. After glancing back toward the stairwell and assuring herself Arnold was nowhere to be seen, Lilly hurried into the counting room.

Mr. Gault was donning his overcoat as she entered the room. "Is Matthew—I mean, Mr. Cheever—in his office?" she gasped while attempting to catch her breath.

He smiled and nodded. "I'm sure he won't mind if you go in," Mr. Gault stated. "Have a nice evening."

"Thank you, and you do the same," Lilly said with a wave. She quickly tucked several loose strands of hair behind her ear. "I hope I'm not disturbing you," she said in a timid voice, "but I've come to ask for your help."

Matthew rose from his chair and walked toward her, his handsome features enhanced by the flickering oil lamp. He offered her a seat and then listened to what she told him. His face revealed emotion from time to time, but he didn't interrupt.

"Will you help?" Lilly inquired as she finished telling him of the plan she had devised to finally bring an end to Mr. Arnold's abuse of his wife and his molestation of the girls in the spinning room.

Matthew gave her a slow smile. "Yes, I'll speak to the elders. But let's keep the particulars between the two of us. No need for others to know what is happening. And I hope for my own sake that you never plot against me, Miss Armbruster."

Lilly gave him a hint of a smile. "Then perhaps you should be very careful how you conduct yourself."

"I'll do my best to keep in your good graces," he replied. "May I walk you home?"

"I don't want to take a chance of being seen by Mr. Arnold," she replied. "But thank you," she quickly added, beaming him a bright smile.

———

The following day, Lilly's apprehension steadily increased. By the end of the workday, an unrelenting queasiness had developed in the pit of her stomach. She shut down her frames and moved a little more slowly than usual to assure she would be the last of girls leaving the floor. "I think it would be safer to meet farther away from the boardinghouse. I'll meet you across the street from St. Anne's. Eight o'clock." She didn't give Arnold an opportunity to reply.

Hurrying home, she attempted to remain calm as she ate dinner and waited. With Mr. Arnold living next door, she decided it would be best if she left the house early. She certainly didn't want to chance an encounter with him before reaching St. Anne's. Fortunately, Matthew was waiting near the church, his carriage one of several lining the street. "You'll be warmer in the carriage," he said, helping her inside.

She didn't argue. "Are the elders going to meet us?"

"They're waiting in the church vestibule. Mr. Sachs is watching for my signal."

"Here comes Mr. Arnold," Lilly said in a hushed whisper. She slipped out of the carriage, and Matthew quickly signaled toward the church doors.

Lilly moved from behind the horses and held up her arm, waving it back and forth. Arnold looked in her direction and headed across the street. He stepped close to her and placed his gloved hand on her arm.

"Thaddeus! So pleased you could make our meeting on such short notice," Elder Sachs greeted as he, Elder Jones, and Matthew stood waiting inside the iron fence that surrounded the churchyard. "Come in," he said, holding open the gate.

"What is going on?" Thaddeus asked under his breath.

Lilly quickly moved away from Mr. Arnold and through the gate, keeping herself distanced from him as they entered the building. His confusion and discomfort were obvious as they sat down in a small room off the foyer.

"We understand you've been good enough to continue paying wages to Nadene Eckhoff so long as Lilly is able to operate her looms at an adequate output. First, we want to tell you we're proud that an elder of this church has acted in such a charitable manner," Elder Sachs stated, his chest puffing out ever so slightly.

Thaddeus gave Matthew a sidelong glance. "Thank you," he mumbled.

"I'm sure you'll be pleased to know that Mr. Cheever has agreed that this arrangement may continue throughout Nadene's recuperation from her injuries. We thank you for that generosity, Mr. Cheever, as I'm sure Thaddeus may have had some concerns about the company's attitude about such an agreement. Wouldn't that be true, Thaddeus?"

Thaddeus's head bobbed up and down, his gaze never leaving the mosaic inset beneath his feet.

Elder Sachs laced his bony fingers together atop the wooden table. "We're attempting to help all of the girls working in the mill, and Lilly has mentioned several girls on your floor who might need some guidance and counseling, particularly regarding how to handle themselves in difficult situations. We were thinking of having a symposium. Of course, it wouldn't be for just the mill girls," he said.

Lilly straightened in her chair. "Perhaps your wife would like to attend, Mr. Arnold."

He met her stare. "She doesn't enjoy socializing in large groups," he replied.

"If she's reticent to attend, I'm sure the elders would be happy to call at your home and encourage her," Lilly replied in a firm voice.

"Absolutely. We would be delighted. And now that we're discussing your wife, I don't believe I've seen her in church for some time. Has she been ill?" Elder Sachs inquired.

"I believe she has, hasn't she, Mr. Arnold? But I'm certain she's on the road to a *complete* recovery. Isn't that correct?" Lilly tilted her head and gave Thaddeus a bright smile.

His thin lips were set in a tight line. "Yes. She should be well enough to attend church by next week."

Lilly realized Arnold was giving his wife enough time to recuperate from the latest beating. But granting him this one concession would be a small price to pay for Mrs. Arnold's future safety. "And I'm sure Mrs. Arnold would enjoy meeting with the ladies for Bible study. Miss Addie tells me a group of them remain for a quilting bee in the afternoons. I'll tell Miss Addie to visit with your wife about attending."

Elder Jones slapped his knee. "Absolutely. My wife attends, as well. She comes home, prepares lunch, and then returns for an afternoon of sewing. Mrs. Jones always has a wonderful time. I'll tell her to make a special effort to invite Mrs. Arnold."

"How grand!" Lilly said.

"I'm glad we've had this meeting," Elder Sachs replied. "I want to do what I can to ensure living in Lowell is a positive experience for these young farm girls. I believe the elders of this church have a duty to them. Their parents have entrusted them to our community, and we must honor their confidence that no harm will come to any of them. Don't you agree, Thaddeus?"

The room was cool, yet a small line of perspiration beaded across Arnold's upper lip. His voice trembled slightly as he said, "Yes, of course. If that's all, gentlemen?" There was a note of hopefulness that they were through for the evening. He leaned forward and rose from his chair.

"I believe so," Elder Jones said, glancing about the table. The meeting quickly adjourned, and Thaddeus made a hasty retreat back in the direction from which he had arrived.

"Did our meeting accomplish everything you had hoped for?" Elder Sachs asked Matthew as they walked from the church.

Matthew nodded and shook hands with both of the men. "I believe everything has been satisfactorily resolved. And I appreciate the trust you've exhibited in me."

Once the men had departed and Matthew assisted her into the carriage, Lilly turned and faced him. "You didn't tell them about his behavior with the girls, did you?"

"No. I merely explained my fear that the behavior of some men in the community toward the girls could become a problem. I told the elders I thought it would be beneficial for them to meet with one or two key supervisors who are members of St. Anne's and reinforce the church's position. It's more likely that the Arnolds' marriage will heal if there isn't gossip about town regarding his immoral behavior."

Lilly furrowed her brow and gave him a pensive look. "I'm surprised you thought about such a thing."

"We humans tend to worry about what other people think about us. In fact, I think half the time folks make decisions based solely upon what *others* may think and the other half based upon their own selfish desires. It's too bad we don't worry more about God's perception of our behaviors and His desires instead. After all, that's the true test, isn't it?"

She was startled by the acuity of his observation, convicted by his words.

———

Lilly didn't permit herself to look in Mr. Arnold's direction as she entered the spinning room the next morning. He made his way up and down the aisles several times, much as he always did. She watched from beneath hooded lids, not wanting him to notice as she observed his movements. This morning his hands remained to himself; there were no unseemly touches or pats, no leaning over and whispering into an ear—only the necessary supervision of an overseer checking production. She relaxed a bit, the tedium of the work calming her roiling emotions. It appeared as if last night's meeting produced the desired effect.

The breakfast bell tolled in the distance, and Lilly slapped the loom handles, the metal foursome shuttering into silence as the buzzing bobbins ceased their whirling. Thaddeus stood in the aisle blocking her departure. She remained frozen in place, unable to speak.

He sneered at her. "My wife would like to attend the symposium. Would you ask Miss Beecher if she would be so kind as to pass along the particulars to Mrs. Arnold once they become available?"

Lilly bobbed her head up and down. "Yes—yes," she stammered. "I'm sure Miss Addie will be most pleased to meet your wife."

He stepped aside, careful there was ample room for Lilly to pass by. She continued staring at him as she inched her way around him, waiting, expecting, certain he would reach out and grasp her.

He didn't. Instead he said, "This isn't over, Miss Armbruster, but I know how to mind my business and bide my time. You'll pay for this."

She chilled and looked into his face. "If you don't cooperate . . ."

"I never said a word about not cooperating. Like I said, I know how to bide my time." He walked away at that, leaving Lilly shaken. Perhaps she'd only made matters worse.

Matthew met Lilly halfway up the stairs. "Are you all right? I was waiting in the mill yard. When I didn't see you come out, I was concerned." He grabbed her by the hand. "Come on, I'll walk you over to the boardinghouse."

"Everything's . . . well . . . Mr. Arnold confronted me a few minutes ago, and I must admit my faith wavered."

"He confronted you?" Matthew pulled her to a halt.

"He blocked my exit in order to make a request."

"What?" Matthew's indignation was obvious.

"He asked if I would have Miss Addie call upon his wife

regarding the time and date of the symposium."

Matthew exhaled and loosened his grip on her arm. "That shows cooperation."

Lilly nodded. "Yes, but he also said this wasn't over. That he knows how to mind his business and bide his time."

"You've wounded his pride, Lilly. It's going to take him time to deal with that. Men don't handle wounded pride very well. I know that firsthand."

She looked up at him, her breath catching in her throat. "I know about wounded pride, as well."

"Time heals all wounds," Matthew replied, his loving gaze upon her.

Lilly struggled with her emotions. Putting on a smile she didn't feel, she said, "Could we move along now? Breakfast will be over before I reach home, and I'm fairly famished."

He laughed as the two of them broke into a run. "I wouldn't want to be accused of causing you to miss a meal, Miss Armbruster."

CHAPTER 27

Christmas morning dawned bright and clear with a fresh covering of snow to make everything look pristine and white. Lilly awakened, not to the sound of the work bell but rather to the sound of merriment. The other girls were giggling and preparing for the day. Some were making short trips home. Others, whose families lived too far for a day's journey, were making plans to celebrate together.

Lilly had been invited to join the Cheevers for Christmas dinner, but her heart wasn't really in it. She thought of this being the first Christmas without her beloved father, and depression washed over her in waves. It had been so hard to lose her mother, but at least there had been the comfort of her father's love. Now there was no one.

"Come on, sleepyhead," Pru teased. "Miss Addie has promised a gay Christmas Day. I'll see you downstairs." She hurried from the room, leaving Lilly alone.

"I'm coming," Lilly murmured, throwing back the covers. The chill of the room nearly made her change her mind and pull the covers tight again. Nevertheless, Lilly forced herself to get up. Sitting on the edge of the bed, she yawned and stretched.

Draped over her trunk was a beautiful gauze-over-satin gown, compliments of Julia Cheever. The woman had arrived the night before with her husband, laden with packages. Christmas gifts for Lilly.

Lilly had tried to refuse them, for after all, she had no gift for the Cheevers. Julia would hear nothing of it. She'd had these gifts specially made, and they would suit no one else. Besides, she told Lilly, it would simply break her heart if Lilly were to refuse.

Hurrying through her morning rituals, Lilly took up the new petticoat and added its warmth to her freezing frame. She'd heard that many women were actually taking to wearing more than one petticoat in order to make their skirts stand full. Lilly thought it rather nonsensical, but she had to admit the material warmed her quite nicely. Two petticoats would probably be even better.

Pulling on the gown of white trimmed in pink, Lilly struggled to do up the buttons before tying the pink waist sash. She would be the height of fashion today, there was no denying that. The gown even boasted the popular puffed gigot sleeves, although Lilly gratefully noted they weren't nearly as full as some she'd seen.

The gown fell to several inches above the floor, trimmed in three rows of pale pink ruffles. No woman in Boston, not even Boott's niece, Isabelle, could boast being more fashionable or up-to-date than Lilly Armbruster.

Taking up the accompanying new bonnet and gloves, Lilly made her way downstairs.

"Oh, your gown is the most beautiful I've ever seen," gushed Marmi. "I wish I were your size—I would beg to borrow it."

Lilly laughed. "And I would let you, of course."

Miss Addie appeared and nodded enthusiastically. "Oh yes. Yes, it's perfect. How positively delightful. Mrs. Cheever has impeccable taste."

Lilly smiled and nodded. "I cannot complain about her taste or the fashion. I do wish she'd saved her money, however. I have nothing to give in return."

Addie leaned in close enough for only Lilly to hear. "It would make quite the gift if you were to marry their son."

Lilly stepped away and waggled her finger. "Miss Addie, you would do well to plan your own wedding."

The girls fussed over Lilly's gown, marveling at the bonnet and expressing their desire to have one made just like it. Even Nadene thought the gown to be most incredible, although she wasn't feeling all that well. Her cough had kept her awake for a good portion of the night, and her burns were still far from healed.

After a delicious breakfast that included a dense cake filled with dried fruits and nuts, which Miss Addie had labored over the day before, Lilly made her excuses and went to take up her cloak. The shabby thing seemed an inappropriate covering while wearing such a rich gown, but Lilly had no choice. She couldn't afford to be wasteful with her money, and the old cloak was still serviceable.

Tying her bonnet securely, Lilly made her way outside. Thankfully, the snow had been shoveled from the walkway. The town was nearly silent, almost as if it were napping. The mills were quiet, and everyone was tucked safely in their homes to celebrate the birth of Jesus.

Lilly walked slowly, considering her mission. She had not gone back to her father's grave since the day of his funeral. For some reason, it seemed very important to go there today. She opened the iron gate to the small cemetery and slipped inside. Making her way through the rows of headstones, she came to the one bearing the name ARMBRUSTER.

This was the final earthly resting place of her parents. Bending down, Lilly pushed the snow from the top of the stone, then stepped back. "I miss you both," she whispered. "It just doesn't feel like Christmas without you." She paused, feeling rather silly for talking to the headstone. She knew her parents were in heaven, but somehow being here made her feel closer to them.

"I don't know what to do," she continued. "I thought I knew what was right. I had a purpose, and that purpose was to cause as much grief for the Associates and their horrible mills as

I could, but now it's different. What little I did do ended up hurting Nadene, and she was already so fragile and sickly. I've only made it worse.

"I know many people here feel just as I do—they hate the mills and the fact that the beauty of the land has been forever spoiled. They feel just as duped as we did. But there are others who see the change as good. The Cheevers have accepted this change and have thrived. Matthew seems very happy." She sighed and shivered against the cold.

"I don't know what to do anymore. I feel lost and confused. I'm so uncertain of the future and what direction to take."

"Seek the Lord in all things. He will guide your steps." She could almost hear her mother's words.

"I haven't been very good about seeking Him or His will for my life. I've been too preoccupied with what I wanted and how I thought it was what God wanted, as well. After all, even though I discontinued my attacks against the mill, the mishaps continued. It surely must have been the hand of God." Yet even as she spoke the words, Lilly wasn't sure she believed them.

"I want to do whatever you want, Lord. I just need some direction." Looking heavenward to the crystal blue skies, Lilly sought her answers. "What is it you want for me? What am I to do?"

"You'll get a stiff neck that way."

Lilly startled as she looked in the direction of the voice. Mintie Beecher stood on the other side of the iron gate.

"Merry Christmas, Miss Beecher," Lilly said, leaving her parents' graves.

"What were you craning your neck to see, child?" The old woman seemed so small snuggled down in her heavy wool coat and bonnet.

Lilly smiled. "The face of God. I thought maybe I could hear Him better if I could see Him. Soul-searching comes in all forms."

The woman's face wrinkled as she pursed her lips in consideration. "Stuff and nonsense, child. It's cold out here, and you'll catch your death in such a thin cloak."

"Why are you out here, Miss Beecher?"

"That's really none of your concern," she snapped.

Lilly shrugged. "I was just being sociable. I meant nothing by it." She thought of the sour woman and how hard it had been for her to deal with her sister's romantic situation.

Mintie softened her expression. "I'm just taking a walk. Nothing more."

"I understand," Lilly said softly. She came through the gate and closed it behind her ever so gently. "I suppose I must get back to the house. Will you be joining us? I know Miss Addie extended you an invitation."

"I'm considering it," Mintie replied, then her voice took on a strained sound. "Although with that John Farnsworth present, she'll hardly notice whether I'm there or not. She doesn't listen to me when he's around."

"Maybe you have your own soul searching to do," Lilly replied gently. "Good day, Miss Beecher. I truly hope you can make it."

Mintie watched the young girl walk away. Her footprints in the snow seemed so small, yet there was a wealth of strength in Lilly Armbruster. There was a great deal of strength in Adelaide, as well. Mintie's shoulders slumped forward, something she never allowed to happen. She felt a sense of defeat wash over her.

Mintie had prided herself on being strong all of her life. She had taken charge of the household upon their mother's death, not even allowing herself time to mourn. Tears that had never been allowed to fall then now gathered in her weary eyes.

"You would not be so proud if you saw me now, Mother," she whispered. She pulled her spectacles from her face and wiped her tears with her gloved fingers. "I am harsh and unfeeling. In my attempt to help direct Adelaide, I have hurt her with my envy and fears."

Lilly Armbruster had spoken of soul-searching, and the words had hit Mintie harder than she wanted to admit, for that had been her very intent upon taking her walk this morning. She needed wisdom and a renewal of strength in order to deal with what most certainly would come. Adelaide would have no reason to put aside this suitor. The Judge would not be around to send this beau away as he had the others.

"And when she marries, I shall be alone," Mintie mourned softly.

You are never alone, my child. I am with you always.

Mintie startled. The words sounded almost audible. Replacing her spectacles, she looked behind her and then across the small cemetery. There was no one. The words had come from no human source.

Then without concern for how it might look or what others might say about her, Mintie very slowly raised her face to the sky. The brilliance of the day hurt her eyes, yet she refused to look away. "Perhaps there's something to this," she murmured. "Perhaps I've not taken the trouble to listen for the truth. Maybe I've sought the wrong companion all along."

Lilly knew the Cheevers would call for her at exactly noon. It gave her time to enjoy the festivities of the boardinghouse and still be able to stand ready when the carriage arrived.

To her surprise, Matthew was the one who called for her. He smiled and greeted them all with great holiday spirit. "Merry Christmas!" he declared as he stomped his boots at the door.

"Merry Christmas, Mr. Cheever," Addie said, coming forward. "Won't you join us for some wassail?"

"I'm afraid not. My mother is expecting us." He turned to Lilly. "Are you ready?"

She nodded, feeling rather weak in the knees. He was so handsome in his long black coat and top hat. "I just need to get my cloak."

He took the piece from her as she pulled it from the peg. "Is this all you have?"

Lilly stiffened. In anger she snapped, "I know it's not very fashionable, but—"

He put his finger to her lips. "Shhh. Remember the day. I wasn't disdaining the fashion but rather the thinness of the material. You'll freeze out there in this."

She calmed her spirit. "I'll be just fine. I walked out to the cemetery this morning and hardly felt the chill." It was a stretch of the truth, but in all honesty her feet suffered more than her body on that walk.

Shrugging, Matthew put the cloak around her shoulders and waited until she'd retrieved her bonnet and secured it atop her head. "Come along. Mother has a feast fit for a king—or in this case, a queen." He smiled in his charming way, and Lilly found her voice completely gone—along with her breath.

He handed her up into the carriage, then climbed aboard and pulled heavy blankets around them both. "Don't scoot clear across to the other side. It's too cold, and your cloak is much too light. We will share our warmth together, and that way you won't catch your death."

"I hadn't planned to catch my death," Lilly said rather snidely. She truly relished the warmth Matthew offered her, but she hesitated to say so for fear of what he might think. Nevertheless, she did as he suggested and moved closer.

The day had gotten much colder than it had been that morning, and now the skies were overcast and threatened snow again. As the wind shifted, Lilly couldn't help but snuggle even closer to Matthew.

"You'd do well to buy yourself a new coat," Matthew said as he snapped the reins. The matched bays strained against their harness and easily pulled the carriage on its way.

Lilly felt a flare of temper but held it in check and decided to tease Matthew instead. "But then I'd have no excuse to sit close to you on carriage rides."

He looked at her for a long moment, his gaze warming her to the bone. His voice came out low and husky. "You never need an excuse to sit close to me, Lilly."

———

That night as Lilly settled into her bed, a hundred memories from the day danced through her head. But none came so easily as her time with Matthew in the carriage. Her heart stirred, and the ache that radiated from that stirring robbed her of any real comfort. She had hoped to remain disentangled—keeping her heart completely safe from harm. But that wasn't the case. And for the life of her, Lilly had no idea how to make it all right again.

"I can't love you, Matthew," she whispered into her pillow. "I simply can't."

CHAPTER 28

Matthew didn't report back to Thurston as arranged. Instead, heeding Boott's advice, he had waited for the man to reemerge. Surprisingly, it had taken a week for Thurston to appear at the Appleton. He'd pushed his way past Mr. Gault and walked into Matthew's office unannounced, his fury evident.

"I specifically remember you saying you would get back with me after you talked to Kirk," William snarled.

Matthew looked up from his paper work. "Good morning, Mr. Thurston. Care to have a seat? I assumed you had returned to Boston for Christmas with your family. I trust you had a joyous holiday."

Thurston crossed the office in two long strides and fell into one of the chairs while maintaining a glowering scowl upon his face. "I didn't come here to discuss Christmas, I came for a reply from Boott."

Matthew looked up from his ledger. "He isn't interested," he said simply.

"What do you mean Boott isn't interested?" Thurston yelled. "I've given him the name of the man who shot him, along with tangible proof to substantiate Mr. O'Malley's guilt, and you tell me Kirk Boot isn't interested? I should have gotten the reward money before I gave you the name. That's it, isn't it? He doesn't want to pay for the information," Thurston growled.

Matthew folded his arms and met Thurston's glare. "You know better than that, Mr. Thurston. That's not Mr. Boott's style. He doesn't plan to use the information. If he intended to make use of it, he would reward your informant."

"This makes no sense," Thurston retorted through clenched teeth.

Matthew shrugged. "I suggest you let it go, Mr. Thurston."

———

Lewis pulled his pocket watch out of his waistcoat several times as he paced back and forth in the foyer of the Wareham House. Thurston was not in his room, nor was there any evidence of him in the restaurant. He was sure Thurston had said to meet him at nine-thirty. He sat down at a table near the window and facing the door—he preferred a good vantage point. The image of a ragged-looking Irish boy, his coal black hair bobbing up and down, reflected on the sun-streaked window of the hotel before the child actually entered the establishment.

A startled look crossed the manager's face before he moved into action, loping around the desk and meeting the child mid-lobby. He was obviously unsettled by the child's appearance. Rightfully so, Lewis thought. The last thing patrons wanted to encounter at the finest hotel and eating establishment in town was a reminder of the Irish clans.

The manager grasped the child by his ear, practically lifting him out of his rundown, shabby boots. "What are you doing in here?" he fumed at the boy.

He held up a dingy-appearing missive. "I've a message for Mr. William Thurston."

The manager glanced toward the child's hand. "He's already checked out of the hotel, but that man in there is waiting on him," he said as he waved in Lewis's direction.

"May I help?" Lewis inquired as he approached the man and boy.

The manager gave Lewis a beseeching look. "This lad has a message for Mr. Thurston. May he leave it with you?"

Lewis extended his hand. "You may feel confident that I will deliver your message to Mr. Thurston. You may tell the writer that you delivered the dispatch to Lewis Armbruster on Mr. Thurston's behalf."

The child handed over the letter and waited, his dark pleading eyes and tattered clothes providing evidence of what was expected. Lewis handed the child a coin, then watched as the boy raced out of the hotel and back toward the Paddy camp.

"Ragged little beggars," the manager snarled under his breath. "Thank you for your assistance," he hastily added, giving Lewis a weary smile.

Lewis returned to his table and placed the correspondence beside his cup of coffee. The writing was crude, apparently scrawled in haste. He wondered who would be delivering mail to Thurston at the hotel. The thought of opening the seal crossed his mind. That idea was quickly followed by the thought of Thurston's possible retribution should he discover such an indiscretion.

Lewis was holding the missive between two fingers, snapping it up and down on the table, when Thurston entered the restaurant and seated himself. Annoyance was etched on the man's face, and Lewis issued a sigh of relief, thankful he hadn't opened the letter.

"Stop that incessant clicking," he ordered.

The letter dropped from between Lewis's fingers and floated onto the table. With his index finger, he pushed the missive toward Thurston. "This was delivered shortly before your arrival."

William eyed the letter and then shoved it into his pocket. Lewis hoped his disappointment wasn't evident. "An Irish lad brought it," he added, hoping to pique his interest.

Thurston showed little curiosity in the added information or the letter. He rubbed the back of his neck and stared out the restaurant window. "I've just returned from a meeting with

Matthew Cheever—regarding O'Malley's involvement in the shooting."

Lewis straightened in his chair. Perhaps this was going to be a profitable day after all. "I hope the reward was generous."

William slammed his fist on the table. The surrounding patrons glanced in their direction but quickly averted their attention when met by William's glowering stare. "He had the audacity to report that Boott was not interested in any of the evidence I presented—not my willingness to testify that it was O'Malley, not the piece of fabric that proves he was in the grove of pines, *none* of it. I even told him I could produce the weapon, but he said Boott didn't want to hear any more allegations against O'Malley."

Lewis was dumbfounded by the revelation. "Why? I can't imagine that Kirk Boott doesn't want to avenge the person who harmed him."

"Cheever wouldn't give me a direct answer. He merely said to 'let it go.' I attempted to discover whether they had received any other reliable information regarding the shooting, but Cheever said he wasn't free to discuss the matter. It's another example of Boott pandering to the Irish. Even if he knows it was O'Malley, he doesn't want to risk admitting he's wrong about those papists. The man's a fool! There's a meeting of the Associates at the end of the week. I doubt whether Kirk will be able to attend, but *I* will certainly be present." William stood, shoved a hand in his pocket, and pulled out the crumpled letter. His eyes now focused on the scrawled writing, and recognition registered in his face. Dropping back into his chair, he ripped open the message.

Lewis watched intently as Thurston read the letter. His jaw appeared to lock, and a slight tic developed in his right eye, culminating in an uncontrollable wink. Thurston rubbed the eye. It continued to flutter. "Do you have any idea what this is?" he asked from between clenched teeth.

"No," Lewis replied. He certainly *wanted* to know. He also knew better than to put voice to his desire.

"Kathryn," he said, brandishing the letter through the air as though it were a double-edged sword. "She's making threats."

Lewis sat silently waiting, hoping for more.

Thurston didn't fail him. "Kathryn has written that if I don't support her on a regular basis, she's going to tell my wife about the child."

Lewis restrained the gasp rising in his throat. Instead, he took a gulp of air and gave William his undivided attention.

Thurston's eyes narrowed as he met Lewis's gaze. "This is going to require your assistance, Lewis. As always, you'll be well paid."

There was an ominous tone to Thurston's voice that commanded Lewis's attention. "I'll do what I can to help. Within reason, of course."

Thurston emitted a dark laugh. "You have no choice, Lewis. You'll do whatever I require—within reason or not." He hesitated, staring out the window at some indeterminate object. "Kathryn and the child are of no consequence to me—they're disposable. My wife, on the other hand, is not. I was accepted into Boston society through my marriage to Margaret. It was her family name that garnered the attention of the Boston Associates and their invitation to join with them and invest in Lowell. I've invested too much time and effort into my success. I'll not permit that Irish tramp to threaten me for the rest of my life. And that's what she would do, continue to make more and more demands upon me until eventually I refused to pay. Then what? After years of handing her money, she'd still go to my wife and ruin my life." He shook his head. "No. I'll not have it. She and the child must both be done away with."

This time it was impossible for Lewis to restrain a gasp. Undeniable horror washed over him. For all his lack of morals and disregard for other people, he'd never had to resort to killing. The very thought made him positively ill.

He didn't want to kill a woman. He couldn't! "You would have me kill the mother of your child?"

"*And* the child," William hastened to add.

Lewis attempted to hide his revulsion. "I'm sorry, Mr. Thurston, but I can't do what you're asking—not a woman and child. I've been responsible for my share of underhandedness, but this goes beyond that. This is well beyond what I'm willing to do for money."

Thurston reached across the table and grabbed Lewis by the wrist. "Don't you tell me what you can't do, Lewis," he hissed. "You *will* kill them. Both of them. And it will be done when and how I tell you. Do you understand me? I have too much information on you, Armbruster. You have no choice in this matter."

Lewis jerked his arm out of William's grasp. "There must be some other way to handle the situation besides killing them," he said in a hoarse whisper.

William's eyes clouded as he spoke, his mind obviously racing to develop some sinister strategy. "It won't be difficult. I'll formulate a plan that can't go awry. Something simple yet effective."

Lewis stood. "I don't like it."

"I didn't ask you to like it. And don't attempt to leave town without my permission, Lewis. I wouldn't want to reveal to Kirk Boott that I was mistaken and that you are truly the person who shot him."

Lewis leaned down across the table and stared into Thurston's eyes. "There's no one who will believe you. You've already pointed the finger at O'Malley."

"You really don't know me very well, do you, Lewis? Do you think me so foolish that I wouldn't have a plan if you decided to betray me? I told you before that I have other contacts who perform assignments for me. One of them was at the scene of the shooting, Lewis. He watched you shoot Kirk Boott; he's willing to testify whenever I say the word. The horse you rode that day? It belonged to another contact. He'll testify to the fact that you borrowed his horse, rode out of town in time to accomplish the deed, and returned his horse in a lather shortly after the shooting was reported. Why, he can even state with authority that you came from the direction of Pawtucket Falls. Combine that testimony with the fact that Boott doesn't believe O'Malley shot him, and any judge would convict you."

Lewis winced. "I'll tell that you were the one who plotted and hired me," Lewis feebly countered.

"*You* have no one who can tie me to the incident, Lewis, nor do you have the funds to buy testimony or silence. In other words, you have no reliable contacts. Now sit down. I believe I've already developed a simple plan."

William wet his lips and leaned across the table, speaking in hushed tones. Lewis listened, his stomach churning as he stared at the puffy lips spewing forth his ruthless plot. "If you follow my instructions, you'll have no difficulty," Thurston said as he finished speaking and leaned back in the chair.

Lewis lowered his head, his chin nearly resting upon his chest. "Is there nothing I can say that would cause you to reconsider?"

"Nothing." William said, pressing payment into Lewis's hand. "Half now and half when the deed is accomplished."

Lewis hated himself for accepting the money. He walked down the street with his mind reeling. Shooting Boott had been one thing—he had shot merely to injure. Killing an innocent woman, not to mention the child, was an entirely different matter. He needed time to think. More than that, he needed something to drink. Bowing his head against the cold, Lewis turned and set off toward Nichol's Tavern, anxious for a tankard of ale.

The remainder of the afternoon was a blur. People came and went while Lewis remained at a corner table attempting to blot out the memory of a dark-haired toddler and his strong-willed Irish mother. By nightfall the ale had done its work—the faces of Kathryn and the little boy were but a fuzzy blur. What he must do, however, had not completely vanished from his mind.

Lewis glanced toward the doorway. A boisterous group of Englishmen entered and seated themselves at a nearby table. Their camaraderie captured his attention as they joked and laughed together. He watched as they were served bowls of steaming fish chowder and hunks of hearty rye bread, and in his inebriated state, he found himself longing for friendship. Only one of the men looked familiar. Lewis recognized John

Farnsworth, who was now pushing aside his bowl and unfurling papers on the table.

Lewis's natural curiosity about the business of others caused him to straighten in his chair and strain to catch a glimpse of what the four men were so intently reviewing. It appeared to be a drawing or diagram, but the picture was hazy, his vision impaired. One of the men spoke of the recent mishaps at the Merrimack and Appleton mills. "These latest mishaps were obviously intentional. Any fool could have seen they weren't accidents but purposefully caused."

"Are you saying they lacked a level of professional talent?" another man said with a laugh.

Intoxicated or not, Lewis's interest was immediately piqued by the comment, and he wondered if John Farnsworth and his English cohorts were numbered among William Thurston's hirelings. He wanted to see what it was these men were studying so intently. Pushing aside his schooner of ale, Lewis leaned heavily on the table and then stumbled from his chair toward the men.

"Hullo, Farnsworth," he slurred, leaning down until he was practically nose-to-nose with Farnsworth. His arm smacked against the papers strewn across the table, sending several fluttering to the floor. Lewis grabbed at one of the pages and swept it upward until it was well within his view. It appeared to be detailed drawings of the power system at the Appleton mills.

"I'll take that," Farnsworth said, pulling the crumpled drawing from Lewis's grasp and handing it to one of the other men. "Appears you may have had one tankard too many, Mr. Armbruster."

"Or not quite enough," Lewis replied, his voice garbled as he staggered out of the tavern, wondering why Farnsworth and his friends were so absorbed in drawings of an already operational power system.

Lewis continued onward, his thoughts shifting from the fine-lined drawing of waterwheels and pulleys to the friendship and harmony exhibited by Farnsworth and the other men. He needed someone in whom to confide, someone who could help him make sense of his unruly life. *Lilly!* Without warning, her name flashed into his mind. Surely she could help him.

His hand balled into a tight fist, Lewis pounded on the door of number 5 Jackson Street. It was nearly ten o'clock, quite late for someone to be calling at the boardinghouse, but he didn't care. He pounded again. The door opened just a crack, and Miss Addie peeked through the narrow opening. Pressing his face near the gap in the doorway, Lewis said, "It's Lewis Armbruster. I must see my sister." The heavy odor of spirits wafted through the night air as he spoke.

Miss Addie sniffed several times, her nose in the air like a bloodhound following its scent. "There's no doubt where you've spent your evening," the older woman admonished. "The girls have retired for the night, but if you care to wait outside, I'll go and see if Lilly is asleep. I won't permit you entry in your condition."

"I'll wait," Lewis said, sliding down onto the front step. "I saw your friend, Farnsworth, at Nichol's," he added.

"John? At Nichol's? Was he by himself?" Addie asked before quickly placing an open palm over her mouth.

Lewis gave her a lopsided grin. The woman was obviously embarrassed by the inquiry. "He was with three other men, all of them engrossed in drawings of the waterwheels and power supply at the Appleton mills. No need to worry, Miss Beecher," he said with as much reassurance as he could muster in his drunken condition. The door closed and he leaned his head against the hard, cold wood. He doubted his sister would appear, but he closed his eyes and waited.

He was unsure how long he had been there when the door jerked open. Lewis fell backward, his upper body sprawling across the threshold. "Good evening, Lilly," he said, staring upward.

"What brings you here at this time of night, Lewis?"

Lewis managed to pull himself into an upright position and meet his sister's gaze. "I need to talk to someone who can help me understand why I've made so many wrong choices in my life." He hesitated a moment. "I thought of you, Lilly. You're the only one who truly knows me. I need help," he whispered.

Lilly glanced toward Miss Addie, who nodded her head. "You may come in, Lewis, but we can talk for only a short time. Boardinghouse rules state I am to be in bed by ten o'clock."

Lewis turned to Miss Addie. She beckoned him in. "I'll wait in my room with the door open, Lilly. No more than ten minutes," she cautioned.

Lilly nodded and then led Lewis into the parlor. "We haven't much time, Lewis. What choices were you alluding to? The boardinghouse girls, your gambling, your drinking, selling the farm . . ."

"You've kept quite a list, haven't you? It would take more time than either of us has to address even those items," Lewis said as he leaned forward on his chair. "And they're not even what I came to discuss. I should leave."

Lilly grasped his arm. "Wait, Lewis. I'm sorry; I know I've been harsh. Tell me why you've come. I'll do my best to help."

He looked at her oddly, wondering why she was so compassionate when he'd been nothing but mean-spirited toward her. Perhaps it was all that religious nonsense she adhered to. Perhaps he looked as bad as he felt. Either way, it didn't matter.

"I've become involved in some matters that are terrible, unforgivable—matters so heinous I dare not speak of them."

"Lewis, you must confide in me if I'm to be of any assistance. *Please!* Tell me what you've done."

Now that the influence of his ale was beginning to wear off, Lewis realized that coming here had been a mistake. What could he do? Tell his sister he was William Thurston's henchman, hired to murder a helpless woman and child? The thought of making such a statement to his sister was ludicrous. Besides, how could Lilly help?

"There's nothing you can do, Lilly, and telling you could place your life in danger. Forget that I ever came here. I don't want to cause you further trouble."

Lilly gently touched his face. "I could pray for you, Lewis. In that regard, I fear I have failed you."

There was an overpowering sadness in his sister's voice that caused Lewis to regret the very essence of who he was and what he had become. "I doubt it will help, Lilly, but I'll not reject your offer of prayer."

Lilly stared at Lewis as he left the room. There was little doubt something sinister was occurring. She knew she must intercede for her brother, pray for his protection and strength to overcome whatever evil had permeated his life. The thought surprised her, yet the urgency to pray was unmistakable—unwavering, overwhelming. A palpable fear for Lewis's eternal salvation consumed her every thought. Falling to her knees, Lilly translated her fear into supplication as she lovingly whispered her words into the ear of God.

CHAPTER 29

A rapping at the front door brought Addie scurrying from the kitchen. "Mintie!" She hesitated momentarily. "I'm surprised to see you."

There were dark circles under Mintie's eyes, and her face was etched in a weariness that gave proof to sleepless nights. "May I come in?" she haltingly asked.

"So long as you understand that I remain steadfast in my admonition regarding John Farnsworth."

Mintie nodded and stepped inside the door. Removing her woolen coat and bonnet, she turned toward her sister. "I've missed your companionship, Adelaide."

Addie gave her sister a guarded smile, still somewhat fearful of Mintie's motivation. "Would you like a cup of tea?"

"Yes, that would be most welcome. I can come into the kitchen if you're busy with meal preparations."

Addie's eyebrows danced upward. Her sister was certainly compliant this morning. "That would be most helpful. I was in the midst of peeling turnips. I'm preparing lamb stew for the noonday meal."

"I'll be glad to finish paring the turnips if it will help,"

Mintie offered as she followed along behind.

Addie's mouth fell open at the suggestion. Mintie offering to assist her? Something was amiss, but for the life of her, she couldn't figure out what Mintie wanted. Handing her sister an apron and a knife, Addie began chopping hunks of carrot and dropping them into a kettle. "Was there something in particular you wanted to discuss?" she ventured.

Mintie nodded, her eyes cast downward as she continued to peel the vegetables. "I've been giving thought to Mr. Farnsworth and his possible predisposition of loyalty to the Crown ever since you told me I was unwelcome in your home."

Addie gave her sister a sidelong glance but didn't interrupt. Instead she silently waited, permitting her sister an opportunity to complete her explanation.

Mintie cleared her throat and continued. "I'll admit I may have jumped to some unwarranted conclusions. However, there were things—still are, for that matter—that give me cause to wonder about Mr. Farnsworth. There's no denying the items I've seen in his room or the men who come to the house—without calling cards," she hastened to add.

"I've spent a good deal of time pondering this situation and seeking the best way to mend our relationship. I don't want an outsider to come between us, Adelaide. After all, we're blood, and we shouldn't permit anyone to cause a breach in our family."

Addie wiped her hands on her stained apron and met her sister's gaze. "Does this mean you no longer suspect he is a traitor?"

Before Mintie had opportunity to reply, Addie's boarders came clattering into the house with their shrill voices filling the air. "Miss Addie, Miss Addie, there's been another accident at the mills," Lilly called, her voice muffled until it finally reached the kitchen.

"Come join me, Lilly," Addie called in return, anxious to hear the details. "What happened?" she asked as Lilly entered the room.

"It's terrible, Miss Addie. Something was jammed in the waterwheel. Several men were attempting to get it loose. When they finally succeeded and the wheel began turning, one of the men lost his footing and dropped into the rushing water below. He was crushed by the wheel," she said in a hushed voice. "The man has a wife and three children. We were told to return home until someone sends for us. Mr. Arnold said it wouldn't be until after lunch for certain and perhaps not until tomorrow."

Lilly's words pierced Addie's heart, each utterance a tiny dart of suspicion. The clattering of Mintie's knife upon the floor caused Addie to startle and whirl around.

"John Farnsworth had diagrams of the Appleton Mill in his room. I saw drawings—large, intricate drawings of the waterwheel and machinery. They were atop his trunk," Mintie hastily added, placing her open palm against her chest. "And to think that only moments ago I was prepared to retract my accusations against John Farnsworth. What folly! I trust you'll now heed my advice and keep your distance from that traitorous man who nearly destroyed our family ties."

Addie stared down at the knife lying on the floor. Her throat constricted. She could not speak, but her mind was racing back to the sight of Lewis Armbruster standing at her front door several nights ago. What was it Lewis had said? *I saw Farnsworth at Nichol's. He was with three other men, all of them engrossed in drawings of the waterwheels and power supply at the Appleton mills.* Why would John have been discussing those diagrams at Nichol's Tavern? Most likely the men who were with him were some of those secretive gentlemen who came calling upon him at Mintie's boardinghouse. A sensation of nausea swept over her. Could the man she had grown to care for be a party to this frightful incident? Surely not. And yet she was filled with apprehension— and questions.

"Did you hear me, Adelaide? Promise me you'll stay away from that treacherous man."

Addie gave her sister a dazed stare. "After listening to any explanation he cares to offer, I'll make my decision. Condemning Mr. Farnsworth without giving him an opportunity to defend himself is contrary to my beliefs, Mintie. I wouldn't want others to treat me in such a manner."

Mintie momentarily perched on the edge of her chair and then rose, her back straight and her neck reaching toward the heavens, as she gave her sister a look of haughty disdain. "You were always a willful child, and it appears you've not changed an iota. What is it going to take for you to realize you are a wretched judge of character?"

"I know I'm a failure in your eyes, Mintie. You consider me no more than an undisciplined child. But you're wrong. I'm a grown woman with my own opinions. The difference between us is that while I tend to see the best in people and situations, you tend to see the worst. You consider that tendency to be a flaw in my character; I consider it a blessing."

Mintie tied her bonnet ribbons into a snug bow beneath her sharp chin. "Once again you're choosing that traitorous Englishman over your own flesh and blood."

Addie watched her sister flee from the house.

———————

Lewis pulled his gold pocket watch from his waistcoat, gently rubbing his thumb over the engraved initials before snapping open the case. Nine o'clock. Tucking the watch back in place, he quickened his step. He noticed a woman and a group of boys on a nearby corner eyeing him suspiciously and cast his gaze downward, hoping the shadows of evening would prevent them from observing his face. He didn't want anyone to remember he'd been to the Acre, especially on this night.

Pulling up the collar of an old tattered coat furnished by William Thurston, Lewis wondered how he had stooped to this level. It was better not to think, he decided. After all, thinking wouldn't change anything, and by now, he was in too deep to dig his way out. Thurston held all of the trump cards.

When Lewis had objected to an early evening arrival at Kathryn's house, William assured him the woman and child would be asleep. With a malevolent grin, Thurston explained that it was Kathryn's practice to sleep in the early evening in order to keep him company during his late-night arrivals. He hoped Thurston knew what he was talking about! Lewis walked the litter-strewn street, seeking the abhorrent hovel Kathryn called home. He listened outside, and hearing nothing, he entered quietly, spying the woman asleep on a crude cot pulled close to the waning fire. The child was slumbering in the crook of her arm. Shadows danced across the room as he silently edged closer and lifted a pillow. He stared down at Kathryn's creamy complexion, her features relaxed in sleep. Paralyzed, he gazed at her unbridled beauty for a moment before gaining a sense of courage and then pressed the pillow tight against her mouth and nose. The shabby covers fell to the floor as she briefly struggled before her body suddenly turned limp. He removed the pillow from her face and stood transfixed, unable to look away from her youthful appearance.

The boy cried out in his sleep, startling Lewis, who had been standing there as if in a trance. The child's waiflike body was restlessly seeking warmth against his mother's already chilling form. The boy couldn't be much over a year old. Lewis shivered. His fingers continued to clutch the pillow, yet he could not muster courage enough to bring it down upon the child's face. A piece of firewood dropped in the hearth. The crackling embers glowed, illuminating a purplish mushroom-shaped birthmark on the boy's arm. Grabbing one of the tattered blankets, Lewis threw it over the child. "If the boy is lucky, someone will find him by morning," he muttered as he rushed out of the room and down the street.

The streets were quiet, with only an occasional passerby to avoid as he hurried toward the Wareham House. He would report to Thurston and hopefully receive the balance of his blood money before morning. For a time he had given thought to refusing the money, thinking that would somehow assuage his guilt. But if Thurston was true to his word, the sum should be large enough to pay his passage to South America and a new beginning. How he longed for a new beginning. Lewis walked past the front desk and up the steps to Thurston's room. He rapped lightly on the door.

William was bare-chested, his shirt dangling from one finger. "I'm preparing to go out. I hope you're bringing me good news," he said as he moved away from the door and stood by the fireplace, his exposed back toward Lewis.

Lewis stared at Thurston's unclothed torso and immediately knew why Thurston had feared Kathryn's threat. William and the child carried the same birthmark on their arms.

"It went as planned. They're both dead," he said, struggling to keep his voice impassive.

William's lips curled into a cruel grin. "Excellent! I still find it difficult to believe that Kathryn had the audacity to think she could hold me hostage to her threats. You know, Lewis, if I didn't already have plans, we'd go and celebrate," he said, quickly changing moods.

Thurston's disdain for the woman who had given birth to his child amazed even Lewis. It was becoming increasingly obvious that Thurston's cruelty knew no bounds. He thought of the little boy, and a tinge of fear crept into his consciousness. "I was considering a trip to South America," he cautiously remarked.

"What? You're joking, of course," William said with a laugh. "We have work to complete right here. Besides, there's no one waiting for you in South America—or is there?" he questioned, making an obscene gesture.

"I merely thought it might be best to keep a low profile. England doesn't appeal to me, and I certainly don't want to move into the western wilderness of this country." Lewis watched as Thurston carefully affixed his cravat. "You mentioned unfinished business. Perhaps it would be best to use someone else since I've been deeply involved in several of your other ventures."

William gave a wicked laugh. "Your involvement is exactly what makes you the perfect person to continue assisting me, Lewis. I won't have you leaving the country. Besides, once I've managed to oust Boott and gain the helm here in Lowell, you'll be my right-hand man. You can't do that from South America. Sit down," he said, pointing to a chair. "I have another half hour before I must leave. I'm sure you've come to collect your money."

Lewis nodded. "I assume you've heard of the difficulty with the waterwheel over at the Appleton?" he ventured.

"You're wanting to know if I'm involved in that disastrous event? Word about town has it that there could be any number of suspects. I'm certainly not among the numbered few being discussed, but I have a feeling there's ample evidence to assure that our Mr. O'Malley is involved in this crime, along with several of his Irish comrades. I do believe that once O'Malley is found responsible for the assault on Boott and the incident at the Appleton, the Associates will be convinced of Boott's incompetence as a leader. Of course, the death of Kathryn and the child will further demonstrate the incivility of the Irish. All things considered, it appears as if matters aren't boding well for the savages. If events don't move in the direction I'm planning, I'll have another assignment for you in the near future," Thurston said as he smiled back at his own image in the mirror.

Lewis felt his heart begin to palpitate rapidly. He didn't want another assignment. All he wanted was to disassociate from this web of horror in which he was now trapped. He watched as William began counting out his money.

"Give up the idea of South America, Lewis. At least for now," Thurston said as he turned and pointed toward the gold lying on the table. "Attempting to remove yourself from my plans could prove—shall we say—fatal? I have eyes and ears everywhere, even along the docks, should you attempt to depart the country against my wishes. Men who enjoy trading information for a few coins. Make no mistake about me, Lewis. If I was unwilling to tolerate Kathryn's demands, I'll not tolerate yours. Do I make myself clear?"

Lewis nodded. "Abundantly," he said. "However, I wasn't attempting to make demands, but I have no desire to run these mills or live in Lowell. My genuine desire is to live in a larger city. Perhaps we could strike an agreement that I'll complete one last assignment for you—then we'll forget we ever knew each other?"

William gave him a thoughtful look. "You have my word."

Lewis gave a nod of affirmation as they shook hands. "I believe I'll go and have an ale before calling it a night. Enjoy your engagement," he called over his shoulder.

Inhaling a deep breath of the cold night air, Lewis knew it was going to take more than one ale for him to forget Kathryn O'Hanrahan and her child. For several hours he sat at Nichol's Tavern, quickly downing one tankard after another, while a conscience he had never before known gnawed at him, prohibiting him from shaking a vision of the woman and child from his mind. Finally weary of attempting to blot out the squalid event, Lewis threw a coin on the table and left. He began walking and then suddenly turned back toward the Acre. He couldn't seem to stop himself; he had to know if someone had rescued the child.

Growing closer, he could hear an increasing commotion as he neared the house. A wagon rumbled by and came to a halt in front of Kathryn's shanty. Moving closer, he stood watching from across the narrow street as a woman pulled herself up into the wagon and then held out her arms toward a child. Permitting the ale to give him false courage, Lewis stepped out in front of the wagon as it began to turn.

"Watch yer step!" the woman cried out, pulling her team of horses to an abrupt halt.

Lewis tipped his hat. "Sorry. I was wondering about all the turmoil and didn't realize you were going to make such a sharp turn. Do you know what's going on over there?" he asked, hoping the woman would take a moment to reply.

Wiping tears from her face with the dirty hem of her dress, she met his gaze. "Me sister's died in her sleep, leavin' this poor child without a ma or pa to love him."

"Truly, died in her sleep, eh?" Lewis said hoping that no one ever suspected the death to be anything else.

"Where are you rushing off to with the child? Must you not see to a proper burial for his mother?" Lewis inquired.

The woman pulled the child close. "I must see to the child's safety. Ya can't be havin' a babe in the midst of death. For sure it'll be causin' a curse upon him. Once I care for the boy, then I'll bury me sister."

Lewis stood watching until the wagon rolled out of the Acre before making his way home to fight the demons who visited him in his sleep that night. The woman had no way of knowing it was too late. The boy already had a curse upon him.

"This had better be important," Nathan Appleton muttered to Tracy Jackson as they waited for the remainder of their colleagues to arrive. "Making a trip to Lowell in the dead of winter is not my idea of pleasure."

"Nor mine," Jackson agreed. "However, William sent word it was urgent, and although the man tends to exaggerate at times, we can't ignore his warning, especially with Kirk still recuperating."

"Yes, I understand. I think I'll acquiesce and let you take control of tonight's meeting, Tracy. Since Thurston contacted you directly, it just seems more appropriate."

The remainder of the men finally arrived and one by one filed into the offices at the Merrimack. When the sound of scraping chairs and murmuring voices had finally quieted, Tracy stood. "Good evening, gentlemen. I thank you for your cooperation and willingness to travel to Lowell for this meeting. Hopefully, we will find resolution to several issues that have been brought to my attention by one of our members, William Thurston." Tracy watched as William's chest visibly swelled when the men turned in his direction and acknowledged him. Clearing his throat, Tracy continued. "Rather than attempt to explain the issues, I think it would be most expedient to read William's missive, which I received earlier this week."

The men listened attentively as Tracy read the allegations, all of which pointed toward Kirk Boott's inability to properly handle the ongoing problems within the community and, in particular, his disinclination to tackle the Irish problem and bring the papists to heel. Murmurs once again filled the room until Tracy finally tapped on the desk in order to regain control of the meeting.

William rose from his chair. "If you have no objection, Tracy, I would be most willing to entertain any questions. But first let me reiterate that I feel Boott has been useless with his sweet talk and promises of a church for the papists. I believe we must make an example of the culprit who committed the shooting. Once that has been done, I believe we must impose severe restrictions and curfews on the Irish. If we force them to use identification passes, cease permitting them to settle in the Paddy camps, and cut their wages, we can keep them from further infiltrating the town. I believe we should hire Americans, even if it requires higher wages and a decrease in our profit. Now, any questions?"

Paul Moody lifted his cigar in the air. "I have one. Is Kirk not attending because he wasn't invited or because he's unable to be here due to his injury? It seems he should have the opportunity to answer these allegations."

"I have presented all of my evidence to Mr. Boott; he is well aware of the involvement of the Irish in all of these incidents. And I would think you, of all people, Mr. Moody, would want these Irish thugs punished. It was one of your most valuable employees who died at the Appleton."

Paul glowered at Thurston. "I don't need you to tell me I've lost a valued employee, William. There's nobody who wants the guilty party punished more than I do. However, when punishment is meted out, I want it to be upon the guilty person."

"You sound like Boott. How much more evidence do you want? It's obviously the Irish, and in fact, I've given you the name of the man who shot Boott and participated in the incident at the Appleton. I've reason to believe he and his cohorts have been involved in all of the mishaps that have been occurring at the mills. This Irish faction needs to be brought under control."

All heads turned at the sound of a closing door and shuffling feet entering the building. "I am deeply touched, William, that you are so doggedly pursuing the criminal who attacked me," Kirk Boott said as he limped into the room. He removed his beaver hat and placed it in Tracy's extended hand. "Thank you, Tracy," he said before continuing. "William is correct. He did send me what he purported was evidence that would convict Johnny O'Malley of shooting me. As some of you know, Johnny is a fine Irish man who is closely associated with Hugh

Cummiskey. He carries a great deal of influence among his countrymen. In fact, he's been vital in securing additional workers from Boston when we needed them for new canal construction."

The men nodded in agreement, all of them having seen the detailed reports Kirk had submitted to the Associates as their projects in Lowell progressed.

"For that very reason, I found William's allegation against Johnny disquieting. After he left, Matthew Cheever and I thoroughly dissected the so-called evidence produced by William. It is all a lie. Had Johnny been located where William purports, it would have been impossible to shoot my right leg."

William jumped to his feet. "Perhaps I misunderstood the exact location, but you can't deny the piece of fabric from O'Malley's coat."

Kirk's resolve was obvious as he pointed his cane toward William. "O'Malley tells me that coat came up missing several days before the shooting, and—"

"And you believe that?" William yelled. "Surely you men can see what I've been saying all along. He's not fit to run this operation."

"Sit down, William," Tracy ordered from between clenched teeth. "You'll have an opportunity to speak when Kirk has finished. Continue, Kirk," Tracy said.

Kirk nodded. "As I was saying, the piece of cloth was found in the clump of trees where William alleges the shooter was located. If he's now changing his mind about where the assassin was hiding, the piece of fabric is of no consequence, is it, William?"

William's face had turned bright red. "Possibly not, but that doesn't nullify the information regarding the incident at the Appleton. I told you I have men who will testify that O'Malley's responsible for the death of Simeon Jones."

"And I have evidence that Johnny O'Malley wasn't even in town on the date of the accident," Kirk rebutted. "Evidence that wasn't bought and paid for."

"What are you saying? That I concocted this whole thing?

That's absurd and you know it, Kirk. You put your evidence before these men, and I'll do the same. We'll see what's been bought and paid for," William challenged.

"Gentlemen, gentlemen," Tracy called out, "let's call a halt to this inappropriate behavior right now. We're all gathered here to resolve this matter. Let's do it in a civilized manner. William, you may present whatever evidence you have to prove your allegations that Kirk is unfit to continue as manager for the Corporation. Kirk, you may then defend your position."

The group recessed while the two men sent for various witnesses to substantiate their allegations. It was growing late when Tracy finally called for a vote. "What say you, gentlemen? Let me have a show of hands. All those in favor of retaining Mr. Boott as manager of the Corporation? Those opposed?" Tracy nodded. "It appears you're the only member opposed to Kirk's retention, William."

The group sat in stunned silence as William pointed his finger at the group. "You've not heard the last of this. You've made a grievous error."

CHAPTER *30*

Lilly watched as Miss Addie glanced across the street toward her sister's boardinghouse. She wondered if the two sisters would ever resolve their differences. The waterwheel incident at the Appleton was still fresh when Mintie's sharp tongue had lashed out against John Farnsworth. Unwilling to abide Mintie's harsh attitude any longer, John had rebuked her for a lack of civility. Offended by his reproach, Mintie had unleashed her wrath upon him before finally accusing him of being a traitor. John had immediately packed his trunk and taken up residence at the Wareham House.

Had it not been for Lilly's intervention, Matthew, now in charge of the boardinghouse keepers, would have immediately fired Miss Mintie as the keeper at number 7 Jackson Street. And had it not been for Miss Addie, Lilly would have bid Miss Mintie a fond farewell. But Addie's despair over the situation had been heartwrenching. "It's her upbringing that makes her act in such a manner," she'd argued on her sister's behalf. "If she loses her position, she's likely to end up in a poorhouse, what with the Corporation unwilling to give her a reference," Addie had wept. "I can't bear to see her brought to ruin."

When Lilly could listen to no more, she had gone and spoken to John, telling him of Addie's anguish. John, in turn, had spoken to Matthew. And Matthew had told Mintie that had it not been for the kindness of John Farnsworth, she would have been sent packing.

In the weeks that followed, very little was seen of Miss Mintie. She remained tucked away in her house, caring for her boarders but doing little else. It appeared, however, that she hadn't entirely given up her snooping. On occasion, she could still be seen peeking out from behind the heavy draperies at the front window.

"You've been very quiet of late, Miss Addie. What's wrong?" Lilly questioned as she walked alongside the older woman while they headed toward town.

"I've been worried about Mintie. She's not socializing at all. I hear she hasn't attended her temperance meetings, and she hasn't been at the sewing bees at the church. In fact, she appears to be sending Lucy to do most of her shopping nowadays. I fear she's becoming a recluse. I'm hoping that once spring arrives, she'll venture out a bit."

Lilly patted Miss Addie's hand. "I fear it may take more than a bit of warm weather to thaw Miss Mintie's heart."

"Most likely, you're correct. She's a proud woman, but deep down, she's a good person, Lilly. I know that may be difficult for others to believe, but it's her spirit that's wounded. She feels unloved and unlovable."

Lilly listened, her mind churning for some way she might encourage her friend. "I'll try to come up with an idea to get her out of the house," she promised, wondering how she could possibly make a chink in Miss Mintie's armor.

"I believed the letter I wrote explaining John's loyalty to this country, as well as the Corporation, would soften her. I even invited her to tea, but she didn't respond," Addie lamented.

"I must admit—I had my own concerns about Mr. Farnsworth at one time," Lilly sheepishly admitted.

Addie gave her an astonished look. "Really? What made *you* question John?"

Lilly smiled. "One night when Matthew's father was escorting me home, I saw John and several men huddled together in a seemingly clandestine meeting; they appeared to be arguing. When Mr. Cheever and I came into view, they rushed off. After listening to Miss Mintie's accusations that Mr. Farnsworth was an English spy, I wondered if she was correct."

Addie shifted her shopping basket to her left arm and smiled. "And what changed your mind?"

"Some time later, when Matthew and I were together, he mentioned Farnsworth and his loyalty to the Associates. I mentioned the meeting and my concerns. He laughed, telling me it was quite the opposite."

Addie leaned in a bit closer, obviously intent on not missing a word.

"He explained that Mr. Farnsworth was unjustly fired from his position in England because the mill owners thought he had been bribed to help Mr. Lowell sneak plans for the looms out of England."

"Did Matthew tell you that John escorted Mr. Lowell through the English mills? It was because of those tours that they accused him of commiserating with Mr. Lowell."

"Their treatment of Mr. Farnsworth was reprehensible!" Lilly declared. "Matthew said that Mr. Farnsworth was so angered by his employer's shoddy behavior that he decided he would come to the United States and help make the mills in New England better than those in the old country. Before he left, he formed an alliance with several of his friends who were being treated poorly. Mr. Farnsworth agreed to pay their passage if, upon their arrival, they brought him additional information concerning the machinery and operation of the mills where they worked in England. They arranged their meetings prior to the men being employed by the Corporation so no one would know of their association with Mr. Farnsworth."

Addie nodded. "That's what John explained to me, also. John feared there might be retribution against the men's families if any word leaked out they knew him. He didn't want the men who were assisting him to face accusations of being spies. So instead of working against American industrialization, John and all of those men were *aiding* the industrialization in New England. I clearly explained those facts to Mintie when I wrote her, but obviously she has chosen to disregard the truth."

"I imagine she's embarrassed, especially since Mr. Farnsworth has proven to be a strong ally rather than a traitor. And since Miss Mintie's so proud, it's easier to seclude herself than face possible ridicule by others."

They continued walking, stopping for a moment to glance in a window along the way. "I can understand Mintie's hesitation to place herself in a position of public ridicule, but I'm her sister. It's almost as if she's unwilling to face the fact that she is wrong."

Lilly thought about Addie's words. "Admitting you're wrong is difficult. I've wrestled with that issue myself. Perhaps we need to concentrate our prayers upon Miss Mintie. What do you think? If we can't soften her, perhaps the Lord will."

A glimmer shone in Miss Addie's eyes. "Is that what helped change your attitude toward the mills?"

"A lot of prayer and several long talks with Matthew Cheever," Lilly replied. "Even if Matthew and I never restore our relationship, he managed to show me that industrialization is a necessity. We can't remain reliant upon England if we're to be a free country. I continue to dislike the fact that East Chelmsford was the chosen spot, but I now accept that the mills are something I can't change. I'm still praying about forgiveness toward those who wronged me. I believe I've come a long way in that regard, but when a day or two passes and I haven't prayed about forgiveness, that same resentment creeps back into my mind. I think it will be an ongoing project for me."

The women entered Whidden's, stopping for a moment to examine a display of newly arrived lace. "Every one of us is an ongoing project that needs God's forgiveness. You've matured in your faith right before my eyes, Lilly. If we can pray Mintie into that degree of maturity, perhaps we can mend our family ties. As for your relationship with Matthew, I believe you two are well on the way to restoration."

Lilly ran her fingers across a shimmering piece of pale blue fabric. "I haven't seen much of Matthew lately. It seems he is always busy with Corporation business and when he is finally available, I'm too tired or have made other plans."

"That fabric would be a good choice for you—perhaps a new gown for the Blowing Out Ball," Addie absently commented. "With Nadene starting back to work on Monday, I'm certain you'll have more energy. I'm pleased she's healed so well. I do admire your loyalty to Nadene."

"It was the least I could do," Lilly murmured, the compliment a reminder of the role she had played in Nadene's injuries. She was certain God had forgiven her willful behavior. Forgiving herself, however, was proving more difficult. "I hope returning to work won't prove too strenuous for Nadene. I know her burns have healed, but her cough seems to be getting worse. Have you noticed?"

"Occasionally she seems to have difficulty breathing deeply, but the last few weeks she has seemed stronger. Besides, she's anxious to get back to work."

The sound of pounding horse hooves, rumbling carriages, and loud voices sent Mrs. Whidden scurrying to the front of the store. "Wonder what's going on out there?" she asked her husband.

Moments later, the bell above the door sounded, followed by laughter and chattering as several patrons entered the shop. Lilly glanced toward the shoppers and felt her knees buckle. She grasped the edge of the display case and steadied herself as she watched Matthew escort Isabelle Locklear into the store.

"This stop wouldn't be necessary if Mother had permitted me ample time to prepare for the journey," Isabelle cooed to Matthew. "I know you didn't want to stop, but I simply refuse to go any farther knowing I've forgotten my hairbrush," she continued. "You are sure a dear to indulge me."

Lilly continued staring at the couple as Matthew patted Isabelle's hand. "We musn't take too long. Bishop Fenwick is waiting in his carriage. He's anxious to get settled."

"I promise I'll hurry," she replied, demurely peeking up from beneath the brim of her silk bonnet.

Lilly wanted to run from the store, but she would have to pass directly in front of Matthew to do so. If she could shrink behind one of the counters, perhaps she could remain undetected until Isabelle and Matthew completed their purchases. She began edging toward a tall display, then stopped and turned toward Miss Addie, who was now overcome by a fit of coughing. Matthew immediately looked in their direction. He appeared startled as he met Lilly's unwavering gaze.

Moving forward, Matthew patted Addie on the back for a moment. "I'll be right back," he said to Isabelle. "Let me get you a cup of water," he offered.

Addie ceased her coughing and gave Lilly a smug grin while Matthew rushed toward the rear of the store. "You were going to hide. But I wanted to be certain he saw you."

Lilly gave the older woman an astonished look. "Why? So I would be further embarrassed?"

"Of course not," Addie chided. "But knowing how you react, I was certain you would avoid Matthew. He wouldn't have an opportunity to explain why he's with that woman, and this whole matter would remain unresolved. There's probably a very good explanation for all of this."

"That's Isabelle Locklear, Miss Addie. Kirk Boott's niece. The one Boott wants Matthew to marry. Matthew told me they had parted company, but it appears he wasn't as forthcoming as I had believed."

Addie gave a gentle cough as Matthew approached. "Don't jump to conclusions," she whispered to Lilly before turning her attention toward Matthew. "I think I'm better, but thank you for your assistance. I believe I will drink that water," she said, taking the cup.

"We need to talk," Matthew whispered to Lilly while extending his hand to receive the emptied cup from Miss Addie. "I'll stop by tomorrow evening."

Lilly opened her mouth to refuse, but Matthew walked away without giving her an opportunity to protest.

334

Matthew slowed his stride to match Bishop Fenwick's as he escorted the rotund cleric up the steps of the Boott residence the next morning.

"I trust you slept well, Bishop," Boott greeted. "I understand the rooms at the Wareham House are quite comfortable."

"The accommodations were satisfactory," he replied. "I'm not sure the weather is going to cooperate for an outdoor Mass. Have you made any alternate plans?"

Boott nodded as he led the visitors into the dining room. The bishop offered a blessing over the breakfast before Boott continued. "I discussed the matter with Hugh Cummiskey and suggested we could make arrangements to hold the services at St. Anne's if the weather was uncooperative. However, Hugh didn't think the Irish Catholics would attend services at St. Anne's. He had some of his men construct a lean-to that will give you some protection. He said they are willing to withstand the elements."

The bishop furrowed his brows. "There's apparently more antagonism than I anticipated. However, I don't want to make anyone uncomfortable. It's been quite some time since a priest has been here to conduct services. There wasn't even a priest available for Christmas mass. So if my people want to meet out-doors, we'll meet outdoors."

"Do you plan to announce the new building after the services?" Kirk ventured.

The bishop slathered a layer of butter onto his biscuit. "So long as we have time to review all of the documents in order to transfer the property prior to departing for the Acre," he replied, licking his finger.

Kirk pushed away from the table. "I had no idea you wanted to complete the legalities this morning, Your Eminence. Matthew and I will finalize the papers for your signature while you finish your breakfast."

The Bishop smiled broadly and nodded his agreement.

"How dare he corner me like this!" Boott exclaimed as he closed the door to his office.

"Apparently he wants assurance everything will be completed to his satisfaction before making the announcement," Matthew remarked.

Boott gave him a look of annoyance. "Obviously! However, I find his tactics heavy-handed *and* insulting. He's determined to secure that extra piece of land. I had hoped I'd have time to convince him otherwise."

Matthew shuffled through the papers and began arranging them in piles for proper signature. "It would appear the bishop has outmaneuvered you this time."

"I've no choice but to sign over the property. I've already told Hugh the announcement would be made this morning. Bishop Fenwick has missed his true calling; he has far too much business acumen for a man of the cloth!"

Thurston opened the door to his room at the Wareham House. "What took you so long? I told you to be here after lunch," he growled.

Lewis pushed past him and entered the room without responding. He was weary of Thurston and his schemes. Worse yet, he was sick of being forced to appear at Thurston's beck and call.

"Have you been drinking, Lewis?"

Lewis flopped into one of the two chairs in the room. "Why do you ask?"

"Your insolent behavior speaks volumes. I won't tolerate drunkenness. You talk too much when you've been imbibing."

Lewis gave a feeble salute. "Yes, sir."

Thurston gave him a look of disgust. "Listen carefully, Lewis. I've brought you here because I've completed my plans to dethrone Kirk Boott. This is serious business, and I need your complete attention."

Lewis grunted and shifted in the chair. "I haven't had *that* much to drink. What is it you're scheming?"

"A fire at the Merrimack," he replied, rubbing his hands in obvious delight. "It will, of course, be your handiwork, but I am going to convince the Associates otherwise."

Lewis gave an ungentlemanly snort. "When are you *ever* going to give up on this nonsense, Thurston? The Associates will never place their trust in anyone but Boott. Can't you see that he's the man they want running their business interests? Why don't you just accept the fact that you're not going to be the manager, go back to Boston, and let me get on with my life," Lewis blustered, his ale giving him artificial confidence.

William jumped up from his chair. His face was red, and the veins along his neck had swelled into a pulsating protuberance. "Don't you begin to tell me what I should or shouldn't do. The fact is, you want to get on with your life and out of your obligation to me. The Associates *will* embrace me as their new leader if you do as you're told. Remember, Lewis, I can be your ruination if you attempt to cross me."

Lewis sighed and settled back in the chair. He knew he had no choice. "So when am I to set this fire?"

Thurston's lips coiled into a satisfied grin. "I think it would be best if we both left town for a period of time before the next 'accident' occurs. I'll send word when the time is right. You can come back to town on the pretense of visiting your sister. Don't forget we've made an agreement, Lewis. I expect to know where you are at all times."

Lewis stood and nodded. "Will you be sending instructions or am I left to my own devices?"

"I'll send specific instructions. You do your best to follow them," William replied in a threatening tone.

There was nothing left to say. Lewis exited the room and walked down the narrow hallway of the Wareham House. He didn't stop walking until he reached the corner table of Nichol's Tavern, where he ordered a bottle of whiskey. Filling his glass with the amber liquid, Lewis quickly downed the contents and poured another. He wanted to forget, and if he couldn't forget, he would at least numb himself of feeling.

Mintie peeked from behind the draperies that covered the parlor windows. She longed to once again have Addie's companionship, yet she could not walk across the street and beg her sister's forgiveness—pride blocked her path. Instead, she pulled Addie's letter from the walnut desk that had once been the Judge's prize possession and sat down in the parlor. Adjusting her glasses, she continued her ritual of reading the letter, just as she had every day since its arrival.

She was now certain the contents were true, that John Farnsworth was not a traitor. Perhaps she had known it all along. But the fear of Addie becoming interested in a man and possibly taking a husband—well, it was more than she could bear to think about. How could their bond remain the same if Addie should marry?

The front door opened, and Lucy bounded in with a smile. "Morning, Miss Beecher. You reading your sister's letter again?"

Mintie quickly folded the letter and tucked it into the desk. "I was merely looking over some of my old correspondence."

"Why don't you write her a letter?"

Mintie gazed over her wire-rimmed spectacles. "And why do you think I should write Adelaide a letter?"

The child shrugged. "Because you like the one she sent you so much. You're reading it most every day when I come in," she replied before skipping off to the kitchen.

Mintie stared after the child. "Perhaps that's exactly what I'll do!"

By the time Lucy had finished the breakfast dishes, Mintie had a penned a well-thought-out note of apology to her sister. "Lucy! I have an errand," she called.

The child came scampering and screeched to a halt in front of Mintie. "How many times must I—oh, never mind. Take this note across the street to Miss Beecher. Tell her you would be happy to wait for her reply."

Filled with a mixture of fear and excitement, Mintie watched out the window for what seemed an eternity. Finally the door opened. Addie stood in the doorway for a moment, then raised her hand and waved before sending Lucy on her way. A smile spread across Mintie's lips as she pulled the drape back a bit farther and waved in return.

"Miss Beecher says she would love to come to tea this afternoon," Lucy said as she entered the front door. "Do you want me to begin dusting upstairs?" the child asked before heading up the stairway. "Miss Beecher?" Lucy turned toward her mistress. "How come you're crying?"

"It's nothing, Lucy. Sometimes folks cry when they're happy. You go ahead and start the dusting. I'll be up shortly."

CHAPTER *31*

Prudence nearly danced into the upstairs bedroom, a mischievous smile lighting her face. "There's someone here to see you, Lilly."

"Who is it? I'm preparing to leave for town."

Prudence giggled. "He said not to tell you."

Lilly squeezed past Prudence, out the bedroom door, and started down the stairs. She stopped midstep. Matthew was standing at the foot of the stairway, smiling up at her.

Hat in hand, he bowed from the waist. "I've come to offer my explanation."

Lilly arched her eyebrows at his remark. "You owe me none. You are free to keep company with Isabelle Locklear or any other woman you so desire. It's none of my concern," Lilly replied as she took her cape from one of the wooden pegs in the hallway. "Besides, I'm on my way to town. I wasn't planning on entertaining a guest."

"That's fine. I'll walk along with you since I'm expected at the Boott residence by eight o'clock."

"Well, I certainly wouldn't want to be the cause of your tardiness. Isabelle might not prove forgiving if you're late," Lilly replied as she tied her bonnet and walked out the front door.

Matthew laughed as he hurried down the walk to catch up with her. "There you go again, letting your jealousy get the best of you."

Lilly skidded to a halt. "What? How dare you, Matthew Cheever! You walk about town with Isabelle Locklear on your arm, you bow and scrape to her every whim and smile as she flutters her eyes, all after disavowing any romantic interest in her. What you hear is not jealousy; it's anger!"

Matthew followed Lilly into the milliner's shop and waited until she had finished. "Well, I think you'll find there's no reason for anger or jealousy," he said with a grin as they left the store. "Mr. Boott asked that I escort Bishop Fenwick from Boston to Lowell. I didn't know Isabelle was planning on making the journey. When I arrived in Boston to fetch the good bishop, he advised me that Isabelle would be accompanying us. Mrs. Locklear has been ill. She recently admitted herself to a sanatorium and insisted Isabelle come to Lowell. If it makes you feel any better, Isabelle is no happier to be in Lowell than you are to have her here."

"I don't give a whipstitch where she is," Lilly protested.

Matthew's boisterous laughter caused Lilly to glare in his direction. "Good! Well, since we've settled that matter and I'm absolved of any wrongdoing, I want to know if you'd do me the honor of attending the Blowing Out Ball with me?"

Lilly stared at him in disbelief. How had he moved from one topic to another so smoothly? Her every inclination was to tell him yes. Instead, she said, "We'll see what happens with you and Isabelle in the next couple weeks."

"I'll take that as a yes," Matthew said, leaning down to place a kiss on her cheek. "I must be off to meet with Mr. Boott," he said, hurrying off before she could wage an objection to his reply or the kiss.

Staggering from the tavern, Lewis zigzagged his way down Merrimack Street until he neared Jackson. He had watched

Matthew kiss his sister's cheek and then hurry away. "Lilly! Wait, I want to talk to you." He attempted to steady his gait while hastening toward his sister.

She stood waiting with a look of expectation etched upon her face. "Lewis, you look terrible. You've been drinking," she said, her voice filled with disappointment.

He guiltily nodded his head. "Do you have a few minutes you could spare, Lilly? I need to talk."

Shifting her parcel, she took hold of her brother's arm. "We dare not go to the boardinghouse with you in this condition. We can walk back to the Wareham for a cup of coffee."

He quickly took a step backward. "Not the Wareham. I don't want to go there," he replied. "The Old Stone House—would you go there?"

Lilly grasped his arm. "I suppose, since I'm with an escort, but we must sit in the eating establishment, not the pub," she replied as they hurried back down Merrimack Street. "Can you tell me what's wrong, Lewis? You're trembling."

Lewis glanced over his shoulder at the sound of footsteps behind them. "I'd rather wait. I don't want to take the risk of being overheard."

A short time later, Lewis located a table situated away from the crowd. He was certain Thurston expected him to leave town immediately, and he didn't want to be seen.

Lilly leaned her head close and took Lewis's hand. "Tell me what has happened."

Holding his throbbing head, Lewis momentarily pondered his decision to burden Lilly with his problems. She couldn't help extract him from this dilemma. Yet he needed a confidant and quickly squelched his noble thoughts of keeping Lilly out of harm's way. "My life is in quite a mess. I've made a lot of wrong choices, all of them selfish and unscrupulous."

"I've made my share of mistakes also; we all have. And I know that in the past you've chosen to turn your back on God and even denounced His existence. But it's not too late to turn your life around. Repentance is difficult, pushing aside all that pride and asking God's forgiveness. But the benefits are overwhelming: you're a totally new person in the eyes of God. Clean! Won't you consider asking God's forgiveness, Lewis?"

The sincerity of her words touched him, and he gave her a gentle smile. "You don't understand the gravity of my sins, Lilly. There isn't enough soap in all of Massachusetts to wash me clean." He patted her arm. "You can't understand the seriousness of my involvement. I'm in a precarious position that forces me to do the evil bidding of another man. I've been hired to set fire to the Merrimack," he blurted.

There was stunned silence. Lilly stared at him in obvious disbelief. "No, Lewis, you can't. Please tell me why. What could possibly—"

Holding up his hand, Lewis shook his head back and forth. "I've already said too much, Lilly. You must forget what I've told you. Promise me that you'll say nothing to anyone."

"Only if you'll promise you won't be party to such a thing. Please, Lewis, promise me. You don't want to be involved in anything else that will cause you more guilt and shame," she pleaded.

Lewis gave her a feeble smile, knowing what he must do. It had been a complete error of judgment to come here. "I promise, Lilly. In fact, I'm going to escort you home, and then I'm going to leave town. I may even head for the wild western frontier. What do you think of that? Do you think I could survive out among those savages we've read about?"

Lilly grasped his hand. "Oh yes, Lewis. That's a wonderful idea. You must leave town immediately. I promise, I'll not breathe a word. But why not consider heading south? Life is gentler and slower in the south, I'm told. I can better picture you as a southern gentleman than an Indian fighter," she said with a grin. "We'd better be leaving, or I'll find myself locked out of the boardinghouse. Will you at least give careful thought to seeking God?"

Lewis gave her a reassuring smile. "We'll see." It was a small concession, the least he could do—he'd been the cause of enough pain in her life.

Lilly tiptoed up the steps to her bedroom, thankful to find her roommates asleep. The girls would have questioned her late arrival, and she didn't want to mention that she had been with Lewis—especially to Prudence, who still believed Lewis would one day be her husband. She settled into the warmth of the bed, but sleep wouldn't come.

It seemed strange not to have Nadene with her. Even though Nadene had planned to go back to work Monday, the doctor had insisted on sending the girl home. Addie had broken the news to the girls.

"The doctor believes Nadene's time is very limited. The consumption has only grown worse, and he feels she is in no shape to return to work." Addie had talked to them for some time, tears streaming from her eyes, as well as from the eyes of the girls who had come to care so deeply for Nadene.

Now Nadene was home, and the loss to Lilly was acute. How difficult it had been to share a bed with a total stranger, yet now how equally odd to be without her. Lilly pushed aside her emotions and tried not to think of Nadene. She prayed for her friend, hoping that the doctor might be wrong—knowing that most likely he was right.

Her thoughts then fell upon the conversation with Lewis, wrestling with the idea that perhaps this fire at the Merrimack would be God's punishment, the answer to all of her once-earnest prayers for the destruction of the Boston Associates. She silently chided herself, remembering the harm that had come to Nadene through the fire at the Appleton. Besides, the Boston Associates wouldn't be the only ones harmed by a fire at the Merrimack.

In one way or another, a major fire at the Merrimack would bring ruination to almost every resident of Lowell, and she didn't want that. After all, if enough tragedy did befall the Associates, Miss Addie might well be out of a job, and Lilly could even find herself out of a home. An idea of what she would do beyond her employment with the mills had never really materialized in her thoughts.

Months ago, I would have been happy at the thought of such destruction, she thought. But that was before, when her heart had been hard and her focus hadn't been God so much as revenge. And hadn't she already resolved those issues and asked forgiveness? Why was she permitting herself to dwell on these thoughts?

Slipping from her bed, Lilly dropped to her knees, seized by an overwhelming sorrow for her brother. She prayed for his protection and ultimate happiness. She prayed he would find a safe haven and loyal Christian friends, that he would seek God's forgiveness, and that God would direct his path toward righteousness.

She crawled back into bed, amazed by her feelings for Lewis. In spite of their past and all of his transgressions, she loved him. Perhaps God would send that same healing power to her brother.

CHAPTER 32

March blew in like a lion, but despite blustery beginnings, the month gradually began to show signs of spring. The night of the Blowing Out Ball had finally arrived, and Lilly actually found herself a mix of emotions. Worry for Lewis reigned uppermost in her mind, but thoughts of Matthew had affixed themselves to her heart.

"Let me see how you look!"

At Miss Addie's request, Lilly twirled about in her pale blue lace-trimmed gown.

"I told you that shade of blue was just right for your complexion when we first saw the fabric at Whidden's," Miss Addie remarked with a twinkle in her eye. "And I was correct. Would you consider helping an old woman with her dress?"

Lilly smiled and gave Addie a hug. "I would consider helping a *very dear friend* with her dress," she said, following Addie into her bedroom.

Addie carefully plunged her arm into the sleeve of her dress. "Matthew has certainly been a frequent visitor lately. And how many times have you been to dinner at his parents' home recently? Seems things are getting serious between you two. Is

347

there anything you want to tell me?"

Lilly ceased buttoning Addie's dress. "No, there is nothing to tell you. Matthew and I are merely friends, just like you and me. And what of you and John Farnsworth? He's been coming to call on you frequently. Do *you* have something to share with me?" Lilly asked with a giggle.

Addie placed a hand on each side of her waist in an attempt to make the buttoning easier. "We have talked about the future—about sharing it—together," she stammered.

"Really? Oh, Miss Addie, that's wonderful. When? Why didn't you tell me?"

"Don't get so excited. I said we've *talked* about the future. We haven't made any decisions, although John has asked me to help him decorate his house once it's finished. They've begun work on it again since the weather has warmed up a bit. He thinks it will be completed by June. We ordered the fabric for the draperies last week."

"Oh, Miss Addie, how exciting. I can't think of anyone who deserves a good husband more than you. And you'll be a perfect wife for Mr. Farnsworth. Addie Farnsworth—that has a nice sound to it. Have you told Miss Mintie?"

Addie shook her head. "Now that we've finally mended our differences, I don't want to do anything to upset her. Until John and I have actually decided we're going to share our future together, it's best I don't say anything to Mintie. Having worked so diligently to heal our relationship, I'm sure you understand how fragile it is. Mintie's made great strides in accepting my relationship with John, but we need more time. And if you hadn't come up with the idea of finding a beau for Mintie, I'm not sure she would have attended the ball this evening."

Lilly nodded as she arranged the layers of Addie's skirt. "Who would have ever thought Miss Mintie and Lawrence Gault would find anything in common? Yet he seems to have a wonderful, calming effect upon her, don't you think? I'm so fond of Mr. Gault, I almost felt guilty when I suggested he call upon your sister," she said with a giggle.

"I must admit that I would never have dreamed such a sweet

man would give Mintie a second glance, but he appears to enjoy her company, and she's like a different person since he's come into her life," Addie said as she handed a string of pearls to Lilly.

"I attempted to convince Mintie to purchase a new gown for the ball, but she wouldn't budge. Stitching a row of new lace around the neckline of her frock was the most I could manage," Addie added with a giggle.

"Not that old brown dress?"

Addie gave an exaggerated nod of agreement, and the two women burst into gales of laughter. "She certainly can't be accused of attempting to turn Mr. Gault's head with her wardrobe."

"That's true. You, on the other hand, are going to turn everyone's head in this lovely gown. And your string of pearls and earbobs are perfect accents."

Addie blushed at the compliment. "Thank you, dear, but the only person I want to please is John. I can hardly wait—we're going to have such a gay time this evening. I can just feel it in my bones. Now, please make sure my sash is straight in back."

Lilly examined the mauve-colored gown to ensure there were no flaws. The full gigot sleeves were quite complimentary on Miss Addie. Lilly straightened the sash and then picked a piece of lint from the shoulder.

"Everything is perfect," she announced.

Prudence and Marmi descended the staircase and gathered in the dining room along with the other girls, all of them admiring one another's gowns, offering to loan a piece of jewelry or pair of gloves to complete an ensemble. The laughter and chattering charged the room with an air of excitement.

"I do wish Nadene could have been here with us," Lilly said sadly.

Addie gently touched Lilly's hand. "I wish she could be here, too, but we must trust that God has it all under control. Nadene would not wish us to be sad tonight. Let us go and share good company in her honor."

Lilly nodded. "She'd like that, I'm sure. Afterwards, why don't we all write her a letter and tell her every detail."

"That's a marvelous idea," Addie agreed.

A knock at the front door sent one of the girls rushing to the hallway. "It's too early for Mr. Farnsworth or Matthew," Lilly commented as she tucked a curl into place.

"Lilly, you have a caller. It's Lewis," Marmi said as she neared the dining room.

"Lewis?" She rushed past Marmi, down the hallway and into Lewis's extended arms. "It's good to see you. You look wonderful," she said, leaning back to look into his face. "What brings you back to Lowell? Not a problem, I hope?"

Lewis gave her an enormous smile. "Everything is fine. I wanted to see my sister, but it appears I've chosen the wrong night to come calling," he convincingly replied. "Is there a party tonight?"

"The Blowing Out Ball. You can attend. It will be great fun. Please say you'll come," Lilly begged. She was surprised at the sincerity of her emotions, but she truly wanted Lewis to attend. God had done a work in her heart—there could be no doubt.

"No, I don't want to interfere with your evening of fun. You go on, and I'll see you tomorrow."

After several minutes of pleading, with Lilly insisting it would only make this joyful occasion more memorable, Lewis finally agreed to attend the ball. After giving Lilly his promise to meet her at the Old Stone House, he departed in order to secure a room at the Wareham for the night.

––––––––

Lilly sat beside Matthew in the carriage, her voice filled with excitement as she told him of Lewis's surprise arrival. "Isn't this perfect?" Lilly asked, clapping her hands together. "Lewis appears to have put his past behind him. I'm so anxious to hear what he's been doing since he left Lowell."

Matthew's face creased with concern. "Please don't be disappointed if you're unhappy with what he tells you. I want you to have a wonderful time this evening."

Lilly nodded her agreement then smiled as she glanced across the carriage toward John Farnsworth and Addie sitting opposite them. It was obvious Mr. Farnsworth was enchanted with Addie's devoted attention, the two of them talking softly as the horses clopped down the street. Catching Lilly watching them, John beamed a smile.

"I nearly forgot to tell you. I received a missive from England. It seems I'm to have company."

"Is your father finally going to join you?" Lilly questioned.

"Not just yet. No, this is from my nephew. My sister's boy, God rest her soul." John's expression sobered. "Sherman Manning, my brother-in-law, passed on a few months back. I didn't know until Taylor sent me this letter. Anyway, Taylor desires a new life in America. His siblings are safely established with his grandmother in London, and he asked to join me here, perhaps to work at the mills."

"We're always in need of another good man," Matthew remarked.

John nodded. "I hoped you'd feel that way. He should be here by the first of May."

"When he arrives and you've gotten him settled in, send him to see me," Matthew replied.

"Oh, look, there's Mintie with Mr. Gault," Addie announced as they stepped out of the carriage. "Mintie!" she called out, waving a gloved hand in the air.

Mintie waved in return, giving them a bright smile. "Good evening," she pleasantly greeted as the foursome approached. "Perhaps we can find a table and sit together," she ventured as they walked in and joined the frivolity.

Matthew took hold of Lilly and led her toward the dance floor. "I believe Lilly and I will begin with a dance. You go ahead and find a place to sit, and we'll join you shortly." The candles and oil lamps cast an enchanting glow throughout the rooms as they whirled about in time with the music.

"There's Lewis," Lilly reported, twisting in Matthew's arms and nearly tripping over his feet as she attempted to keep her brother in sight. He glanced in her direction, and she excitedly waved in return. "He's coming this way."

Lewis tapped Matthew's shoulder. "Would you mind if I cut

in, Matthew? I promise to return her quickly."

Matthew smiled as he released Lilly to her brother. "I don't think I have a choice," he said with a laugh. "She's been tripping over my feet since you arrived. I think she was afraid you would dance with someone else first."

"That's not so. Lewis may dance with anyone he wishes," Lilly protested.

Matthew slapped Lewis on the back. "It's good to see you, Lewis. I hope we'll have time to visit a little later."

"Thanks, Matthew," Lewis replied as he grasped Lilly's hand and began to move across the dance floor.

Lilly gave her brother a winsome smile. "You look wonderful, Lewis. I want to hear everything. Tell me where you've been and what you've been doing, because whatever it is seems to agree with you."

"Thank you for the kind words, Lilly. I took your sisterly advice and went south, although not very far," he said with a laugh. "I've been in Philadelphia working with some men who are developing a new import and export business." Lewis glanced about the dance floor and then back toward his sister. "You are by far the most beautiful young lady in attendance this evening, Lilly—but you always *were* a pretty girl."

Lilly felt an overwhelming affection for her brother. "Why, Lewis? Why have we had so many years of ugliness between us? Why did you . . . hate me?"

He frowned and turned her effortlessly. "I wish I could take back those years—I truly do. Upon reflection, I can only say that my actions were born out of jealousy and fear."

"Jealousy and fear of what?" she questioned, watching him intently, as though she might ascertain the answer from his expression.

"I was jealous of you and fearful that our parents would no longer have any use for me after you came along. You were so lovely, like a little doll. People were always commenting on it. I felt misplaced. I'd had Mother and Father's undivided attention, and suddenly I had to share."

"But I adored you," Lilly said, shaking her head. "I used to plead with Mother to tell me why you were mad at me. I wanted so much for us to be close."

An expression of pain crossed Lewis's face. "I suppose it's too late for that now."

Lilly squeezed his hand. "Of course it's not too late. We've already grown closer just in the past few months. Remember when you showed up here in Lowell? I wanted nothing to do with you. The past, and all that stood between us, was too much to contend with. You were planning to use the girls for your greater gain. . . ."

"Which I did and am now deeply ashamed."

"What made the difference, Lewis?"

He made a halting step but quickly recovered. "Coming face to face with who I am and what I'm capable of doing made me realize just how far I'd sunk. I can't change the past, Lilly, and I'm certain there is no future—not for someone like me."

"But . . ."

He shook his head. "Let's forget such sad things and enjoy the music. I'll soon be returning to Philadelphia, and I desire to enjoy a pleasant moment with you before I go."

They continued dancing through several musical arrangements, Lewis seeming to enjoy Lilly's company. He spoke of his excitement over his new business venture and beginning his life anew while Lilly listened attentively, thrilled by his report.

Returning her to the table where Matthew sat, he said, "I think I should dance with Prudence. I believe I owe her an explanation of my disappearance," Lewis told Lilly. "You need not fear. I don't plan to woo her, merely tell her I've moved to Philadelphia."

Lilly gave Lewis an endearing smile, watching as he walked toward the table where Pru and several other girls were seated.

"If he weren't your brother, I believe I would be overwrought with jealousy," Matthew softly remarked as he and Lilly approached a table laden with punch bowls and silver trays filled with tiny sandwiches and cookies. "Your face is fairly aglow with love."

Lilly took a sip of her punch. "There's been such a wonderful change in Lewis. It appears he's finally become the man God intended him to be. I can't believe the change."

"I must admit he appears to be happy and content. And from the cut of his suit, I'd say his new business opportunity has already proved financially successful." Matthew glanced about and said, "Don't look now, but Thaddeus Arnold and his wife are walking in this direction."

Lilly stiffened. "He's never made good on his threat that things weren't yet resolved." She continued to drink her punch, even as she watched the man from across the room.

"I'm telling you, Lilly, his threats were probably nothing more than manly pride. Men don't like to have their plans altered—especially by women."

"Well, he does appear to treat all of the girls on our floor with dignity and is evenhanded in his decisions. *And* I can now sleep at night without fear of hearing his wife crying out in pain during the night."

Matthew held up the punch ladle and raised his eyebrows. "More?" he inquired.

Lilly nodded and held out her cup. "Good evening, Miss Armbruster and Mr. Cheever," Mrs. Arnold greeted as she came alongside them. "Mr. Arnold stopped to talk with one of the men. I thought I would have a cup of punch," she explained. "And I wanted to thank you," she whispered to Lilly.

Lilly snapped to attention at the word of thanks. "For what?" she cautiously questioned.

"Well, I'm not sure I rightly know the truth of it, but I know you had something to do with the change in Mr. Arnold." She smiled and lifted the cup of punch. "Sometimes he still loses his temper, but he's never laid a hand on me since the day he came home ranting and raving something about you and the church."

Mrs. Arnold's face revealed how the years of worry and harsh treatment had taken their toll. Lilly patted her arm. "I cannot take credit for anything. I'm just glad to have your company in church and at our ladies' social gatherings. Your quilting puts them all to shame."

Mrs. Arnold blushed. "Oh . . . I . . . well, thank you."

Thaddeus Arnold arrived at that moment. He looked at Matthew and nodded before fixing his gaze on Lilly. Lilly shivered, recognizing his dislike of her.

"Miss Armbruster. Mr. Cheever. Good to see you both." He looked to his wife. "If you two will excuse us, I intend to dance with my wife."

Lilly watched the smiling woman put down her cup. She took hold of her husband's arm with a cautiousness born out of experience. Lilly wondered if the woman would ever have a truly peaceful life.

Matthew finished his plate of sandwiches and held out his hand to Lilly. "I believe this dance is mine."

Lilly pushed aside her thoughts of Mrs. Arnold and nodded. Allowing Matthew to lead her onto the dance floor, Lilly relished the gaiety of the moment. "This is one of the happiest days of my life. I see the work God has done in my heart, and I can only thank Him. And Lewis! Would you believe that before he left Lowell, he told me he was going to set fire to the Merrimack? And now he's—"

"What?" Matthew interrupted, stopping midstep. "Lewis threatened to set fire to one of the mills, and you didn't tell me? Why would you withhold such vital information, Lilly?"

"Could we continue dancing before we cause a spectacle?"

Matthew jerked into motion. "Well?" he insistently questioned as he began to maneuver her through the crowd of dancers.

"Lewis told me he had become entangled with a disreputable scoundrel who threatened to ruin him if he didn't set the fire. He believed he had no options, but after we talked, he decided he would leave Lowell and begin his life anew somewhere else. When he left town that night, I saw no reason to tell anyone. Lewis wouldn't tell me any of the particulars or the name of anyone else involved. He feared I would come to harm if I knew too many details. Besides, the threat to the mills and the possible destruction of human life were gone. To taint Lewis's name when he'd actually done nothing would have been unfair."

"I suppose you're right. Still, I wish you had confided in

me," Matthew replied as the music stopped. He took hold of Lilly and led her toward their table. "So what brings him back to Lowell? Can the threat have passed so quickly?"

Lilly gave him a look of consternation. "He said he was anxious to see me. I believe he wanted to show me he was doing well and had begun making changes in his life. How silly of me! I should have realized he was putting himself in harm's way and immediately sent him on his way. Instead, I all but forced him to come to the ball and make a public appearance."

Matthew gently pressed his thumb along a crease in Lilly's brow. "It's a beautiful night and a lovely party. We shouldn't be discussing anything more distressing than the fact that the punch is overly sweet. Forget my thoughtless prying," Matthew said, giving her a tender smile. "Why don't we step outside for a moment and get some air?"

Lilly nodded her head in agreement, anxious to push the unpleasant thoughts into the recesses of her mind. Lewis had returned a changed man, and nothing else mattered right now.

They stepped outside, and Lilly shivered from the chill of the night air but said nothing. She wanted very much to sort through her feelings for Matthew and to better understand his for her. Still, it was hard to speak her mind. She was enjoying a tender balance of emotions and actions on both her part and Matthew's. She had come a long way in learning to control her temper and had come to realize that Matthew's choices had not been as unwisely made as she had originally believed. With that thought in mind, she turned to face Matthew.

"I want to apologize," she said.

"For what?"

"I've treated you poorly these last few years. I've blamed you for the inevitable changes on the land. I pushed you away in my bitterness."

"I never wanted to see you hurt, Lilly. I never realized what my choices would mean to you," Matthew replied softly. "Given the fact I intended to marry you, I should have discussed the entire matter more thoroughly with you."

Lilly felt warmed by his words and looked away. She didn't

know if she could bear to talk about what she'd lost with Matthew. She shivered again and rubbed her arms.

"Come on, let's get you back inside," Matthew said, reaching out to take hold of Lilly. "We've had enough confessing and apologizing for one evening."

Lilly smiled and nodded. "Besides, we might have people talking if we stay out here too long."

Matthew chuckled. "Let them talk. Better yet, maybe we should give them something to talk about."

CHAPTER 33

The swirl of colorful dancers blended with the lively music. They were dancing a reel, swaying in and out of the aligned ranks, when Lilly and Matthew came back to the room. Addie and John seemed to be enjoying themselves immensely, which to Lilly was no surprise. What was surprising, however, was the fact that Miss Mintie and Lawrence Gault were among the dancing couples. Furthermore, Miss Mintie was actually laughing out loud. Lilly couldn't help but smile and motion to Matthew.

"It's amazing what the right man can do in the life of a lonely woman."

"I've heard that to be very true," Matthew said, leaning close to her ear. "And likewise, the right woman can completely fill the heart of a lonely man."

Lilly met his gaze, his lips only inches from hers. She wanted very much for Matthew to kiss her—for him to be the right man who would forever change her loneliness. Moving a fraction of an inch closer, she prayed he might understand.

"Fire! Fire! The Merrimack!" A chilling silence momentarily quieted the frivolity of the ball. Then suddenly chair legs began scraping across the wooden floors as the men jumped to their feet and rushed from the room.

Lilly pulled away, looking frantically around the room. "Where's Lewis?"

Matthew took a moment to survey the crowd. "I don't see him, Lilly. I must get over to the Merrimack."

"Do be careful," she urged, watching as Matthew hurried off with John Farnsworth and a limping Kirk Boott, who followed behind.

Lilly grasped Addie's arm, hoping her friend would provide a steadying influence. "I must find Lewis."

"I'm sure he's gone with the other men to help put out the fire. There doesn't appear to be a man left in the room. Even Mr. Whiting's gone to help," she soothingly replied.

Once again scanning the room, Lilly took Addie's hand and moved away from their table. "Let's find Prudence. Lewis was going off to dance with her about an hour ago. I didn't see him after that."

Addie pointed toward the door. "There she is—with Marmi."

Stretching up to wave, Lilly called out and quickly crossed the room. "Pru, where's Lewis? Have you seen him?" she asked, silently praying that Prudence would say he had been with her all evening.

Prudence shrugged her shoulders. "I don't know, Lilly. We only danced one dance. He apologized for treating me boorishly last winter. He also told me he had moved to Philadelphia and said he wasn't going to be in Lowell for long. I accepted his apology, and we parted after the dance. After that, I'm not sure where he went."

"Shouldn't we go over to the fire? Perhaps there's something we can do to help," Lilly suggested while silently praying that Lewis's reappearance in Lowell and the fire were merely a co-incidence.

"I don't know that we can be of much assistance, but at least we can see how much damage has been done," Addie replied.

Clustered together, they scurried off toward the Merrimack

with Mintie and Addie leading the way. Smoke filled their nostrils as they hastened down French Street. Mintie slowed her pace as soot showered down from the glowing sky. Several small explosions filled the air as windows shattered and leaping flames engorged with fresh air soared toward the heavens. Fire illuminated the mill yard as the harried men frantically worked to extinguish the blaze. As they approached, several men could be seen leaning over a moaning figure.

Pointing a finger toward the groaning form, Prudence turned toward Lilly, her face etched in horror. "Lilly, look—someone's been burned!"

Lilly felt a deep sense of dread. As she pushed closer, edging through the congregated men, she feared the worst. Although he was burned almost beyond recognition, Lilly knew it was the body of her brother. She fell to her knees beside Lewis, tears in her eyes. His breathing was shallow and irregular as he lay unconscious on the cold ground.

"Oh, Lewis, no," Lilly moaned.

The quiet murmur of conversation was interrupted by William Thurston's determined voice rising above the crowd. "I, for one, can attest to what happened here tonight. I was out for an evening stroll as I am wont to do on evenings when I need to clear my head and think," he pontificated.

"Has anyone sent for a doctor?" Lilly shouted toward the men that encircled her brother's body.

"Yes, yes, of course," William Thurston replied, obviously irritated by the interruption. Loudly clearing his throat, he regained the attention of the crowd. "As I was saying, I was out for my evening stroll when I came upon Lewis wrestling with several Irishmen—apparently the ones who had set fire to the building. It appeared Lewis was unable to apprehend the culprits. As I quickened my pace and drew closer, I saw Lewis rushing forward, attempting to douse the blaze. It was then his clothing caught fire, leaving him in this tragic condition."

Lewis groaned, his eyes fluttered open, and he began mumbling, beckoning Lilly closer, but someone held her back.

Lilly looked up to see William Thurston's intense expression.

He gripped her shoulders to keep her from drawing closer to Lewis and dropped to one knee. "Don't talk, Lewis. You need to save your strength," he said, the words a hushed command. He looked to Lilly, saying, "It's for the best."

"Mr. Boott wants to talk to you, Mr. Thurston. He heard you were privy to some information regarding the fire," a soot-covered worker called out.

Thurston hesitated. "Don't say anything, Lewis," he ordered. "Do you hear me? Nothing!" He stood and straightened his coat before strutting off to meet with Kirk Boott.

Lilly looked after the man momentarily before turning her attention back to her brother. "Lewis, can you hear me?" Lilly whispered. "Please don't die," she begged, choking back her tears.

Her brother's eyes opened a mere slit. He moved his mouth, but she couldn't hear him. She bent her ear to his lips. "I . . . did . . . the best I could." His words were interrupted with weak coughing spasms. "I . . . set . . . the fire at night . . . so no one . . . would be injured," he rasped in a barely audible tone. Lilly raised up and looked at him in disbelief. Surely he couldn't have said what she thought he said.

"Step aside. Let me get to him," Dr. Barnard said, moving toward Lewis's side. He stooped down beside Lewis and performed a cursory examination before requesting the aid of several men. "We need to get him to my office. Quickly!"

William Thurston came rushing back as the men moved Lewis onto a board. "What are you doing?" he hollered as they hoisted Lewis into the air.

Lilly remained close to Lewis's side, certain that her brother's life was hanging in the balance. "Taking him to Dr. Barnard's office for treatment," Lilly replied.

Thurston hastened to Lilly's side. "I can't let you do this alone. Lewis has been a loyal friend, and I want to be with him until the . . . well, uh . . . until he regains consciousness," he stammered.

"Don't you think they need you here, helping put out the fire?" Lilly inquired. "I can stay with my brother."

Thurston remained close by her side. "No, I won't hear of it. I won't desert a friend in his time of need. Besides, you shouldn't be alone right now, either, Miss Armbruster."

"Lilly!" Matthew called out. "I'll join you at the doctor's office as soon as possible." Lilly turned and waved.

"No need, Cheever, I'll accompany her," Thurston replied.

Lilly wished Matthew would call Thurston back to fight the fire. She didn't like William Thurston, and she certainly didn't want him accompanying her to the doctor's office.

Once they reached Dr. Barnard's office, he instructed the two to wait outside. "My wife will assist me. If I need further help, I'll call you."

The two of them waited. Nothing Lilly said could persuade Thurston to leave. Finally she ceased her attempts and began to pray for her brother. She wanted Lewis to live, but if that wasn't to be, she at least wanted one last opportunity to talk with him. There were questions that needed to be answered before her brother left this world.

Lilly startled when Dr. Barnard entered the room. "I wish I had better news to bring you. Unfortunately, I think Lewis is going to slip from his state of unconsciousness into death very soon."

Thurston jumped up from his chair. "You're certain he won't regain consciousness?"

The doctor solemnly wagged his head back and forth. "It doesn't appear likely," Dr. Barnard replied and then turned toward Lilly. "I'm so sorry. Even if I had arrived sooner, there would be nothing I could have done. His burns are too severe."

Thurston had donned his coat and top hat and stood with his gloved hand covering the front doorknob. "I'm sure you'd like to say your good-byes in private, Miss Armbruster," Thurston said quickly before departing.

"You can come back and sit with him if you'd like," Dr. Barnard offered.

Lilly followed the doctor and took a chair beside the bed. The smell of burnt flesh again reminded her of her own misdeeds. She desperately wished she'd never succumbed to her need for revenge. Although Nadene had recovered physically from her burns, Lilly knew the pain and misery suffered could never be wiped away.

She wanted to soothe her brother but realized there was nothing she could do that would make him more comfortable. So she bowed her head and began to pray, silently at first and then softly out loud, asking God to ease her brother's pain.

"Lilly, is that you?" Lewis's voice was a mere whisper.

"Lewis . . . oh, yes, Lewis, it's me."

He groaned as he turned his head toward her. His voice was low and gravelly. "You were always a good sister, Lilly. I don't know how you tolerated my treatment of you. . . . I was a terrible brother, and I've been a terrible man." He gasped for air, making an awful wheezing sound, chilling Lilly to the bone.

"Shh, Lewis, don't be so hard on yourself. It was my belief in God that enabled me to endure. However, I must admit it wasn't always easy." She smiled and gently touched his singed hair. "Sometimes you certainly put my faith to the test, but God was true to His word and sustained me. Lewis, I need to know—have you accepted Christ? Have you invited Him into your heart as your Savior? Have you repented of your sins and asked God's forgiveness? All you need do is ask," she fervently explained.

"You don't know . . . the depth of my sin. I couldn't ask to be . . . forgiven of the heinous crimes I've committed. Jesus won't forgive me, even if I asked," he replied, his voice fading.

"Lewis," Lilly urgently whispered. "Lewis, can you hear me? Lewis!" She leaned over his face until she felt his shallow breath upon her cheek. He had slipped back into unconsciousness, but he was still alive. She sat down, covering her face with her hands, and wept. *Please, Lord, let him live until he realizes there's no sin you won't forgive,* she silently prayed.

She didn't know how long she had been praying when Lewis once again moaned her name. Bending near, she whispered in his ear. "Lewis, just ask God's forgiveness."

"Irish woman, she's dead . . ." he muttered.

"Lewis, you need to ask Jesus to forgive you," she sighed.

"Baby still alive . . ."

Lilly couldn't believe the words. "Lewis, what are you saying? Do you have a child? A baby? Where's the child, Lewis?"

"Yes, baby . . . a boy. Alive. Paddy camp. He has a mushroom birthmark . . . on his arm," he replied, wheezing for breath.

There was no doubt Lewis was growing weaker by the moment, yet she hadn't confirmed if he had asked God's forgiveness. Desperation rose from deep within her. "Lewis, do you understand that God will forgive *any* sin—you have but to ask. Do you understand?"

"Yes, Lilly, I understand," he whispered.

"Have you accepted Christ into your heart, Lewis?" she urgently questioned. "Lewis, please answer me."

Lewis exhaled, emitting a soft gurgling noise before his head turned against the pillow.

He was dead—without telling her if he had accepted God's grace, without saying if he'd asked for forgiveness. She grasped his charred hand, her tears flowing freely as she mourned her brother's passing.

Someone touched her shoulder. "Lilly, how can I help?" Matthew gently asked.

She jumped up and fell into his arms. "Oh, Matthew, he's gone. Lewis is dead. He died before telling me if he had accepted Christ," she said through her tears.

Pulling her close, Matthew held her for several moments, then led her from the room. "There's nothing more you can do here, Lilly. Let me take you home. Look, I've brought your wrap. Miss Addie thought you might need it." Gently, he helped Lilly on with her cloak and directed her toward the door.

Lilly turned around. "I should tell Dr. Barnard I'm leaving," she murmured.

"I talked with him when I came in. He knew I was going to escort you home."

The smoky air filled Lilly's nostrils. "The fire, Matthew? Were you able to save the mill?"

"We won't be able to evaluate the actual damage until daylight, but the fire is out. Most of the damage was to the printworks. Mr. Boott and Farnsworth and I will assess the damages first thing in the morning," Matthew explained. "It doesn't appear we'll be shut down for more than a week or so."

Lilly sighed. "I hope it won't be too long. The girls can't afford to pay their room and board when they're not receiving wages."

"I'm certain the Corporation will make arrangements to protect the girls," he said.

The two of them walked in silence until they neared the boardinghouse. "Matthew, I believe Lewis has a son," Lilly blurted.

Matthew stopped and gave her a look of surprise. "What would give you such an outlandish idea?"

"He mentioned a baby on his deathbed—a boy. I don't think a man lies while on his deathbed, do you?"

"No, I don't suppose a man would have much reason to tell falsehoods on his deathbed, but what did he actually say?"

Lilly gave him a thoughtful look. "He said the mother was dead. It's a boy. I don't know how old he is, but he has a birthmark, a mushroom-shaped birthmark on his arm," she recounted.

"Anything else?"

"He said the child is in the Paddy camps. I assume the mother was Irish."

Matthew rubbed his jaw and gave her a thoughtful look. "I do recall several occasions when I saw Lewis around the Acre. I wondered why he was there. Perhaps he did have more reason to be there than I imagined, but he never mentioned anything to me. You should remember, however, that his words might have been the delirious ramblings of a dying man. Please promise me you'll not worry any further. I plan to spend a good deal of time in the Acre over the next few days, and if I find any evidence of a child, I'll tell you."

"Oh, Matthew, would you? Thank you so much," Lilly replied, giving him a weary smile. "But why are you planning to spend time in the Acre?"

"Didn't you hear William Thurston say he had observed Lewis fighting with some Irishmen who were supposed to have started the fire? I need to investigate his allegations."

Lilly thoughtfully considered his reply. "I don't think you'll find anyone to substantiate Thurston's claims. Lewis admitted he started the fire," Lilly said, her voice barely audible.

Matthew held her by the shoulders. "Lewis *told* you he started the fire?"

"Yes. He said he set the fire at night so none of the workers would be injured. Somehow he felt it was the one noble thing he could do if he was going to set the fire," she said, beginning to weep. "Oh, Matthew, I'm truly alone in the world now. My entire family is gone. Even though Lewis and I weren't close, he was my brother. And just as he was beginning to turn his life around, he's snatched away. When my father died, I didn't think the void could be any greater. Now I know I was wrong. I have no one."

Matthew pulled her into his arms, and Lilly relished the comfort of his embrace. It felt so right to be with him. Perhaps he would speak words of reassurance, even love.

"Everything's going to be fine, Lilly."

Lilly looked into his eyes. She had once loved this man and had pushed him away in anger. Her own pain had made it impossible to continue their relationship. Now her pain made her desire that relationship more than anything.

Matthew gently touched her cheek. "You needn't feel alone. God is always with you, and besides that, you have Addie—and the girls here at the house are your friends. And you know how much my family cares for you."

Lilly felt a wave of disappointment. Stepping back, she wiped her eyes. "Thank you for helping me tonight. It was good of you to see me home from the doctor's. Good night, Matthew."

She walked up the stairs, remembering Matthew's words and wondering why he had failed to include himself among those who cared about her. When he had asked to escort her to the Blowing Out Ball, she was certain he had romantic feelings for her. Better still, she finally felt that she might be ready to accept her own feelings for Matthew, maybe even open her heart to him. Obviously she had once again misinterpreted his intentions.

CHAPTER *34*

Matthew bounded up the front steps of his parents' home, still wondering if he had done the right thing. He had wanted to declare his feelings for Lilly the night before, but it seemed inappropriate to avow his love when she was grieving her brother's death and the loss of all familial bonds. Holding back was the hardest thing he'd ever endured—short of losing Lilly in the first place.

Julia Cheever rounded the corner of the parlor as Matthew entered the front door. "What a wonderful surprise, Matthew. You're just in time for breakfast," she greeted, her hair perfectly coiffed and her pale green dress setting off the color in her eyes. She embraced her son, kissing him lightly on his cheek as he bent obediently to receive her greeting.

"Do you miss living on the farm, Mother?" Matthew inquired as they walked to the dining room.

She turned and gave him a puzzled look. "Why are you asking about the farm?"

"I suppose because life seemed much more simple back then."

Julia patted his hand. "That's because you were a child,

Matthew. Life has complexities in varying degrees throughout the years; where you live is of little importance. It's *how* you handle the difficulty that really counts. How we deal with life's problems gives evidence to our love and compassion as well as our relationship with God. Don't you think?" she asked. "Good morning, Randolph," she said as her husband entered the room.

Randolph pulled out a chair and seated himself at the table. "Good morning, my dear. Matthew, this is a pleasant surprise. To what do we owe this unexpected visit?"

"We were just discussing the complexities of life," Julia replied.

Randolph gave her a hearty laugh. "That's a rather profound subject for so early in the morning, isn't it? Is that truly why you came over here this morning, son?"

Matthew gave his father a grin as he helped himself to a piece of ham. "Not exactly. I came to tell you that Lewis Armbruster died last night—from the injuries he sustained in the fire at the Merrimack."

"Oh, Matthew, how sad. When your father returned home last night, he told me Lewis had been injured. I didn't realize it was so serious."

Matthew nodded. "Lilly is distraught. With Lewis gone, she has no family. Added to that is the fact that Lilly wasn't sure where Lewis stood before the Lord prior to his death. She's feeling an overwhelming sense of loss."

"And well she would, Matthew. I can't believe you took her back to that boardinghouse. Why didn't you bring her here to be with family?" Julia chided.

Matthew stared at his mother momentarily. "Because we are *not* Lilly's family, Mother," he said in a patronizing tone.

"Exactly!" Julia replied, giving Matthew a stern look while pointing a serving ladle in his direction. "When are you going to set aside your foolish pride and make Lilly your wife?"

"My foolish pride? It's Lilly who's filled with pride and won't admit that she's in love with me!"

"Well, of course not. She did that once and what did it reap? You went off to school and came back filled with pride and arrogance, telling her that life on a farm was a foolish dream. Then you prance about town with that uppity Boston socialite who's related to Kirk Boott holding on to your arm. And you expect Lilly to declare her love to you while you sit back and wait? Such foolishness, Matthew!"

Matthew looked toward his father, hoping for some assistance. It was obvious none would be forthcoming. Instead, while propping his chin in one hand, his father grinned and remained silent. Turning toward his mother, Matthew took a sip of coffee. "I wanted to tell Lilly of my feelings last night, but it didn't seem the appropriate time. After all, Mother, she had just lost her brother."

Julia stirred a spoonful of sugar into her cup of tea. "You always find one excuse or another to wiggle out of tying the knot," Julia scolded.

"I don't think a funeral would make a very romantic setting for a proposal," Matthew countered. "And what about the proprieties? Why, proper society would surely be of the opinion that Lilly remain out of social settings for at least six months."

"Oh, bother with proper society," Julia replied. "Sometimes love must overrule society."

Julia continued stirring and gave Matthew a stern look. "You know, Matthew, there are some distinct differences between men and women. Obviously, you don't know how women think and what makes them happy. I, on the other hand, know that a bit of good fortune is exactly what Lilly needs. I'm sure she's bereft. I can't think of anything that would cheer her more than . . ." Julia hesitated and met Matthew's gaze. "Did you say *proposal*?"

Matthew nodded and continued eating his breakfast.

"So you *are* going to ask Lilly to marry you?"

Matthew gave her a winsome smile. "Yes, Mother, if she'll have me."

Julia appeared to digest the affirmation before bounding from her chair and embracing Matthew.

Matthew pulled back. "But I intend to give her time to think this through. I don't want her to marry me simply because she's feeling her loss over Lewis. I want her to marry me because she loves me."

"Of course she loves you, darling boy," Julia said, hugging him close again. "Who wouldn't love you?"

———————

Lilly wandered through the early June blanket of grass that covered the cemetery until she stood before the small granite stones that marked her parents' graves. Only a few scattered blades of grass could be found on the freshly turned earth that marked Lewis's final resting-place. Lilly picked up a clump of the dirt and sifted it through her fingers, watching the fine soil drop onto the grave. She would save enough money to purchase a proper marker for Lewis, she decided.

Why had God taken him? she wondered. Hadn't the death of her parents been enough without the loss of her only other relative? And Nadene's death only days after Lewis's death had been equally devastating. Lilly had wept bitter tears when the letter had come from Nadene's mother. It had simply stated Nadene had succumbed to death, no longer able to fight the debilitating illness that had caused her cough and weakness through her final years.

For a time Lilly had avoided everyone. The pain of her loss threatened to eat her alive, and dealing with her ragged emotions consumed her time. Work had become nothing more than routine, but at least it filled her days. Nothing, however, had filled the lingering void in her heart. She prayed for God to fill the emptiness, and yet she continued to yearn for something more, something that seemed unobtainable: family.

The birds chirping overhead as they built their nests served as another reminder of her isolation. "Why, Lord?" Lilly murmured. "Just when Lewis was beginning to change his ways, when we could have resolved our problems and drawn closer— why did you take him then, Lord? Why did you leave me all alone?"

Gazing heavenward, Lewis's dying words came to mind. Something about a child, a boy, in the Paddy camp, he had said.

"I *do* have family," she announced to the sky. "I have a nephew—and somehow I will find him!"

———————

"I know you think me rude, but you'll enjoy the day if you only get out and give it a try," Miss Addie stated as she fairly pushed Lilly ahead of her.

"You sound just like Matthew. This morning after church, he said that I needed to get out and enjoy myself, that I had been mourning far too long."

Addie nodded in agreement. "That young man has a good head on his shoulders. You listen to him," Addie clucked. "He's been more than patient in waiting for you."

"Lewis has only been dead three months, Miss Addie. I'd hardly say I've been in mourning too long," Lilly contradicted. "Besides, what do you mean Matthew's been patient in waiting for me?"

Addie began fussing with the bow on Lilly's dress, pulling it first in one direction and then another. "You're a young woman, Lilly, and I think mourning three months for a brother who spent his entire life tormenting you is sufficient. I know, I know," she said, holding up her hand, "you and Lewis had begun to reconcile your differences, and he was changing his ways. I commend him for his repentant behavior, Lilly. The fact remains, however, that moping around here with your chin on your chest every day is not going to bring your brother back, and it certainly doesn't help you. Now go out and have a little fun," she said, giving the bow one final twist.

Lilly reached down and embraced Addie in a hug. "Thank you."

"You are most welcome," Miss Addie replied, opening the front door. "I believe your young lady is ready," Addie said to Matthew with a sweeping gesture.

"Matthew!" Lilly gasped.

Matthew held out his arm to Lilly. "Our carriage awaits," he said with great formality, which caused all three of them to laugh. "It's good to hear you laugh again, Lilly," Matthew said as he helped her up into the carriage. "There's a place not far from Pawtucket Falls where I thought we could picnic."

"That's private property, Matthew. Are you planning to trespass?"

He gave her a smile. "I think we'll be safe," he replied as he urged the horses onward. "I've been concerned about you, Lilly. You've been so withdrawn since Lewis's death."

She nodded. "I realize that's true, Matthew. I've been feeling so alone, floundering for some sense of identity. I know it may sound feeble, but I've been dwelling on the fact that I'm the only Armbruster left. Then the other day I went to the cemetery and was praying, wondering why God had permitted Lewis to die, questioning why I had to be completely alone, without family. It all seemed too unfair. I didn't want to be alone."

Matthew pulled the carriage to a halt. "Good! I'm glad to hear you don't want to be alone, because that's what I want to discuss with you," Matthew replied as he helped her down and retrieved the picnic basket.

"Really? Well, let me tell you what God revealed to me the other day," she said, her words gushing forth. "I'm not alone. I have a nephew, Lewis's child. I want to find him, Matthew. I know you asked a few questions at the Acre shortly after Lewis died, but you didn't *really* look for the child. I want to find the boy. He's an Armbruster. Will you help me find him?"

Matthew placed a cloth on the ground and began to spread out their picnic luncheon. "Sit down," he said, patting the blanket and waiting until she seated herself. "I would be willing to help you find the child if you would agree to help me in return," he said. "Is that something you think you could agree to?"

Lilly gave him a quizzical look. "I can't imagine how I could possibly help you with anything, but I promise to do my very best."

Matthew nodded and slowly pulled a small box from the inside pocket of his coat. He carefully arched his hand over the box, and although Lilly tried her best, she was unable to peek around his fingers.

Matthew gave her a solemn look. "Now, remember what

you've promised," he said with finality.

Lilly was beginning to question the propriety of her decision. Surely Matthew wouldn't ask her to do anything inappropriate, would he? "I remember," she meekly answered.

Matthew handed the box to Lilly. Nestled inside was a beautiful sapphire ring. "This ring once belonged to my grandmother," he said.

"It's beautiful," Lilly replied, handing it back to him.

He smiled. "I'm pleased you like it, because my grandmother gave me the ring so that I could one day give it to my wife, Lilly."

It took a moment before she understood the full impact of what Matthew was saying. She gazed at him in disbelief. "Are you—do you—I mean . . ." she stammered.

"Yes, Lilly, I'm asking you to marry me. I want you to become my wife."

Tears streamed down Lilly's cheeks. Matthew wanted her to be his wife. She was going to belong to someone—have a family.

Matthew softly brushed away her tears. "I know I can't make up for all you've lost, but I'm determined that together we can create an even better life. It won't replace your old family, and that's not what I want to do. You need to keep your memories. But I want to make you happy. I want to build new memories with you, Lilly. I want you to be my wife." He paused and gave her a look so full of love and longing that Lilly thought her heart would burst. "I love you, Lilly. I've never stopped loving you."

"Oh, and I love you, Matthew. I did you wrong by blaming you for everything that happened here in Lowell. I wanted so much for life . . . for us, to go on as it had always been. It was safe and I was happy."

"I want to make you happy again. Will you marry me?" He paused and gave her a roguish grin. "Don't forget your promise that you'd do anything I asked."

Wiping away a stray tear, Lilly permitted Matthew to slip the ring on her finger. "It would make me very proud to be your wife, Matthew," she said, gazing down at the ring. Tears of joy spilled over and trickled down her cheeks. "Yes, yes, I'll marry you," she said, lifting her lips to accept his kiss.

"I'm not sure how I'm going to hide my ring," Lilly said, gazing down at the sparkling stone as they arrived at the boardinghouse.

Matthew gave her a look of surprise as he pulled the horses to a halt. "Why would you want to do that?"

Lilly took hold of Matthew's hand as he helped her out of the buggy. "I thought you would want your parents to know our plans first—before I told Miss Addie or any of the girls here at the boardinghouse."

Matthew pulled her into an embrace. "My mother won't care who knows first, so long as I've asked you to marry me and you've accepted," he said, leaning down and kissing her lightly on the lips. He pulled away and added, "She's been quite enthusiastic about this for some time." He kissed her a little longer this time, then pulled away again to say, "I must say, I'm getting quite enthusiastic about the idea myself." This time he kissed her quite soundly.

Lilly giggled and melted into his arms, the warmth of Matthew's lips against her own and his strong arms surrounding her enchanting. But then she remembered herself and quickly pulled away. "Miss Mintie is probably hiding behind her curtains watching every move we make," Lilly whispered. "And I have no desire to be the talk of the town."

Matthew tilted his head back and laughed, an enthusiastic, resonant chuckle. "Well, I hope Mintie Beecher gets her eyes full!" he said as he pulled Lilly close for another sweet, lingering kiss.

CHAPTER *35*

Sunday, September 6, 1829

"Didn't I tell you you'd be married before a year was out?" Addie teased as she helped to adjust Lilly's wedding veil.

"Yes, you did, but it's actually been a few days beyond a year," Lilly replied.

Addie laughed. Standing on tiptoe she checked the top of the veil. "Well, I'll not begrudge you a few days over. The important thing is that you're marrying your true love." She stepped back and shook her head. "And aren't you the picture of perfection?"

Lilly gazed at her reflection in the mirror and could scarcely believe the image she found there. "I look so . . . so . . . ."

"Beautiful!" Addie declared.

Lilly studied the gown as she turned first one direction and then the other. The layered muslin rippled gently. She liked the way the pleated bodice had been trimmed with white satin ribbon. "I'm just amazed at the workmanship of this gown. Mrs. Cheever arranged to have it created for me, and I simply can't imagine what it must have cost her."

"That's unimportant," Addie told her. "She knows the worth of the woman inside the gown. That will always be much more important." She smiled and put one more pin in Lilly's upswept hair. "There, now that should hold."

Miss Addie had given her the lace piece that acted as her veil. "This lace is exquisite. Oh, Miss Addie, I'm so happy I could cry."

"Well, they say if you don't cry on your wedding day, you'll cry for the rest of the marriage. But I'm not of a mind to believe it. I'd refrain from crying," Addie admonished. "You don't want to go to your bridegroom with puffy red eyes."

"I can't believe I'm actually marrying Matthew. It seems like a long-forgotten dream, and now it's coming true," Lilly declared, turning to Addie. "You've been such a dear friend throughout this ordeal. I'm so blessed to have your friendship. I hope you know you'll be welcomed in our home anytime."

"Oh, my dear, I'm the one who has been blessed. You taught me to cook and made my boardinghouse one of the most sought after in all of Lowell. I'll have no trouble filling your vacancy, but I'll miss your company more than I can say."

"Then we'll have to make certain we share tea at least once—no, two times a week," Lilly declared. "No matter what, we mustn't lose touch or let time separate us."

"Agreed," Addie said as though making an earnest pledge.

With Addie and John to stand with them, Matthew and Lilly were joined in marriage in a quiet ceremony at St. Anne's. Lilly listened to the solemn tones of the minister and felt Matthew's reassuring touch. With her friends from the mills present to witness their vows, Lilly felt quite blessed and loved. She knew her parents would have smiled upon the union and felt confident in the knowledge that she was doing the right thing.

A noise from the congregation brought Lilly out of her reflective thoughts. She glanced over her shoulder to find Julia Cheever sobbing into a lace-edged handkerchief. Had she not known better, Lilly would have fretted that the woman was unhappy. Matthew's father smiled reassuringly at Lilly and put his arm around his wife in a loving manner. Lilly smiled and returned her attention to the man at her side. If he were half as compassionate as his father, then Lilly knew he would be a prize.

The minister issued a series of commands regarding marriage, prayed a long, intense prayer over the union, then pronounced them man and wife. In a matter of moments the ceremony was over and she was Mrs. Matthew Cheever.

Matthew kissed her soundly but didn't linger. He winked at her as they pulled away. He whispered, "I'll make up for that later."

Lilly felt her cheeks flush. In the months that had passed since her acceptance of Matthew's proposal, she had known some very long, lingering kisses. Matthew wouldn't be obliged to make up for anything, but Lilly rather hoped he would try.

The congregation hurried from the church and arranged themselves to greet the couple. Lilly watched as Lawrence Gault guided Miss Mintie from the sanctuary. The woman was actually wearing a gown of powder blue with black trim. The color alone took years from Miss Mintie's face and frame, but her smile accomplished even more. And Lilly couldn't be sure, but she thought perhaps Miss Mintie had added little wispy bangs to fall upon her forehead. She giggled at the thought of how decadent Miss Mintie must have felt in doing such a thing. Lilly strained to get a better glimpse, but the bonnet Miss Mintie wore was rather wide brimmed.

"Are you ready?" Matthew questioned, pulling Lilly possessively to his side.

"Absolutely."

They moved down the aisle of the church and out the door.

"Here they are!"

A rain of rice came down upon them as Matthew and Lilly moved toward their awaiting carriage. "I'll soon have us away from here," Matthew said, taking up the reins.

Lilly waved behind her. "Don't forget, they're all coming to the boardinghouse for the reception. We have to be there for that."

"Says who?" he questioned as he gave the reins a flick of his wrist. The horses, a matched pair of black geldings that were a gift from his father, stepped into motion.

"Matthew, they'll be expecting us. We can hardly just drive about Lowell hoping they'll not notice we're missing," Lilly said, laughing.

The day had turned out to be quite beautiful, with just a hint of fall crispness to the air. Lilly knew that soon the leaves on the trees would change and the countryside would be a riot of color. She had come full circle. Only a year ago, as Miss Addie had pointed out, she had been bitter and angry, ready to do harm to those who supported the mills.

The only explanation was that God had changed her heart. She had not come willingly into His submission—not at first. She remembered her anger and cringed inwardly. Such hatred could never have been used to serve a God of love and justice.

Lilly had been so deep in thought that she didn't realize Matthew had stopped the carriage. She looked up to find him watching her, one brow raised ever so slightly as if to try to read her mind.

"You looked almost sad," he said softly. "You aren't regretting your decision already, are you?"

Lilly smiled and shook her head. "No. I could never regret you."

"You did at one time. I remember feeling quite overwhelmed by the regret and anger you hurled my way."

"I know and I'm sorry."

He pulled her into his arms. "I know that, silly. I know, too, that your heart has changed. You're not the same woman you were a year ago. I like the soft, sweet creature who has come to take her place."

He lowered his mouth to hers, his lips warm and tender. Lilly felt her breath catch in her throat as he tilted her head to better meet his kiss. His touch did strange things to her, and Lilly marveled at the sensation that spread out from her stomach and seemed to warm her entire body.

"I'm so happy you're finally mine," he murmured as he pulled away ever so slightly. He kissed her nose and cheeks, then recaptured her lips.

Lilly melted against him, completely forgetting where they

were. The rest of the world no longer existed. It was just the two of them together—alone.

Abruptly, Matthew pulled away and tugged down his top hat. "I think we'd better get to the boardinghouse now, or I might be inclined to forget it altogether."

"Oh, Matthew. You are such a tease."

He looked at her with a gaze that revealed there was little teasing in his words. Lilly found herself caught up for a moment, then licked her lips and nodded. "Yes, we'd better go now."

Matthew turned the horses and directed them toward town. "I hope you know I'm very serious about doing whatever is necessary to find Lewis's son. I'm only sorry we haven't already accomplished the deed. There simply isn't much in the way of evidence to lead us."

Lilly felt tears come to her eyes. "Thank you so much for caring about the boy. I know it won't prove easy to locate him, or we'd have already found him."

"But we will find him. You mark my words. And when we find him, we'll raise him as our own son."

"Perhaps one day we'll have our own son, as well." She felt her cheeks warm at the thought of bearing Matthew a child.

Matthew looked at her and laughed. "Indeed, Mrs. Cheever. In fact, I'd like at least a dozen."

Lilly's mouth dropped open. Matthew roared with laughter and pulled her close.

"I didn't mean we had to have them all at once. One a year will be just fine."

Lilly picked up easily on his playful spirit. "Just for that, maybe I'll only give you daughters."

Matthew looked at her for a moment, then shrugged casually. "As long as they're as beautiful and smart as their mother, I suppose I can bear it. Although when they're of an age to court, I'll be hard-pressed to let them out of the house. I think we should make a rule that our daughters will not be allowed to take a suitor until they're . . . umm . . . say, thirty years of age."

"I'm sure they'll have something to say about that," Lilly

replied. "Besides, I'm just twenty-one, and look at the plans you have for me."

Matthew nodded. "Exactly my point." He grinned wickedly. "I know exactly what I have planned for you, Mrs. Cheever."

Lilly grew flushed again and buried her head against Matthew's shoulder. What a wonderful, marvelous wedding day. What a loving and perfect spouse. She couldn't ask for anything more. She stood in awe of the grace and mercy God had extended to her and relished the blessings that had come in the place of what she truly deserved.

As they rounded the corner and headed toward Jackson Street, Lilly smiled. She had once dreaded the very sight of the mills. Now they didn't hold such a threat against her. The past was laid to rest, sleeping neatly in a bed of what might have been. The future, however, rose up before them, and like a weaver to the loom, they would yet choose to make the patterns of what would be. But no matter what might come, Lilly knew with great confidence that God would guide those choices—not toward a road of revenge and destructiom but rather to a path that would lead them into hope and love. A path that would draw them closer to Him and to each other.